Such Sweet Sorrow

Katie Flynn

Such Sweet Sorrow

arrow books

Published by Arrow Books 2008

2 4 6 8 10 9 7 5 3 1

First published in Great Britain in 2008 by
Arrow Books
Random House, 20 Vauxhall Bridge Road,
London SW1V 2SA

www.rbooks.co.uk

Addresses for companies within The Random House Group Limited can be
found at: www.randomhouse.co.uk/offices.htm

The Random House Group Limited Reg. No. 954009

A CIP catalogue record for this book
is available from the British Library

ISBN 9780099521778

The Random House Group Limited supports The Forest Stewardship
Council (FSC), the leading international forest certification organisation. All
our titles that are printed on Greenpeace approved FSC certified paper carry
the FSC logo. Our paper procurement policy can be found at
www.rbooks.co.uk/environment

Mixed Sources

Product group from well-managed
forests and other controlled sources
www.fsc.org Cert no. TT-COC-2139
© 1996 Forest Stewardship Council

FSC

Typeset in Palatino by Palimpsest Book Production Limited,
Grangemouth, Stirlingshire
Printed and bound in Great Britain by CPI Mackays, Chatham ME5 8TD

For Barbara and Noel Hughes,
just in time for your Golden Wedding
(when the last thing you will be
doing is reading this book!).
Much love, Katie Flynn

Chapter One

1939

'Well I never, if it isn't our Miss Wainwright! Sorry, I should have said Mrs Sheridan, of course. Good gracious, it must be all of two years since you popped into Gowns to say hello. And this will be your little girl; why, she must be seven or eight and this is the first time I've set eyes on her ... Libby, isn't it? She don't favour you, love. I suppose she must be like her da ... though I can't see no resemblance meself. Christmas shopping, are you?'

Libby, who had been carefully licking the pink sugar off an iced bun and watching through Lewis's window the snowflakes whirling down from the threatening grey sky, jumped at the strident voice and turned to stare at the speaker. It was a tall, heavily built woman, wearing a pair of gold-rimmed glasses, and she was beaming at Marianne Sheridan as though they were old friends, though Libby was sure she had never set eyes on the woman before. However, being a well brought up child, she would have greeted her politely had the woman so much as glanced in her direction, but the stranger's attention was focused upon Marianne, the small brown eyes in the heavy face flicking over Libby's mother as though searching for something.

1

'Oh, Miss Harding, how you startled me!' Marianne said. 'I have visited Gowns several times, actually, but you haven't been around. Libby's come in with me a couple of times to meet the staff . . . but I'm forgetting my manners! Would you care to join us? As you say, we've been Christmas shopping, but when it started to snow we decided it was time for some elevenses, especially since Libby fancied some lemonade and a cake. It's really lovely to see you . . . do sit down and I'll order another pot of tea. Goodness, Miss H, fancy you remembering Neil. I'm sure you only saw him at our wedding, and that's getting on for eight years ago now.'

Libby crossed her fingers beneath the starched white tablecloth and willed Miss Harding to refuse the invitation. The cake stand in the middle of the table still held a chocolate eclair and a macaroon, as well as a couple of fairy cakes, and Libby had intended to go for the eclair if her mother suggested she might like a second cake. Of course it was possible that, if Miss Harding did join them, more cakes would be forthcoming, but it was equally possible that her mother might say there was a war on and offer the cakes to the newcomer.

Miss Harding, however, pulled out a chair and sat down heavily upon it, then pushed up the sleeve of her coat and peered short-sightedly at her wristwatch. 'We-ell, it won't hurt to take the weight off me feet for five minutes, only I don't want to be late. I dare say no one's told you, queen, but I retired a year or so back. Well, I had ever such a nice letter from Mr Eccles – he's the floor manager, new since your time – telling me that what with the young men joining the armed forces and the young girls queuin' to get into factories he were desperately short of staff, and wondered whether I'd consider comin' out of retirement. He's offerin' a full wage though the job's part time: ten in the mornin' till four in the afternoon, and no weekends.'

'Golly!' Marianne said. 'But I suppose he would have to offer a decent salary because the girls in the factories are really well paid, I believe. But what about your pension?'

'That's why I'm here today,' Miss Harding said. She was staring very hard at the plate of cakes. 'Chocolate eclairs! Ooh, I'd ha' done murder for a chocolate eclair when I were a kid. As for the pension, it's to sort out such details that Mr Eccles sent for me.'

Marianne stared at Libby and made a little jerk of her head which Libby understood all too well. She leaned forward and propelled the cake stand towards the newcomer. 'Would you like one, Miss Harding?' she said politely. 'I'm afraid we don't have a spare plate but you can use mine if you like; I've finished.'

'I don't mind if I do,' Miss Harding said. She extended a plump, very white hand and took the eclair without a second's hesitation, then turned to Marianne. 'You've not been approached, I suppose? But of course it's so long since you worked here that I dare say you aren't even on the books any more.'

'No, I've heard nothing, but I'm sure you're right and they've forgotten me,' Marianne said cheerfully. 'But I don't think I would come back even if they asked me to. You see, it's not war work, and like everyone else I'd rather help the war effort if I could. If it wasn't for Libby here, I'd join one of the services. Neil's in the Navy so I rather favour the Wrens . . .'

'Someone told me Mr Sheridan's an officer, as I recall,' Miss Harding said, rather thickly. She had demolished the eclair whilst Marianne was speaking and Libby was forced to admire the speed at which she had gobbled it up and the fact that not one speck of cream had managed to escape to mar her bright pink lipstick, or her powdered cheeks and chin. 'I remember him at your weddin'; best-lookin' feller I ever set eyes on, apart from fillum stars of course.' She had been carrying a large handbag which she had pushed under her chair when she sat down, but now she hooked it out, opened it, and produced a tiny powder compact, flicking it open and peering anxiously at her reflection. She patted her hair, then replaced the compact in her bag and turned once more to Marianne. 'That reminds me. Didn't it say on the wireless that children were to be evacuated to the country as soon as war started? Surely little Libby should have gone with her classmates?'

Libby sighed. It was a remark she had heard all too often back in September and October, although it was voiced less frequently now that a great many parents had reclaimed their children from their foster families. Libby knew that everyone had expected bombs to start falling from the moment war had been declared, and when this had proved not to be the case a large number of children had returned to their own homes. Schools which had been shut down would open again in the New Year, but Libby knew that this phoney war, as they were calling it, could not last for ever. Her father was a first lieutenant on a corvette which protected the convoys bringing supplies from the United States of America. The merchant ships in his charge had been harassed and attacked by both U-boats and German warships, and he had told Libby the last time he was in port that she would have to leave the city as soon as things began to hot up.

But Marianne was answering her old colleague's question as patiently as though she had not done so over and over in the weeks that had elapsed since 3 September. 'Oh, Libby would have gone all right, but on the very day the children were told to assemble at Lime Street station she threw out a rash. It was measles, and she had a really bad attack followed by tonsillitis, and when that had cleared up the poor little soul got chicken pox. She wasn't out of quarantine until November, so Neil and I talked it over and decided that I would concentrate on building her up to her former state of health before we let her go anywhere without us.'

'My goodness!' Miss Harding said, looking properly at Libby for the first time. 'Now you mention it, she does look a bit peaky. Still, it's best to get all the childish ailments over in one go. I don't suppose I ever told you,' she added, turning her gaze back to Marianne, 'but the reason I wear glasses were measles. I gorr'em when I were fifteen and though me mam telled me to lie quiet in a darkened room I had me sister Edna smuggle me in copies of *Peg's Paper* and the like and read 'em by candlelight, or pulled back the curtain a little way so's some light could come in. I knew me eyes ached like anything, but I didn't stop, and by the time I were well enough to gerrup me sight were affected.' She turned back to Libby. 'I dare say your mam warned you as how measles could ruin your eyesight?'

Libby, who had indeed been nagged on the subject, said that she had been deprived of books from the moment the first spot appeared. At the time she had felt badly done by, but her mother had spent hours reading aloud to her and now, seeing how Miss Harding had had to peer at her wristwatch through her ugly little spectacles, Libby was grateful that reading had been impossible for her. 'And I don't have any brothers or sisters to smuggle anything up to my room,' she added.

'Well, I'm sure it's grand to be an only child,' Miss Harding said rather doubtfully. 'I were one

6

of nine kids so I wouldn't know. But you must let me pay you for that eclair, Miss Wain – I mean Mrs Sheridan,' she added, making a half-hearted attempt to open her handbag again.

'It's quite all right, Miss Harding,' Marianne said immediately. 'Goodness, look at that snow! It looks as though we shall be having another white Christmas, and they said 1938 was the first one for eleven years.'

'Oh, I do hope so,' Libby said, clasping her hands like the heroine in a fairy story. 'Daddy expects to be in port for Christmas and I've asked for a sledge because when Daddy was a little boy he went sledging in the hills, and he's promised to take me if the snow is right.'

'Me and me brother Sid – he were the nearest to me in age – used to take trays to Havelock Street. You had to station someone on Netherfield Road so's you could shout to whoever were comin' down on the tray if there were vehicles approachin'. Eh, it were grand whooshing down the hill with the wind tryin' to tear off your scarf and everyone screamin' wi' the excitement of it all.' Miss Harding got ponderously to her feet. 'Well, listen to me gabblin' on! It won't make a very good impression on Mr Eccles if I'm late, for though I've been tellin' meself it ain't an interview I reckon it is really. Fancy me bein' late for me first interview in twenty years! Bye-bye, Miss Wain – I mean Mrs Sheridan. Bye-bye, chuck. Wish me luck!'

Both Libby and her mother did so, though Libby

still felt a trifle resentful over the chocolate eclair. They watched the older woman disappear through the big glass doors, turning to wave as she headed for the lifts, then Libby picked up her glass of lemonade and drained the last mouthful. Her mother glanced at her wristwatch, then examined the cake stand. 'It's only twenty past eleven and we don't have to be at Gammy's till one.' She smiled at her daughter and hailed a passing waitress. 'Could you bring us another chocolate eclair, please? And a little more hot water.'

The waitress complied and presently Libby was finishing off the extra eclair whilst her mother ate the macaroon. 'You're a really good girl, Libby,' her mother said when Libby thanked her for the pastry. 'I knew you wanted it, of course, but you behaved just as you should and never even looked wistful when Miss Harding took it. And as soon as we've finished, queen, I think we ought to do a bit more shopping because if this weather keeps up we shan't want to come out more than we have to.'

'But I thought we'd nearly finished,' Libby said, struggling with the last button of her coat. 'Who haven't we bought for? Oh, Mummy, do you think I'll get that sledge?' The two of them had made their way out of the café and down the stairs and were now hovering just inside the big doors which led to the street. Libby, staring out at the huge snowflakes, wondered why they looked grey against the sky as they floated to earth, even though everyone knew that snowflakes were just about as pure white as anything could be. 'You bought Daddy the book you said he wanted and the beautiful curly pipe and I bought him the packet of tobacco, and we're both giving Gammy the lovely blue cardigan you knitted . . . who's left?'

'Darling, you can't have forgotten your Aunt Fiona,' her mother said incredulously. 'She's your only aunt!'

'But you said the woolly hat and scarf were for Auntie Fee,' Libby said reproachfully. 'You said that not everyone could wear yellow, but it suited her perfectly.'

Libby had always loved shopping with her mother, but they had been at it since early morning, and it was a fair way to Gammy's little house in Crocus Street. What was more, the last time she had visited her grandmother she had left a half-finished storybook on the kitchen table, and she knew that if they went straight to Crocus Street she would be allowed to read whilst Gammy chipped potatoes and Mum laid the table.

'Ye-es, but Fiona's my only sister and she does love pretty things,' her mother said now. 'Daddy and I can give her the hat and scarf, and you can give her . . . some really nice earrings.' They were both carrying various packages, but at least earrings would not add much to the weight of their burdens, Libby thought, following obediently as her mother turned away from the doors and headed for a display of costume jewellery. 'Why, you can choose earrings in a second and then we can scoot for the tram and be in Crocus Street before you can say knife.'

But in fact the display of earrings was so enticing that it was a good twenty minutes before the final selection was made. Libby had wanted to purchase a pair of large gold hoops studded with chips of artificial diamond, but her mother was in favour of two tiny gold hearts with a green leaf depending from each of them. 'But Mummy, Auntie Fee's got such masses of hair and it's so long that your little earrings won't show,' Libby pointed out. 'You'll be able to see those lovely big hoops even when she's just washed her hair and it's all puffed out round her face.'

Marianne laughed. 'The thing is, my love, that Fee has to tie her hair back for work and though I do agree that the gold hoops are very striking, I don't think she could wear them in an insurance office.'

'Oh, but they're so pretty,' Libby said mournfully. 'She could wear them when she goes to the Grafton, or one of the other dance halls. Still, I expect you're right. We'll buy the gold hearts.'

So presently they left the store with the little earrings in a tiny velvet box, wrapped around with tissue paper and pushed into her mother's smart leather handbag. Outside, the huge flakes were still falling and Libby wasted several moments, tongue extended and eyes crossing, trying to catch them as they whirled earthwards. She caught a couple, remarking to Marianne that they tasted exciting, but then she saw the tram they wanted to catch clattering along the road, and the pair of them hurriedly crossed over to the stop, dodging the traffic and clutching their various parcels.

In fact, they need not have hurried since there was a fairly lengthy queue. 'I don't believe we'll get on this one,' Libby grumbled, as people began to edge forward. 'If I was by meself, I'd squiggle past everyone else and get aboard first, but it's only kids that can do that. Folk would shove a grown-up back and tell them to keep to their bleedin' place.'

'Libby!' Marianne said on a gasp. 'I never thought to hear my little girl swear. And as for jumping the queue, don't you dare let me catch you doing such a thing.'

'I wasn't swearing, Mummy, I was repeating what I've heard people say when a grown-up shoves their way to the front,' Libby said placidly. She thought to herself that her mother did not know the half of it and perhaps it was a good thing. When her mother and father went off for a weekend, or to visit her paternal grandparents, they usually left her with Gammy, which meant of course that she played with the children living in Crocus Street. Libby was well aware that her mother would not have approved of a good many of the pastimes in which she indulged when staying there. She went with the other kids to the Saturday Rush, though she seldom had to relinquish her fourpence. One of the boys would go in through the foyer and make his way straight to the fire exit. The rest of them would squiggle down the outside of the cinema until they reached the double doors, which would be opened from the inside to let them in. Naturally, the boy would charge everyone a penny for his services, but even so this would leave Libby with threepence to spend on ice creams, popcorn or her favourite sweets, sherbet lemons.

There were other ploys, which Gammy took for granted but Libby knew her mother would not condone. Getting a free ride by hanging on to the back of a tram – skipping a lecky, the kids called it – or begging fades from the stallholders in St John's market, or carrying shopping or doing messages for the elderly of the court in return for a penny, or even a ha'penny. Libby, who got sixpence a week pocket money, never revealed to the other children that she had no need of the money and besides, it came in useful. Sometimes, when she had fetched water for old Mrs Bradshaw, she would accept the ha'penny the old lady gave her, but carefully conceal three or four pennies amongst the crocks on the draining board waiting to be dried up and put away. It made her feel like Robin Hood, but she would never have dreamed of admitting what she did to the other kids, let alone boasting about it. Mrs Bradshaw, notoriously vague, would assume that she herself must have dropped the money there when sorting though her purse, and would be a little better off as a result.

But right now, Marianne was saying, in a shocked voice, that the rules were the same for grown-ups as for children; one waited one's turn and never, never pushed ahead.

'No, Mummy, I never do. It's what I've seen other kids do,' Libby said virtuously, crossing her fingers in her white woollen gloves. 'Downstairs is full . . . well, almost; shall we go up?' She clattered up the stairs and, glancing behind her, saw her mother following. Then she looked down the aisle and saw to her dismay that almost all the seats were taken up here too. However, there was one right at the very front and another half a dozen rows back, so she hurried up the aisle whilst the tram was still stationary, took her place on the front seat, and saw her mother slide into the other vacant one.

Then she settled back to enjoy the ride, for the front of the tram was her very favourite place. She reflected that not even the tram driver had a better view, and hoped that the falling snow would not stick to the glass. Unfortunately, it did so, but the side window remained clear, and when the large and bewhiskered man seated next to it saw her trying to peer past him he grinned cheerfully at her. 'Hang on, queen. If you want to sit agin the window, then we'd best swap places,' he said. 'I'm gerrin' out in another half-mile or so, an' it takes me all me time to walk the length of the tram and geddown them 'orrible stairs wi'out fallin' flat on me face. If I'm on the outside seat I'll gerra head start.'

Changing places, Libby thanked him very prettily, dug in her pocket, and produced an Everton mint, which he accepted after an initial pretence of reluctance. Then she pressed her small nose against the glass and began to scan the shop windows and the scurrying crowds. For the first time she realised that there were a large number of men on the pavement below, many of them in naval uniform, and this made her think that probably a ship, or ships, had just docked. How lovely it would be if she spotted her father; after all, he had hoped to be home for Christmas so it was perfectly possible that his corvette, the *Marjoram*, might be in port right now. Naturally, the thought made Libby stare harder than ever, planning as she did so how, if she saw him, she would bang on the glass, then run as fast as she could towards the stairs, shouting the news to her mother, ringing the bell to warn the driver, and diving off at the very next stop. And how thrilled Daddy would be to find his little girl rushing towards him through the thickening snowflakes! She would make him get aboard the tram and join her mother on the top deck, chattering away to him as she did so, clutching his hand, helping him with his Gladstone bag and not asking him whether he had brought her a present for, though he always tried to do so, in wartime it was not always possible.

But of course all of this depended on her seeing her daddy and she realised, with a little dismay, that identifying someone when you could only see the top of his head would not be easy. In fact she had resigned herself to simply enjoying the tram ride when a man in naval uniform, strolling along the pavement, removed his cap for a moment to knock the snow off it and she caught a glimpse of thickly waving dark gold hair. For that second she truly thought that it was her father.

The tram had come almost to a halt, hemmed in by another tram just ahead, and the crowd on the pavement had also slowed their pace, including the naval officer. Libby jumped to her feet and would have run to join her mother except that she saw that Marianne was occupied. The conductor was issuing their tickets and her mother was counting out pennies and ha'pennies into his hand. Libby sighed, tried to catch her mother's attention, failed and returned to her seat.

The old man who had given her his place grinned at her as she sat down beside him once more. 'Did you think it were your stop, queen?' he asked her. 'You don't never want to gerroff a tram between stops 'cos you might break your leg, or get yourself squashed flat by another vehicle.'

Libby grinned back. 'You're thinking of that poem my gammy taught me,' she said. '*Oh Mummy dear, what is that mess that looks like strawberry jam? Hush hush, my child, that is Papa, run over by a tram.*'

The old man's grin broadened. 'Well there you are then. I reckon that were writ by the poet lorry whats-isname, and you can't get no truer than that. So if it weren't your stop, what was you a-doing of, eh?'

'I don't think Mr Masefield – he's the poet laureate – wrote that,' Libby observed, smothering a giggle. 'He writes about a tall ship and a star to steer her by; we learned that in school last term. My daddy often quotes his poetry, and actually I jumped up because I thought I saw him through the window . . . my daddy, I mean, not Mr Masefield. He's aboard a corvette, the *Marjoram*, and she's due in port any time now, so it could have been him. Only the conductor was in the way and my mother was paying for our tickets.'

The old man got to his feet and patted her shoulder as he began to make his way along the narrow aisle. She followed him in order to give her mother's sleeve a tug. 'Mummy, this gentleman is getting off the tram so why don't you come and sit next to me up at the front?' As her mother nodded agreement and began to collect her packages together, Libby raised her voice to address her erstwhile companion. 'Goodbye, sir, and thank you for your company.'

She thought her mother would be proud of her for being so polite and was surprised, and none too pleased, when Marianne propelled her smartly back to her seat, saying, a trifle breathlessly: 'I saw you chattering away and making the old fellow laugh, but you do know, don't you, pet, that you really shouldn't speak to strange men? Oh, I'm sure your whiskery friend was perfectly harmless, but sometimes there are people on trams who aren't harmless at all. So in future, if you sit next to a stranger, try not to chatter.'

Libby heaved a deep sigh. Sometimes she felt that being a child was far more difficult than being a grown-up. She was bidden on the one hand to be polite and respectful to all adults, yet it now appeared that she must hold aloof from some without knowing why. She opened her mouth to question this latest rule, then remembered the man she had seen as the tram had juddered almost to a halt. 'Yes, all right, I'll try to remember,' she said rapidly. 'But Mummy, just when the conductor was taking your money, I thought I saw Daddy. He was walking along the pavement carrying that navy blue Gladstone bag he bought last Christmas. I jumped up and started to run down the aisle, only I couldn't get past the conductor and I couldn't catch your eye, and whilst you were still counting out our fares the tram jolted and moved on. Did you look out of the window, Mummy? Oh, and if it was Daddy, then he'll be home before us and he'll be so disappointed to find the house empty. Do you think we ought to get off this tram and catch one heading for the Croxteth Road? I'm sure Gammy will understand.'

'Oh, Libby, darling, we can't possibly do that. Gammy's expecting us, remember, and anyway, there are heaps of naval officers in the city, you know. Remember, you were looking at him from a very unusual angle and could easily have been mistaken.'

'I suppose you're right,' Libby said slowly. 'Only, if it was Daddy . . .'

'We could have our lunch with Gammy and then go straight home to Sydenham Avenue just in case he's there,' Marianne said. 'I had planned to do some more shopping but we can come out again tomorrow. I certainly wouldn't want your daddy to have to spend the afternoon alone in the house.' She leaned across to give her daughter a quick hug. 'I'm beginning to wish you'd not been looking out of the window at that particular moment, queen.'

'Oh, Mummy, I'm so sorry,' Libby said remorsefully. 'But the more I think about it, the more I think you're probably right and it wasn't Daddy at all. And even if it was, he'll be happy enough to spend the afternoon in the nice warm kitchen, and you know how he hates shopping.'

To Libby's relief, the anxious crease left her mother's brow and she smiled. 'You're absolutely right, pet. So we'll forget about rushing home, go and see Gammy, and then finish the shopping. We've no more presents to get but I did think we might nip into St John's market for a bag of oranges. And you could do with some nice thick woollen stockings; your old ones are getting thin at the heels. We can buy them a good deal cheaper on Scotland Road than in the big stores.'

Libby was about to remark that the stockings she was wearing were a trifle shrunk from constant washing, and pinched her toes, when the conductor shouted the name of their stop and people began to leave their seats. She and her mother followed suit, clattering down the stairs and pushing their tickets into the slot provided for that purpose. Then they jumped off the platform straight into what seemed to Libby to be a blizzard. She gasped, then lowered her head and seized her mother's hand, and the two of them began to hurry along the pavement, heading for Crocus Street. They turned the corner and Libby immediately realised that Stanley Road was in fact sheltered compared with Crocus Street. The wind was howling and the snowflakes stung her cheeks. She was wearing a red beret but now the wind tugged so fiercely at it that she feared for its safety – it was a new acquisition – so she released her mother for a moment to tug it down, unbecomingly, so that it covered her ears and eyebrows, and she saw that her mother, too, was pulling her own hat more firmly on to her head and turning up the collar of her navy blue coat. Then the two grabbed hands again and fought their way down the street, for Gammy lived at the Commercial Road end.

Mother and daughter turned thankfully into the jigger and scuttled round to the gate into the yard. They pushed it open and and headed for the kitchen door, knowing that Gammy would be there expecting them, for no member of the family would have dreamed of going to the front door. When they burst into the kitchen Gammy was at the sink, peeling potatoes. She looked up and dropped the potato and the knife, wiped her hands quickly on her wraparound apron, and hurried over to help

Libby out of her coat and to take the now rather soggy parcels from them both.

'I were just beginning to wonder whether you would take one look at the weather and head for home,' she said, opening the door again to shake the snow off Libby's coat and hat on to the cobbles of the back yard. 'But of course it weren't snowing when you set out 'cos it didn't even start till after eleven. My, my, I thought you was a couple of snowmen when you came in just now.'

'I feel like one,' Marianne said, shivering. She hung her coat and hat on the hooks beside the back door but Gammy, tutting, shook her head and bustled across the kitchen to lower the drying rack from its place against the ceiling.

'We'll purr'em up here, then mebbe they'll dry out by the time you have to leave,' she said, spreading both coats and both hats across the rack and then heaving it ceilingwards once more. 'My, but it's a foul day! However, it may ease off later.' She glanced at the clock on the mantel. 'I think we'll have our grub a bit early, like; then if there is a lull in the storm you'd better make a dash for the tram. That is, if your coats is dry by then. If not, I could lend you me big black umbrella, only that means I'll have to come all the way out to your place to gerrit back.'

Marianne laughed. 'Oh, Mum, as if I'd let you do that! But quite honestly, an umbrella would be torn to shreds by the wind before we even reached the tram stop. How many of us will be eating today? I know Fee's at work and won't be back until evening, but what about the lodgers?'

Her grandmother, Libby knew, had three lodgers: a father and son, Tomas and Eamonn McNally, who shared the front bedroom and worked at the Tate & Lyle factory in Eldon Street, so were unlikely to be home for the midday meal; and old Mr Parsons, who had worked at Ogden's tobacco factory up the road and was now retired. He might well come home for dinner. Inside herself, Libby sighed. Her mother always referred to the midday meal as lunch, but Gammy called it dinner, and the evening meal, which Gammy called supper, or even high tea, was dinner as far as Libby's parents were concerned. To add to the confusion, she had heard the children who went to the Daisy Street school just up the road refer to elevenses as lunch.

Gammy was answering her daughter's question. 'No, it'll be just us. Didn't I tell you? Mr Parsons has got a temporary job at Ogden's. They called him back because wi' so many men joining the forces they're desperate for workers. Believe it or not, they're paying him the same wage as the full-time workers, though he's doing much shorter hours, so of course he agreed to go back like a shot.'

'Well, if that isn't a coincidence!' Marianne said. She was laying the table, or at least gathering plates, cutlery, cups and saucers, but now she took the kettle off the hob and pulled it over the fire, then went across to the sink. 'I'll chip the spuds, Mum, if you'll peel them.'

'What's a coincidence?' Gammy said plaintively. 'Wharra one you are, queen, for startin' a sentence an' never finishin' it.' She turned her head to address Libby. 'You finish layin' the table, love, and fetch out the salt and vinegar from the pantry, while your mam and meself gerron with the dinner. Tell me when the kettle boils so's I can make a pot of tea, 'cos the kettle's way too heavy for a kid o' your age.'

'Right, Gammy,' Libby said. 'Have you got any milk or do you want me to get down a tin of conny-onny?' Libby knew her grandmother often put condensed milk into drinks when she had run out of fresh, and was not surprised to be told she'd best bring out the opened tin of milk which she would find on the slate slab.

Libby spread the plates and cutlery out on the table as her mother spoke. 'No wonder I never finish a sentence with you talking non-stop, Mum. It's a coincidence because I met Miss Harding in Lewis's restaurant this morning. She retired a year ago, but had been asked to return to work and was going for an interview. She asked me if I'd been approached, but of course it's years since I worked there, so I've heard nothing. Even if I did, I wouldn't go back. When Madam here is evacuated, I mean to get some sort of work which will help the war effort. I might even join one of the women's services, only I'd like to be sure I don't get posted somewhere far away.'

Gammy peeled the last of the potatoes in the bowl and turned to smile approvingly at her daughter. 'That's right. We all want to do our bit,' she said. She was a small, plump woman, with a round jolly face. When Libby was little she had been intrigued by Gammy's false teeth, which were very large and white and shiny, and seemed far too big. Her nose was short and turned up at the tip, and her upper lip was short, too, so that unless she closed her mouth very firmly, which only happened when she was cross, or concentrating fiercely, it was usually slightly open. Her hair, which was light brown and streaked with white at the temples, was pulled back from her face and fastened into a large soft bun on the nape of her neck. Her eyes, however, were beautiful; very large and a deep velvety brown, and fringed with curly lashes which many a girl half her age might have envied. She turned to Libby. 'If you look under the bottom shelf in the pantry, you'll see two bottles of Corona. The cherryade has been started – Eamonn's that fond of cherryade – so you'd best bring that out.'

'Right, Gammy,' Libby said, her mouth already watering at the thought of cherryade – she, too, was fond of that particular flavour – egg and chips, and the pudding which she knew would follow, for she had glimpsed a treacle tart lurking beneath the wire mesh dome next to the slate slab.

The three of them worked quietly away and presently Gammy tipped the chipped potatoes into a pan of briskly bubbling fat and, when they were beginning to turn golden brown, produced her frying pan and broke three eggs into it. Very soon they were sitting down to their meal, Libby pouring a dollop of ketchup on to her plate, with a wary eye on her mother who rarely allowed tomato sauce to be used in her own house, except as a special treat. 'There's no point in my providing good, nourishing food if you mask the taste with pickles and sauces,' she was wont to say. 'I always salt the cooking water before I add the vegetables, so they shouldn't need anything more. Besides, too much salt is bad for you and I'm sure that sauces must contain a great number of other nasty things as well.'

Dipping her chips first into the golden yolk of her egg and then into the puddle of bright red sauce, Libby reflected that her mother almost never made chips at home, either, which made them even more of a treat. And though Marianne had not helped herself to ketchup, she had shaken vinegar and salt over her plate with a prodigal hand. Libby sighed at the complexity of grown-ups. Mummy and Auntie Fee had been brought up by Gammy, so they must have eaten a great many chips, bought pies and battered fish, types of food which her mother now said would give her spots and make her hair greasy. Yet Marianne was acknowledged to be a very beautiful woman – her skin was pale as milk and as clear, with not a spot in sight – whilst Auntie Fee was not only very pretty, but

24

also what her mother described as 'striking'. Libby was not certain what this meant, but thinking of her aunt's cloud of red-gold hair, big hazel-green eyes and wonderful creamy skin, scattered with tiny golden freckles, she knew it must be a compliment of no mean order.

'Well, if the snow makes you that hungry, young lady, we'll have to hope it don't last for too long,' Gammy observed, piling up the empty plates and heading for the sink. 'I trust as how you've got room for a slice of my treacle tart with a nice helpin' of custard over it? I made it special, knowin' you've got a sweet tooth, but I dare say Fiona and Eamonn will polish it off if you can't manage none.'

'So that's where the milk went!' Marianne said gaily. 'I thought the milkman would have delivered before the snow started. But I won't have any, Mum. I've eaten far too much already.'

'It's home-made,' her mother said, a trifle reproachfully. She knew Marianne did not approve of bought cakes or pies and usually baked her own bread, but Gammy, working part time in the Manchester Laundry at the corner of Snowdrop Street, not a hundred yards from her house, did not always have time to bake. The laundry employed her to iron difficult and delicate garments. But even the knowledge that her mother had made the treacle tart specially did not tempt Marianne, though she accepted a second cup of tea.

Presently, when Gammy and Libby had finished

their pudding, Marianne took her cup over to the window and peered out through the misted pane. 'It's snowing worse than ever,' she said gloomily. 'Well, that puts paid to any more shopping, queen, because there's absolutely no point in Gammy drying out our coats just to get them soaking wet again.'

Gammy got up from the table and joined her daughter at the window. 'It ain't coming down quite so fast,' she said, though Libby thought she sounded doubtful. 'Tell you what, you give me a hand to wash up and clear away, and if it hasn't stopped we could bring the big jigsaw through from the front room and have a go at it on the kitchen table. If it still ain't stopped by the time we've finished the jigsaw, then I reckon the two of you had best get a taxicab what'll take you straight to your door. I know it's a bit pricey, but you won't mind that.'

'Oh, Mother! How can we possibly do that?' Marianne asked in a scolding tone. 'It's not as if taxis cruise up and down Crocus Street. We'd have to walk to the Stanley hospital, and we might not get one even then. No, if it hasn't stopped by the time we've washed up, we'll have to brave the elements, I'm afraid. You see, there's always a chance that the *Marjoram* might have docked and Neil could be waiting for us at home. I wouldn't want him worrying.'

Gammy heaved a sigh but agreed that they had best follow this plan, though she did say that she

26

would not let either of them go out into the storm without so much as an umbrella.

By the time they had washed up and cleared away, however, the wind was no longer howling and the snow was falling in a much more leisurely fashion. Gammy and Marianne turned from the window and Gammy bustled across to the drying rack. 'It looks like the worst is over,' she said cheerfully. 'If the weather's real bad tomorrer, I shan't be going to the laundry, so you can keep my umbrella for a day or so. But if you mean to finish off your messages, then you could either pop into Fiona's office and leave it wi' her, or bring it back to me when you've a spare moment.' As she spoke, she was lowering the drying rack and helping Libby into her coat and beret, though she tutted when she realised that her grand-daughter had not got a scarf. 'Still, with me umbrella, you and your mam will get home without being soaked through,' she said with satis-faction. She handed her daughter the big black umbrella which stood by the back door. 'Now don't forget, queen,' she said, 'hang on to it if the weather's foul agin tomorrer. I ought to keep a spare but somehow I've never got round to it.'

'Well I will,' Marianne said gratefully, buttoning her coat and jamming her hat well down on her smooth silky hair. Libby admired her mother's hair, which was not red-gold like Fiona's but a beautiful rich brown, like the shiny horse chest-nuts the kids played conkers with in the autumn.

Libby had secret hopes that her own straight, limp hair might turn from ordinary brown to gleaming chestnut as she got older, but so far it had shown no sign of changing, and when she had asked her aunt whether she might one day become a redhead Auntie Fee had just laughed and said she should be grateful to have nice brown hair and no freckles.

As Marianne began to tug at the back door, Gammy held out her arms to Libby. 'Give your old gammy a kiss, chuck,' she said. 'If it hadn't been for your daddy maybe comin' home I'd ha' made you stay the night, but that ain't on.'

Libby kissed her grandmother's soft pink cheek and returned the hug. She was beginning to say how much she would have liked to stay over when Marianne got the back door open, picked up her various parcels and caught hold of Libby's gloved hand. 'Oh, Mother, for all we know the snow could be even worse tomorrow,' she said briskly. 'I'm sure we're doing the right thing in leaving during a lull.' She turned and gave her mother a quick kiss. 'And thank you for our dinner and the umbrella; I promise to bring it back either tomorrow or the next day.'

'Tell you what,' Gammy shouted, as Libby and her mother began to cross the snowy courtyard, 'why don't you pop in and have your tea wi' us tomorrer? If Neil's home, he'll be very welcome, as you know, but if he ain't, a trip out will take your mind off worryin' over him. How about that, eh?'

'We'll see what the weather's like, Mother,' Marianne shouted. 'Bye for now.'

28

They were lucky; as they reached the Stanley Road the tram they wanted came slowly along. It was not crowded, but when Libby tried to head for the stairs her mother pulled her back. 'No you don't, young lady,' she said. 'There's plenty of room inside and those stairs are terribly slippery in wet weather.'

Libby sighed but obediently slid into a seat about halfway up the aisle and rubbed a clear space in the misted window. She peered out at the people hurrying past, but saw no one she knew, not even when they changed trams at the Pier Head.

They reached the Croxteth Road and made their way from the tram stop to Sydenham Avenue. Marianne clicked open the little green gate and they trudged through the snow which had piled up between the house wall and the fence, reaching the back garden with considerable relief. It was immediately obvious that there was no one at home, for none of the blackout blinds had been drawn, and had Neil arrived in their absence he would scarcely have sat in the dark. When her mother unlocked the back door and let them into the empty house, Libby accepted that she must have been mistaken.

'Oh well, that just proves it wasn't Daddy I saw,' she said rather sadly. 'Never mind. Perhaps he'll come tomorrow.'

'I'm so sorry you're disappointed, darling,' her mother said gently. 'What would you like for your tea, love? How about baked beans on toast? You've already had one egg today, and that's quite enough.'

'Yes, baked beans would be fine,' Libby said, glancing contentedly round the bright and cosy kitchen. Her mother had pulled the blackout blinds and turned on the light as soon as the back door was safely closed, and then drawn the gaily patterned curtains.

'Right,' Marianne said briskly, going across to the pantry. 'While I get your tea you can nip up to your bedroom and fetch your school books, because you don't want to fall behind your class-mates, do you?'

Libby pulled a face. 'I bet they aren't working half as hard as me,' she grumbled. 'I remember hearing on the wireless that evacuated children were sharing schools with the kids already there, so they work either mornings or afternoons, not both. Must I, Mummy? I'm quite tired, and it's been a long day, wouldn't you say? Besides, I'm conva . . . conva . . .'

'Convalescing,' her mother supplied. 'But that doesn't mean lazing about doing nothing, so off you go and fetch your books down. When you've had your tea, we'll do schoolwork for an hour or so and then I'll read you another chapter or two of *The Railway Children*.'

Libby bounced to her feet at once. She could read the book for herself, of course, but she much preferred her mother's rendering, for Marianne did all the voices differently and made it very exciting. 'OK, Mummy,' she said, heading for the stairs. 'I shan't be two ticks.'

'OK is slang . . .' Marianne began, but Libby, already halfway up the stairs, did not bother to reply. Everyone used slang, from Gammy to the other children at school, so why should she be different? Breaking into song as she thundered along the landing, she began to plan how she would tackle the threat of evacuation when her mother next spoke of it. I am not going away, and if they send me I'll find my way back in a week, she told herself, bursting into her bedroom and seizing her satchel. It was bulging with school-work, which one of the teachers who had been left behind had promised to mark. If Mummy goes off to join the forces, then I shall jolly well live with Gammy!

Chapter Two

Marianne woke early the next morning. Though she had tried to play down any hint of anxiety over Neil's arrival, she was beginning to wonder whether he would in fact be in port for Christmas. Libby adored her father and she would be bitterly disappointed if he did not get home. Neil was the sort of father every child should have, Marianne thought, one who would sacrifice his own pleasures to give his daughter treats such as trips to the theatre, walks in the country, or days out at the seaside. Last summer he had taken his small family to a delightful guest house in Llandudno, and for a whole week Libby had played on the sand, creating huge castles with his help, whilst Marianne lazed in a deckchair and read. Neil had taught Libby to swim, had taken her up and down the beach on her favourite donkey, and had paddled in the rock pools with his trousers rolled up, turning over rocks and naming every sea creature they came across. Yes, an ideal father and a wonderful husband. If he did not get home, Christmas would be spoiled for them both.

Today was 22 December, which meant there was

still time, and if she got all her shopping done today and Neil arrived by this evening, they would have all Saturday and Sunday to prepare for the great day itself.

Marianne glanced at her small alarm clock. It was only just after eight o'clock, but if she meant to get her shopping done she had best get a move on. She threw back the bedclothes, giving a little shiver as she did so, crossed to the window and pulled up the blackout blind, sighing as she realised that during the night the window had been covered with frost flowers. She placed her warm palm on the pane and peered. The snow had stopped, but a good deal must have fallen during the night for it lay several inches deep, as far as she could see. She could tell, however, that there was no wind, for the snow had not blown off the small conifers which grew in next door's garden. She should be able to do her shopping and take her mother's umbrella back without getting soaked to the skin.

Marianne left the window and padded across the pretty pink carpet to where her dressing gown hung on the back of the door. Usually she would have gone straight to the bathroom and washed in the hot water provided by the geyser over the bath before rousing her daughter, but this morning she decided she would go down first to open the stove and make sure that it was burning brightly so that Libby would not have to eat her breakfast in a chilly kitchen.

When she was halfway down the stairs, however, the kitchen door opened and her daughter appeared, carrying a filled cup in one hand. Libby uttered an exclamation of disappointment when she saw her mother. 'There! I was bringing you a lovely cup of tea in bed, Mummy, as a special treat. Oh, why don't you go back to your room, then I could bring it up anyway?'

'No, I don't think I'll do that if you don't mind, because if we're to get all our messages – all our shopping, I mean – then we must both get a move on,' Marianne said tactfully. 'But Libby, darling, you've been told over and over not to touch the kettle when it's hot. Indeed, I didn't know you could so much as lift it.'

'Oh, I didn't,' Libby said tranquilly. 'I used the water from the hot tap in the kitchen. I thought it would be just as good.'

Marianne looked at the pallid, lukewarm liquid in the cup and was thankful that she would not have to drink it. 'That's very sweet of you, my love. Now you nip upstairs and wash while I riddle the stove and make up the fire. I'll have the tea while I work,' she finished consolingly, if untruthfully.

Libby handed over the cup and hurried up the stairs, and Marianne went into the kitchen. There was a puddle of milk on the draining board, but otherwise the room looked as it should. The curtains had been pulled back and the blackout blind rolled up, and Libby had got the oats and the loaf out of the pantry and stood both ready on the table. Thank God she didn't try to make the porridge or the toast, Marianne thought gratefully, tipping the unappetising tea down the sink and beginning her usual morning tasks. But of course she was only trying to help, so I mustn't grumble. I think I'll suggest that we just have porridge and tea though, because I would really like to catch the nine o'clock bus. I'll take my big marketing bag and buy all the Christmasy fruit and vegetables from St John's market. Then we'll go to Gammy's and give her back her umbrella. It might be an idea to take some fish and chips, since she won't be expecting us at lunchtime.

Presently she heard Libby thundering down the stairs and checked with her eye that everything was as it should be. The porridge simmered gently on the back of the stove and the bread was sliced and buttered, so all that remained for Libby to do was laying the table. She said as much as the child joined her, then hurried upstairs to get herself ready for the day ahead. In the bathroom, it occurred to her to wonder how Libby had managed to light the geyser since she was forbidden to handle matches, but a hand on its stout white side told her that the contraption had not been used; Libby had washed in cold water. She is a good child, Marianne told herself, for all she says she'll defy me and refuse to be evacuated. Besides, I know she won't do it. But just to make certain, I'll get Neil to have a talk to her when he comes home.

Satisfied that Libby would listen to her beloved father, Marianne lit the geyser, turned the tap and began to wash.

By the time they had done their marketing, bought the fish and chips and staggered off the tram at the Crocus Street stop, Marianne was beginning to regret her impetuous plan. The fruit and vegetables were dreadfully heavy, and though Libby was carrying the fish and chips in a string bag, Marianne herself had the huge flapping umbrella trapped under one arm and was uneasily aware that the pavement was slippery with melted snow and ice. What a mess she would make of her silk stockings and her warm overcoat if she measured her length.

However, they were nearly at their destination, and as she and Libby turned into the jigger which ran behind the Crocus Street houses she felt a pleasant glow of anticipation. It would be lovely to get into Gammy's cosy kitchen and see her pleasure when they handed over the fish and chips. Marianne knew that even when Gammy was working at the laundry she always came back for her dinner, so there was no fear of finding her not at home.

And, indeed, so it proved. Her mother was in the kitchen, making a pot of tea. She turned as the door opened, a welcoming beam spreading across her rosy face. 'There, and I was just wonderin' whether you'd brave the cold and come a-tabberin' upon me door later this afternoon,' she said joyfully, sweeping her granddaughter into a tight embrace and then giving Marianne a smacking kiss on the cheek. 'Oh, you good girl, you've brought back me umbrella! Not that I'll need it, tomorrer being Sat'day, 'cos even old Mrs Fazakerley wouldn't expect me to work at a weekend. I did go in this morning, early, and finish off all the fine stuff for 'em, so now I'm at your service, young ladies. I've not cooked a hot meal, but —'

'Tan-tara!' Libby carolled, pulling the newspaper-wrapped package of fish and chips out of the string bag and plonking it down on the kitchen table. 'Mummy bought half a dozen pieces of fish and loads of chips, just in case your lodgers was in, but if they're not you can always hot it up for their supper tonight.'

Gammy bustled across the room and began getting plates and cutlery out of the sideboard, chattering away as she did so. Marianne was replying to a question about the price of fruit at the market when the back door burst open and Fiona came into the room. She was speaking as she entered. 'Is everything all right, Mam? You got me message? Only I didn't want you to worry . . .' Her eyes fixed themselves on Marianne, flickered to Libby and returned to her elder sister. 'Good Lord, Marianne, what on earth are you doin' here? Mam said you were poppin' in yesterday for your dinners but she never said no word about today.'

'Didn't she?' Marianne said, considerably

surprised. 'That's rather odd, because if the weather had been really bad I was supposed to bring Gammy's umbrella up to your office. Didn't she even tell you that?' She swung round on her mother, laughing. 'That's carrying forgetfulness a bit far, wouldn't you say?'

Gammy began to answer, but Fiona cut across her words. 'I had to work late last night – so did Mary and young Vi – and because of the blizzard, Mary and Vi said I could have a shakedown on their floor. You know what the trams are like, they stop runnin' if the weather is really bad, so I thought stayin' over with them were a good plan. Mr Pinfold's secretary lives on Stanley Road, though, and she weren't workin' late, so I give her a note for Mam, explaining what I were doin', so she wouldn't worry.' She giggled. 'We had a grand time, the three of us. The boss went out and bought everyone fish and chips, and then we gorron with the work. We didn't get away from the office till after nine, and of course we were hungry again by then, but young Mr Oliver – he's one of the clerks, and keen on Mary – had gone out earlier and mugged us to a lovely sponge cake from the baker's up the road.' She giggled again. 'It seemed only polite to ask him back so he could share the treat. It were like the midnight feasts in them schoolbooks we used to read: cream cake and hot cocoa and a lorra laughs. It were midnight before I got me head down, but we got to the office on time this morning, and the boss said we could

38

leave at twelve, 'cos there weren't much point in working later with Christmas so close.'

Marianne heaved a deep sigh. 'What a one you are, Fiona. Midnight feasts, sleepin' on folks' floors . . . anyone would think you were Libby's age, you great big kid!' She turned to her mother. 'I take it you got the message, Mam, and didn't have to worry.'

'That's right,' Gammy said calmly. She was used to Fiona's erratic lifestyle, Marianne knew, and even had she not received the note would have guessed that no harm had come to her daughter.

As she talked, Fiona had taken off the fawn-coloured scarf and the long coat which she had been wearing. She hung them up, then removed her shoes and slid her feet into the slippers which stood near the back door, regarding the shoes critically as she did so. 'If I'd known it were goin' to snow I'd have worn me boots,' she observed. 'I meant to buy some grub, knowing you wouldn't be expectin' me this early, Mam, but I'd no sooner stepped out of the office than a tram came along and I hopped aboard without thinking.'

'It's a good thing you didn't buy anything, since Libby and I have brought fish and chips,' Marianne observed. 'I hope you like 'em, queen, since you had 'em last night as well.'

Fiona beamed. 'I *thought* I smelled fish,' she said triumphantly. 'Fish and chips is a thing you can't never have too much of.' She was still holding her shoes in one hand, and now she waved them at

39

Marianne. 'These are me best, or were me best rather. Patent leather don't take kindly to being soaked through.'

Marianne reached out a hand and rumpled her glorious red-gold curls. 'Trust you to wear dancing pumps to the office,' she said, laughing. 'Did you mean to go the Grafton after work? If so, you should have taken your pumps in a bag and changed when you reached the dance hall. Honestly, Fee, you just don't think.'

Fiona was beginning to answer when someone knocked on the front door. Instantly, she shoved the shoes into Marianne's hands. 'I'll answer it; it'll be Paul Hill. We were supposed to be going to the flicks last night. I sent him a message, but I expect . . .' She was already heading to the front door, so Marianne sighed and ran up the stairs to put the shoes in Fiona's bedroom, reflecting that it was just like her sister to ruin what was obviously a brand new pair simply through thoughtlessness.

She was halfway down the stairs again when she suddenly gave a shriek and almost flew down the rest of the flight, pushing Fiona aside so hard that her sister thumped against the wall and uttered a squeak of protest. 'Steady on, Marianne!' she gasped. 'Don't forget Neil's me brother-in-law so I'm entitled to be pleased to see him, same as you are.'

Marianne, safe in Neil's arms, detached her lips from his and turned to smile at her sister. 'Sorry, queen. I didn't mean to be rough,' she said remorse-fully. 'But I was so worried that he wouldn't make it in time for Christmas, and so thrilled to see him . . .' She pulled herself out of her husband's arms and bent to pick up his Gladstone bag as Libby came hurtling out of the kitchen and hurled herself at her father, chattering wildly as he bent and lifted her up.

'Oh, Daddy, Daddy, Daddy, I just knew you'd be here in time for Christmas,' she squeaked. 'We haven't decorated the front room or the tree yet because Mummy said to wait till you got home, but I were getting worried in case you didn't arrive in time. We made some really pretty decorations out of cardboard and silver paper – stars and moons and things – and I'm longing to see how they look on the tree . . .'

Neil entered the kitchen, where Gammy, wreathed in smiles, was waiting to greet him, and stood his daughter down. He began to struggle out of his greatcoat. 'Well, we'll get the tree in as soon as we get home,' he promised. He hung coat and cap on the peg, hugged Gammy, then turned to Marianne. 'I take it last year's tree has continued to thrive? But will it be possible to dig it up with all this snow on the ground? Only, as the tram came along Stanley Road, I spotted a feller selling Christmas trees. We could get one of them and leave last year's where it is for the time being.'

Marianne smiled lovingly at him. 'It might save a lot of bother to buy another tree,' she admitted.

41

'But how did you know where we were, love? You poor thing, you must have traipsed all the way out to Sydenham Avenue only to be disappointed. I really should have left a note on the kitchen table saying where we'd gone, but we left in rather a rush to catch the nine o'clock tram. So go on, what made you end up here?'

'Deduction, my dear Watson, plus my sheer brilliance,' Neil said, grinning at her. 'There was one hell of a blizzard yesterday – sorry, love, didn't mean to swear – and I thought you wouldn't have gone out in that, but today it's not too bad at all so I guessed you'd be doing your last-minute shopping. I went into the centre and had a quick look round in Lewis's and Blackler's. Then I thought you might be having elevenses, so I popped into Fuller's and Cooper's. And then, because it was getting near lunchtime, I thought I'll bet they've gone to Gammy's, and I was right, wasn't I?'

'Yes, you were,' Libby cut in, beaming at him. 'But was there a blizzard at sea as well as on land, Daddy? Oh, don't say you were in Liverpool yesterday and didn't come home to Mummy and me! Because I thought I saw you, only we were upstairs on the tram and it moved on before I had a chance to get your attention . . . if it was you, that is.'

Neil looked startled, then pulled a rueful face. 'I don't know whether it was me or some other handsome sailor,' he said jokingly, 'but you've been and gone and ruined the surprise, young lady.' He turned to Marianne, taking both her hands and shaking them gently to and fro. 'Yesterday, I came before the Promotions Board. It's a long-winded business but the upshot was that I've got my own command. I'm captain of the *Sea Spurge* and sail with her when she leaves on the sixth of January. I hope you're proud of me, best of wives.'

'Oh, darling Neil, I'd be proud of you if you were just a stoker, but captain of your own ship!' She laughed exuberantly. 'I shall have to buy a new hat because I'm sure my head has just grown at least two sizes bigger.'

'But why didn't you come home last night?' Libby piped up. 'Surely you could have, Daddy?'

Neil laughed, but shook his head. 'No I couldn't, pet. Because it's wartime, the Board had to sit very late indeed, long after the trams had stopped running . . . and there was that blizzard, remember. So I got myself back to the good old *Marjoram* and spent the night aboard.' He turned to his mother-in-law. 'I'm sorry to land you with an extra mouth to feed, Gammy, but bread and cheese will suit me fine, or I could nip out and buy a meat and potato pie from Sample's.'

His mother-in-law, pouring tea into five large mugs, began to answer, but Marianne forestalled her. 'It's all right. Libby and I bought fish and chips, and we got extra in case the lodgers were home,' she told him. 'Was it you that Libby saw, Neil? Mind you, the blizzard was at its height, which made it difficult to recognise anyone. The tram was quite near the docks, though, and it was around noon.'

Neil took a mug of tea from his mother-in-law with a word of thanks and sat down on a wheel-back chair, pulled up to the kitchen table. 'I honestly don't know, darling, but I suppose it might have been,' he said. 'My appointment was a late one but there's always a deal to do when we dock. 'No, thinking it over, I doubt if it were me; I reckon we only docked around noon.' He took a long swallow of his tea, then put an arm round Libby's shoulders and kissed the side of her neck, making her giggle. 'I'm sorry to disappoint you, chick, but I don't think it could have been your old dad you saw. And how's my girl? I won't ask if you're looking forward to Christmas, but how are you going to like going off into the country and being with all your pals, eh? Oh, I know you don't want to be evacuated, but a port is no place for kids in wartime.' He turned to Marianne. 'And it's no place for their mothers, either,' he said firmly.

Marianne sighed, then stroked a hand over his golden hair. 'Dear Neil, this is neither the time nor the place to start a serious discussion,' she said. She turned to her sister, who was leaning negligently against the end of the table and looking, Marianne thought, both sulky and bored, which was typical of Fiona when she was not the centre of attention. 'Do give Gammy a hand with laying the table and so on, Fee,' she said. 'I don't know if you've noticed, but it's started snowing again, so the sooner we've eaten our meal the sooner we can get on the road home.'

'Leaving Mam and me with the washing up, I suppose,' Fiona said waspishly. 'I don't see why you're in such a hurry to get home, Marianne. You've done all your shopping and you're coming here for Christmas dinner, so you won't have much preparation to do until Boxing Day. You could easily stay here, have your tea, and go home after that.'

She still sounded distinctly grumpy and Marianne's eyebrows shot up. Fiona rarely showed that particular side of her nature when they had company, and though Neil was a relation by marriage Marianne knew that her sister liked him and always did her best to impress him. She opened her mouth to ask what the matter was, but was forestalled by Gammy, who was clattering heated plates on to the table and beginning to dish up the fish and chips whilst Libby ran backwards and forwards fetching salt, vinegar and bread from the pantry. 'Fiona, fetch the cutlery, and stop givin' yourself airs,' she said briskly. She turned to Marianne. 'The truth is, Madam here has promised to put up me paper chains in the front parlour this afternoon. I guess she thought you'd give a hand, which would make it more fun, and mean she wouldn't be the only one balancing on the stepladder and getting pricked by the holly. And now get eatin' because there's still some of that treacle tart left, enough for a small piece all round.'

'That's wizard,' Neil said, eyeing his plate with enthusiasm. Then he turned to Fiona, grinning at the younger girl. 'You're just jealous because your sister is married to the captain of the best corvette in the British Navy, and you've never been out with any officer higher than a first lieutenant,' he said teasingly. 'Well, I'll see if I can fit you up with one of my fellow skippers. And now let's get outside these fish and chips.'

And very soon they were all enjoying the hot food and talking happily of the holiday to come.

The Sheridans left as soon as the washing up was finished. Snow was falling gently but persistently and Neil, burdened with his Gladstone bag and Marianne's marketing, decided that they would take a taxi if there was one available when they reached the Stanley hospital. 'I'd buy a tree only the truth is I don't think I can carry anything more,' he said ruefully, as they drew level with the salesman and his firs. 'So it looks as though I'll be spending most of the afternoon digging in our back garden.' Libby however pointed out that she was quite capable of carrying a Christmas tree as far as the nearest taxi, so Neil produced some money and handed it to her, telling her to choose a tree with a good shape. 'You and your mother can carry it between you,' he said. Fortunately they didn't have to juggle with their awkward burden for long before they saw, ahead, a taxi cab disgorging its passengers. Neil dumped his bags on the snowy pavement, told his womenfolk to stay just where they were, and set off at a sprint. 'I'll get the driver to come back and pick you up,' he shouted over his shoulder. 'Shan't be two ticks.'

Libby was staring after her father anxiously when her mother gave a small sneeze, then snapped her handbag open and began to delve inside, obviously searching for a handkerchief. Plunging her hand into the pocket of her overcoat, Libby was about to offer her own when her mother found what she was looking for and hastily produced the hanky as another sneeze overtook her. The hanky was lace-trimmed and pale pink, and as Marianne flourished it something small and white flew out of its folds and fell towards the ground. With a squeak of dismay, Libby lunged forward, for her mother was standing close by a drain. But she was too late: the small white object fell between two of the iron bars of the grid and even as Libby dropped to her knees she knew it was too late. Melted snow water swirled along the drain and there was no sign of the object from Marianne's handbag.

'Libby Sheridan! What on earth are you doing down on your knees in this slush?' Marianne said indignantly. 'That coat cost a great deal of money and your stockings weren't cheap either. Did you drop something?'

Libby scrambled to her feet. 'I didn't drop anything, Mummy, it was you,' she said reproachfully. 'When you pulled your hanky out of your bag, a little packet fell out. I don't know what it was but I tried to save it, only I wasn't quick enough and it went down the drain.'

'Something came out of my handbag? A packet? I can't imagine what it could have been,' Marianne began, then gasped and clapped a hand to her mouth. 'Oh, my God! Don't say I've been and gone and lost Fiona's earrings. I popped them into my bag for safety yesterday rather than putting them with the rest of the shopping, and then I forgot they were there. Oh, Libby, darling, whatever can we do? I really don't want to come out again tomorrow, especially now your father's home. I'll just have to ask the driver to drop me off at Lewis's so that I can replace them.'

The taxi drew up beside them and Neil jumped out. He and the driver began to load their shopping, placing the Christmas tree in solitary splendour on the front passenger seat. As they settled on to the cracked leather upholstery, Marianne explained breathlessly what had just happened. 'So if you'll get the driver to drop me off as we pass Lewis's I'll nip in and replace them and come the rest of the way by tram. They were awfully pretty, Neil, and they were Libby's present. I'm sure she'd feel badly if she had nothing to give her aunt.'

Libby was not at all surprised when her father agreed, though he refused to even consider that Marianne might then catch a tram home. 'We'll either park or drive round until you're ready to be picked up,' he said firmly. 'I'd offer to go in

48

your stead, but having never seen the earrings in question, I'd probably come out with something totally unsuitable.' He leaned forward and shot open the glass panel which separated the driver from his passengers, and gave the man instructions.

Libby, clamouring to be allowed to go too, was told firmly to stay just where she was. 'I'll be a great deal quicker on my own,' Marianne told her. She lowered her voice to a whisper. 'Taxis cost quite a lot of money, queen, even when they're standing still, so I promise I won't keep you waiting a moment longer than necessary. After all, there's no choosing involved this time.'

As she spoke, the taxi drew to a halt right outside Lewis's and the commissionaire rushed out to open the taxi door and usher the customer inside. Libby leaned back in her seat and took Neil's hand. 'The earrings were *ever* so dainty,' she informed him. She turned her most beguiling smile on him. 'Daddy, it's still snowing pretty hard. I wonder if I'm going to get a sledge for Christmas? Only, if I am, and the snow is still thick tomorrow . . . well, it might melt by Christmas Day . . .'

Neil laughed and pinched her nose. 'Good try, young lady,' he said mockingly. 'But Santa Claus delivers on Christmas Day and not a moment before.'

'Oh, all right,' Libby said resignedly.

'Ah, here comes Mummy – wasn't she quick?'

Marianne slid into the seat beside her daughter.

'Darling, the store had sold out of the earrings I chose,' she said. 'But there were still some of the ones you picked out at first – the hoops – so I bought them. And do you know, I believe you were right? I think Auntie Fee will prefer them, truly I do.'

Libby beamed. 'Thanks, Mummy,' she said gratefully. 'Oh, don't I hope it stays snowy until Christmas Day, because you never know, I might get a sledge!'

They reached home in good order and went round to the back of the house. Libby had often complained that hiding the back door key on the lintel just below the little half-porch was unfair, because she could not reach it, but recently she had taken to standing on two earthenware plant pots which brought her up to within arm's reach of the key. It was the first time Neil had seen her perform this feat and it made him laugh, though Marianne always worried that she and the pots would come crashing down together. 'You might break a leg as well as the plant pots,' she had told her daughter the first time Libby had fetched the key down for herself. 'I suppose I shall have to hide the key somewhere else, then you won't be tempted to do acrobatics.'

So far, however, it had remained in its accustomed hiding place and now Libby thrust it into the lock, turned it swiftly, hopped inside and held the door for her burdened parents. 'In you come, Mummy and Daddy,' she said cheerfully. 'Will the trams be running on Christmas Day? Because if not, it's an awful long walk to Crocus Street and back.'

'We could always get a taxi again,' Neil said cheerfully. 'Now let's get organised. The stove hasn't gone out so at least the kitchen's warm, but since we'll be spending the evening in the front room I'll nip along and put a match to the fire in there whilst Mummy makes us all a nice cup of tea.' He rubbed his hands together and chucked Marianne under the chin before beginning to struggle out of his coat. 'I know a cup of tea is the first thing any woman thinks of when she enters her kitchen, isn't that so, Libby?'

He got his coat off as he spoke and Libby, feeling very grown up and sensible, wagged a reproving finger at him when he went to hang it on the pegs by the door. 'It'll take hours to dry there, Daddy,' she said importantly, crossing the kitchen and beginning to lower the drying rack. 'Just drape it over here and put mine and Mummy's on as well, and they'll be dry by the time we need them for church tomorrow.'

The weekend passed quickly. The family went to church on Sunday morning, but instead of the hot dinner they usually enjoyed Marianne presented them with cold meat and mashed potatoes, followed by a hot pudding, because Neil loved jam roly-poly and Marianne considered that he needed feeding up. After that, Neil went up to the loft and got down the Christmas decorations and paper chains, with which he proceeded to festoon the front room. Then he planted the Christmas tree in a bucket covered in bright red crêpe paper, and he and Libby enjoyed themselves very much hanging glass balls, silver tinsel and tiny artificial birds and beasts on every branch. Meanwhile, Marianne made afternoon tea and wheeled it through on her trolley. She had made scones and a Battenburg cake since she did not intend to serve supper that evening. 'Knowing Gammy, we shall be eating non-stop tomorrow, so I think it's best if we take it easy today,' she informed her husband and daughter. She turned to Libby. 'I know you drink tea at Gammy's but I do prefer you to drink milk, darling, because it's better for you. Help yourself to sandwiches.'

Despite Libby's fears, she was not packed off to bed early. Neil interceded for her, saying that she would never sleep for excitement. 'We'll have a couple of games of snap and then I'll read to you for half an hour; that's bound to send you to sleep,' he said, laughing at her. 'Because you know the rules: Santa Claus only visits sleeping children, not naughty little girls who deliberately stay awake so that they can get a good look at him.'

'And you'd best have a bath before going to bed,' Marianne decided. 'The hot water will make you sleep like a top. Now go and get the cards, queen; they're in the dresser drawer.'

Libby, hurrying to obey, cast a satisfied glance

at the room as she left it and thought it looked wonderful. She wished the little candles on the tree had been lit but both Daddy and Mummy were very fussy about what they called 'naked flames' and never lit the candles until Christmas Day tea, extinguishing them as soon as the meal was over. Gammy, however, was not nearly so fussy. Libby knew that when they entered the Crocus Street house tomorrow morning, the candles on the tree in Gammy's parlour would be blazing away, the bowls on every available surface would be full of nuts, raisins and fruit, and friends and neighbours would be popping in and out, accepting drinks and wishing each other season's greetings. When it's our turn to have Gammy and Fiona for Christmas Day it's always very quiet with just the five of us, so it's nice to have a change, Libby told herself, getting the snap cards out of the dresser. I do love Christmas Day at Gammy's, even though Mummy says all the noise and comings and goings give her a headache. Yes, I really love Christmas in Crocus Street.

Libby woke at the crack of dawn on Christmas morning, as all right-minded children do, and carried her stocking through to her parents' room. She wriggled into their bed, thumped them both unceremoniously until they sat up, wished them a Merry Christmas and then began to attack the stocking.

'I thought we were going to get a nice cup of

53

tea to wake us up,' Neil teased. 'Didn't you think so, Marianne?'

'I thought it would be a hot cooked breakfast at the very least,' Marianne said, giving Libby a squeeze. 'What *is* the time, darling? It still feels like the middle of the night and it isn't the blackout blind because your father rolled it up and opened the window before coming to bed. I told him the snow would blow in and we'd probably be found frozen stiff in the morning, but he said he couldn't sleep in an airless room so I had to give way.'

'It's seven o'clock, or it was when I went down and looked in the kitchen,' Libby said. 'I knew you'd ask the time, Mummy, so I checked, and it's still snowing. Oh, oh, a clay pipe to make bubbles with! And a little mouth organ! Isn't Father Christmas kind?'

'Not to parents he's not,' Neil said, groaning. 'I remember the year you got a penny whistle and nearly drove your mother demented by sneaking up behind her and blowing it in her ear.'

'Never mind that now,' Marianne said, slipping her feet into her furry slippers and beginning to don her dressing gown. 'Since I'm awake, I might as well make that cup of tea. We'll drink it cuddled up warm in bed, but as soon as it's gone we really must get up.' She turned to Neil. 'I'm doing your favourite breakfast, darling, bacon, kidney and scrambled egg, and the trams are running a Sunday service, so if we want to get to Gammy's in good time we'll need to catch the eleven o'clock at the latest.'

'Gammy never gets Christmas dinner on the table until three in the afternoon,' Neil pointed out. 'If we arrive earlier we shall have to give a hand.'

He sounded so despondent that Marianne laughed. 'It won't hurt you to do women's work for once,' she said. 'And Libby loves to help, don't you, pet?'

Libby put her pudding spoon down with a sigh of contentment and beamed at Gammy across the table. Neil had been right as usual: dinner had not even started until a quarter past three, so eating had been accompanied by the king's Christmas address to the nation, and it had been almost four when they had cleared the dinner plates and begun to serve Gammy's delicious, home-made Christmas pudding. So now Libby spoke with real feeling. 'Gammy, that was the best dinner I've ever had,' she said earnestly. 'I'm so full I might easily burst, but let's get on with the washing up and clearing away because then it'll be time to open the presents, won't it?'

Neil wagged a reproving finger at his daughter, then turned to where the McNallys and Mr Parsons were seated, faces glowing from all the good food. 'You wouldn't believe that this girl has already received a lovely sledge from her mother and myself, a postal order for ten shillings from her grandfather and grandmother in Devon, and lots of little presents from friends and neighbours,' he said. 'Yet she's still eager for more. *What* a greedy child!'

Fiona, seated next to him, thumped his knee, making him give a shout of pretended pain. 'She ain't greedy, you horrid feller,' she said. 'It's natural to want to know what's in a parcel; I'm as bad meself. I always nag me mam to let me open mine early, but she never will. So don't you go callin' names, Neil Sheridan!'

It always took an age to clear away after Christmas dinner, but it was done at last, and family and lodgers trooped into the parlour and present-opening began. The beautiful blue cardigan was much admired and Gammy promised to wear it next day when the Wainwrights would go to the Sheridans' place for another, though less Christmasy, dinner. Libby was hopping with excitement, as much over the giving of her gifts as the receiving, and Fiona was just as excited as she handed her own presents round.

'Open mine next, Auntie Fee,' Libby shouted, pushing the small, gaily wrapped packet into her aunt's hands. 'I'm sure you'll like . . . what's in there.' Fiona untied the ribbon and smoothed it out, then did the same with the outer wrapping and the tissue paper. 'Don't you love them?' Libby said, as the gold hoops were revealed.

Fiona pounced on her, giving her a kiss. 'Oh, Libby, darling, them's the nicest present I've had this Christmas! I bet you chose 'em yourself, didn't you? They'll look wonderful, all glittery, even when me hair's loose. Oh, you are a clever kid!'

'Yes, I chose them and I'm so glad you like them,' Libby said proudly. 'Put them on, Auntie Fee.'

But Fiona was already standing in front of the mirror, putting the new earrings into her ears, turning her head from side to side in order to see them better. Then she swung round on the rest of the company. 'Well, fellers? What do you think?'

'You look like a fillum star,' Eamonn said. 'You'll knock their eyes out next time you go to the Grafton.' He turned to Libby. 'You certainly know what suits your auntie!'

Fiona glanced across to Neil and gave him a mock salute. 'What do you think, Captain?' she asked with a giggle. 'D'you think they suit me?'

'Very nice,' Neil said. 'And now I'll open one of mine!'

The rest of the day passed far too quickly and presently the Sheridans found themselves homeward bound once more. They reached Sydenham Avenue, and after stowing away her presents Libby was quite happy to be tucked up in bed. And tomorrow Gammy and Auntie Fee will come to us, even though the snow doesn't look much like stopping, she told herself. And Daddy has promised that he'll take me and my new sledge into Prince's Park. I expect Auntie Fee will come as well, and maybe Mummy too, though I don't think Gammy will risk it. It's a pity the lodgers won't be coming, but Mummy says they aren't family, and anyway they go to their pals' houses, so I suppose they enjoy that more. But of course it's one reason why the day at our house is so much quieter than a day at Gammy's.

And the day after Boxing Day I shall have to write my thank you letters, especially to Grandpa and Grandma Sheridan. I don't suppose we shall be able to visit them for a summer holiday next year because of the war. Oh dear, and I do love getting on the train and going all the way to Plymouth, and then being picked up in Grandpa Sheridan's lovely car and taken to Darland House, with the beach and the great huge garden, and the little pony in the stables, poking her head over the half-door and asking for an apple.

Mr Sheridan senior had been a high-ranking naval officer before the war, and now he had a shore job doing confidential and important work. He was based in Plymouth, which was fortunate, since the family home was only a couple of miles outside the town. Mr Sheridan was tanned and handsome, with a thick thatch of blond hair streaked with white at the temples, and very blue, very shrewd eyes. Libby knew he was a magistrate – whatever that might mean – and she had soon learned to love him and his slender, good-looking wife. Why should she not? As their only grandchild, she held a special place in their affections and knew that they would be as disappointed as she if the summer visit failed to materialise.

But since the trains are still running so that children can be evacuated, I suppose they'll still be taking people from Liverpool to Plymouth, Libby told herself drowsily. I'll ask Daddy in the morning. I know he'd be awful disappointed if we couldn't see Grandpa and Grandma Sheridan until the war was over. And on that thought, Libby fell asleep.

Despite Libby's secret fear that Gammy and Auntie Fee – and her parents for that matter – would not consider going across to the park when they saw how deep the snow had become during the night, they had a really good day, to begin with at any rate. Gammy and Auntie Fee arrived eager to please and be pleased, and Marianne had worked hard all morning so that there would not be much to do when the Wainwrights arrived. They were having roast beef and Yorkshire pudding, followed by an orange jelly into which Marianne had emptied a tin of mandarins, saying that after all the eating they had done on Christmas Day a light pudding would be best.

She intended to serve fresh fruit salad after a supper of cold beef and potatoes in their jackets, but when Gammy offered to make pancakes instead she took one look at Neil's hopeful face and agreed with a good grace. 'It's not that I want to see Neil go hungry,' she had explained as she outlined her meal plans for Gammy's approval, 'but they feed them so much stodge aboard ship that it's a wonder he doesn't weigh twenty stone.'

'But he's norra bit fat,' Gammy pointed out rather indignantly. 'It's an old saying but one you want to take serious, my girl. The way to a feller's heart is through his stomach. Suppose some woman comes along and woos him from your side wi' suet puddin's, jam rolys and the like? You'll regret them salads an' all that fruit, I'm tellin' you.'

Marianne laughed and Libby, listening, laughed too. She knew her father well enough to realise that he would soon speak up if he objected to any of Marianne's menus and she knew, also, that her mother would agree to anything which made Neil happy. She said as much, then began to lay the table in the dining room, for though the Sheridans usually ate in the kitchen, when they had company they used the small, square dining room with its polished mahogany table and the French windows – seldom opened – which led on to a tiny terrace and thence into the back garden.

Fortunately for Libby, the snow ceased after lunch, and when she began to press for a sledging expedition her father agreed at once to take her, though Gammy said firmly that she meant to have a snooze before the parlour fire and would thank them not to disturb her until tea was ready.

Fiona was keen to join them. She said she remembered sledging in Prince's Park when she was young, though she assured Libby that they had not been grand enough for a proper sledge, but had made do with trays.

'I remember that well,' Marianne said, her eyes kindling with pleasure. 'In fact last Christmas Libby and I took my big tray and went across to the park and had a fine time, didn't we, queen?

Neil wasn't home, but even so we enjoyed ourselves.' She turned to Gammy. 'Would you mind if I deserted you for an hour? Only I've been stuck in the house for so long that a breath of fresh air will do me the world of good.'

Fiona stared at her. 'I thought you had a headache,' she said, almost accusingly. 'The cold ain't good for headaches, Marianne, nor the dazzle from the snow either. Are you *sure* you want to come?'

'Of course she'll come,' Neil put in, giving his wife a squeeze and a kiss on the cheek. 'As for the headache, that came on yesterday when we were playing those noisy games, but it was quite gone by this morning, wasn't it, love? So is it decided, Gammy? I shall accompany my gaggle of girls to the park, choose a safe but exciting spot, and push them down the hill one at a time on the new sledge. And I won't bring them back until you've had a lovely snooze and are feeling refreshed and ready to go.'

Having seen Gammy comfortably established in her chair before the parlour fire, the women and Neil got their coats from the hallstand and were heading for the kitchen when Marianne was struck by a bright idea. 'I'm going to bring the big tray that Libby and I used last Christmas,' she said gaily. 'It will mean less time hanging around waiting for our turns. Why, we could go down two at a time!'

'Oh *yes*, wharra super idea,' Fiona said excitedly.

'We could race one another; we used to do that when we were kids, didn't we, Em?'

Marianne nodded. 'Yes we did, but please don't call me Em. I like the name Marianne because it's unusual, but when you used to call me Em, or Emmy, folk thought my name was Emily, which isn't unusual at all.'

'But everyone calls me Fee,' Fiona pointed out, buttoning her coat, then turning to help Libby into hers, addressing the child as she did so. 'And everyone calls you Libby, though your proper name is Elizabeth, so why shouldn't your mam be Em, eh?'

'Because she doesn't like it, and doesn't want us to call her that,' Libby said at once. 'I like being Libby, it's much nicer than Elizabeth, and you must like being Fee, or we'd soon get given the rough side of your tongue, as Gammy says.'

This made them all laugh, particularly Neil. 'It's odd how some people are given nicknames and others aren't,' he said thoughtfully. 'I bet if my name was Michael I'd get called Mike, or Mickey, but Neil isn't so easy to shorten.' He turned to his wife, who had both arms wrapped round an enormous tin tray. 'Give me that, goose. It's far too big for you to carry. And now let's get a move on or it'll be dark before we even reach the park.'

Chapter Three

Marianne had joined the sledging party on impulse, and as they headed for the park along the snowy and almost deserted pavements she wondered why on earth she had left the warm house for the chill of the outdoor world. She reflected that whilst her sister still had a strong streak of the child in her make-up, she herself had grown up as soon as her daughter had been born. No, even earlier than that, she reminded herself, for from the moment she had met Neil she had begun to change from the thoughtless, fun-loving girl she had been – a girl very like Fiona now – to someone mature and sensible, who thought hard before taking any action and always did her best to appear in command of any situation.

The truth was, she had loved Neil from their very first meeting, but had had to acknowledge that he came from a very different background from her own. He spoke as the announcers on the wireless did, and seemed never to be at a loss for the correct thing to do. She had been careful to suppress her Liverpool accent when she had been taken on at Lewis's, but until she met Neil she had never used what she considered her 'posh' voice at home or in the street. After meeting Neil, however, she began to speak properly all the time. He had even influenced her choice of clothing, and instead of the bright, primary colours she preferred she had begun to take his advice and go for softer, subtler shades, colours which emphasised her very blue eyes or the chestnut glints in her hair.

In the early days of their courtship, too, she had used both lip rouge and make-up, seldom venturing from the house without painted lips, darkened brows and lashes, and a great deal of Pond's face powder. But then Neil had taken her to New Brighton for the day and the pair of them had splashed in the waves, made castles on the sand and eaten fish and chips from newspaper, and Neil had told her that she had skin like milk, lips like cherries and eyes as blue as the sea. 'You've got assets given you by nature that most girls would kill to possess,' he had said, eyeing her teasingly yet with an underlying seriousness. 'You don't need paint, you beautiful creature, so why use it?' She had said, falteringly, that she supposed it was because the staff at Lewis's were expected to look their best, but Neil had laughed at her and told her that in his opinion she looked her best when he could actually see her face without clouds of powder and lipstick. 'One of these days I shall take you to meet my parents and I'd like them to see you as you really are,' he had said. 'I know they'll love you, as I do, and think you as pretty as a picture.'

It had been the first definite sign he had given her that his intentions towards her were serious, and Marianne had gone home that evening lit up with excitement and determined to do nothing of which the handsome young officer would disapprove. She had followed his advice over what suited her best and had stopped twisting her hair up in curl papers, allowing it instead to fall straight and shining like silk to her shoulders, where it turned under naturally in a pageboy style.

She had been diffident at first about taking him to the small house in Crocus Street, afraid that he would despise her mother and think her twelve-year-old kid sister a graceless hoyden, but this had proved not to be the case. She thought afterwards that had he disapproved of Mam and Fiona she would not for one moment have continued their friendship, for she knew that her mother was a marvellously warm and loving person and was sure that her sister would grow out of her wild ways as she got older. But fortunately Neil had liked and approved of both of them, never criticising either of them by so much as a word or a look. He had popped the question to Marianne within six months of that wonderful day in New Brighton, giving her the prettiest engagement ring – a cluster of sapphires, the same colour as her eyes – and promising to take her to his home in Devonshire so that she might meet his parents and make arrangements for a June wedding.

Marianne had been so happy that even the

enormous hurdle of meeting the Sheridans had not seemed insurmountable, and in fact it had not been the ordeal she had feared. The house had been tremendously imposing, but Neil's parents had welcomed her with great kindness. Mrs Sheridan had told her she would think of her as the daughter she had always longed for and Mr Sheridan had seconded the remark and taken her out in his beautiful car to meet members of the family.

She had had a lovely time with them and had returned home even more determined to do everything Neil suggested. He was eight years older than her and much better educated, and had taken her house-hunting in a far more expensive area than any Wainwright would ever have considered. The house in Sydenham Avenue had been one of the last properties they had seen and they had both loved it, though the rent asked by the landlord had seemed frighteningly high to Marianne. Neil, however, had taken it in his stride. 'We'll rent for a few years while I save up and then we'll buy,' he had told her. 'But that won't be for some time yet.'

'Marianne, what a dreamer you are! Neil just asked you if we should join them kids there, or go a bit further afield. What d'you think?'

Marianne, brought back to the present by her sister's voice, jumped, then looked measuringly at the shallow slope before her, realising that they had reached the park whilst she was lost in her own thoughts of long ago. 'Sorry, Fee. I was thinking back to when we were kids,' she said,

66

rather untruthfully. 'D'you remember coming up here with Stocky Bellis and Stevie? We had one tray between the four of us and as I remember you were so little and light that when the sledge stopped at the end of the slope you flew on like a perishin' bird and my didn't you howl!'

'I skinned me knees; anyone would have howled,' Fee said reproachfully. 'But you've not answered me question: do you want to stop here or go further?'

After a short discussion, they agreed to go on. Presently they found an uninhabited hillock, trudged to the top of it and began, tentatively at first, to slide down on sledge and tray, whooping with delight as they grew more confident.

By the time dusk was beginning to fall, Marianne was flushed, excited and as noisy as any other member of the party. She had descended the slope on the tray whilst Fiona took the sledge, and had won the race even though she had ended up head first in a snow drift. Neil had heaved her out of it, laughing helplessly, and had kissed her on her snow-covered nose. Then she and Libby had gone down the slope, both perched on the sledge, whilst Neil and Fiona, with much grumbling and shouting, had somehow managed to climb aboard the tray. This time Marianne and Libby, being so much lighter, had not managed to win, but, as Libby had pointed out when her father and aunt had emerged from the snow drift, this was not such a bad thing. They had had another couple of contests, swapping partners each time, but then Neil had looked up at the darkening sky and decreed that they should return home.

He carried the sledge and the tray under one arm and put the other round Marianne's waist, whilst Libby and Fiona raced ahead, laughing and shouting and occasionally stopping to pelt each other with snowballs. Marianne suddenly realised how tired she was and began to feel vaguely ashamed of her childish behaviour, but when she said as much to Neil he stopped in his tracks, turned her in his arms, and gave her a real and very loving kiss. 'Darling Marianne, just for one afternoon you turned back into the delightful, unselfconscious girl I fell in love with,' he said tenderly. 'You forgot you were a married woman with a child of almost eight and let your hair down, as the saying goes. Oh, I know the country's at war and you will have a great many problems to tackle, but you must never forget how to enjoy yourself. Why, I behaved like a lad myself, and your sister could have been the same age as Libby.' He glanced ahead to where his daughter and sister-in-law were now rolling a huge snowball ahead of them. 'I guess those two mean to make a snowman, but I fear I shall have to put a stop to that. I'm dying for a cup of tea; let's hope Gammy's got the kettle on.'

By the time the Wainwrights left that evening, it was full dark, so Neil insisted on walking them up to the tram stop. He had offered to go down to the end of the road and telephone for a taxi from the box on the corner, but Gammy and Fiona looked shocked at the unnecessary expense and said they would just as soon catch a tram. Marianne said she would run Libby's bath so that the child would be in bed by the time her father returned, though Libby thought this very unfair. 'I want to go with Daddy and see Gammy and Auntie Fee off; it's Christmas and I always stay up late at Christmas,' she said petulantly. 'It's not fair, Mummy. And why should I have a bath? Sunday night's my bath night.'

'You'll have a bath because you've been playing in the snow and getting cold, and I want to make sure you're nice and clean before you get between those sheets,' Marianne said. 'As for going to bed late at Christmas, it's half past nine now, which is nearly two hours after your normal bedtime, so don't argue, young lady, or you'll find yourself in bed by seven tomorrow.'

Libby began to wail again that it was not fair, but Neil crossed the room, gave her a playful slap on the bottom and turned her towards the stairs. 'It is fair, because you're tired out, and that's why you're so cross and unlike yourself,' he told her, gently propelling her upwards. 'I can't read you a story tonight, pet, because if I try to do so your Gammy and auntie will miss the last tram, but I'm sure Mummy will deputise for me – unless you fall asleep before she can get a word out.'

*   *   *

When Libby woke on Wednesday morning the room was still in darkness, and she remembered that she had been so tired the evening before that she hadn't asked her mother to roll up the blackout blind. For a moment she lay still, aware of the warmth surrounding her and knowing full well that her room would be freezing cold, but it was not in her nature to stay in bed when she could be up and doing, so she threw back the covers and took a long leap, landing only a foot or so away from the window. Quickly, she jerked the blind cord, then breathed on the frosted glass to make herself a peephole, and saw that the sky overhead was a dark and depressing grey, the snow had become deeper overnight and more flakes were descending.

Libby sighed, crossed the room and glanced towards the bathroom. The light was on and the door open, and as she padded along the corridor, her toes wincing at the touch of the ice-cold linoleum, she saw that her father was shaving, one half of his lean jaw smooth and clean whilst the other half still wore a fluffy beard of white foam which Father Christmas himself might have envied. Libby reached the doorway and waited until the razor was well clear of his face before saying, 'Morning, Daddy!' When Neil cut himself whilst shaving it made him cross and he wore little bits of toilet paper stuck to the cuts, which did little to improve his appearance. As it was, he jumped, then turned to grin at her.

'Morning, pet! Mummy says she has to go shopping and I'll go down to the docks. The *Sea Spurge* is in for a refit, but as her captain I have to keep an eye on things. I told Mummy I'd meet the pair of you at Cooper's and buy you lunch. Then if Mummy hasn't finished her shopping and doesn't need us, you and I can go round the museum or the Walker Art Gallery until she's ready to come home.' He gave her a conspiratorial smile. 'I hate shopping.'

'So do I, and I'd love to go round the museum,' Libby agreed fervently. 'I expect Mummy will be ages buying food, because there wasn't much left over yesterday, was there?'

Neil chuckled. 'No, there wasn't, and what there was your mother packed up in a tin so that Fiona could take it for her lunch at the office. And rationing starts in less than a fortnight and you won't be able to nip into a shop for half a pound of butter or a bag of sugar then, so careful housewives like your mother will be wanting to get stocked up on anything going while they can.'

The three of them left the house together immediately after breakfast. They parted when they reached the shops, Neil to make his way to the docks whilst Marianne and her daughter, both armed with stout canvas bags, began their tour of the shops. As Neil had said, a great many women were buying up goods which would soon be on ration. The more expensive shops still seemed to have plenty of nice things on the shelves and Libby

71

thought that this would probably always be the case. 'Why can't you buy your rations wherever they've got the most food?' she asked and was quite surprised when Marianne explained that this would not be possible.

'You have to select and name the grocer of your choice, and he will be the only person from whom you can buy rationed goods,' Marianne told her. 'It makes sense to choose the shop nearest your home because wherever you go you won't get any more than the government allows you, even by paying over the odds.'

Libby thought about this and decided it was probably fair. 'But I hope they never ration sweeties,' she said anxiously as, their shopping completed, they turned their steps towards Cooper's. 'They wouldn't do that, would they, Mummy? It would be awfully cruel to children.'

Marianne laughed. 'Since they are rationing sugar, I imagine it will only be a matter of time before you're having to hand over sweet coupons for an ounce of aniseed balls or a toffee stick,' she said. 'You see, darling, we don't grow sugar cane in England, nor cocoa beans for making chocolate. These things have to be brought in by sea, and some of our ships are getting sunk by the Germans. So the supply of goods from overseas is beginning to shrink.'

As she spoke, they reached Cooper's and ascended the stairs towards the first-floor restaurant. They reached it and saw that many of the

72

tables were already occupied, but Libby gave a crow of triumph. 'Daddy's here already, and he's bagged us a table!' she cried. She turned to her mother. 'Will you come round the museum with us, Mummy? Or would you rather go straight home? I'm sure Daddy would put you and the bags into a taxi so you wouldn't have to carry everything yourself.'

'Libby Sheridan, you're a little horror,' her mother said roundly, but Libby saw that she was smiling. 'You can't wait to get rid of me so you and Daddy can have time to yourselves! Well, I don't mind, but we'll see how we feel when we've eaten our lunch.'

To Libby's delight, everything went according to plan. After a delicious lunch, she and Neil put Marianne and her shopping into a taxi and waved her off. Then they went to the museum and made their way slowly round every exhibit, Libby clinging to her father's hand and listening with real enjoyment to his explanations. Afterwards they had tea and walnut cake at Fuller's and then they, too, caught a taxi. Libby, who felt she did not want the afternoon to end, would have preferred a tram ride, but Neil explained that he meant to meet a couple of his crew for a drink later that evening, so needed to be home in good time.

They reached Sydenham Avenue and Marianne greeted them lovingly, listening to their description of the fun they had had. She had made a cold high tea in case they were late, and when the meal was over Libby suggested that they might play with the new board game she had been given for Christmas. Marianne, clearing away, said she was willing, but Neil shook his head. 'No can do, sweetheart,' he said regretfully, and went off to get ready for his night out with his pals at a pub down by the docks.

When her father had kissed her goodnight and left the house, Libby challenged Marianne to a game of Snakes and Ladders. They played happily for an hour before Marianne sent Libby up to bed, announcing that she must get on with her knitting.

Libby slept at once but was awoken, what felt like hours later, by the sound of raised voices coming from the kitchen downstairs. Intrigued, she slipped out of bed, slid her feet into her slippers and donned her dressing gown. It was a good excuse to join her parents – she would say that they had made so much noise that they had woken her. What was more, if she added that she would never get back to sleep again without a little something in her tummy, she was pretty sure that hot cocoa and biscuits would be forthcoming.

She was almost at the foot of the stairs before she realised that far from having a friendly discussion of what each had been doing that evening, Marianne and Neil were quarrelling, an unheard of event. For a moment Libby considered returning to her bed and pretending she had heard nothing. But then she heard her own name. She hesitated, listening, then sat down on the bottom stair. They were discussing her future, so it was not sneaky to listen, since they would have to tell her whatever was decided, and very soon she was so intrigued that she could not possibly have returned to her bed with her curiosity unsatisfied.

'. . . I'm telling you, my dear, that it's our duty – ours, not just yours – to send Libby away to somewhere safe, out of danger. And by the same token I want *you* to be safe. Liverpool is probably the most important port in England at the moment, and you must realise that once the Luftwaffe get themselves sorted out they'll obliterate the city from the map.'

Marianne muttered something about the docks, saying that Sydenham Avenue ought to be perfectly safe, but Neil cut across her words.

'. . . don't be such a fool, Marianne! I'm sure the Germans have had plenty of practice in placing their bombs, but it's not an exact science, you know. They'll be given targets but that doesn't mean to say they don't know the psychological advantage of razing an important city to the ground. Look at Madrid! And after all, you must want to be with your little girl, so why not go as well? I know some mothers accompany their children; I've heard chaps saying that their wives have done just that. Can't you do as I ask, so that I don't have to worry about you all the time?'

'No I can't,' Marianne said roundly, her voice sharp now and as loud as her husband's. 'How d'you think I would feel, hiding away in the country, unable to make a home for you when the *Sea Spurge* was in port? And anyway, the government evacuated mothers of very young children, or babies, not those whose kids were nearly eight years old. And what would happen to our house?'

'It's not our house, it's only rented, and we'd close it up of course and simply pay the landlord a retainer,' Neil said, but he no longer sounded quite so certain. He dropped his voice and his tone became more conciliatory. 'Look, darling, I simply want you to be safe. If you won't go with Libby when she's evacuated, and you want to help with the war effort, then why don't you join one of the women's services? You'd be able to see Libby from time to time – and probably me as well – but they don't billet Wrens, or Waafs, or ATS for that matter, anywhere dangerous. Or there are other places needing war workers . . .'

'I don't want to leave this house,' Marianne said obstinately. 'It's my home, Neil, and I love it. To be frank, I don't want to leave my mother or my sister either, for that matter. I've thought of asking them to move in here because Crocus Street is right by the docks, in a far more dangerous position than this house . . .'

'I've already suggested it, but your mother won't budge because of her lodgers,' Neil said icily. 'I told her she was a silly old woman, but she just laughed. As for Fiona, it's my belief that she'll join up. No reason why she shouldn't because there's nothing to hold her in Liverpool, and if she does I think your mother might see sense and move in here and look after the house for the duration – though the lodgers would make that difficult, I suppose.'

Marianne gave a crow of triumph. 'If it's safe for my mother, then it's safe for me, and you clearly think it's safe for her,' she said. 'And you're right, of course: I have every intention of doing some sort of essential war work, and nothing you can say will stop me. One of my old friends is working in a factory making wireless parts for aircraft, another has joined the WAAF and is being trained as what she calls a plotter, and Edie Brown is making uniforms for the armed forces. I could do any of those things. If I *did* decide to join one of the services they might teach me to be a driver, and I'd like that. But it will be *my* decision, Neil, and not yours. For the first time since we got married, I shall make up my own mind and I'm afraid you'll have to lump it.'

A short silence followed this remark, and Libby could just imagine the expressions on the faces of the two combatants. Suddenly she realised she was tired out, and also upset. Daddy and Mummy never quarrelled, but they were doing it now, and even as she turned to remount the stairs she realised that she would never sleep unless she was sure her parents were friends once more.

She stole to the top of the stairs, then turned

and descended again. The voices from the kitchen were still raised, but stopped abruptly as she burst into the room. She hurled herself at the nearest person, which happened to be Marianne. 'Mummy, Mummy, you and Daddy mustn't quarrel! Your voices were so loud I woke up, and you were arguing.' She gave her mother a hard hug then transferred herself, limpet-like, to her father. 'Daddy, say you're sorry, say you're sorry!' she demanded. 'Please, please, please don't be cross with each other. I know some mummies and daddies have rows, but you *never* do.'

Neil immediately picked her up and sat down in the fireside chair with her on his lap, murmuring that they hadn't really been quarrelling, it was just a difference of opinion. Libby looked up at his face, which was red, then across at her mother, who was pale and angry-looking. She said, placatingly: '*Please* don't be cross with each other.'

The angry look faded from Marianne's face and she held out her hand to her daughter. 'It's all right, pet; we were both being rather silly to tell the truth, and tempers got a bit frayed. Would you like some cocoa and biscuits? Only Daddy and I were about to go to bed, so if you're not thirsty . . .'

'Oh, but I am,' Libby said quickly. 'One of the teachers at school was always telling her pupils that they mustn't let the sun go down upon their wrath. Cocoa and biscuits would be nice, but it would be nicer still if both of you would say "sorry" and "didn't mean it". Give each other a big kiss and say you're friends or – or I'll never get to sleep, I know I shan't.'

Marianne began to speak, then stopped as Neil laughed, stood Libby down and got to his feet. He crossed the room in a couple of strides and took his wife in his arms. 'I'm sorry, darling,' he said, his voice as soft and loving as though they had never quarrelled, Libby thought contentedly. He turned to his daughter, still holding Marianne. 'Will that satisfy you, young lady?'

'Yes, but Mummy must say it too,' Libby said firmly. 'It's only fair, because you were both shouting, weren't you?'

Marianne heaved a sigh. 'I'm very sorry, Neil, that we disagreed, and I promise you that when I come to a decision I'll let you know, so we shan't have to quarrel again,' she said. Then she reached up, pulled Neil's head down to hers and kissed him before turning to her daughter. 'And just how long were you listening outside that door before you burst in on us?' she asked suspiciously. 'I can't deny we were shouting, but I shouldn't have thought even shouts would have penetrated two closed doors.'

'My bedroom door was open,' Libby said quickly, not wanting to answer her mother's first question. 'Can I have some cocoa, Mummy? I'll take it up to bed if you like.'

Marianne and Neil got ready for bed rather quietly. Marianne reflected that her daughter had spoken no more than the truth. They never quarrelled, and now that she thought about it she realised guiltily that, as Neil had said, he had only been thinking of her safety when he had begged her to move away from the city. She gave an enormous sigh, rolled over and slid both arms round her husband's neck. 'Oh, my darling, I'm so sorry,' she whispered. 'But I can't let my country down any more than you could. I agree that Libby must go away, but I've heard you say that only rats desert sinking ships and I won't be a rat for anyone.'

Neil chuckled sleepily. 'I suppose you're right, but let's talk about it some other time. And now we'd better go to sleep or we'll be a couple of wrecks by morning.'

On 6 January the *Sea Spurge* sailed, with her new captain in command. Neil went aboard with a case full of the little extras that Marianne always supplied, though she told him, ruefully, that it would not be so easy to acquire luxuries in future. Before he left, he implored her again to try to get war work away from the Pool, but Marianne simply said, evasively, that she would see what was on offer. 'And do get Libby evacuated as soon as you can,' he begged her earnestly.

In this matter, at least, Marianne was able to assure him that she would do so. However, because of the severity of the weather, the children who had come home for Christmas were still in the city, and many mothers had decided to keep them there. This meant that schools were opening again, and though Libby's convent was still closed her mother had dragged her along to the local primary and registered her there on a temporary basis. Libby had been furious at first but speedily made friends. She found the schoolwork easy, and ended up begging her mother to allow her to stay both in Liverpool and at the new school. Marianne, however, had every intention of keeping her promise to Neil, for she would be unable to do war work if she had a child not yet eight needing her at home.

After Neil left, Marianne took Libby to Crocus Street, for though she did not disbelieve her husband she did wonder why her mother had been so determined not to move into their house in Sydenham Avenue. Mrs Wainwright, however, made it clear to Marianne, as she had to her son-in-law, that she had no intention of being, as she put it, 'druv out of me home by them bleedin' Jerries'.

'I've me lodgers to think of. Oh, I know Eamonn's been an' gone an' joined the Navy, but Mr McNally and Mr Parsons like to be near their work and wouldn't take kindly to being dragged to the other side of the city,' she said. 'Besides, I've gorranother lodger startin' next week. He's an old feller bein' brought back as a warehouseman down by the docks. He's a nice chap; in fact I've known him for years, and I reckon you'll remember him,

81

queen. Limpy Smith, they call 'im, because he were involved in an accident of some sort an' gorra crushed foot. He walks wi' a stick, but apart from that he's pretty fit and very strong. After his wife died and he retired, he went to live with his daughter over the water, but it's too far to travel in each day.'

'Oh, I remember Limpy,' Marianne said at once. 'You've done well to get him for a lodger, Mam, because he's strong as an ox and a real helpful bloke. But where's he going to sleep? I take it Fiona's still in the little room? I know Eamonn and his dad shared, but you can't expect Limpy and Mr McNally to do the same, surely?'

Gammy chuckled. 'I'm callin' me daughter's bluff,' she said frankly. 'She keeps saying she's goin' to join the WAAF or the Wrens – she don't like the ATS uniform – but so far as I know, she's done nothin' about it. So I've told her she's got to move in wi' me until she leaves, which means sharin' my creaky old bed, and hangin' her clothes on hooks 'cos me wardrobe's pretty well full. What d'you think of that?'

Marianne laughed, then sobered. 'You are awful, Mam, to drive your youngest away from home,' she said reproachfully. 'Not but what it's time she left. I'd been married a couple of years by the time I was her age. But, you know, you shouldn't let your lodgers dictate where you live. I bet you haven't even sounded them out about a move.'

The two women were in the kitchen, Gammy

preparing vegetables at the sink and Marianne lining a pie dish with some of the pastry she had just made. Libby was playing out, though Marianne guessed she would be in soon, probably accompanied by several small friends, since children seemed to know by instinct when it was time for elevenses. Gammy plopped a peeled potato into the pan and turned to give her daughter a knowing grin. 'Didn't have to. They must ha' guessed what was in the wind when your Neil came calling, with neither you nor the kid in tow, saying he had a favour to ask. I dunno if they listened at the door or what – I took Neil into the parlour – but the minute he left, old Mr Parsons spoke up and said he hoped as how I weren't thinkin' of desertin' 'em. So naturally I said I weren't, 'cos no bloody Hun would make me shift, and that were that.' She looked shrewdly at her daughter. 'And if you've a mind to join up, like our Fiona, then I'll give an eye to Libby wi' real pleasure. Once her aunt's gone, she can share my room and go to the Daisy Street School, like what you did.'

'Libby is being evacuated to somewhere truly safe, in the country, as soon as it can be arranged,' Marianne said firmly. 'And I don't believe I will join up. I'll stay in my own house, volunteer for fire watching or something similar, and get work which will help the war effort. As for letting Libby come to you, with the docks within spitting distance, I wouldn't dream of it. Neil would kill me for a start. Oh, Mam, I do worry about you.' She picked up the basin of precooked meat, tipped it into the pie dish, and began to cover it with the pastry lid. 'But perhaps you'll think again when things, as Neil puts it, begin to hot up.'

On the way home in the tram, Marianne told Libby that Gammy would not be moving in with them. 'But it won't affect you, love,' she consoled her small daughter, 'because soon you'll be off. I'd love to take you myself, just to see where you'll be living, but I don't think I'll be able to. I'm going for an interview in a few days, at a factory making parts for aeroplanes, and once I'm working there it won't be possible at first to get two or three days off altogether, which I may need if you are to be billeted some distance away. Don't worry, though. You'll be going with a teacher and some other children, and you'll be safe as houses. I'll give you a postcard to fill in, saying how your journey went and giving me your new address. You must put it in the letter box as soon as you arrive.'

Libby pulled a face. 'I don't want to go,' she said sulkily. 'Other kids are staying; most of the kids in my school hated being away from home. They said the food was rotten and the ladies they lived with were rude about their clothes, and the kids in the local school called names. Honestly, Mum, I'll be really good and helpful if you'll only let me stay.'

Marianne had noticed, with some dismay, that Libby called her 'Mum' now, and often used very ungrammatical speech, but she realised that this was merely protective coloration since at home she was still 'Mummy', and Libby never said 'gorrago' or 'ain't it?' when under her own roof. So now she smiled at her daughter and gave her a hug. 'Remember, darling, you'll be evacuated to the same place as the rest of your convent school, so though you may miss your new friends for a little while, your old friends will be delighted to see you again. And now let's talk about something else. I suggest we go to the park this afternoon and feed the ducks, and you can have a go on the swings, and then this evening we'll both write nice, newsy letters to Daddy.'

Libby turned and beamed at her mother. 'Ta ever so much, Mum,' she said, and Marianne tried not to wince.

'Have you got everything, darling? Remember to take off your scarf and gloves when you get in the train or you won't feel the benefit later. Goodness, it's cold! I put your postcard right on top of your clothes in the suitcase and your sandwiches and some fruit are in the little string bag. And for good-ness' sake don't lose your gas mask. Don't put it down for a moment, because if you pick up the wrong one it won't fit you and – and that could be rather unfortunate. Now don't forget, the most important thing is to post the card just as soon as you arrive.' Marianne bent and hugged Libby convulsively. 'Oh, my darling, I'm going to miss you so dreadfully, but I'm sure it won't be for long.

You've got a clean handkerchief? There are two in your case, but I'd rather you didn't open it until you've reached your destination. I haven't packed you anything to drink because Miss Lamb says she'll buy everyone lemonade or milk when the train pulls into a station where someone is selling such things. Are you sure you're all right?'

'No I'm not,' Libby said crossly. 'I don't want to go, and if I hate it I shall come straight back, so there.'

'If you hate it you only have to write and tell me and I'll make arrangements for you to be moved somewhere else, but not back to Liverpool,' Marianne assured her. 'Ah, here comes Miss Lamb.' She smiled at the tall, grey-haired woman approaching. 'Good morning, Miss Lamb! This is my daughter, who will be in your charge. Now hop aboard, darling, or you'll be left behind.'

Libby climbed reluctantly into the carriage, closely followed by the teacher. The guard came along the platform, blowing his whistle and slamming doors. Marianne waved vigorously until the train rounded the bend and could be seen no more, though she had the distinct impression that her daughter was not waving back, but had moved away from the window as soon as the train began to pull away.

Marianne had known she would feel awful sending her only child off into the unknown, but to her secret shame she was guiltily aware of a feeling of relief. Libby had been a perfect little terror ever since arrangements for her evacuation had been completed. She had refused to help at all in the house, and had twice wandered off and been gone for hours, causing Marianne to worry over her whereabouts. She had deliberately brought back to the house some truly dreadful children and on one occasion had taken money from Marianne's housekeeping purse, for the tram fare, and sneaked off to Crocus Street. There, Gammy had said, the child had spent at least an hour nagging her to persuade Marianne to keep her at home. Naturally, Gammy had refused to do any such thing, and the episode had ended when Fiona got home from her office. She had laughed at what she called 'Libby's cheek', but had quite agreed with Gammy that such behaviour was downright naughty.

'Your mammy will be mad with worry,' she had said, thrusting Libby aboard the tram. 'If she were a normal mam she'd tan your perishin' backside till you couldn't sit down, but knowing my sister she'll just tell you off and send you early to bed. However, queen, I won't have you upsetting your Gammy the way you done this afternoon, so if you try it again, I swear I'll wallop your sit-upon so's you'll be eatin' your grub off the mantelpiece for a week.'

Fee's threat had impressed Libby into better behaviour, and though she had been quiet and sulky for the last couple of days she had not behaved outrageously again and Marianne was glad of it. Libby had always been a sweet and tractable child and Marianne hoped devoutly that she would become so again once she got back with old schoolfellows, for she blamed the rough and tumble of the pupils at the local school for her daughter's sudden bad behaviour.

She hurried along Lime Street, feeling almost carefree. She would start her new job at the factory the following Monday, and realised she was looking forward to it. She would be working with young women of her own age, doing her duty as a British citizen, with only herself to please, except of course when the *Sea Spurge* came into port. Then, she dreamed, life would be a second honeymoon. She and Neil had married in early June and within a couple of months she had realised that she was already expecting a child. She had been eighteen, no age at all really, but though they had both been delighted at the thought of parenthood, carefreeness had flown out of the window. It would be good to enjoy Neil's company, to talk freely, even to argue, without the constant presence of their small daughter. I'll go to Cooper's and buy myself lunch before I head for home, Marianne told herself, and broke into song. *A cigarette that bears a lipstick's traces, an airline ticket to romantic places, and still my heart has wings, these foolish things remind me of you.*

Libby had always enjoyed train journeys, but on previous occasions she had been with her parents either going to Devon for a holiday with Grandma and Grandpa Sheridan or returning home. She had never before ventured into the unknown with a number of strangers. Furthermore, her journeys had always been undertaken in the summer whereas now the snow lay thickly as far as the eye could see, and though the train was stuffy, the air outside was bitterly cold. Libby looked timidly around. She knew only one of the children who shared the carriage with her: a girl at least two years older than herself, who had always seemed to despise younger girls and had scarcely glanced at Libby when she sat down next to her. Libby knew her name was Elsie, but she doubted if the other girl knew who she was, so was surprised when Elsie leaned forward and peered through the mesh of Libby's string bag, saying hopefully: 'Gorrany chocolate, chuck? Me mam don't get up too early of a mornin' so I didn't get no breakfast. I could murder a Mars bar, so I could.'

Libby was tempted to ask if the older girl usually had chocolate for breakfast, but decided it would not be wise; Elsie was hefty and Libby did not fancy making an enemy of someone both older and stronger than herself. She had never met Miss Lamb before, but very soon realised that, despite her gentle appearance, the teacher was a force to be reckoned with. Whilst Libby was beginning a faltering explanation – that her lunch consisted only of sandwiches and fruit because her mother thought chocolate bad for her teeth – Miss Lamb leaned across and addressed Elsie in a tone which brooked no argument. 'Everyone may open their packed lunches when I say so and not a moment before. And everyone will eat the food their mother has provided and will not start swapping. Because this is not part of a general evacuation, we shall have to change trains in about half an hour. If we have time, I shall buy everyone a drink – probably tea, or maybe milk – and those of you with pocket money may use the slot machines to get yourselves chocolate bars, but you must not stray from our group. Is that understood?'

'Where's we goin', Miss?' Elsie said bluntly. 'You've gorra know, you're in charge. I don't see why . . .'

'I know the name of the station at which we shall disembark, but I see no reason why I should share that knowledge,' Miss Lamb said crisply. 'It's not as though any of you will be remaining there. You will be going on by car, or bus, or perhaps by pony and trap, because the town has already absorbed its quota of evacuees.' She looked, consideringly, at Elsie. 'When the train stops and we get off, you shall be my second in command, since you seem to be the oldest member of the group. I shall have to leave you in charge whilst I get everyone something to drink. All right?'

Libby hoped that Elsie would not blame her for Miss Lamb's attention, but when they got off the train and clustered round the slot machines she realised that Elsie was thoroughly enjoying wielding her new authority and was doing it quite well, too. A group of boys had also got down from the train and begun milling around and eyeing the girls, but Elsie shepherded her charges away from them. And presently, when they got aboard the next train, she organised a game of I Spy and the children grew easier in one another's company. Libby and a small shy girl named Freda sat together and chatted and, to Libby's surprise, time passed quite quickly, though the train was a slow one, so that it was afternoon when they reached their destination.

Miss Lamb herded them into the waiting room, where a short white-haired man wearing heavy horn-rimmed spectacles, and the boys they had seen earlier, awaited them. A woman with a clip-board joined them, greeting the teachers and saying that she had a list and would be able to accommodate them all, though some – indeed most – would have to travel quite long distances to reach their billets.

'I'm not staying, you know,' the male teacher put in quickly, 'though I believe this lady will be needing a billet. I'm just delivering these boys. They all missed the first evacuation for some reason, but no doubt you've been told how things stand.'

The lady with the clipboard looked doubtful. 'Oh well, I trust they'll behave themselves even without a teacher. We've hired a bus for the first part of the journey. I and . . . Miss Lamb, is it? . . .

shall travel with the children, but I suppose you will want to catch the next train back to Liverpool.'

Libby, who knew very few boys and was afraid of the ones she did know, clung to Freda and suggested that they should sit near the front of the bus, which turned out to be easy because the boys made a concerted rush for the back, pushing and shoving and behaving like the savages Libby thought them. Miss Lamb's voice sounded small and thin against the babble of talk from the lads, but the bus driver, a big burly man with tightly curled grey hair and a gap-toothed grin, had a voice like a foghorn, which rose well above the shouts from the back of the bus. 'The next boy to open his mouth will find hisself walking,' he bellowed, 'and them hills is where we're headin'. Ever walked up hills? Well, one more peep out of you and you'll be wearin' out your shoe leather on some pretty rough ground, I'm tellin' you.'

From the immediate silence which followed, it was clear that no one fancied walking. The bus travelled for several miles before stopping in a village where a group of people waited beside a row of small shops. The lady with the clipboard stood up. 'Mrs Evans-Bread?' she called and a woman in a dark coat, with a headscarf tied beneath her chin, stepped forward.

'Two boys, we're 'avin'. Brothers, mebbe?'

Miss Lamb surveyed the boys, sitting remarkably quietly at the back of the bus. 'Any brothers? Ah, you two.' The pair pushed to the front and she examined their labels. 'Bobby and Jim Sullivan; right, lads, you'll be stayin' with the lady in the red headscarf. Off you get.'

In this manner, she disposed of a good few of the children, then signalled to the driver to start up once more. The bus stopped several times and Libby grew anxious. Both Freda and Elsie had been claimed and there were only a couple of boys and no girls at all, apart from herself, remaining on the bus. To her relief, most people took either boys or girls, so it seemed unlikely that she would find herself sharing accommodation with one of the lads. But when the bus stopped again and both boys were claimed by a large man in gaiters and riding breeches, it was a white and frightened face that Libby turned to Miss Lamb. 'What's happening?' she quavered. 'I'm the only one left. Doesn't anyone want me?'

Miss Lamb gave a reassuring chuckle, patted Libby's shoulder and then took the seat beside her. 'It's too bad of me,' she said remorsefully. 'But the fact is, my dear, you were not at the same school as the other children on this bus, and your mother was keen that you should join some of the pupils from your old school, if it was at all possible. Unfortunately, no one could offer a billet in the village where your friends have been placed, but we found you somewhere. I understand we'll be met, though you'll have quite a journey to school and back each day, further than you could walk, I think, but I dare say there's a bus . . . I can't tell you much more, I'm afraid. I'll leave you with Miss Eluned Williams to settle in for a couple of days, and then I'll come and visit you, make sure you're all right.' Even as she spoke, the bus drew to a clattering halt and Libby saw, through the gathering dusk, that a horse and cart was drawn up at the side of the road, with a burly-looking man standing at the horse's head. 'Oh!' Miss Lamb said. 'Oh, dear . . . that doesn't look like a Miss Williams.'

'Indeed it is not,' the bus driver interrupted, with a soft chuckle. 'Looks like old Dewi, what gives a hand with the cattle.' He turned to smile kindly at Libby. 'He'll give you a ride as far as Tregarth Farm, and no doubt Miss Williams will be waiting to greet you with a nice hot supper.'

Libby grabbed her now empty string bag and her small suitcase and scrambled off the bus, bidding the bus driver and Miss Lamb farewell, and realising as she did so that the snow was thicker here in the hills than it had been in Liverpool. The man holding the horse's head said something in a foreign language to the bus driver, hefted Libby's suitcase into the cart and lifted her in after it. Then he climbed on to the driving seat, picked up the looped reins and turned his head to address her. 'Afternoon, cariad. I said as how I'd pick you up for Miss Williams, bein' as how it's milkin' time. I'm Dewi Jones. I works for Miss Williams sometimes.'

'I'm Libby Sheridan,' Libby said, then clapped

a hand to her mouth. What was it her mother had said? *Don't speak to strange men*. But surely that could not apply when one was being driven along in a horse and cart? If she did not answer when he spoke he would think her dreadfully rude, and though she had not had a chance to take a good look at him, she had got the impression of a round, red face, twinkling eyes and a friendly smile. She cleared her throat. 'Is it far, to Tregarth Farm, I mean?'

'Three mile, mebbe four,' Dewi Jones said laconically. 'A pretty road, it is, in summer, though in winter, with the trees bare and the river runnin' in spate, it can seem a bit grim like.'

For a short while they chatted inconsequentially, but then Libby grew silent, staring around her. She could hear the river to her left but could see nothing for the trees which crowded close on either side. They seemed to be in a narrow valley, between two steeply wooded hills, but it really was growing dark now and Libby could make out very little. Indeed, she never even saw the house as they approached it.

Dewi drove the horse and cart round the bulk of a grey stone dwelling and into a smallish courtyard surrounded by low outbuildings. As the horse clattered to a stop, a door opened at the back of the house and golden light streamed over the snowy yard, and Libby saw that icicles, glittering like diamonds, hung from the eaves around her. The open door led into what looked like a kitchen.

She recognised a large blackened range, its front open to reveal the red glow of a fire. And then the driver was lifting her down, handing her the suitcase and shouting something in Welsh – Libby guessed it was Welsh – to whoever had opened the door.

Hastily, she bade her new friend goodbye and hurried across and into the kitchen, pulling the door shut behind her. The woman who had obviously heard them arrive and flung open the door began to speak, but Libby interrupted her. 'You showed a light!' she said accusingly. 'They say if you show a light, aeroplanes will come and they'll bomb our houses flat. I think they can put you in prison for showing a light.'

The woman chuckled. 'I dare say you're right, but who's to tell on me? And what aeroplane is going to waste a bomb on an old farmhouse tucked away in the Welsh hills? Nevertheless, you are right. I should have pulled the curtain across before opening the door, but I wanted to light you in since you're a stranger in these parts.' She held out a brown, work-roughened hand and took Libby's. 'I'm Miss Williams and you've come all the way from Liverpool. What's your name, child?'

'I'm Libby Sheridan,' Libby said shyly. She took a good long look at the woman clasping her hand. She had thick white hair cut short in a bob, and the skin of her thin lined face was brown and weather-beaten. She had very dark eyes, a rather beaky nose and her mouth looked stern, but even as she thought this, Miss Williams gave her a smile of great sweetness.

'Know me again?' she asked, and Libby blushed, realising that she had been staring, knowing that staring was rude. She opened her mouth to say she was sorry but Miss Williams, tutting, took her suitcase from her and stood it down, then began to unbutton Libby's coat. 'You've come a long way and I expect you're cold,' she said. 'Come and sit by the fire. I'll pour you a bowl of hot soup and you'll soon thaw out.'

Libby had not realised how very cold she was, but now her numbed feet and hands began to make themselves felt, tingling and aching. She looked doubtfully up at her hostess. 'I think I'd better sit up to the table because my hands are too cold to hold a bowl of soup,' she said.

Miss Williams shook her head in self-reproof. 'I'm a stupid old woman sometimes,' she observed. 'I should have thought of that.' As she spoke, she poured what Libby guessed must be the soup from a small blackened saucepan into a blue pottery bowl, which she stood on the table. She placed a spoon alongside it, then gestured to Libby to take the kitchen chair nearest the bowl, and Libby obeyed with alacrity, for the soup smelled marvellously good and it was a long time since Miss Lamb had given the order to start their packed lunches.

Miss Williams went over to a big Welsh dresser, standing against one wall, and cut a hefty slice off a round fat loaf of bread. She did not bother with a plate, but handed it straight to Libby, then turned her head and said, 'Do you want some soup, Matthew? I know we ate earlier, but I dare say you could do with another helping.'

Libby jumped and stared round wildly, for she had not realised there was anyone else in the room. Following Miss Williams's gaze, she saw with a shock that there was a boy sitting in the shadowy end of the kitchen. Because he was sitting down she could not see how tall he was, but she thought he looked older than herself. He had a thin, pale face with a fringe of dark hair hanging over his forehead, and it occurred to Libby, though she could not have said why, that he did not look in the best of health. He must have noticed how Libby jumped, though, when she saw him sitting quietly there, for he grinned at her with a touch of malice so that when she smiled back, it was rather doubt-fully. How odd that she hadn't noticed him ... how odd, for that matter, that he hadn't drawn attention to himself before. 'Matthew!' Miss Williams said again.

'Sorry, Miss Williams. Yes, I'd like some soup, please,' the boy said.

Libby took her eyes off him and glanced across to where her hostess was cutting another slice off the loaf, and when she looked back at Matthew she saw that he was now sitting at the table and beginning to spoon soup.

'You are a devil, young Matthew,' Miss Williams said, handing the boy the bread. 'I didn't realise that Libby hadn't seen you. Still, she's done so now so she knows what an odd fish you are.' She turned to Libby. 'How's the cawl? It's made of every sort of vegetable you can imagine, though of course it's all winter vegetables at the moment. In summer we make it with fresh peas, beans and young carrots, but at this time of year we have to make do with dried peas from Mr Mostyn's shop in the village and root vegetables from the clamps.'

Libby stared at her uncomprehendingly, but before she could ask the question which hovered on her lips Matthew leaned forward and tapped her bowl with his soup spoon. He was grinning. 'Miss Williams doesn't often slip up, knowing I don't speak Welsh,' he said. 'But just now and then she forgets. Cawl is just vegetable soup. And for your further information, tea is té, bread is bara and milk is llaeth.' He finished his soup, then picked up the remains of his piece of bread and wiped it round the bowl. Libby stared at him. He spoke in the "posh" voice which one heard on the wireless, yet he had mopped up the last of his soup with a bit of crust in a way which, Libby knew, both her parents would have condemned. Once again, he saw her staring, and instead of pretending he did not know the reason he commented at once, 'Oh, I know mopping up soup with bread is bad manners, but in this house we don't waste anything. Remember, there's a war on.'

'And another good reason for not wasting any food is that I'm the one who has to carry heavy bags up from the village,' Miss Williams put in. 'It's not so bad in the summer, but in winter the lane is treacherous, what with the snow and the ice, so I put on my gumboots and take a good deal of care, or get a neighbour to do my shopping for me. But when I was a girl, "waste not, want not" was dinned into my head, and I won't see good food fed to those fat lazy pigs if I can avoid it.'

Libby looked at Matthew to see how he liked being called a fat lazy pig, but he seemed to realise that she had got hold of the wrong end of the stick, for he leaned across and tapped her knuckles lightly with his spoon. 'Miss Williams keeps pigs, real ones,' he told her. 'She has two sows and four fatteners.' He turned towards the older woman. 'You cure your own bacon, don't you, Miss Williams? It's the best I've ever tasted.'

'Aye. Just about everything we eat comes from the farm,' she told Libby. 'Now, just you rub that crust round your bowl and gobble it up, and I'll show you up to your room. I'm sure you'll be tired out, and no need to wake early tomorrow because you won't be going to school for a day or so.'

Libby, after only a moment's hesitation, did as she was bid, reflecting that she was entering upon a very different life from the one she lived with her mother in Liverpool. The very thought sent a wave of homesickness over her, but she did her best to ignore it and went and got her suitcase, looking expectantly at her hostess. 'I am rather tired,' she said. 'Um . . . can I have a drink of water by my bed, please? And can you show me where the bathroom is?'

Matthew gave a rude crack of laughter. 'There is no bathroom,' he said baldly. 'But we're allowed to come down to the kitchen to wash, because it's so cold in the bedrooms now. The water comes from a pump in the yard, which you'll have to learn to work so's you can fill the buckets we keep under the sink. I can do it,' he added, and Libby wondered why the last few words sounded – oh, proud, somehow.

However, she did not mean to let him know that 'no bathroom' had struck a chill into her heart. 'Lots of people don't have bathrooms; my Gammy doesn't, for instance,' she said loftily. 'And she has an outdoor privy.' She turned a rather anxious face towards her hostess. 'I expect you have an outdoor privy too, don't you? Should – should I visit it before I go upstairs?'

Miss Williams looked at her doubtfully. 'We-ell, there's a chamber pot under your bed which you can use, and a slop bucket beneath the washstand,' she said. 'But if you'd rather use the privy . . .'

'I would,' Libby said fervently. She could just imagine horrid Matthew suddenly bursting into her bedroom and catching her sitting on the chamber pot. 'Is your privy very far from the house?'

Miss Williams sighed, went over to the dresser and produced a small and rusty-looking torch. Then she unhooked a dark and voluminous cloak off the back door and swirled it round her shoulders. After that, she thrust her feet into a pair of enormous gumboots and watched whilst Libby struggled back into her own coat. Then she turned to Matthew. 'Do you want to pay a visit?' she enquired bluntly. 'If so . . .'

'I don't, thank you very much,' Matthew said quickly. 'You take little Miss Townmouse and show her the ropes. I'll wash up the soup bowls and the pan, and put them away while you've gone.'

As soon as they were out in the dark and snowy yard, Miss Williams took hold of Libby's hand. She led her into what she told Libby was a garden, though at the moment it was simply obliterated by the snow. At the end of the garden there stood a small shed-like construction which Libby guessed must be the privy, for the snow here was well trodden. Miss Williams handed the torch to Libby as she opened the privy door. 'I guess you'll want to see where you sit and where the paper hangs,' she said calmly. 'Tell me when you're through.'

Libby took the torch, thanked her and entered the small space, shutting the door firmly behind her. She flashed the torch and saw an ancient bolt but decided not to slide it across; the prospect of being unable to slide it back and having to spend the night in here was one she could not face. Another quick flash of the torch revealed a bunch of newspapers and magazines, cut into strips, threaded with hairy string and hung on a nail, and, as she settled herself, she found she was smiling.

It was so like Gammy's privy in Crocus Street! Even the newspapers and magazines were familiar and the sight of them made her remember, guiltily, the number of times her mother had rattled on the door and accused her of sitting there reading unsuitable material instead of doing whatever she had to do and giving others a chance to use the facilities. Naturally, Libby had always denied that she was reading, although of course she was, but now, mindful of poor Miss Williams hanging about in the cold, she yanked her clothing into position, picked up the torch and emerged back into the snowy night.

Miss Williams took her hand once more and hurried back to the kitchen. 'There's a bit of water left in the washing-up bowl; you can rinse your hands in that,' she said briskly. 'Good boy, Matthew, to think of leaving it in the sink. Now let me see, Libby, you want a glass of water by your bed, so I'll carry that up and you can bring your suitcase and you, Matthew, can . . .'

'I'm not going to bed yet; I've just got to the exciting part of my book and if I don't finish the chapter, I'll never sleep tonight for wondering what happens next,' Matthew said quickly.

Miss Williams nodded. She had picked up a small lamp and kindled it from the fire, and now she made her way past Matthew and out through a doorway which led into a small hall. Then she began to mount the stairs, with Libby close on her heels. Normally, Libby would have had a good look at her surroundings, but tonight she was far too tired and simply followed the older woman into a tiny whitewashed room in which there was just space enough for a bed and a washstand. The blackout blind was down so Miss Williams stood the lamp on the floor. 'My room is directly opposite this one, if you need anything in the night,' she said. 'I put a hot water bottle in your bed earlier, but I dare say it'll have cooled by now.'

'It doesn't matter,' Libby said, beginning to tear off her clothes. She looked round for somewhere to hang them, but there was nothing, so she laid them on the end of the bed, snapped her suitcase open, and dragged out her long white winceyette nightdress. Miss Williams had tactfully left the room, pulling the door to behind her, so Libby put the nightdress on over her vest, liberty bodice and knickers, jumped into bed – the bottle was still deliciously warm – and called out to her hostess that she was ready to sleep now. Miss Williams returned so quickly that Libby realised she must have been hovering outside the door. She picked up the lamp and turned it off, then walked over to the window and rolled up the blind so that Libby would not be left in total darkness. Then she came over to the bed and looked down at Libby for a moment, as though unsure what she should do or say, but Libby solved the problem for her by curling up beneath the covers and muttering a sleepy 'Good night'.

Miss Williams replied in kind and left the room,

shutting the door behind her. As soon as she was alone Libby, who had been facing the door, rolled over, got cautiously out of bed and padded over to the window. Outside there were trees, black against the snow, and a roof, which she supposed must belong to a porch. She tried peering first to the right and then to the left, to see whether her room overlooked the front or the back of the house, but realised she was being foolish. Besides, it was bitterly cold and she knew from past experience that icy feet can keep one awake for hours. Accordingly, she climbed back into bed and realised that the glass of water she had asked for was on the washstand. There was no bedside table or cabinet, however, and if she put it on the floor she might knock it over during the night. Sighing, she placed her feet firmly on the hot water bottle, and then turned her face into the pillow and began to cry. This was all so strange, so different from her life back in Sydenham Avenue! She had stayed with Gammy on numerous occasions, when her mother and father had wanted time to themselves, but that was very different. She had shared Fiona's bed, or Gammy's, and had never suffered from the horrid feeling which was assailing her now: a sort of dragging misery which she supposed must be what people called homesickness. She remembered her determination to run back home if she was unhappy, but even the thought of doing such a thing was absurd, she realised now. She might get as far as the village but she would certainly never find her way back to that small railway station, let alone traverse the many miles which separated her from Sydenham Avenue.

However, all was not yet lost. Her mother had promised that if she was unhappy she could be sent elsewhere . . . but Miss Williams had been kind. Libby sniffed and wiped her tear-wet face on the rough linen sheet. It smelt of lavender. Perhaps she would wait awhile before deciding anything. She glanced towards the window and saw the sky clear and speckled with stars, and a crescent moon peering down on her through the frosted branches of a great tree. Presently, she slept.

Libby was awoken next morning by what sounded like someone tapping on the door. Sleepily, she wondered who could be calling so early, then concluded that her mother would hear the knock and answer it. She listened for footsteps descending the stairs and crossing the hall, and for the front door opening, but the only sound she heard was the tap, tap, tap. Reluctantly, Libby opened her eyes and was so shocked by what she saw that she shot right up in bed, heart hammering, and stared wildly about her. Even as she took in the tiny whitewashed room, the washstand and the small window through which she could see the branches of a tree, she remembered. She had left her home in Sydenham Avenue the previous day and this was her little room at Tregarth Farm. Pale sunshine streamed through the window and even as she watched, a big fat drop of melting ice fell past the glass. Tap, it went, and was speedily followed by others, tap, tap, tap.

Libby remembered that Miss Williams had told her she might lie in this morning since there would be no school for her today. For a moment, she was tempted to snuggle down once more, for the bed was warm and well supplied with blankets. But she knew that even if she did so she would be unable to go back to sleep, so she scrambled from beneath the covers and went over to the wash-stand. She looked rather doubtfully at the water in the jug, then remembered her hot water bottle; the water in it would no longer be hot, but she knew from past experience that it would be a good deal warmer than that in the jug. She had a bit of a struggle to unscrew the cap, but did it at last, had a hasty wash, then dressed and headed for the stairs.

Reaching the hall, she turned at once towards the kitchen and saw that the door was not quite closed. Warmth came out to meet her as she pushed it open, suddenly realising that she had no idea of the time. However, the first thing she saw when she entered the room was Miss Williams stirring something in a large black saucepan, and the boy, Matthew, was sitting at the table, eating something out of a pottery bowl. 'Morning, Townmouse,' he said cheerfully. 'You're in luck; Miss Williams makes the best porridge in the whole of Wales and you're just in time to have your share.'

At this moment, however, Miss Williams turned and smiled, though she raised her brows. 'Well I never! I looked in on you earlier and you were so sound asleep that I told Matthew here I doubted you'd stir before noon,' she said. 'Well, well, you're just in time for your plate of porridge.' She turned and wagged a reproving spoon at Matthew. 'No second helpings for you today, young man.' Seeing Libby hovering uncertainly, she tutted. 'Sit down, child, for the Lord's sake! I take it you drink tea?'

Libby would have liked to say she preferred milk but decided that since she was a guest such a remark would be impolite, so she just said, meekly, that weak tea would be very nice, thank you. Then she sat herself down on the chair she had taken the previous evening and began to eat the porridge which Miss Williams had placed before her. To her surprise, it was absolutely delicious, with a thin sprinkling of brown sugar and a trickle of milk round the edges. Heartened, she finished it up in no time, though she looked rather doubtfully at the mug of tea which Miss Williams had plonked on the table beside her. If this was her hostess's idea of weak tea, she was glad she had not asked for strong.

Matthew followed her glance and grinned. 'You can't have sugar in it because of rationing, but you can have a saccharin tablet,' he said, pushing a small bowl containing the familiar little white tablets towards her.

Libby, however, shook her head. 'It's all right;

if you drink without breathing in you can hardly taste it,' she said, and wondered why Matthew smiled. Another morning, she decided, she would drink the tea before eating the porridge.

'Finished? Good. Well, I've work to do outside, so you two can wash up and put away and so on and when that's done, Matthew, you can show Libby round, which won't take long. After that you can amuse yourselves until I come in to prepare the midday meal.' Libby was about to ask why Matthew would not be going to school, but Miss Williams was already at the back door, her cloak round her shoulders, a most disreputable man's cap pulled firmly down on her head and gumboots on her feet. 'Is that clear? See you at lunchtime then.'

She disappeared through the doorway and Libby, deciding that the snow was probably too deep for Matthew to wade all the way to the village, stood up, picked up the porridge bowls, and headed for the sink. To her total astonishment, Matthew, carrying their two tin mugs, was there before her, still sitting in his chair. She gasped, looking down at him, wondering how on earth . . . and then realised that Matthew was in a wheelchair and had simply propelled himself from the table to the sink. He clattered the mugs on to the left-hand draining board and then, as she watched, swivelled expertly and propelled himself back to the stove. He picked up the big kettle from the hob and returned much more slowly and carefully to the sink, where he splashed boiling water into the washing-up bowl, stood the kettle on the draining board, and heaved up one of the buckets, tipping cold in with the hot until he was satisfied that the temperature was right. He began to wash the crocks with the aid of a little mop, standing them to drain and turning to grin at his companion. 'Refill the kettle, will you?' he said cheerfully. 'I can do it but it's awkward and I usually manage to spill some. Then you can get one of the tea towels and dry up, only I'm afraid you'd better wash the porridge pan because I never seem to get it completely clean. The sink's at the wrong angle, or something.'

'I think you're jolly clever to wash up at all,' Libby said admiringly. 'Are you – are you in that wheelchair all the time? I mean, can't you walk at all?'

'Not a step, but my arms are very strong,' he assured her. 'I got some horrible disease when I was only a nipper – my parents died of it – but I don't mean to give up. I exercise when I'm lying in bed and I rub my leg muscles like fun. One of these days I'll walk again, see if I don't.'

'That's good,' Libby said. She finished drying the porridge saucepan and turned to take her coat from the hook. 'Do you have a jacket, Matthew? Only I can't see one hanging up here.'

'I do, but I've got Miss Williams's old cloak for the farmyard,' Matthew said. He looked disparagingly at Libby's coat. 'If you wear that on the farm you'll ruin it in no time. Tell you what, put it on for warmth and cover it with that old black oilskin. It'll keep the worst of the mud off. I take it you've got gumboots?'

'Yes, I took them off when I came in last night, but I don't know where . . . oh, there they are, the smallest pair in that line,' Libby said thankfully, slipping her feet into them. 'Which are yours, Matthew? I'll bring them over.'

'Pair next to yours,' Matthew said briefly. 'You can put them on for me if you like; it'll save time.'

Libby felt rather shy, but though he seemed to have no movement in his feet or legs she got his boots on without any trouble, pulled the old oilskin down over her smart navy coat, and flung the back door open.

Matthew promptly trundled out into the yard, Libby following close behind. All around them the snow was turning to slush and icicles were dripping, and when they ventured to take a peep into the lane they saw that it looked more like a stream. They returned to the yard and Libby was gazing around her when Matthew gave a shout, slewed his chair round, and pushed her half a dozen feet ahead of him only just in time. An enormous slab of snow and ice came rocketing off the roof of the farmhouse and Libby realised that had Matthew not given her a shove, she would have received the full impact. 'Phew! That was a close shave,' Matthew said. 'As I expect you've realised, Tregarth isn't a proper farm any more. We've got

111

two sows and four fatteners in the pigsties, two rather elderly sheep in the orchard, and four cows who are in the cowshed for the winter. The hens wander loose all day, but have to be penned up at night because of foxes. Most of Miss Williams's living comes from the eggs – the steady money, I mean, because the pigs bring in quite a bit, I think. But then she has to pay Dewi from time to time, and though Miss Williams has the farm the estate kept most of the land, so she isn't nearly as well off as people think. That's why she likes us to clear our plates and never to refuse food or ask for something different.'

'I see,' Libby said slowly. 'The porridge was lovely, though.'

Matthew nodded. 'Yes, her porridge is always prime,' he agreed. 'And we get it every morning, even if she can spare an egg, because she says porridge lines our stomachs. She works terribly hard, as hard as a man, so I do whatever I can to help and you must do the same.' As he spoke, he was ushering her into what turned out to be the cowshed, for when the occupants turned their heads to gaze at the visitors Libby saw four small, fudge-coloured cows with gentle brown eyes and neat little hooves. 'The one dribbling is Bluebell, the one beside her is Buttercup, then there's Daisy and Pansy,' Matthew informed her. 'They're what they call Jersey cows and they produce very rich milk.' He lowered his voice. 'Miss Williams has to send most of it to the dairy, but we keep some

112

back for our own use and make butter, which is delicious.' He looked wistful. 'I'd love to be able to milk and heaven knows Miss Williams has tried to teach me, but it's the damned wheelchair. One day I will do it, but not yet.' He eyed her consideringly. 'She'll teach you, I suppose, lucky beggar. And when spring comes, you'll be able to get the eggs when the hens lay astray. Ah well, there's a lot I can do, and I'm sure I've got stronger every day since I came here.'

Once they had admired the pigs and the big old carthorse in the stable, they returned to the house and thawed out in front of the kitchen fire. 'We have bread and cheese and apples at lunchtime, and a hot meal in the evening,' Matthew told her. 'As I remember it, you'll have a postcard addressed to your parents which you're supposed to fill in and send as soon as you can, so if you nip up to your room I'll lay the table and then help you to write the card – if you need help, of course,' he added.

Libby gasped, a hand flying to her mouth. She had completely forgotten the postcard and felt very guilty since she had promised her mother to send it the moment she arrived at her new home. However, when it was done, Matthew pointed out that she would be unable to reach the village until the weather cleared. 'If you'd been able to ride old Dobbin, Miss Williams might have let you take him, but at the moment, with the snow on the hills melting, the lane is far too dangerous, even for the horse,' he told her. 'Why, the milk lorry can't come up to collect the churns when it's really bad, so a neighbour picks them up and takes them down to the village on his tractor. But I expect one of the teachers will write to your mother and explain, so she won't worry.'

Libby thought, privately, that her mother would worry a great deal if she knew that her daughter was marooned in an old farmhouse completely cut off from civilisation, but in fact Miss Williams, returning for the midday meal, took the card from her and promised that it would be on its way to Liverpool by that very evening. 'You two stay indoors. I'm going over the tops,' she said briefly. 'I'll be home before dark.'

As soon as she had gone Libby settled herself to asking questions. 'How long have you been here, Matthew?' she asked baldly. 'I do like Miss Williams, but she puzzles me. She talks like someone on the wireless, but she doesn't . . . well, she doesn't look the way she talks, if you understand me.'

'I've been here since war broke out. I was in the first wave of evacuees,' Matthew said. 'And Miss Williams is – oh, absolutely grand. Well, she took me in, didn't she? They carted me round half North Wales and I heard every excuse under the sun – it's awful to feel so bloody unwanted, if you'll excuse my French – and then word came that a Miss Williams of Tregarth would take me on and I came here. She never made me feel a useless cripple, the way they did down in the villages, and she never says "you can't", or "don't strain your-self," and even my gran said things like that from time to time. You're lucky, I'm telling you; she's simply the best.'

'Ye-es, but that doesn't explain the way she talks and looks . . .' Libby began, but Matthew said that it was too long a story to tell now, and would she like to stop chattering and help him lay the table. Libby, sensing the firm closing of a door behind which he did not mean her to pry, accepted the rebuff and asked no more personal questions that day, though when Miss Williams returned to say that the postcard was on its way, Libby did ask what their hostess had meant by 'over the tops'.

'I meant over the hills,' Miss Williams said. 'I was born and brought up in these hills, and know them like the back of my hand. If you keep high you can get to the village via the castle, but it's no road for children or strangers. However, when summer comes, I'll maybe show you the way.' She grinned suddenly, her expression as mischievous as a child's. 'You wouldn't want to miss school because the lane was impassable, would you?'

Libby and Matthew both smiled. Missing school whenever the weather was bad was a treat unknown to city children but one which Libby, at least, would embrace eagerly, she thought. She was heartily glad that the village had been full and that she was billeted with Miss Williams and Matthew at Tregarth Farm.

Chapter Four

Marianne started her job, making wireless parts for aircraft, a week after Libby left, and though it seemed strange at first she soon began to enjoy both the company of the other girls and the work itself. The journey, however, from Croxteth Road to Long Lane was a lengthy one. First she had to catch a number 15 tram to the Pier Head, where she changed to one going to Walton Avenue. She got off at Stopgate Lane and then had to walk until she reached Long Lane and the factory. Until March arrived her shifts sometimes meant that she left home before day had dawned, but even in daylight it was still a wearisome journey. Crocus Street was much closer and twice, when she was working a double shift, she went to her mother's house and slept on the sofa, realising how much easier her life would be if she moved in there, at least when she was working a night shift.

Libby's eighth birthday was towards the end of March, so Marianne applied for unpaid leave in order to visit her. Miss Williams met her in the horse and cart and at first Marianne too was puzzled by the contrast between her cut-glass accent and her appearance, but Matthew had decided that Libby could be trusted with the story and was happy to explain it to them both once the first rapturous greetings were over and he and Libby were showing Marianne round the farm.

'Miss Williams inherited Tregarth from her father, but he could not leave her the castle or anything like that because of a thing called an entail,' he said. 'An entail means the property has to go to a male heir, and since Miss Williams had no brothers everything went to a cousin she had never met. Her father had taken most of the Tregarth land into the estate because he always expected his daughter to marry, so when she inherited it the farm had no more than maybe six or eight acres of land – not enough to grow crops, anyway. But I don't believe Miss Williams really minded. She just began to work extremely hard so that she would be independent. She works like a man, you know, and doesn't have money to spare for smart clothes or shoes.'

Matthew was twelve, but seemed older, perhaps because of his disability, and Marianne thought him delightful, as well as intelligent. 'One should never judge by appearances,' she admitted. 'And I agree with you, Matthew, Miss Williams is grand.'

'Yes,' Matthew said. 'I think Libby and I are really lucky because Miss Williams treats us as if we were her own kids, and makes sure we're happy and well fed. Isn't that so, Libby?'

Libby nodded vigorously. 'She's nice,' she confirmed. 'And Matthew and I get on ever so well, don't we, Matt? The kids at school are OK, and the man who farms at the head of the valley has a son called Rhys – Rhys Evans – who pops in and picks Matthew and me up so that we get safely to school and back each day. We manage pretty well, really, and it will get easier when summer comes.'

When Marianne left Tregarth Farm, she was happy in the knowledge that Libby had fallen on her feet and was learning new skills into the bargain. Her daughter had told her that Miss Williams was teaching her to milk, to tell a broody hen from one which was just cross, and to perform simple tasks such as pumping water, feeding the hens and the pigs, and even driving Dobbin, though this required little skill since he knew the way to the village and back quite as well as the children did.

'I am so happy here, Mum,' Libby had said. 'I wouldn't move away for anything, except to come back to you, of course.'

Three days after Marianne returned to Sydenham Avenue, Neil came home, announcing that he would be with her for a couple of days. Marianne greeted him as warmly as ever, though since he was always tired and often spent a good deal of time criticising his wife's determination to remain in Liverpool, these periods were not as pleasant as they might have been. She was glad to be able to point out that having visited Libby she knew for certain that leaving Liverpool to be near her was out of the question, since the farm was so far from any factory which might have employed her.

Unfortunately, she could not take more time off

while Neil was home, and when she admitted that she'd twice spent the night with Gammy in Crocus Street his frustration boiled over and he became really angry, reminding her of the nearby docks and the danger. 'You'd all be a good deal better off in the country,' he said for the umpteenth time. 'Why oh why won't you *listen* to me?'

'It was only two nights, when I was on a double shift, and when you say "all", I take it you aren't including Fiona?' Marianne said coldly. 'She did just exactly what you advised her to do: she joined the Wrens, and instead of being posted up to Scotland or down to Cornwall she's working right here in the centre of Liverpool, and jolly near the docks too.'

Neil shrugged. 'I can scarcely tell your sister what to do, particularly now she's a member of His Majesty's Forces,' he said crossly. 'Well, I'd sooner you didn't stay in Crocus Street. You were the one who was so keen to keep our house on, but now you're quite happy to sleep on your mum's sofa, not two minutes' walk from the docks, when you know how I worry.'

'You might worry about the journey I have to undergo, particularly when the weather's bad,' Marianne pointed out. 'Honestly, Neil, it's not a good idea to do a double shift and then have that long journey to Sydenham Avenue. Besides, Gammy feeds me, which is a real treat after returning home tired out only to have to start preparing a meal for myself.'

They were in the kitchen of the Sydenham Avenue house, and when she looked into his weary face, at the strain lines round his mouth, she rushed over to him, throwing her arms round his neck and pressing herself close. 'Darling Neil, don't let's quarrel,' she said urgently. 'I promise you that if the Jerries start bombing Liverpool I'll think again, but you know my job is nearly as important as yours. The boss says I'm the fastest, neatest and most accurate worker he's got, and he's not a man to hand out praise as a rule. He says I'll make supervisor before we're through.'

She had expected to see his face soften, to feel his arms go round her, but instead he stiffened and pushed her away. 'You won't be a supervisor for long if you're in Crocus Street when a bomb misses the docks and flattens your mum's house,' he said, and before she could reply he was heading for the stairs, calling over his shoulder that he would have a bath and be down for supper in about forty minutes.

Marianne was bitterly hurt by his rejection, and though he apologised and was very sweet to her when he came downstairs once more, she knew she would never be able to forget his words. She also knew that when his ship sailed the following day she would be working, and was guiltily glad that she would not have to wave him off when they were so at odds with one another.

She was still brooding over the argument when Mr Reynolds, the factory manager, called her into his office. Marianne wondered what she had done, expecting a reprimand, but instead he told her that he wanted her to take charge of an extension to the existing factory. 'You'll have a dozen or so girls working under you and I'm afraid you'll have to teach them their job, since, as you know, our present staff are fully occupied at the moment. For the time being, you and Janet Brown will be in charge of the girls, though you will be in overall command. Naturally, your salary will reflect your increased responsibility. The extension has been furnished with benches and so on, and arrangements have been made for the tea lady to service the premises once she's finished with the main factory building. I take it you're prepared to accept your new position? You are? Good! Then if you'll follow me, I'll show you round your future domain.'

Marianne was delighted with everything except the information that Janet Brown would be her assistant. She could not deny that Janet was good at her work, but she was a loud-mouthed, arrogant woman, who liked to browbeat and bully any girls who seemed unlikely to fight back. I'll have to keep my eye on her with a dozen new girls on the workbenches, Marianne told herself, looking with approval at the shiny surfaces and apparatus in the clean and airy room.

She returned to her bench, bubbling with excitement, and received hearty congratulations from most of the girls with whom she worked, though some of them tightened their lips and muttered.

Janet Brown was clearly delighted by her own promotion, but sneered sotto voce that Marianne's elevation was due to her posh voice and fancy ways.

Marianne's friend Betty, however, who supervised the trainees in her section, told her to ignore spiteful criticism and think practically. 'If you've got any brains at all in that head of yours, queen, you'll move in with your mam, for the first few weeks at any rate,' she said. 'You know what it'll be like. You'll be workin' overtime at both ends of the day to make sure your girls don't send poor work through to the finishers. It's a helluva long journey from here to Sydenham Avenue and I bet your mam would welcome you wi' open arms.'

Marianne agreed that this was so and decided to visit Crocus Street when her shift ended that very day. If Neil had not been so dictatorial, she told herself, she would have put up with the daily journey out to Croxteth Road, but now she felt, defiantly, that she had a perfect right to please herself. Why not? Neil said he worried about her, but did she not worry about him? Of course she did, along with every other married woman whose man was serving in the armed forces.

So when she finished her shift, she caught the tram to Stanley Road, anxious to talk to her mother. Her sister would probably be in too, for Fiona, who was now a writer – which was what the Navy called their clerical workers – at naval headquarters, usually worked office hours. It was seven in the evening as Marianne turned into Crocus Street and hurried along the pavement before diving down the jigger. As she crossed the back yard, ducking under the washing on the line, she mentally rehearsed the request she intended to make, and wondered how Gammy – and Fee, of course – would react.

She burst into the kitchen. Gammy was bending down and extracting a pie from the oven, Fiona was draining a pan of potatoes over the sink, and the three lodgers were sitting at the table, their expressions so hopeful that they made Marianne think of three puppies watching their dinner dish descend. Not that any of the men were young, but when food was in question she guessed they would have all the eager anticipation of boys. Gammy backed out, put the pie down in the middle of the table, and beamed at her eldest daughter. 'You're just in time for supper – mutton and onion pie, spuds and mashed swede,' she said triumphantly. 'Take your coat off, queen, and sit down. You look excited. Whazzup?'

Before Marianne could reply, Fiona had turned from the sink, still holding the heavy pan of potatoes. 'Is your Neil home?' she asked. 'No, he can't be; the *Sea Spurge* has only just gone to sea, hasn't she?'

Marianne frowned. 'No, it's nothing to do with Neil. Mr Reynolds has put me up to supervisor – well, more than that, really. I'm to be in charge of a new extension, starting on Monday. I'll get girls who've never worked on a production line, so I'll have to train them. And my salary will go up quite a lot, which is good.'

'Well, congratulations!' the lodgers said, almost in chorus.

Marianne put her hands to her hot cheeks. Her mother, having disposed of the pie, came over and hugged her. 'You've done well, chuck,' she said approvingly. 'I'm proud of both me gals. Young Fiona here works for the top brass – her job's real important – and now you're makin' your way up to management, 'cos I reckon that's where you'll end up.'

Marianne laughed and took her place at the table as her mother began to cut the pie into six large slices. 'I doubt that. Well, I hope the war will be over before I have time to rise to such giddy heights. But Mam, this job will make a difference to the hours I work, for the first few weeks at any rate. I've got to be at the factory at least half an hour before my girls get in, and I'll probably leave a good half-hour later than them as well. I know it's putting a strain on you, but it would make my life a lot easier if I could sleep on the sofa here for a short time. I'd help in any way I could, obviously – and I'd give you my ration book, of course – but to come home to a hot meal is such a treat and the journey to Long Lane from Crocus Street is nothing compared to the trek I do at present. And it isn't as if it'll be for ever; just until I grow accustomed to the new job.'

Gammy began to say that there was nothing she would like more than to have both her daughters under her roof, but Fiona, who was dishing up the potatoes and the mashed swede, interrupted. 'Sorry to disappoint you, Mam, but for some time I've thought it would be more convenient if I moved in wi' me pal Mandy, who lives almost cheek by jowl with me workplace,' she said. 'She asked me ages ago but I didn't do nothin' about it because of leavin' you in the lurch. However, if I move out and Marianne moves in, no doubt she'll pay you the same.' She beamed round the table, then turned to her sister. 'How many spuds can you manage, queen? Three? Four? They ain't big 'uns.'

'Oh, three, please. But I'll only be here for a few weeks,' Marianne said anxiously. 'What'll Mam do then?'

'I dare say I'll manage,' Gammy said, with un-impaired cheerfulness. She wagged a reproving finger at Fiona. 'You've been talking about leavin' home ever since the war started. When you joined the Wrens I expected you to go. But even if you were to stay, we could make up a bed for your sister in the parlour. So that's settled.' She pulled her chair up to the table. 'As for your rent, young Fee, that's neither here nor there, so don't you go worritin' about that. What concerns me is how Neil'll take it. He don't like the idea of anyone livin' so close to the docks, lerralone his wife.'

'I shan't tell him, and anyway, it's only tempor-ary,' Marianne pointed out. 'If the Luftwaffe target Liverpool, the whole lot of us can move back to my place, but honestly, Mam, I think Neil is just being over-cautious. So it will be all right, particularly if he never finds out! The truth is, the war in the Atlantic is hotting up and he's not able to come home nearly as often as he did before Christmas. In fact the two days he was home recently were the first for . . . oh, for weeks.'

'Well, if you're sure,' Gammy said comfortably. 'I don't want to have me son-in-law buzzin' round me ears like a demented bluebottle. You start this new job Monday, is that right? Then Fiona and meself will come over to your place Sunday and give you a hand packin' your stuff. You'll be sharin' my bed, of course, so you won't need sheets or pillowcases, but you'd best bring any food what might go bad if you left it, and all your work things, and a dressin' gown so you don't shock me lodgers by appearin' in your nightie.'

'That would be a great help,' Marianne said gratefully, and when the meal was over and the three women were washing up and clearing away, she began to tell her mother and sister about her visit to Tregarth, as this was the first time she had seen them since returning from North Wales. 'Miss Williams is an odd-looking woman. She dresses pretty much like a farm worker, cuts her own hair into a very rough sort of bob, and has really weather-beaten skin because she spends almost all her time out of doors. But she's got a heart of gold. She baked Libby a cake to celebrate her eighth birthday; you never saw anything like it! It was about as even as the lane up to their house, with as many dips and furrows as a ploughed field, and the middle wasn't cooked at all, though the outside was burnt.'

Gammy and Fiona both laughed. 'She's no cook then,' Fiona observed. 'How does she feed the child? I don't recall that Libby would eat any old rubbish.'

'She's got two evacuees, Libby and a lad called Matthew, and she feeds them very well,' Marianne assured her sister. 'She makes wonderful soup, delicious stews and very good porridge, but Matthew told me that until he interfered, boiled eggs were always cooked until they could bounce on the floor without shattering and sometimes potatoes ended up as mush because she forgot to take them off the flame. Bread's a bit of a problem, though. When the children are in school, they pick up a loaf from the village shop. Miss Williams tries and tries to make her own bread but it always goes wrong. Still, she made soda bread while I was there – that's the stuff you make without yeast – and though it was a bit hard, it was nice with her home-made cheese and some of the onions she pickled last autumn.'

'I reckon bakin' – scones and sponges and fruit cakes and that – is something we can all live wi'out, even though they're tasty,' Gammy said. 'Bakin' of that sort is the kind of thing your mam teaches you; you can't just pick it up like you can makin' soup or stew.'

'You're right, and she does all the farm work, with only occasional help, so she doesn't really have time for much else,' Marianne agreed. 'She is a funny old thing, though. She talks really posh, like the announcers on the wireless, and yet runs the farm like clockwork and is greatly respected by everyone in the neighbourhood.' As she spoke, Marianne looked up at the clock on the mantelpiece and gave a squawk, flying across to take her coat down from its hook. 'Look at the time, Mam! If I don't get a move on I'll miss the last tram, and I don't fancy having to walk from the Pier Head.'

Marianne found her new job absorbing despite the fact that Janet proved to be as difficult as she had feared. She countermanded Marianne's instructions whenever she thought she could get away with it and tried to persuade the girls on the assembly line to follow her example, though with very little success. Feeling herself unappreciated by the new workers in the extension, Janet took to sneaking away whenever the opportunity occurred, in order to spend time with the girls who had been her buddies in the main building. Of course, this increased Marianne's own workload, but she was so glad to be relieved of Janet's presence from time to time that she did not complain.

Eventually, however, the day came when Mr Reynolds, who must have suspected something, came into the extension at a time when Janet was not around. He examined the work the girls were doing, congratulated them on the speed with which they had learned, and then asked with seeming idleness how they got along with Miss Brown. Most of the girls let their expressions speak for them, but one or two were more forthright. 'She's norran easy person to work for,' little Violet Duke said. 'If you gerrit right she don't say nothin', but if you gerrit wrong she jumps on you wi' her welly boots on.'

Mr Reynolds smiled and moved on to the next girl, and after ten minutes turned to Marianne. 'Where's Miss Brown now?' he enquired. 'I know it's a fair walk from here to the Ladies, but by my reckoning she's been gone getting on for half an hour.'

'She might have gone to the stores, I suppose,' Marianne said cautiously. She knew full well what her assistant was doing, because she had followed her only the previous week, curious to know just what Janet was up to. The other woman simply followed the tea trolley, which meant that when she entered any of the production rooms everyone abandoned their benches and clustered round her for their ten-minute break. Marianne had known that if she stopped Janet's expeditions it would mean that the girl was always in the extension and would probably be sulky and even more difficult. Now that the matter was in Mr Reynolds's hands, however, things might change, for surely Janet could not blame Marianne because the boss had found her out?

Mr Reynolds did nothing that day, rather to Marianne's relief, but the following morning the office boy bounced into their room and announced that Mr Reynolds wanted to see Miss Brown in his office.

Janet, already halfway to the door and no doubt heading for the tea trolley, stopped as though she'd been shot. For a moment she stood frozen to the spot, then she glanced uneasily at Marianne. 'What does he want?' she enquired belligerently. 'Have you been tale-clatting on me, Miss Sheridan?'

Janet always called Marianne 'Miss', plainly considering that by so doing she was reducing the other woman to single status once more. Marianne had tried correcting her but had given up, realising that it pleased Janet to believe Marianne was being needled by her behaviour. Now, however, she said frostily: 'No, I have not said a word about you to anyone. But Mr Reynolds was in here yesterday, checking the girls at work, and he asked where you were.'

'Yeah, an' I suppose you went and told him some bleedin' lie,' Janet said aggressively. 'Tryin' to get me into trouble . . .'

'No she did not,' Dotty Carruthers said. Her voice shook a little, for she had frequently been the butt of Janet's spite. 'She said you'd gone over to the store for components, so you didn't oughta blame her, Miss Brown.'

Janet sniffed and seemed about to argue, then changed her mind and marched stiffly out of the room. She did not return for half an hour, and when she did so she was plainly in a flaming temper. She stalked up and down the room, criticising everything everyone did, and when the hooter sounded for the end of the shift she strode into the middle of the room and addressed everyone at the top of her voice. 'Mr Reynolds wanted to see me to say me work here was finished 'cos you don't need any further training. You know more or less what you're supposed to do. So I'm goin' back to me old place, amongst me friends, which I'm real glad of. I'd like to say I'll miss you, but I shan't.' And before anyone could comment, she had turned and stomped out of the building.

When she had gone, Marianne looked round at the girls and saw the smiles on their faces, and knew that her own eyes must have lit up. Working here without Janet's destructive presence would be truly pleasant; life would be much easier for them all. However, she had one piece of news that might not be quite so popular, so she clapped her hands to get everyone's attention and then spoke up. 'Well, girls, it's grand news that Mr Reynolds no longer thinks of you as trainees, but as part of the workforce helping to win the war. However, this means that we start shift work as from next Monday, and unfortunately our first week is on nights. Miss Blenkinsop told me earlier in the day, knowing that you might have to make special arrangements, but because of Miss Brown's leaving I decided not to mention it until she'd actually gone. Now, has anyone any questions?'

Naturally enough, the girls wanted to know whether there would be transport available for night shifts and were told that a bus would drop them off just before ten o'clock and another would pick them up just after six. 'But if you live close enough to the factory to walk, please do so in groups,' Marianne advised. 'It's not too bad at this time of year, but when winter comes we don't want anyone lying in the snow for half an hour with a broken leg. If you're with friends, they can get help, but if you're alone, say on a dark February morning . . . well, I'll leave it to your imaginations.'

Marianne had now been staying in Crocus Street for nearly six weeks, though she went back to her own house at weekends, sometimes accompanied by Gammy and sometimes alone. She had not seen Neil since starting her new job but had received a couple of hastily written letters from him, explaining that the turn-round at the Liverpool end of his Atlantic convoys did not allow him time to come ashore. She had accepted this, and had told him that he must let her know when he *was* able to come home so that she might make arrangements, since her shifts were often awkward because of her new position. He had congratulated her wholeheartedly, said he was proud of her and promised to be in touch just as soon as he could grab a few hours off, but so far this had not happened. So once a week Marianne returned to Sydenham Avenue, lit fires, polished furniture, made sure there was food in the pantry, and usually spent at least one night in the marital bed, though Gammy always resolutely refused to stay over, saying she had her lodgers to consider.

On the Monday they started their first night

shift, Marianne decided she would spend the day in Sydenham Avenue. She had gone there at the weekend and had been dismayed to find four boys playing with a football, made of rags tied together, in her back garden. When she had asked the children, sharply, what they thought they were doing the oldest boy, who was probably around ten, had given her a sly look from under his lashes. 'No one don't live here,' he had announced. 'It's empty, ain't it, Alfie? So we's got as much right as anyone to play footie in here.'

Marianne had told him, even more sharply, that he was quite wrong. 'My husband and I live here, but he's the captain of a corvette and I work shifts in a factory, so we're not here all the time,' she had told them. 'If I find you here again, I shall send for the scuffers and they'll go round to your parents' houses and see that you're given a whipping. Do you understand me?'

'We aren't doin' no harm, missus,' the boy who had been addressed as Alfie had whined. 'Our mams won't lerrus play on the road and the park keeper at Seffy drove us off the grass 'cos he said it were too wet and we'd ruinate it.'

'Yes, and you're ruining my grass as well,' Marianne had said severely. 'Go on, off with you!'

She had smiled to herself as they had scattered, but when she had gone into the house and found a broken window and some ornaments missing she had been less amused, wishing she had taken the boys' names and addresses. She had visited the police station and explained the situation, and was told that the local bobby would keep an eye on the house, but the desk sergeant had advised her to pop in unexpectedly whenever she could and to alert the neighbours, hence her decision to visit Sydenham Avenue before her night shift.

Accordingly, as soon as breakfast was over on Monday, she caught a tram to the Pier Head and changed on to a No. 32. Downstairs had already filled up so she went straight to the upper deck and, gazing incuriously out as the tram swung into Park Lane and slowed, she saw a familiar bush of red-gold hair with a Wren's hat jammed on top. Smiling to herself, Marianne tapped on the window, hoping to get Fiona's attention, but her sister did not look up. Marianne tapped again on the glass, but then the tram moved forward and she lost sight of her sister.

Heaving a sigh and leaning back in her seat once more, Marianne began to make a mental list of the things she would do in Sydenham Avenue, but before she had got very far a hand landed on her shoulder. She looked round and there was Neil, smiling down at her. 'Sweetheart!' he said exuberantly, slipping into the seat beside her. 'Well, if this isn't my lucky day! The turn-round has been delayed for twenty-four hours, so I've left my number one in charge. But I thought you'd be at work. What's happened? Don't say you've thrown in your lovely job?'

'No, but we start nights tonight,' Marianne

134

explained. 'Oh, Neil, it's marvellous to see you . . .' She cast a quick glance behind him but saw only a very large fat man in seaman's uniform, trying to squeeze past Neil in order to get the last seat up at the front. She turned back to her husband. 'Didn't I see Fiona just now? Were you with her? I tapped on the window, but . . .'

'Oh, Fiona. Yes, you did see her. She was on her way to work so she came with me as far as the tram stop and saw me aboard, and then went off to naval HQ.' Neil slid an arm round her shoulders and gave her a quick squeeze. 'She did warn me that you'd probably be at work, but you know how it is; the thought of a home-cooked meal and a night's sleep in my own bed was irresistible. To find you actually at home was more than I dared hope.' He lowered his voice to a husky whisper. 'To have you all warm and cuddly in my arms for a whole night would make my time ashore perfect.'

'Oh, darling, I told you I'm working tonight,' Marianne said, dismayed. 'And there's absolutely nothing I can do about it because it's our first night on shifts and I'm in charge.'

Neil's shoulders drooped, but then he brightened. 'I've got an idea, sweetheart. When we've had lunch, let's go to bed. That way you'll be rested when your shift starts and I'll have my lovely cuddlesome girl for at least a few hours. Tell you what, I'll get up when you do and take you by taxi right to your factory so we don't miss a moment together, because I have to be back at the *Sea Spurge* by eight tomorrow morning, worse luck!'

It was on the tip of Marianne's tongue to say that she would have to let Gammy know, then remembered that Neil had no idea she was staying with her mother. She sighed to herself, remembering the old saying: *Oh what a tangled web we weave, when first we practise to deceive.* How true it was! But Gammy would just assume she was spending longer at the house because of the youngsters who had broken the window and stolen her stuff; no need to worry that her mum would think she was in some sort of trouble. If she, Marianne, remembered that she was supposed to be living full time at the Sydenham Avenue house all should be well.

And indeed, so it proved. She made an excuse for the lack of fresh food in the pantry and nipped into the nearest chip shop for fish and chips for lunch, and as soon as these were eaten she and Neil went to bed. He was very warm and loving towards her and afterwards, despite her inner conviction that she would never be able to sleep in daylight, she dropped off at once, waking a couple of times when Neil mumbled in his sleep or turned over, but otherwise having quite five hours of slumber.

Neil had offered to accompany her to work, but when the alarm woke them at eight o'clock she looked at his tired face and ordered him to stay in bed. 'I can manage perfectly well on the trams, and where d'you think you'd find a taxi in this neck of the woods?' she asked him. 'You stay in bed, my darling, because you look as though you've had a really tough time and need all the sleep you can get. Now listen; my shifts may change about a bit, but if I know in advance when you'll be home – you can ring the factory and leave me a message – then I'll try to arrange something. Mr Reynolds appreciates everything I do and will really help us to see each other from time to time. But now I must go, because to be late would make me seem unreliable, and I've worked fearfully hard to convince management that I'm not.'

Fortunately, she had kept a spare pair of work overalls in her wardrobe and she donned these, struggled into her winter coat and a thick head-scarf, which all the girls wore, kissed Neil warmly and set off at a run for the tram stop.

It seemed no time at all before the factory loomed up, dark against the stars, and Marianne, clocking in all by herself because she was early, decided to nip up to the kitchen to see whether she might wheedle a cup of tea out of whoever was up there. As she went, she glanced at the door of one of the production rooms and saw, through it, Janet laughing at something the girl next to her had said. I don't believe that woman laughed once whilst she was working in the annexe, Marianne told herself. Mr Reynolds knew what he was doing when he sent her back to her old job, though I expect she misses the extra money. Oh well, no one can have everything.

* * *

Marianne was pleased with their night's work and told her girls they had done well. 'Go home and try to get five or six hours' sleep, then do your housework or shopping and have another snooze before your next shift,' she advised them. 'That's what I mean to do, anyway.'

The girls nodded wearily and Marianne saw them out, then glanced round the tidy room. Quickly, she switched off the lights, then went round letting up the blackout blinds, for the new intake of trainees would not want to fumble their way across the darkened room before starting their day's work at eight o'clock. She left the factory and took a deep breath of the soft early morning air. If she went as far as Stopgate, she could get the 19A tram from the terminus and be in Crocus Street in reasonable time.

Resolutely, she began to walk, surprised that there was no one about. She was passing a dark entry between two buildings when she became aware of movement to her left. She turned her head . . . and someone came charging out with such force that they cannoned into her. She began to apologise, knowing it was not her fault but anxious to avoid a confrontation, and felt her hair grabbed, felt someone seize both her arms from behind. She tried to scream but a large hand muffled her mouth.

Chapter Five

Thinking the attackers must be after money, she stood still, knowing her handbag contained little more than her tram fare; then she saw a balled-up fist coming towards her face and only just managed to duck in time. She also bit the hand muffling her mouth, causing her attacker to give a cry of pain. Then she heard a voice hissing: 'Gerr'er on the ground! Go on, Edie, you gerr'er legs.'

Marianne recognised that voice and knew she was in for real trouble. Janet Brown and her pals had been lying in wait, and if she didn't do something quickly, it would be too late. Marianne had not fought anyone for years, but she began to fight now and to her astonishment landed a good few telling blows. She used her feet, her fists, her teeth, but realised she was unlikely to win against so many – there were three or four of them, all strong hefty girls, who must know that this attack would lose them their jobs if she was able to identify them later to management.

Someone grabbed her by the back of her coat and heaved. Buttons popped and she fell backwards, landing on top of the attacker. Then she screamed, so loudly that she even startled herself.

She began to try to struggle to her feet and saw Janet outlined against the now paling sky, leaning over her with something bright in her hand. A knife? A broken bottle? Marianne tried desperately to squirm away, saw the raised hand begin to descend . . . and then there was another, larger shape, and an angry voice, and Janet was pulled roughly away from her. 'What's all this?' a man's voice enquired wrathfully. 'Four to one, eh? I'll learn you, you wicked buggers . . . my God, if they ain't all gals!'

He bent over as the sound of running footsteps began to recede into the distance. 'You all right, gal? No point in chasin' 'em. Here, can you sit up?'

'Yes. I can probably stand if you'll give me your arm,' Marianne said breathlessly. 'I think you just saved my life; that girl had a knife, or a broken bottle, or something.' She shuddered. 'Surely they can't have meant to kill me?'

The man, helping her to her feet, shook his head. 'No, it weren't a knife nor a broken bottle. I think it were a belt buckle. But whatever it were, she meant more harm than good. Know 'em, do you?'

'Yes, I think so,' Marianne said, her voice gaining strength. 'I think they work at the same factory as me. One of them – the one with the belt buckle – was my assistant on a training scheme, but she got taken off it when management realised she was more hindrance than help.'

'Ah, I see; the little bitch had a grudge,' the man said gruffly. 'Not that she were little – dammit, she 'ud make two of you. But you just catch a hold of my arm and we'll get aboard the tram what ought to be waitin' at Stopgate. Then we'll go straight to the Stanley hospital and they can see how bad you're hurt.'

Marianne took his arm but shook her head at the suggestion of hospital as they began to walk slowly towards the tram stop. 'You came along before they'd had a chance to do much,' she assured him. 'I'm bruised and scratched and battered, but I'll be fine once I've cleaned myself up a bit.' She gave a rather watery laugh, then fished out a handkerchief from her coat pocket, blew her nose and wiped her damp cheeks, before coming abruptly to a halt. 'Oh, goodness, I must have dropped my handbag at some stage. It's got all sorts in it, though not much money. Would you mind awfully going back?'

'Course not, though whether it'll still be there I wouldn't like to guarantee,' her rescuer said. 'Gals like that would steal the gold fillings out of their grandmother's teeth. Still an' all, if there were no money in it to speak of . . .'

'I thought they were after money when they first jumped me,' Marianne admitted. 'That was why I didn't fight back at once, but I didn't see them taking my bag . . . ah, there it is, see?'

They retrieved the handbag and set off for the tram once more. Marianne hung back slightly as they approached the vehicle, whispering to her rescuer that she must look an awful sight. The man chuckled. 'Well, there isn't a button on your coat and your hair's come down from its coil, but otherwise you look fine,' he said reassuringly. 'Besides, them dim blue lights in trams make us all look like ghoulies and ghosties, so I shouldn't worry if I were you.'

They took seats upstairs and, for the first time, Marianne was able to have a good look at her rescuer. He was very tall and broad, with clumpy reddish hair which looked as though he had cut it himself with garden shears. He had a craggy face, weather-beaten skin, a broken nose and small hazel eyes, which twinkled responsively when he met her gaze. 'Well, now you know the worst, queen; I ain't no handsome prince, even though I did rescue a beautiful lady,' he said gallantly. 'They don't come much plainer'n me; me mam used to say I were an ugly bugger but me heart were in the right place, an' I reckon that says it all.'

Marianne laughed; she could not help it, and he was right . . . well, he was certainly not a handsome chap but when he grinned at her, revealing white but uneven teeth, she saw that he had his own sort of attraction. 'Men aren't supposed to be beautiful,' she told him. 'Oh, but I don't even know your name! I'm Mrs Sheridan – Marianne Sheridan – and at the moment I'm living with my mother on Crocus Street. And you are . . . ?'

'Bill Brett,' her companion said. 'I lodge in Pansy Street.'

'Oh, you're not far from Crocus Street.'

Bill chuckled. 'That's right. I thought you looked familiar; I've probably seen you making your way to the tram stop on Stanley Road, off to do your marketing. I'm a tram driver, you see, so you'd not notice me.' He added: 'They say all scuffers look alike, an' I reckon all tram drivers do an' all.'

'But what were you doing on Long Lane at that hour?' Marianne enquired. 'And wasn't it lucky for me that you came along and saw what was happening? They meant to do me real harm, you know, because they must have realised I would recognise at least one of them – and in actual fact, thinking back, I believe I know them all.'

'Any feller would have given you a hand as soon as he realised what were up,' Bill said. 'I'd been to visit an old pal of mine. He broke his leg gettin' off the tram one frosty morning and he's still takin' it easy, though normally he's as spry as any sparrow, for all his seventy-five years. I spent the night there because his wife had gone to visit her sister, and was on my way to work.' He turned, courteously, to face her. 'You're in a factory; I guessed that much. What d'you do? Make uniforms? I know you aren't in munitions, 'cos that work turns girls yeller as daffy down dillies, and from what I can make out your skin's a normal colour.'

Marianne laughed. 'We assemble radios for the RAF,' she said.

Her companion turned and gave her the benefit of his wide, almost childlike smile, which looked odd in his wind-burned face. 'That's good war work,' he said. 'The fact is, if I tek you to the Stanley, then they might insist on stitching you and to my way o' thinking you'd be best off wi'out a line of holes in your face.' He looked closely at her. 'Or mebbe they wouldn't stitch it, 'cos now as I looks properly, it ain't that deep. I reckon in a month you won't know it were ever there.'

Marianne, who had leaned forward, endeavouring to see her reflection in the window glass, leaned back again. 'Well, you have relieved my mind,' she admitted. 'My husband is a captain in the Navy and quite the handsomest man I've ever met. I don't know what he'd do if I had to tell him I was scarred for life, because he never wanted me to take a job in a factory in the first place; he wanted me to get away from Liverpool. He says the port is dangerous in wartime. But I want to help with the war effort and I could scarcely do that hidden away in the countryside.'

'Your husband's right; but you don't have to be in the city to help the war effort,' Bill observed. 'There's factories makin' engines, aeroplanes an' so on, tucked away in the country where they hope they won't be noticed. But I reckon Liverpool will be your husband's home port.' He smiled at her as the tram crossed Commercial Road and got to his feet, reaching out to pull the strap which would ring the bell and alert the driver that a passenger wished to alight. 'And you want to be able to look after your feller when he comes into port; right?'

144

'That's right,' Marianne said as the tram clanked to a halt. They both disembarked and Marianne expected him to bid her farewell and climb back aboard, but he made no attempt to do so. 'Oh, Mr Brett, it's most awfully good of you to bring me this far, but you should have got back on the tram,' she said. 'You've done quite enough for me already. There's absolutely no need for you to come any further.'

'I'll see you into your mother's house and make sure she's got something to put on that cheek,' Bill Brett said firmly. 'And then I'm coming with you back to your factory. I can say what happened to you if there's any doubt in the matter, where the attack took place and so on. It's up to your boss if he wants to inform the police, but I think you should do so. Gals as vicious as those four are dangerous.'

'Oh, but I can't tell the police,' Marianne said, dismayed. 'I know it was a wicked thing to do but they might send them to prison and the factory needs all the workers they can get. I'm pretty sure they'll lose their jobs and have to go into some other type of work, and as it happens, Jan – I mean, the ringleader is one of the best assemblers we have.'

As they talked, Marianne had turned the corner of the jigger and opened the gate into Gammy's little back yard. They went into the kitchen, where Gammy was wrapping the lodgers' carry-outs in greaseproof paper and the men, who had clearly breakfasted earlier, were already in their coats and hats, queuing up to take their snap. Everyone turned as Marianne and her companion entered the room. Gammy began to speak, then gave a cry of distress and hurried across to take her daughter's face between her plump little hands. 'Oh, queen, wharrever have you done?' she asked. 'Run into a bramble bush by the looks of you.' She held her daughter away from her, her shrewd little eyes taking in every detail of Marianne's appearance. 'Oh, me darlin', your lovely coat! The mud'll brush off but it'll be a real job to replace the buttons, 'cos they've clearly been ripped off an' took material with 'em; and the only place for them stockin's is the dustbin . . . oh, your poor knees! Wharrever happened? Don't tell me, you've been knocked down by a perishin' tram!'

Marianne meant to laugh gaily and to wait until the lodgers had left before explaining, but the laugh came out more like a little sob and as soon as she began to speak tears flooded her eyes and trickled down her cheeks. Gammy looked at her, then up at her companion, and then told her lodgers, rather sharply, that they had best be getting off to work. 'You've got your grub and it won't do for any of you to turn in late for no reason,' she said. 'You can hear the tale when you come home this evenin'. Off with you now!'

As she spoke, Bill Brett had led Marianne to the basket chair nearest the stove and sat her down, but only when the back door had closed behind the lodgers did he speak. 'It's all right, missus, there's no real harm been done,' he said reassuringly. 'But this young lady's real shook up. I think a strong cup of tea, well sugared, is a good idea, if you've such a thing handy. And while Mrs Sheridan here drinks it, I'll tell you what happened.'

Half an hour later, Gammy was in full possession of the facts and sure that Mr Brett was right: Marianne must go straight back to the factory with him and tell Mr Reynolds what had occurred. Marianne said, feebly, that she could go alone and that poor Mr Brett should get back to his tram depot, but Gammy pooh-poohed the idea. 'Our friend here is what they call an unbiased witness,' she said firmly. 'I aren't sayin' your boss wouldn't believe you 'cos I'm sure he would, but I reckon you've got no option but to inform the police, queen. And once the scuffers get involved, you'll need a reliable witness.' She grinned at Bill Brett, now sipping a large tin mug of tea, though without the sugar. 'It's rare good of you to tek care of my girl and I reckon, when he next gets into port, young Neil, her husband, will want to thank you an' all. So when you've done your duty I'll be much obliged if you'd come back here and let me know how to gerrin touch wi' you when you're not working.'

Bill agreed to do this, since he said he intended not only to accompany Marianne to her factory and to the nearest police station, but to bring her back to Crocus Street so that he and Gammy between them could see she had a proper sleep. 'I reckon, meself, that your boss will put you on a different shift if he's got any sense. Though if he means to sack them wicked girls . . . but no point in frettin' over it till we know what's what.'

The visit to Mr Reynolds went pretty well as Marianne had guessed it would. He agreed that the police must be called in and asked if Marianne would give a statement naming the guilty parties, and setting down in writing what they had done. When he saw the names, however, he tutted and then surprised her. 'Janet Brown has had a warning and will of course get her cards. And her three companions are all girls of very bad repute, whom we shall be glad to lose,' he said. 'But in my opinion, Mrs Sheridan, I shall not be called upon to sack them. They'll simply not turn in for their shift tonight and we shall never see them again. With workers so desperately needed, they'll simply make their way to an inland town, probably, where they can earn good money in a factory, and no questions asked. But wherever they go they'll have to mind their Ps and Qs for a bit, because their names will be on record and if they get into any sort of trouble again it'll be prison, not just a fine or a reprimand.'

'Well, if Janet and co. won't be around, I suppose I might as well stay with my girls and work their shifts with them,' Marianne said, though rather doubtfully.

But Mr Reynolds shook his head. 'No, no; I always thought it would be a waste of your talents as a staff trainer to let you remain with your intake,' he said. 'Besides, Miss Brown now has a double grudge against you. I'm told she has frequently boasted about having found herself a "soft billet" in this factory, and losing it might easily cause her to plot something else against you before she sets off for pastures new. I think you should take the rest of the week off – we'll call it sick leave – and then start to assist Miss Nolan with the new intake in the main building. I know for a fact that she will be very glad of a helping hand.'

All the while this was going on, Bill Brett was sitting quietly with his cap in his hands, his gaze going from face to face. Now he spoke up. 'Excuse me, Mr Reynolds, but I'm sure you're right and Mrs Sheridan will be a deal safer on a day shift, for a few weeks at any rate. I wish I could say I'd meet her out of work when the hooter sounds, but we tram drivers work shifts same as your employees do, so I reckon it 'ud be best if she worked days. Cowards like them girls won't attack in broad daylight.'

Marianne murmured that she would be very careful not to walk to the tram terminus alone in future. 'And I know Betty Nolan pretty well because we were at the Daisy Street school together when we were kids,' she said. 'She lives in Harebell Street so we'll be able to go to and from work together whilst we're on the training scheme. No one is likely to tackle two of us.'

When they left the factory, the oddly assorted couple visited the police station, where Marianne told her story once more. She displayed her badly grazed knees, her bruised shins and the purple finger marks on her wrists, but did not have to say anything about the cut on her face since Gammy and Mr Brett had agreed that it would heal best kept clean and uncovered, and it was therefore the first thing the desk sergeant noticed when they walked across to his counter. He was a pleasant, fatherly man who heard their story with a sad shake of the head. He took down the statements rather laboriously, and when Marianne read hers and signed to say it was a true record she saw that he had included every word she had said, and was satisfied that, if it ever came to court, Janet and her cronies would be in deep trouble.

Marianne had not expected to enjoy either the visit to Mr Reynolds or the trip to the police station, but she was truly surprised to find the repetition of her story upset her so much that she was shaking like a leaf by the time the ordeal was over. Mr Brett seemed to understand exactly how she felt for he took her along to the nearest café, sat her at a corner table and plied her with tea and newly baked scones. 'I've enjoyed your company,' he told Marianne, 'but the place for you right now is your bed, and as soon as you've drunk the tea and eaten the scones I'll take you back to your mam in Crocus

Street. I'll write down my address and how I can be contacted, and then I'll leave you to sleep.'

Presently, as they made their way back to Gammy's, Marianne tried to thank her companion once again for his help and support, but he just shook his head at her, smiling. 'What else would anyone have done?' he enquired. 'Do you think another feller would have walked by on the other side, and I'm the only good Samaritan in these here parts? I'm tellin' you, anyone would have done the same.'

'Maybe you're right, but most people would have thought their duty was done when they put me aboard the tram,' Marianne pointed out. 'I don't think I would have had the courage to visit Mr Reynolds and the police without your support. Honest to God, Mr Brett, I'm so grateful! I wish I could do something for you. If you ever need someone to do you a big bake, you've only got to say the word.'

'There is one thing you could do for me,' her companion said. 'Will it be all right if I pop in from time to time to have a bit of a jangle wi' you and your mam, check up how you're going on? And if you think your husband mightn't like it, he's only got to look at this ugly old phiz of mine to know you're safe as houses.'

Marianne laughed, but felt her cheeks grow hot. Neil would not like it, she knew instinctively, but he would jolly well have to lump it! So she said gaily: 'Very well, Mr Brett, I'll try to remember, and my husband isn't the only one who'll be grateful to you. I've an eight-year-old daughter called Libby; she's been evacuated to North Wales, but when I tell her how you rescued me she'll be as thankful as I am.'

Marianne was not sure why she had mentioned Libby, but Bill beamed at her and said that he liked kids. 'And there ain't no cause for your husband to come searchin' me out to thank me for only doin' what he would ha' done himself if the situations had been reversed. It's just foolishness to spoil his time ashore tryin' to find me so's he can tell me what I already know.'

'It's true that he doesn't get much time ashore, and often spends a good deal of it sleeping,' Marianne said. 'It may be months before he is able to thank you, but you won't mind that, I dare say.'

Bill chuckled. 'No, I shan't mind,' he assured her. 'But mebbe we'll meet at Crocus Street when I pop in to see how you're gettin' on.'

'Maybe,' Marianne said, and realised she had no intention of telling Bill that her own home was just off the Croxteth Road, though she knew she must move back there soon or incur Neil's severe displeasure. Life, she decided, was quite complicated enough without giving Bill her home address and risking his turning up there when she was alone, or, worse, when Neil was back for a few hours.

They reached Gammy's house for the second time that day, and entered the kitchen. As promised, Bill wrote out his address in case they needed to contact him.

Gammy, who was making a big pile of sandwiches, set the plate down on the kitchen table with a clatter. 'Help yerself, la'; tea's a-brewin',' she said.

Bill helped himself to a sandwich. 'My, Mrs Wainright, these are good, but I hope I'm not doin' your lodgers out of their grub. Tell you what, next time I come calling I'll bring you a big bag of cookin' apples so's you can make 'em a pie.'

Gammy assured him that no one would go short on his account and produced some rock buns and a jar of honey. 'Go on, dig in,' she commanded, seeing him hesitate. 'Me rock buns is famous and Mr Parsons has an old cousin what sends him a jar of honey from time to time, 'cos she's got her own bees. Just you eat up.'

Marianne enjoyed her week of sick leave, but even more, as time passed, she found herself enjoying Bill's undemanding friendship. She had been truly grateful for his timely intervention when the girls had attacked her, but she had supposed that his championship of her would end there. Instead, she reflected now as she came out of St John's market and saw him approaching along the pavement, he had become a very good friend indeed. And his friendship was altruistic, never expecting any sort of return for the favours he offered so freely. He mended leaking pipes, put new glass in a window

153

broken by an over-enthusiastic football player, borrowed a ladder so that he might replace slates which had been blown off in a storm, brought them vegetables from his allotment, and was always on hand to tackle any little job which proved to be outside the capabilities of either Marianne or her mother. Gammy and Marianne did their best to repay him by baking an extra pie or cake from time to time, and they had invited him in for a meal on more than one occasion, since any fear that he might get the wrong impression had been banished when he made it plain that he knew Marianne was a happily married woman and that he was a great believer in marriage, having been wed to his Dora for more than a dozen years before she died.

He had not mentioned this sad fact either, until curiosity had got the better of Marianne and she had asked him why he had never married. She had said, half apologetically, that he was clearly ideal husband material and his sandy eyebrows had shot up in astonishment at her words, but then he had smiled ruefully before answering. 'Fancy you thinkin' me a bachelor,' he had said. 'No, I'm a widower, queen. Me and my Dora got wed in twenty-six. We were both young, but we knew our own minds and never regretted it. In fact the only thing we regretted was that we'd no children, 'cos we'd ha' liked a fambly, but it weren't no one's fault, just one of them things. And when she got ill I reckoned it were as well we'd no kids, for how could I have coped? My poor little Dora took up all me time whilst she lived, and later . . . no, I reckon most things in life work out for the best in the end.'

'I'm so sorry. I shouldn't have asked,' Marianne had said humbly, but Bill had only said that he liked talking about Dora because it seemed to bring her back just for a moment, and before Marianne could say anything else he had added that spending time with her and Gammy made him feel like a family man again. 'One of these days I'd like to meet your Neil,' he had finished. 'He must be a grand feller. Well, I reckon you're a good chooser because you've chose me to be your pal,' he stuck out his chest, 'which just shows you're a young woman of descrim . . . descrim . . . oh, dammit, a young woman what's got good taste in fellers.'

It was true that Neil had said he must meet Bill and thank him, but his times ashore were so short that Marianne feared the meeting would never happen – or not until the war ended, at any rate.

But right now, there was Bill, in his driver's uniform, giving her his slow familiar grin. 'Mornin', queen. You're shoppin' early,' he said. 'Are you headin' for home? If so, I'll give you a lift with that bag, some of the way at least.'

Marianne smiled. 'Thanks, Bill, but it's not heavy, and anyway I'm not going home yet; I'm meeting my sister Fiona for lunch and some window-shopping, since I'm on a late shift. Thanks for the offer, though.'

'Ah, righty-ho. I'd best be off then,' Bill said with unimpaired cheerfulness.

One of the nicest things about him, Marianne thought, was his air of unruffled calm. He would have been pleased to carry her bag and have her company as far as Crocus Street, but he was equally pleased that she was going on a shopping spree with her sister. A bus drew up alongside them and Bill gave her a hasty wave and jumped aboard. 'Enjoy your shoppin' trip,' he shouted as he did so. 'See you later, maybe.'

Marianne met Fiona as arranged, and when they had ordered their lunch the talk turned almost immediately to the fate of the girls who had attacked her. Fiona had been very much shocked when she heard of the assault, and had expressed a desire to meet Bill Brett herself so that she, too, might thank him. 'It's all very well, queen,' she said earnestly now, gazing at her sister across the round, marble-topped table, 'but you could have been killed, you know. Girls like that – in a gang – can get carried away. Why, if someone trod on your face acci-dentally, you could still wake up as dead as if they'd done it on purpose. So I hope you and our mam are treating him like a hero.'

Marianne laughed. 'We're doing that all right. But let's forget it; Mr Reynolds and the police said the girls would never dare to show their faces round here again. As for Mr Brett – Gammy and I call him Bill now – he's one of the best.'

At this point, the waitress put their food in front of them with a flourish, and when she had gone Fiona gave an irresistible gurgle of amusement. 'I can't get used to bein' served by nippies what are old enough to be me mam,' she said. 'Of course, it's the war, but it still seems odd.' She dug her fork into a potato and rolled her eyes heavenwards. 'This is much better'n sarnies. Now tell me, is this Bill Brett a handsome feller? How old is he? You said he were a tram driver so I reckon he's no spring chicken or he'd have been called up.'

'I don't actually know how old he is, but he broke his ankle very badly a couple of years ago, so when he tried to join up the medical board rejected him, and aren't I glad! He's got clumpy reddish hair and a broken nose, and I imagine he's around forty, but I've never asked. I won't pretend he's an oil painting, in fact I suppose he's quite plain, but he's so nice that after a bit you forget what he looks like.'

Fiona, who had been eating rapidly, pushed her plate away and began to struggle to her feet. 'Shame he isn't handsome,' she said vaguely. 'His wife can't be all that fussy.' She giggled. 'I dare say she were the one what broke his nose!'

Marianne opened her mouth to tell Fiona that Bill was a widower, but her sister was putting on her coat, announcing as she did so that she would have to run all the way back to Lime Street or risk a black mark for being late. Marianne, donning her own coat, said teasingly that Fiona's conscience must have grown more tender since the two of them had shared a house. 'You never worried about being late before,' she said, as they hurried along Church Street. 'And your excuses were always accepted, even when they were a bit wild, like the time you said you'd rescued a little boy's puppy from under a dray horse's hooves and had to take it back to its owner, who lived quite half a mile from your office. I can't imagine anybody swallowing that one.'

Fiona stared at her, her lips quivering into a tiny smile. 'If you're goin' to tell a little white lie, the first thing you do is convince yourself that it's true. By the time I reached the office, I knew which street the boy lived on, what clothes he was wearing and how his mother looked when she came to the door and I thrust the puppy into her arms.' By now they had reached naval headquarters and she turned to give her sister a valedictory pat on the arm. 'Bear that in mind next time you intend to tell a whopper and everyone, even meself, will think you're speakin' the gospel truth.'

Marianne had half expected to resent her return to the factory but instead she found she was happier than ever. Betty Nolan, a large sweet-tempered girl with no aptitude for issuing commands, insisted that she did not want the job of supervisor and went to Mr Reynolds, imploring him to promote Marianne in her place. 'She don't mind tellin' folk what to do, and I hate it,' she explained. 'Mrs Sheridan could do the job standin' on her head – well, didn't she prove it in the annexe – and the girls work better for her than they ever did for me. So please, Mr Reynolds . . .'

Mr Reynolds was happy to agree to the exchange and Betty, who lived in Harebell Street, just a stone's throw from Crocus, was happy to accompany Marianne to and from work. 'Not that them girls would dare to come within a mile o' the factory,' she assured her friend. 'And if they did they'd have two of us to tackle, which wouldn't please 'em, not by a long chalk.'

So work went well, and Marianne put off returning to Sydenham Avenue, and hoped that Neil would understand.

June approached, and it became clear that France would fall, the Maginot Line being overrun by Germany's Panzer divisions. It was vital to rescue the British Expeditionary Force so that they might regroup in Britain, both to defend their country and to attack the enemy once more. The call went out that any sea-going vessel capable of crossing the Channel should do so, in order to rescue the troops lining the beaches of northern France.

Marianne was still living in Crocus Street and Fiona came to visit, anxious to give them the latest news of what was being called the evacuation of Dunkirk. 'You won't be seeing your Neil for a bit,' she said, 'because the *Sea Spurge* is off to

France, along with every other vessel in the Navy, I should think.'

'Oh, but what about his convoy duty?' Marianne said, dismayed. 'It's dangerous enough chasing fat merchant ships back into the convoy when they've strayed out of it, but going across to territory which is in German hands must be worse. Are you sure, Fee?'

'Course I'm sure,' Fiona said briefly. 'If the *Royal Daffodil* and the *Iris* are going – and they are – you can be sure warships will be needed to fight off the wolf pack.'

The sisters were sitting out in Gammy's yard, enjoying the sunshine, for the weather was brilliant, and had been so for days. Fiona squeezed Marianne's hand and smiled into her eyes. 'Don't *worry*, you goose! Neil will be safe as houses and probably he'll even get some time off when he gets back. Well, he's bound to, because they'll need to sort out the convoys and regroup, and that means time ashore for the crews.'

And sure enough, Fiona was soon proved right. One night in early June Marianne was in bed, though unusually wakeful, when she heard somebody come slowly and falteringly across the yard. Then she heard a tentative tap on the back door. Telling herself that it could not possibly be Neil, for she still had not told him that she was living in Crocus Street, she went quickly down the stairs and pressed her face to the kitchen window. A tall figure, cap in hand and blond hair shining in the

160

moonlight, leaned wearily against the doorjamb. Marianne gave a squeak of joy and rushed across to unlock the back door, and Neil practically fell into her arms, saying groggily: 'Oh, God, I'm so tired, my darling! It's been hell, but I'm home safe now . . . I didn't mean to wake you. I'll sleep on the settee . . . God, I could sleep for a week . . . a month . . .'

'Sit down, my love, and I'll put the kettle on,' Marianne said, keeping her voice low with an effort. 'How thin you are, Neil . . . just let me pull down the blackout blinds and then I can light the gas, stoke up the fire and get you a hot drink.'

Neil leaned back in his chair as Marianne bustled around, pulling down the blinds and stirring up the fire. She filled the kettle and set it on the flame, then went and got the biscuit barrel and extracted some ginger snaps, of which she knew he was extremely fond. She made the tea, poured two cups, and took the chair opposite her husband's.

She waited until he had drunk the tea and eaten several biscuits, then spoke gently. 'Fiona told me you'd gone to France to help rescue the soldiers. I've been praying for you – and the others, of course – because I guessed it was most dreadfully dangerous. There have been newspaper stories about the little boats and the naval ships which were trying to defend them, and of course I've talked to neighbours who've got back safely. I asked about the *Sea Spurge* and Jim Doughty – d'you remember him, Neil? He lives in Snowdrop

161

Street – could only tell me that he'd been on board one of the big ships – I think it was the *Scotia* – when it was bombed, and sank within two minutes. He was one of the lucky ones actually on deck when it happened. One of the little boats picked him out of the water and took him to a destroyer, and though they were constantly attacked he got back all right. He said he thought he'd seen the *Sea Spurge* but couldn't be certain. Oh, Neil, it must have been hell!'

'It was,' Neil said. 'And of course we didn't get them all off, not by a long chalk. And fellers were telling us that they'd left practically all their equipment behind because it's always more important to save men than machines. But it's going to make things pretty hard. I reckon everyone – even you, my sweet – will be asked to double the output of everything they're making towards the war effort. The army will need munitions and the air force will want many more planes than we've got at present. As for the Navy . . . we're short of pretty well everything, the same as the others, because it wasn't just the Royal Navy's ships that got bombed but merchantmen too, the ones who have been bringing us supplies from America. *Mona's Isle* – that's the Isle of Man steamer – went down with all hands; she hit a mine. But we've just got to accept our losses and work like mad to build up again.' He gave a rueful smile and leaned across to take Marianne's hand. 'My poor darling, first I try to make you quit your job and join Libby in

162

the country, and now I'm telling you to stay in Liverpool and work twice as hard because I've realised that even being bombed won't be as bad as life under the Nazi jackboot.'

Marianne gave a deep sigh of relief; now was the moment to tell Neil that though she was still training she would be going back on shift work quite soon. This time they were talking about twelve-hour shifts, and living at Gammy's was the only way she would be able to cope. So she got to her feet and went and sat on Neil's lap, putting her arms round his neck and rubbing her face against his, though the stubble made this a rather rough experience. 'Darling Neil,' she said, and began to tell him how much easier her life would be if she stayed in Crocus Street.

Neil heard her out, making the appropriate comments, and agreeing wholeheartedly that she must continue to live at Gammy's. He said that he would speak to the landlord of the house in Sydenham Avenue and see if he could find them a tenant willing to take it on as a furnished let.

'But what will happen when things settle down and you get a proper leave?' Marianne said plaintively. 'I didn't tell you, but we had a window broken and some bits and pieces stolen a few weeks ago. It was kids, of course, but folk taking on a furnished let won't look after our nice things the way we would ourselves, and you said if the bombing started and Crocus Street was hit, we should all move back to our place, even the lodgers.'

'You're right, I did. I'll discuss it with the land-lord – I'll go and see him tomorrow – and let you know what we decide,' Neil said. 'But right now I need to sleep. Get me a couple of blankets, pet, and I'll doss down on the sofa in the front room. What time is it? Good God, it feels really late, but it's only midnight. I should get a good seven hours' kip before your mum comes downstairs and starts making breakfast, and she won't need to come into the parlour anyway, so I can have a bit of a lie-in.'

Marianne fetched blankets and a pillow from the cupboard, and saw her husband comfortably bedded down before she suddenly remembered something. 'Neil, how did you know I was here?' she asked curiously. 'I know I never told you in my letters that I'm living in Crocus Street, because I didn't want to worry or upset you. The trams would still have been running when you docked, or you could have walked up to the hospital and picked up a taxi to take you to Sydenham Avenue. What made you come here?'

There was an appreciable pause before Neil replied. 'D'you know, I begin to suspect I must be psychic,' he said slowly. 'I simply felt that coming to Crocus Street was what I ought to do. Of course, it's a good deal nearer than Sydenham Avenue, but that wasn't the reason. It was just a strong feeling that I'd find you here.'

Marianne beamed at him. 'That's the nicest thing you've ever said to me. And I must share your psychic feelings, since I usually fall asleep the moment my head touches the pillow, but tonight I was wide awake and alert when I heard you crossing the yard. Good night, best of husbands! See you in the morning.'

Slipping back into bed, being careful not to touch her mother's warm flesh with her own ice-cold feet, Marianne jumped when a voice spoke close to her ear. 'Where's you been, chuck? Had to pay a visit, did you? I disremember when you left me bed, but it were a while back, I'm thinkin'.'

'Oh, Mam, you made me jump a mile! I'm so sorry to have disturbed you,' Marianne said remorsefully. 'But Neil's home! I made him a cup of tea, got out the biscuits, and then sat and talked to him for a while. He looks worn to a bone, but he thinks he'll be ashore for several days whilst they sort out the convoy situation.'

'Oh aye? And what made him come to Crocus Street? I know you ain't told him you're livin' wi' me, because you said he'd worry.'

Marianne began to say that he had followed an instinctive feeling that he would find her with her mother, then changed her mind. Instead, she said: 'It's a long way to Sydenham Avenue; it was easier to come here first. Anyway, I took the opportunity to point out that it was a long way for me as well and explained that I found it very much easier to live here, especially when I'm on shifts.'

'Oh I see; that's good,' Gammy said drowsily. 'Lucky for him you're a light sleeper – lucky for him you really *are* livin' here, because I reckon he'd

165

have had to knock the back door down before me or the lodgers would have wondered what was up.' She chuckled sleepily. 'I bet the captain never thought of that! Or perhaps he thought Fiona was still here, though that wouldn't have done him much good since she sleeps like a perishin' log and wouldn't leave her warm bed just because someone was knockin' . . . knockin' . . . knockin' at the . . .'

Marianne waited for her mother to finish the sentence, then smiled as Gammy began to snore instead, and settled herself more comfortably. She had a great deal to think about and resigned herself to lying awake for hours, but in fact she slept almost at once and did not wake until the alarm bell shrilled.

Chapter Six

Libby woke to find sunshine streaming in through her open window, along with the scent that she considered the most beautiful in the world, the smell of sun-baked grass. She jumped out of bed and looked out. The sky was pale blue and clear and she gave a little skip and hugged herself with glee, for the estate was haymaking and needed every helper within miles. Poor Miss Williams did not have sufficient land to grow hay, but in this at least the estate was generous. Other farmers were paid for their help by reciprocal work on their own acres, but Tregarth was paid in hay, which Dewi stacked and thatched and used for winter feed.

Libby did not have a watch and had not bothered to wind her alarm the previous evening, since to her delight and astonishment school always closed when farmers needed their children on the land. When she had been gloating over this fact to Rhys and Matthew, Rhys had laughed and said she would soon change her tune when winter came. 'You'll find yourself picking sprouts after the first frost, when the plants is up to your waist and every perishin' sprout you pick deluges you with icy water,' he had told her. 'And pickin' main crop spuds; that's filthy work, that is, 'cos the plough turns up the taters and we have to dig down with our fingers, pick out every single one, and put 'em into the bucket, which gets heavier and heavier the more you harvest. Then there's opening up the clamps – that's mucky work too, and really cold. You'll have chilblains all over and after a day or so you'll begin to think kindly of a nice warm classroom, a decent school dinner and finishin' off at half past three – sometimes earlier – so you can get home in the light.'

Libby must have looked a trifle dismayed, for Matthew had given her a cuff. 'He's havin' you on, girl,' he told her. 'It's true that we do help to pick the spuds and sprouts, and it can be cold, dirty work, but they never ask us to open up the clamps, and now that the estate has half a dozen land girls I doubt they'll need extra hands for spuds and sprouts either. No, we'll miss school in winter all right, but it won't be in order to work on the land, it'll be the weather. Miss Williams says that up this end of the valley we can be snowed in for weeks – well, last January and February I didn't get into the village once. So you can look forward to that.'

But right now, Libby was not worrying about winter, for haymaking did not seem like work at all. Miss Williams had acquired some blue denim dungarees for her, since even the best and most delectable of hay can sometimes contain thistles or nettles, and everyone wore trousers to protect their legs from close contact with such painful plants. Libby dressed quickly, deciding to wash when she returned from her day's labour, though she did brush her teeth before clattering down the stairs.

Matthew had thought at first that he could be of little assistance in the hay field, but Dewi had tutted and said that he had a job all lined up, and as soon as they reached the meadow he had lifted Matthew out of his wheelchair, sat him on the broad back of the horse harnessed to the cart, and told him to guide Duke to the rick yard when the cart was full.

Matthew had pretended to sigh, but Libby had read his gratified expression and knew that he had been delighted to be useful, for it was galling for him to be always a bystander and never a part of the action. And he soon proved his worth, taking the job seriously and getting the mighty horse to move off only when the cart was piled so high that to add any more hay would be downright dangerous.

Rhys and Libby, of course, did yeoman work in the meadow, raking the hay into piles, though they did not attempt the task of loading the carts, since this called for considerable strength and quite a lot of skill. And of course all of them, including the land girls, did an equally sterling job when Mrs Hodges and one or two of her helpers came down to the field with huge baskets of food and cold tea for the workers.

Libby shot into the kitchen to find Matthew already there, spooning porridge, and Miss Williams cutting bread, buttering it, and smearing home-made jam on every slice before clapping them together to form sandwiches. With the speed born of much practice, she wrapped them in greaseproof paper and pressed them into the empty cake tin before her. 'Keep the wasps off,' she remarked, pushing down the lid. She turned to Libby. 'Nip into the apple loft and fetch down half a dozen eaters, there's a good girl; save my legs. Then you can come back and have your porridge.' She chuckled. 'I'll dish it up so it can be cooling while you're away, like the porridge in *Goldilocks and the Three Bears.*'

'Right you are, Auntie,' Libby said. Two months ago Miss Williams had told the children, with a mixture of shyness and brusqueness, to call her Auntie instead of Miss Williams, 'since it's shorter and easier to say,' she had added gruffly. But Libby sometimes forgot, especially when Dewi, or another farm worker, referred to her as Miss Williams.

The apple loft was above the stable and Libby ran up the rickety stair, sniffing appreciatively, for the apples were carefully laid out on hay and old newspapers, and the air smelt sweet. Her dungarees had two large pockets, so she selected six of the biggest, firmest apples, put three in each pocket and then checked the others, finding two which were going rotten and putting them aside to take down to the pig bucket. Miss Williams – Auntie – had impressed upon them the importance of checking the apples every time they visited the loft. 'Because, though I'm very careful, a good apple only has to touch a bad one to become infected.'

Matthew had grinned at Miss Williams. 'One bad apple spoils the whole barrel,' he had said. 'Teachers are very fond of sayings like that, but you mean it literally, don't you, Auntie?'

Auntie had nodded approvingly. 'That's it, Matthew,' she said. 'So you'll remember, when you go up to the apple loft, to pick out any bad fruit and feed it to the pigs.'

They had been in the kitchen at the time, the children watching Auntie peeling cookers, which she would stew and serve with custard. Apple pie would have been lovely, but their hostess was no hand with pastry. Libby had opened her mouth to remind Auntie that Matthew could not climb the stair up to the apple loft, then had closed it again. Their hostess knew perfectly well that Matthew could not reach the loft, but she always tried to treat him as she treated everyone, and Libby knew he appreciated it, so had said nothing more.

Now, having checked all the apples, she ran lightly down the stair. The pigs enjoyed the rotten fruit, greeting it with grunts of delight, and Libby returned to the kitchen feeling that she had done her duty both by Auntie and the livestock. She fished the good apples out of her pockets, laid them on the table, and then sat herself down to attack her porridge. 'There were a couple of bad 'uns, which I put into the trough,' she announced as Auntie picked up the apples and pushed them into the cake tin. 'They snuffled them up in no time. Are you ready to go, Matthew? Only Dewi said they'd start early, being as this is the last of the estate meadows to be cut.'

Matthew, with a slice of somewhat blackened toast in one fist, said he could go as soon as she herself had finished her porridge, and presently they set out, with Libby unobtrusively pushing the wheelchair whenever they came to difficult ground. Matthew liked to propel himself, but he was sensible, accepting help with his usual placidity; and since he was carrying their lunch in the cake tin he needed to be able to grab it when the ground was bumpy. All the haymakers brought a snack for lunchtime, the men often making do with a hefty slice of bread and a raw onion, as well as the inevitable bottle of cold tea, but Auntie said this was not enough for growing children and always packed them sufficient for a meal.

Working on the estate fields meant climbing out of the valley to get there, so Libby, who had been chattering gaily to Matthew on a variety of subjects, fell back in order to push the wheelchair, and stopped talking since she needed all her breath for the climb. She guessed that Rhys would be at the field before them. His father's meadows were the next to be cut, so he and his parents would want the estate work completed as quickly as possible. Libby reflected that she could have done with Rhys's help now, since the wheelchair – and Matthew – seemed to get heavier as she neared the top of the incline. As if on cue, someone panted up behind her and a pair of strong brown hands seized the wheelchair, pushing her quite roughly to one side. 'Shove over, and let the dog see the rabbit,' Rhys said breathlessly. 'No work for a girl it is, pushin' this lot uphill.'

'Oh, thanks ever so much, Rhys,' Libby said gratefully, relinquishing her place and walking beside Matthew once more. 'We can manage pretty well as a rule, me and Matt, but he's got our dinners in that tin, and a bottle of milk wedged down beside him, so he can't push his wheels like he usually does. Wish we had an engine on this wheelchair, don't you, Matthew?'

Matthew grinned but shook his head. 'An engine? No bloody fear! If I had an engine I should have to go to school in all weathers. Probably Auntie would expect me to let you two sit on my lap so that the three of us could get into the village even if the snow was three foot deep.'

Rhys and Libby laughed, Rhys a trifle breathlessly. Then they were at the top of the hill and could see the hay meadow spread out before them, with Duke and Duchess, the two great shire horses, just approaching along the lane which led from the estate stable yard. 'Goody, we're not late,' Matthew said exultantly. 'Run ahead, you two. All

I need to do now is apply brakes to the wheels if I start catching you up. Be a sport though, Rhys, and take our dinner tin, because if it slides off my lap when I'm alone I shan't be able to pick it up.'

Libby would have offered to stay with him but knew he would tell her not to be daft, so she and Rhys set off at a gallop over the smooth grass and presently arrived at the meadow, where they stood chatting whilst they waited for the horses and carts, laden with workers, pitchforks and rakes, to arrive so that everyone could start work. 'That Matthew, he's a real card,' Rhys said as they watched Matthew coming sedately down the slope. 'He told me he was brought up by his nain after his mam and da died. He said they died of that disease, something or other paralysis, the same thing what crippled him. Has she visited him yet? His nain, I mean . . . that means granny in case you didn't know.'

'Know, when every kid in the village talks about their nain and taid, even to us ignorant English?' Libby said derisively. 'And I'd like to know how his nain could possibly visit him, since she's dead. Didn't he tell you' she lowered her voice, 'didn't he tell you that he was put in a children's home last summer, because with his nain gone there was no one to look after him? He absolutely hated it and as soon as war broke out, he insisted on being evacuated.' She looked rather apprehensively into Rhys's strong brown face. 'He's never said he didn't want anyone to know and I'm sure he

174

wouldn't mind my telling you, only just in case, Rhys, don't tell anyone else, and don't let on to Matthew that I told you.'

'Not a word will I say; I'm no clapgi,' Rhys assured her. 'Poor old Matthew though, hate it he would. Different it is for kids brought up in them homes since they was babbies, because they've known nothing else, but I reckon Matthew's folk were quite classy.'

'You're right there; his father was a doctor – what they call a consultant really – and his mother a hospital sister. I reckon he gets his brains from them 'cos he's awfully clever, isn't he? I mean, when you think of the schooling he's missed, yet he still comes top in practically every subject when his class has examinations.'

Rhys gave a snort of amusement. 'Not sayin' much that isn't, when you think how thick the boys and girls in our class are,' he said. 'But Matthew would come top even at the grammar school, if only he could get there. A pity it is that he can't, because it means he'll have to leave school at fourteen, same as the rest of us. Now if he were to live with someone in the village . . .'

'They wouldn't have him; the billeting lady tried all over but the only person who said she'd take him on was Auntie – Miss Williams to you – and even if someone in the village wanted him now, he wouldn't go. He studies at home, you know, and Auntie sends away to some old cousin or rela-tive of hers, and the relative sends Auntie text books. He was a teacher once, this chap, and he's offered to send Matthew all sorts of questions – maths, history, geography, that sort of thing – and to send Auntie the answers in a different envelope.' She giggled just as Matthew, looking rather pink, came to a halt beside them. She turned to him. 'Matthew, tell Rhys what Auntie said when that old schoolteacher offered to send her answers to the questions he was going to give you.'

Matthew laughed as well, saying: 'She said, "What a bloody cheek! I'll have Cousin Hubert know that I'm not yet in my dotage and can answer any question a mere schoolteacher is likely to set his pupils."' This was said in a very fair imitation of Miss Williams's voice and set Rhys to laughing.

'Very good, and likely true as well,' Rhys said, grinning. 'But are you sure you've got it right, boyo? Never have I heard Miss Williams use slang, let alone swear words. She must have been annoyed.'

'She was,' Matthew said simply. 'She went to Bangor university, you know, and got a first class honours degree, which means she's entitled to put BA after her name.'

'Well I never,' Rhys said, clearly much impressed. 'Knew she was clever, of course, common knowledge that, but I didn't know she went to university. I remember my mam telling me once that Miss Williams was one of them suffer-somethings, but she never mentioned university.'

'D'you mean suffragette?' Libby said incredulously. What a lot she was learning! 'They were demanding votes for women, weren't they? Wasn't their leader a woman called Mrs Pancake?'

The boys guffawed. 'It was Mrs Pankhurst, you owl,' Matthew said. 'Ah, here come the workers!'

As soon as the carts had been unloaded, work began. The grass was cut and turned, and laid under the hot sun until it was dry and could be taken to the stack yard, where the men skilled in such work – Dewi was one of them – would make it into ricks. The meadow was the largest they had worked in so far and when the time came to break for the midday meal, everyone was hot, tired and grateful for a rest. There were a number of large oak trees in the hedgerow which cast a pleasant shade, and the workers, including Auntie herself, congregated there, knowing that they had completed more than half of the task before them and pleased with the results of their toil, for the grass was well grown and sweet-smelling.

As befitted her years, Auntie had found herself a fallen log to perch upon, and she sat there like a queen, discussing farming matters with the men and women around her. Everyone else swigged straight from their bottles, but she had brought a Thermos and sipped her tea from the cap, much to the amusement of the three children. They teased her, Matthew actually remarking that she was far too ladylike to drink cold tea straight from a bottle. Auntie vigorously denied the charge but said that cold tea in a Thermos stayed cold and did not go tepid and Matthew, drinking lukewarm milk, had to admit that this was desirable. He was sitting in his wheelchair whilst the others sprawled on the grass, but had just announced he would join them as soon as he had finished eating when there was a stir and a murmur from the workers and Linda, the land girl nearest them, poked Libby in the ribs. 'The big cheese has come to make sure we're not slackin',' she hissed. 'Ever met Mr Ap Nefydd? He's the owner of the estate.' She giggled. 'If you'd asked Dewi or Ieuan, or any of the older workers, they'd have said: "the new owner", 'cos he only inherited when the old feller died ten years ago.'

'Which one is he . . .' Libby began, then interrupted herself. 'Don't tell me, don't tell me, he's the tall grey-haired one wearing the open-necked white shirt and breeches. Who's the other one, though?'

'Oh, him,' Linda said, and there was a world of dismissal in her tone. 'That's Ifor Jones, him that they call Cod's Eye, though God knows why.'

'I've no doubt God do know. Most of us is in on the secret too,' Rhys said, leaning forward and lowering his voice. 'They say someone chucked a snowball at his dad when he were just a kid. There were a stone in it, see, but anyway it were packed hard. It hit him in the eye, an' ever after, that eye swivelled around any old which way, so they called him Cod's Eye, see?'

'But that was his father, not him,' Libby pointed out. 'This feller's eyes look all right.'

Rhys chuckled. 'In Wales, nicknames go from

father to son until no one can remember how they started,' he told her. 'And because so many of us share the same surnames, it helps to identify which Jones or Williams you're talking about.'

Libby opened her mouth to ask Rhys what his own nickname was, but at that moment Mr Ap Nefydd approached them. 'Afternoon, Ellie,' he said in a deep and rather pleasant voice. 'Surely you haven't been haymaking? It's time you took things a bit easier, my girl.'

Libby and Matthew exchanged startled glances. Ellie? Miss Williams was always addressed with great respect by both villagers and farm workers, and this man, whose name they had never heard so much as mentioned before today, must be as strange to her as he was to them.

Auntie, however, bristled. 'Good afternoon, Francis,' she said coolly. 'May I remind you that I am not yet in my dotage and am perfectly capable of working in the hayfields. I see *you* haven't used a pitchfork today, however, and if you must use my given name, may I remind you that it's Eluned.'

'You may indeed,' Mr Ap Nefydd said courteously, sitting down on the log beside her. 'And may I remind you, my dear cousin, that my name may be Francis, but I prefer to be known as Frank.'

'I'll bear it in mind, though I dare say it would be more correct if I were to call you Mr Ap Nefydd and you were to call me Miss Williams,' Auntie said. 'However, I'm sure you did not come over to discuss what we should call one another.' She finished the tea in her cup, then picked up the greaseproof paper in which one sandwich still reposed and held it out. 'Would you care for a sandwich, Frank?'

Mr Ap Nefydd stared curiously at the proffered sandwich, then shook his head. 'I'm sure it's absolutely delicious – did you make the bread yourself, my dear? but I mustn't deprive you,' he said. 'Cod's Eye – or perhaps he would prefer to be known as Ifor Jones – and I lunched half an hour ago. We had a salad, a good many slices of rare roast beef and some new potatoes, served with butter and parsley. If I had known you meant to come and give a hand to bring in my hay, I would have asked you to share our repast. However, cousin – not that we are exactly close relatives, of course – I could still invite you to dine with us tonight.'

'How kind!' Auntie said. Libby heard the sarcasm in her voice and cast a wary glance at Mr Ap Nefydd, fearing that he might be annoyed to have his invitation treated in so cavalier a fashion. Auntie, however, must have regretted her tone for she added politely: 'However, as you know, I have a great many tasks to perform every evening, quite apart from the fact that I now have two young people to feed. But how remiss of me! I've not introduced you. Libby and Matthew, this is Mr Francis Ap Nefydd, who owns the estate.' She turned to the man seated beside her. 'Frank, meet Libby Sheridan and Matthew Hawke.'

Mr Ap Nefydd leaned forward and held out a large and very clean hand, first to Libby and then to Matthew. 'The invitation extends to your house guests, naturally, Eluned,' he said. 'Though the castle can hold no interest for you, these young people might like to explore its rather faded splendours. Another evening perhaps?'

Libby and Matthew exchanged longing glances but knew better than to say a word. The invitation had plainly been aimed at Auntie; she must answer for all of them, and they knew already what that answer would be. However, Miss Williams clearly did not mean to be outdone in the politeness stakes. 'Thank you, Frank; perhaps some other time, when we are not all so extremely busy,' she said. 'But why don't you come down to Tregarth? I can't offer you an exquisitely cooked meal since I don't have a cook – and don't think I failed to notice that dig about the bread in my sandwich because I'd be the first to admit that a loaf made by me would be as useful in a siege as a cannonball, and just as hard. But if you, my dear cousin, would deign to try your hand at bread making, I dare say one bite would break every tooth in your head.'

'You're probably right, but then I've never pretended to be a practical man,' Mr Ap Nefydd said ruefully. He got leisurely to his feet. 'Well, if you're sure you won't dine with us tonight, I'd better take myself off so that you can continue with your work.' He turned away with a casual lift of his hand, then turned back. 'One of these days I'll take you up on your invitation to visit Tregarth. Last time I called, if you remember, no one answered my knock. Next time, I shall be sure to see that you are at home before I so much as set foot in your yard.'

Libby saw their kindly hostess tighten her lips, but also saw a pink flush creep up her neck. She was about to ask Auntie why she had turned down Mr Ap Nefydd's invitation when everyone began to return to their work. Dewi came up and lifted Matthew out of his wheelchair as though he weighed no more than a small child, and sat him astride Duke. Then he began to hand out tasks to everyone else, and presently Libby found herself raking up the hay into piles and chatting to the land girls around her.

As soon as she was able, however, she attached herself to Rhys, and asked him if he knew why Auntie had been so unfriendly to Mr Ap Nefydd. Rhys shrugged. 'I don't really know,' he said guardedly. 'There's all sorts of stories but I never took much notice meself. Still, when you think about it, it's no wonder she's a bit caggy like with him. After all, the castle was her home until her da died. Then old Mr Pryce came and didn't do the estate no good. My mam says he were all take an' no give, which was hard for Miss Williams, having to see what her father built up brought low, if you get me. Then this 'un took over, knowin' nothin' about the land, only he went an' employed Cod's

Eye as his estate manager, so things got a bit better, but everyone says if Miss Williams had had her rights, it would never have sunk so low.'

'Oh, I *see*,' Libby said, though in fact she was not sure that she really did. 'But Rhys, it's not Mr Ap Nefydd's fault that he inherited the estate, is it? And he can't help not knowing very much about the land. Or are you trying to say Cod's Eye isn't a good estate manager, and Mr Ap Nefydd chose the wrong man?'

Rhys turned and stared at her, his brow wrinkling. 'Cod's Eye not a good estate manager?' he said incredulously. 'Why, he's the best! The problem is, there's not much money because old Pryce milked the estate, like I told you. But they're doing their best, the two of 'em.'

'I think I see,' Libby said slowly. 'But I still don't understand why Auntie – Miss Williams – was so rude to Mr Ap Nefydd. Shouldn't she be glad that he's trying to make the estate work properly? It's what she does at Tregarth, after all.'

Rhys leaned on his rake for a moment, pushing his fingers through his hair until it stood up like a cockerel's comb. 'Hit the nail on the head, you have,' he said triumphantly. 'Miss Williams isn't afraid to get her hands dirty. She milks the cows, takes care of the pigs, cleans out the hens . . . well, she does everything a farmer should do, whereas Mr Ap Nefydd simply gives orders, or lets Cod's Eye do it, and never puts a hand to the plough, as they say.'

'Oh I *see*,' Libby said again, and this time she really did understand for she knew how Auntie had to plot and scheme in order to pay Dewi's wages when she needed his help, whereas, though Rhys said that money was short at the castle, there was still sufficient to pay not only an estate manager, but a great many other workers, including the half-dozen land girls. 'But Rhys, that doesn't explain why Auntie pretended to be out when Mr Ap Nefydd called at Tregarth. Or was she really out? She might have been visiting in the village, or taking the cows back to pasture, I suppose.'

Rhys snorted. 'I dunno. You may be right, but most folk think she guessed it were him so never came to the door,' he said. 'He tried three times, so he says. Still, Tregarth is all Miss Williams has got left, an' if she don't want him visiting, the simplest way to keep him out is not to answer the door.'

'But that's really rude, and unkind as well, and I don't believe Auntie is either of those things,' Libby said indignantly. Then she laughed. 'It reminds me of that poem we learned the other week. *"Is there anybody there?" said the traveller, knocking on the moonlit door* . . . Only of course it wasn't night-time when Mr Ap Nefydd came knocking, was it? And I think it was in the poem. But this afternoon Auntie invited him to come to Tregarth; everyone heard her. And I'm telling you, Rhys, that if Mr Ap Nefydd comes calling when

Matthew and I are about, we'll let him in and make him welcome.'

Rhys grinned at her. 'You just want to go up to the castle and have a good poke around the ruins,' he said. 'All girls is curious as cats; me mam says so, an' she should know.' He surveyed the pile of hay. 'We'd better get a move on or we'll miss the cart, 'cos the second wagon is almost full.'

'Well, we couldn't ask for better weather than we've had these past few days,' Auntie observed that evening, tucking into her plate of stew. 'And I'm not only thinking of the haymaking, but of the evacuation of our troops from the Continent. All the reports say the sea has been as calm as a millpond, which must have helped the hundreds of little boats which went over to bring them home.' She turned to Libby. 'I've no doubt your father's ship will have sailed across the Channel and saved a great many of our brave soldiers.'

'Well, at least we've got men to fight off the invasion which they keep saying is going to come,' Matthew observed. 'I know we want fine weather for the hay, Auntie, but now the troops are back, the fine weather will aid the enemy, won't it? We could do with a good storm, like the one which wrecked the Spanish armada when Philip of Spain decided to add England to his conquests.'

'Yes, you're right, but I don't think for one moment that the enemy are in any state to invade, because they will have used all their strength to try to prevent the men from returning,' Auntie said hopefully. She chuckled. 'Orders have gone out that all direction signs are to be painted over so that if the enemy do land, they won't know where the devil they are.'

'Air supremacy's the thing,' Matthew said wisely. He was an avid reader of any newspaper which came his way, and listened with far more attention to bulletins on the wireless than Libby did. 'I'm really sad about France because they weren't just our allies, they were our friends, and it's always hard when a friend turns against you.'

There was a moment's awkward silence whilst Auntie used a piece of bread to wipe round the last smears of stew on her plate, gaze fixed on the task in hand. Then she looked across at Matthew, meeting his eyes squarely. 'I know what you mean when you say it's hard to have a friend turn against you,' she said quietly, 'and I expect you're thinking that I wasn't very nice to Mr Ap Nefydd earlier today. I don't know if you guessed that we were once close friends – or someone may have told you that that was the case – but things went wrong between us years ago, and I'm afraid I find it diffi-cult to forget the past. It's rather a long story and, like everything else in my life, a trifle complicated. Are you sure you want to hear it?'

Matthew hesitated, then glanced at Libby, who gave the tiniest little nod of her head. Matthew turned to Auntie: 'If you don't mind telling, I'm sure Libby and I would be most interested,' he said politely. 'We'll even make the tea so you don't have to get up.'

Auntie laughed but got somewhat stiffly to her feet. 'I'll make the tea, since I prefer to handle a boiling kettle myself,' she said firmly. 'But you two can wash up and clear away. Libby, there's a seed cake in the blue tin on the pantry shelf. Because of the haymaking, I've not made a pudding, so that will have to do instead.'

Libby glanced quickly at Matthew and saw him smothering a grin, for neither child liked seed cake. They would have refused their portions except that they did not want to take Auntie's mind off her story. Libby handed the tin over and watched as Auntie poured three cups of tea and cut three generous slices of cake. Then they all sat down again and Auntie took a deep breath and began her story.

'As you know, I was an only child, but a very happy one. I had loving parents, a wonderfully romantic home – or so I thought – and friends all around me. Even then, I was deeply interested in the home farm . . . in fact in agriculture generally. In those days we had a huge flock of sheep, a great many dairy cattle, and pigs and poultry.

'Then, when I was ten years old, my father heard of the death of a distant cousin and his wife. He had not known his cousin well, but when he realised their son was now an orphan, he and my mother decided to offer the boy a home. As you will have guessed, the boy who came to live at the castle was Frank Ap Nefydd. He was a couple of years older than myself and at first he was very unhappy, for he had never lived in the country. Despite the name, neither of his parents nor the boy spoke Welsh, for they had been born and bred in Liverpool, where Mr Ap Nefydd was a partner in a firm of solicitors. They had lived in a large house near the centre of the city and Frank had attended a smart school. In fact, because he was a clever boy and had no interest in the land, my parents sent him to boarding school, where he was very happy and did extraordinarily well. It was because of his enthusiasm that I agreed to go to boarding school too, and eventually we both got university places and gained our degrees.

'I was very happy, both at school and at university, but I always intended to return to the castle and help my father to run the estate. Frank came home in his vacations, as I did, and announced that he meant to practise as a solicitor, joining his father's old firm in Liverpool.'

At this point Auntie, who had been dunking her seed cake in her cup of tea, finished the last squishy portion and spoke rather thickly through it. 'Frank and I had always been good friends and I must suppose that, no longer knowing anyone in Liverpool, he had formed the idea of taking someone with him: me, of course.' She looked sharply at Libby, then wagged an admonitory finger. 'No, Libby my dear, I know it sounds excessively romantic, but it was not so in the least.

I thought of Frank as a brother and he thought of me as a sister, and I had not the slightest intention of pretending otherwise. If Frank had been sensible and admitted that he simply wanted a companion in his new venture, we might have remained friends, but he told my father he was in love and wanted to marry me, and to my absolute horror, my father believed him. First he tried to persuade me, and then he tried threats, reminding me of the entail and explaining that, unless I married, I would find myself penniless after his death.'

'And you never did marry, though I expect lots of people wanted to marry you,' Matthew said, exhibiting rare tact, Libby thought, for she simply could not imagine Auntie as ever having been young, let alone beautiful. 'Did your father realise that Mr Ap Nefydd would inherit the castle and the estate one day?'

Auntie gave a short bark of laughter. 'No, he didn't. In fact no one, including Frank himself, had the slightest idea that it would happen. After my father died, Nathaniel Pryce, another distant cousin of some sort, inherited. I had been teaching, but came home to be with my mother, who was in no state to be left alone. We moved into Tregarth, which had been in my mother's family for a great many years, though the estate had bought most of the land.'

'Didn't Mr Pryce offer to let you stay at the castle?' Libby asked as Auntie paused for breath.

'Oh, I know all about the entail, Matthew explained it to me, but surely, knowing it had been your home all your life, and that your mother had lived there ever since she married your father, Mr Pryce must have offered to let you stay?'

Auntie smiled rather grimly, but shook her head. 'I don't suppose it even crossed his mind because, relative or not, I don't mind telling you that he was really a nasty old man. The estate workers used to say that he was a taker not a giver, which means that he milked the estate for every penny he could get out of it, and never put anything back in. So you see, Mother and I were better off at Tregarth.'

Matthew had been frowning, clearly puzzled by something, and now he cut in. 'But was Mr Pryce Frank's father, since Frank inherited next? And if so, why are the surnames different?' He took a deep breath then puffed out his cheeks and expelled the air in a long whistle. 'Phew! You said it was complicated, Auntie, and you were right!'

Auntie laughed. 'If you think this is complicated, wait till I get a bit further on,' she said. 'No, Mr Pryce had never met Frank, so far as I know.'

'Gosh!' and 'Golly!' the two children said in unison.

'In fact, the death of Mr Pryce put the lawyers in a quandary, for there seemed to be no obvious male relative to inherit. But they worked very hard for more than two years and eventually came up with Francis Ap Nefydd. By then, he was running a very successful law practice in Liverpool and we thought he would probably put a manager in charge and never come near the place himself. I think he might have done so had the estate been flourishing, but when he came here to look the place over he was appalled by what he found. Remember, he had known the estate in my father's day and had no idea how Nathaniel Pryce had run it down. He spent the first year sharing his time between his law practice and the estate. Then he appointed Cod's Eye, who was not only to manage the estate but would teach Mr Frank everything he knew.'

'And did he never go back to Liverpool?' Matthew asked. 'For all we know, he might be in the city nine-tenths of the time, because we've never seen him before, have we, Libby? Of course we've heard the workers call him "the boss" and "the old man", but we've not heard his name or seen his face before.'

Auntie reached out for their empty plates. 'For two young people who detest seed cake, you managed to get that down to the last crumb,' she observed. 'As for Mr Ap Nefydd, I believe he rarely leaves the estate, though he does visit his firm from time to time, when he feels they need him. You see, a good deal of the money which has helped to bring the estate back into full production comes from the firm of Nefydd, Mortimer & Briggs, so he likes to keep his eye on things.' She carried the crockery over to the sink, then returned to the table, poured herself another cup of tea, and reached for the depleted seed cake. 'I'll pop this back into the tin, and I think you two had better leave the washing up and go and collect the eggs and shut up the hens for the night. If you're not too tired, that is.'

'We're not a bit tired,' Matthew said, speaking for both of them. 'Come on, Libby. I bet I find more eggs than you.'

As the two youngsters disappeared into the yard, Auntie carried the stew pot over to the sink. She had decided she would do the washing up herself for a change, since they had all worked hard in the twenty-acre and she guessed the children, not used to such work as she was herself, must be very tired, however indignantly they denied it. She carried the kettle over from the range and poured boiling water into the washing-up bowl, then added cold from the bucket under the sink, shook in some soda and began to wash the plates.

As she did so, she reflected that she had told the children the truth, though not quite all of it, for she had not mentioned what had happened during the two-year gap between Mr Pryce's death and the solicitors' discovery of Frank Ap Nefydd. When she had realised that, left to itself, the estate would simply fall apart, she had moved back into the castle and taken over. Because there was no money, Nathaniel Pryce having spent it all, most of the workers had had to leave, but, she told herself defensively now, she had done her very best. Indeed, she had left Tregarth to fend for itself whilst she had strained every nerve to at least keep the estate from complete ruin.

And, she considered now, she had not done too badly. She had borrowed money from the bank to pay the remaining workers, and bought seed to grow corn, barley and other such crops. In the castle itself, after a hard day's work on the land, she had cleaned, replaced broken windows and, in winter, lit fires not only in the kitchen, but in each of the main rooms by turn. She had made butter and cheese in the big modern dairy which her father had built, and sold it in the nearest market town.

When she had heard that Frank was to be the new 'lord of the manor' she had been pleased, though extremely surprised, for he was such a distant relative that it had never occurred to her that he might one day inherit. She had assumed that he would be grateful that she had stepped into the breach and managed the place for two hard years, but of course he had not seen the property during Mr Pryce's reign and so had no idea of the good she had done. Oh, he had thanked her, to be sure, but perfunctorily; had offered his help with the task of bringing Tregarth 'up to scratch' as he had put it, and had then simply moved into the castle and taken over. She had wanted to offer advice which she knew he would need, but he had told her, kindly but firmly, that he meant to employ an estate manager and had appointed Cod's Eye.

193

This was a decision with which she could not possibly argue, for Cod's Eye had, as he put it, learned estate management at his father's knee. No one could have been better suited to the task but, illogically, she had felt criticised, unappreciated and passed over, all the work she had done for love counting for nought.

Now, she told herself ruefully that she had been foolish to believe, as she knew she had, that Frank would ask her to take over the estate for him whilst he returned to his law practice in Liverpool. When this had not happened, when he had taken up residence in the castle and made it plain that he did not need her advice, she had been hurt and furious, unable to meet him without showing the antagonism she felt.

Finishing the washing up, she reflected that she had meant to be pleasant, to accept that she must make do with Tregarth and leave Frank up at the castle to make his own mistakes and to learn from them, but even after years her resentment still smouldered, and whenever they met she found herself making sharp comments and saying things that she afterwards regretted.

Perhaps she should have been warned by what had happened when Nathaniel Pryce had first come to the castle. He had resented her because she had frequently visited him, advising him, interfering with his workers, trying to explain what one did and didn't do, until he had forbidden her to so much as set foot on estate land. As if that had

194

not been bad enough, he had decided that Tregarth should by rights be part of the estate, and had gone to court, accusing her father of sharp practice, suggesting that he had claimed the farm illegally so that his wife and daughter might have somewhere to live after his death.

Fortunately, old Mrs Williams eventually traced the documents which proved that her family had not only owned Tregarth for at least two hundred years, but actually built it, which had ended the court case and Eluned's secret fear that they might be turned out. It had also, she believed, ended her mother's life, for the suspense and worry had brought on a heart attack from which the old lady never recovered.

Outside in the yard, the children shouted to one another. The fat white hen always laid in the stable block, and had done so today. Matthew had collected a dozen eggs and was disputing Libby's right to claim fourteen because he could not see into the mangers from his wheelchair, nor get across the ditch to take the eggs which had been laid in the hedge. Smiling, Auntie opened the door and looked out, just as Libby said placatingly: 'Yes, all right, Matthew; tell you what, I'll fetch the ones from the proper nesting boxes in the henhouse and you can count them as your finds. Then I'll go into the hay barn and everything I find in there will count for me. Is that fair?'

'It's very fair indeed and you shall have two boiled eggs apiece for your breakfast tomorrow,'

Auntie called, 'and I'll use Matthew's egg-timer and watch it like a hawk so they don't go hard on me. Or would you rather have eggy-bread? Only boiled eggs are quicker and they'll be cutting Rhys's father's long meadow tomorrow and praying the fine weather lasts until all is safely gathered in, as it says in the hymn.'

Both children turned and beamed at her. 'Boiled eggs will be fine, Auntie,' Matthew shouted. 'If the hens go on laying the way they're doing at present, we can have eggy-bread another day. Only my mother used to call it French fried bread.'

'Ah well, your mother was a smart city lady who knew all the posh names for things, I expect,' Auntie said tactfully. 'I'm like your young friend; we call a spade a spade, don't we, Libby? And bread soaked in egg and milk and then fried is eggy-bread to us. And now you'd best come in if you've finished your work, because I'm about to make our bedtime cocoa.'

Chapter Seven

1940

It was an icy November day and Marianne was shopping in St John's market, searching for onions which for some reason were almost unobtainable. With a sigh, she visited the last stall, then abandoned her quest, stepping out on to the pavement and wincing as the cold bit at her unprotected face. There were other greengrocers in the area, of course, but she was willing to bet that none of them would have onions. She had almost decided to give up and go to the nearest café for a cup of something hot, when she heard herself hailed.

'Mrs Sheridan! Hang on a minute so's I can catch you up.'

Marianne looked round and saw an elderly neighbour, her breath forming a cloud of steam as she came hurrying towards her. It was Mrs Shepherd, who lived next door but one to her in Sydenham Avenue. Folk there tended to keep themselves to themselves, but not Mrs Shepherd. She was a lovely lady, always eager to stop for a chat whenever Marianne was passing her gate.

'Hello, Mrs Shepherd. You're looking fit and well! Is everything all right at home?' Marianne asked rather anxiously. She tried to keep an eye on the house and did so whenever she could, but she had not been back for a fortnight and a lot could happen in that time.

'Everything's fine, but you know that; I saw you and your hubby goin' in by the front door only . . . what, four or five days ago?' Mrs Shepherd said blithely. 'You was wearin' a new coat, dark blue, or mebbe navy, with the collar turned up and a matching hat; very smart I thought you looked. Mind you, it were growin' dusk and very overcast.' She chuckled. 'You didn't see me, but I saw you.'

Marianne felt her heart give a huge, uneven jump and only just stopped her hand from flying to her mouth. She knew very well that she had not visited the house for two weeks, and when she had done so it had not been in Neil's company. But it would never do to say so; Mrs Shepherd, nice though she was, must have made a mistake, been looking at the wrong house, or been thinking of another occasion. So she put her hand to her brow and frowned, pretending thought. 'Oh? And – and I was with Neil? I don't remember . . . ah, yes, that would have been . . . let me see . . . last Wednesday or Thursday?'

'Were it?' Mrs Shepherd said. 'I know your hubby had hard work gettin' the key in 'cos he fumbled with it for a moment before it turned. I were about to shout out that he ought to try a spot of oil when there were a click and the door swung in. I opened me mouth to have a word but I reckon

I were hidden by that there conifer Mrs Nicholls put in a couple o' years back, and by the time I'd moved sideways, like, so we could see each other, he'd followed you in an' were closin' the door behind him.'

'Oh!' Marianne said feebly. 'You're quite right, that lock needs oiling badly; I'll do it the next time I visit Sydenham Avenue. In fact, I'll do it today, because I've just remembered that Mr Soames, on the corner, sometimes has a few onions for sale and my mother wants a couple for a stew. Then, whilst I'm there, I'll just warm the place through because it doesn't do to let a house get damp at this time of year.' She looked hard at Mrs Shepherd; just how much would it be safe to say? How much would she give away if she asked the wrong question – and how much might she learn if she asked the right one? But her neighbour was looking at her enquiringly, so Marianne plunged in recklessly. 'We – we only popped in just to check that everything was all right and those kids hadn't broken in again; we didn't have time to warm the place through.'

'That's very sensible, my dear. Though I didn't see you leave,' Mrs Shepherd said, sounding disappointed. 'If I'd known you weren't going to stay over, I'd have asked you round for a cuppa and a nice round or two of toast, but I didn't like to butt in, if you see what I mean.'

'You are kind,' Marianne said gratefully, glad now that she had spoken. 'But I'd better be on my way. I'm on the night shift later and I'd like to have a couple of hours' sleep before I set off for the factory.'

Mrs Shepherd's face fell. 'There, and I were about to suggest poppin' into Lewis's for a nice cup o' tea an' a jangle,' she said rather reproachfully. 'How about it? My treat, of course.'

Marianne shook her head, falsely regretful. 'It's awfully kind of you, Mrs S, but I've got rather a lot to do before my shift starts, especially if I'm to light the kitchen fire. I promise you that next time I'm in Sydenham Avenue, I'll give you a knock. Then we can share a hot drink and a gossip while I check that the house is all right.'

Mrs Shepherd agreed to this, to Marianne's great relief, and she hurried to the nearest tram stop and began her journey, her mind in a whirl. A hundred thoughts had rushed through her head. Burglars! But no, the man had had a front door key. And though Mrs Shepherd had not said so, she assumed he must have been a naval officer. Then another thought occurred. Neil had been unable to persuade the landlord to allow them to sub-let, and had said it seemed wrong to leave the place empty when so many people, particularly naval personnel, had nowhere to stay when their ships docked, save for the Sailors' Home which was almost invariably as full as it could hold. Yes, of course! Neil would have lent the key to a fellow officer, told him to make himself at home for the duration of his leave – might even have gone to the house with him.

Yes, that would be it. No doubt Mrs Shepherd, seeing two figures at the front door, had leapt to the obvious conclusion. However, she felt indignant at the thought that Neil had lent their home without at least mentioning it to her first.

She was actually getting down off the tram and walking towards Sydenham Avenue before something else occurred to her. If Neil's shipmate had been in Liverpool, that meant that Neil himself must have had at least some shore leave. Why had he not delivered his friend to their house, seen him comfortably settled, and then got himself out to Crocus Street to spend at least a few hours with his wife? Unless of course his companion had not come from the *Sea Spurge* but from some other ship; then he might only have had time to dump the man on the doorstep and return, hastily, to set sail once more.

By now, Marianne was at the front door, which she opened with her own key. Usually she went round the back, but because of Mrs Shepherd's information she felt obliged to follow in the footsteps of whoever had entered the house four or five days before. Because she rarely used the front door, she had not bothered to oil the lock and knew that the key always stuck and had to be persuaded to turn, which it usually did with a loud squawk. Today, it turned soundlessly and without effort, and, slipping inside, Marianne thought grimly that Mrs Shepherd's unspoken advice had not been necessary; someone had oiled the lock.

In the darkened hallway she paused for a moment, her heartbeat quickening. Then she set off for the kitchen, telling herself crossly that she had no need to feel an intruder in her own home, yet knowing it was this reaction that had caused her to hesitate. She went quickly and quietly along the corridor, glancing into the dining room on her left and the sitting room to her right. Both, of course, were empty, as she had known they must be. She reached the kitchen door, turned the handle slowly and quietly, and then flung the door wide as though hoping to surprise whoever, or whatever, lay behind it. But the kitchen was empty. Marianne stalked into the room, bristling. She opened the pantry door, half expecting to find the remains of a loaf of bread or a jug of curdled milk, but there was nothing. She checked the food, which was mainly tins and packets, and was fairly sure that everything was as she had left it, two weeks before. Then she went across to the Aga, which she had not lit on her previous visit, since she had been merely popping in, but the range was clean and cold, and still laid with paper, sticks and small pieces of coal, so that whoever needed to do so could just put a match to it.

After a prolonged study of everything in the kitchen, dining and sitting rooms, Marianne was sure that neither thieves nor inquisitive small boys had found their way into the house. Indeed, she was beginning to doubt the evidence of Mrs Shepherd's eyes, for if Neil had loaned the place to a fellow officer, he had not made a meal, lit a fire, or left any other sign of his brief occupancy. However, there was the oiled lock . . .

Marianne sighed deeply, then headed for the stairs. She would just check the bedrooms . . .

Libby's room and the spare one were just as she had left them. She went into the room she and Neil shared and it, too, seemed simply empty, in no way as though a stranger had used it. Marianne frowned. She decided Mrs Shepherd really had mistaken the house, for she had said that it had been growing dusk when she had spotted the couple. Yet it was not like Mrs Shepherd to make such an obvious mistake, particularly since she had mentioned the conifer growing in the garden of the house next door.

Marianne glanced once again at the bed, went to leave the room, then turned back. She snatched at the beautiful bedspread, which her godmother had made as a wedding present, then folded back the eiderdown, blankets and top sheet, and stared very hard at the pillows, looking for a dent where a head had lain, or a stray hair, or some other sign. She remembered changing the bedlinen the last time she had slept here and bent over the nearest pillow to check that it still smelled of lavender.

It did not. Was there the faintest trace of perfume, not the one she habitually used? If so, it was very faint. Marianne sat down on the bed with a thump. Had Mrs Shepherd been right? Had someone visited her house and Neil not breathed a word of it to her? He could have dropped her a line, even if he had no chance to visit. Next time she saw him she must remember to ask, for if he was letting fellow officers use the house he must tell her. What a chance he had taken! She could have gone quietly into the house, heard movement upstairs and rushed to the telephone box on the corner to contact the police with news of an intruder.

Having thought that far, she told herself that Neil's only real sin, if you could call it that, was in not telling his wife that he had lent the house to a fellow officer and that officer's wife. Or girlfriend. Oh, heavens, or trollop!

Marianne sighed and remade the bed, went downstairs, checked that the windows were all closed tightly and that the back door was locked, then let herself out through the front door and made for the tram stop.

As she climbed aboard the tram, however, a solution to her problem presented itself. Neil was her one true love and would never deliberately deceive her. He must have lent the house to a friend and not had time to tell her, or done so in a letter which had failed to reach her. Yes, that was the logical explanation and one which she would simply accept. She need say nothing to Neil to let him know that she had visited the house, or been told of the clandestine visit. But there was one thing which she could do without offending anyone. She would have the locks changed, explaining that she had lost their spare key.

Having made up her mind how to act, she felt a good deal better and was able, when she returned to Crocus Street, to greet her mother perfectly normally and go off to work that night with a semblance, at least, of her usual calm authority.

Two days before Christmas, Marianne returned to Sydenham Avenue, her arms full of Christmas decorations, including a small branch of mistletoe and a slightly larger one of holly. The city had been the victim of sporadic raids by the Luftwaffe ever since the summer, but two nights previously it seemed that the Nazi bombers had finally got their measure, for the raids at the weekend had been heavy, though obviously aimed largely at the docks.

Marianne had hoped to be able to get Libby home just for the festivities; indeed, it had all been arranged. But on the morning of the 21st she had sent a telegram to Miss Williams at Tregarth, saying that her plans had been altered and that she would not now be fetching her daughter back to Liverpool for Christmas. Instead, she had parcelled up Libby's presents and despatched them, hoping that they would arrive in time but sure, anyway, that she had made the right decision. She knew that aircraft only took off when skies were clear and last night had been deeply overcast, with hail and even flakes of snow blowing into her face as she traversed Long Lane. But one could not rely upon the weather and she had no intention of putting her daughter's life at risk. On the other hand, she did not want Libby's Christmas to be ruined by fears that her mother, Gammy and Auntie Fee were in danger, so she said nothing of the raids. They had been reported on the wireless, of course, but the danger played down, since anything else would have been bad for morale.

She reached Sydenham Avenue and went through the front gate and down the side of the house to the back door, letting herself in and shivering slightly at the chill of the once warm and lively kitchen. Never mind, it would soon be warm and lively again, for one good thing had resulted from the recent bombing raids: Gammy had agreed that the whole family, including the lodgers, would spend Christmas here. The lodgers had demurred at first, saying they could not impose, though only Limpy Smith and Mr McNally would actually be with them over the holiday. Mr Parsons had a whole week's leave and meant to stay with his married daughter in Christleton, a small village just outside Chester.

Marianne was on leave herself, so, since she was not travelling into North Wales to fetch Libby home, she meant to make the house as welcoming and festive as possible. Her first act was to light the fire in the stove and to begin cooking, for she had been saving up both her rations and anything else she could buy for weeks and weeks and intended that everyone should eat really well whilst they were staying in Sydenham Avenue. By four o'clock, the baking was finished, the decorations were in place and she had even dug up the Christmas tree from the back garden, put it in a bucket with plenty of earth round its roots and carried it into the sitting room. Had it been possible she would have decorated it too, but not being possessed of four pairs of hands she had been unable to bring the decorations from Crocus Street. She knew there was a box of tree ornaments stowed away in the attic, but fetching them down would mean ascending a rickety ladder and searching by torchlight through the cobwebby loft space and Marianne, who was terrified of spiders, decided that decorating the tree would have to wait until she had raided Gammy's things next day.

It was when she realised that a long and empty evening stretched ahead of her that Marianne decided she simply could not face being in the house all alone. She knew she would think of nothing but the puzzle of the oiled lock, so she stowed her baking in the pantry, banked down the stove, locked the back door and took her coat and hat from the hook. She glanced into the dining room, which she had decorated with the paper chains she and Fiona had made when they were Libby's age, then went into the sitting room to check that the fire was almost out, pulling the guard in front of it although it seemed to be largely composed of greying ash. After that, she let herself out through the front door, locked it, and got out her small pocket torch. She knew she would soon get her night eyes, but she wanted to make sure that the gate was properly latched when she left the house behind.

As she turned into Croxteth Road, she saw a tram approaching the stop and began to hurry. Climbing aboard, she found herself wondering whether Neil might get home for a few hours at least over the holiday. She knew he would do so if he possibly could, since she had written to him telling him that Libby would be home and would be thrilled to bits if he could get back. He had replied that he would certainly try to do so, believed it might be possible, and sent them both his love. Of course the lure of Libby's presence no longer applied, but there was no way of contacting him until the *Sea Spurge* next came into port, and anyway, she guessed he would understand and would applaud her decision not to bring Libby back into danger.

She reached Crocus Street, realising that she was very tired, and was thrilled to be met by a wonderful smell of baking and the warmth of her mother's kitchen. Gammy was sitting by the fire, mending socks, her spectacles perched on the end of her nose, a cup of tea steaming gently in the hearth. She looked up when Marianne came in. 'Eh, it's grand to see you, queen. Your sister arrived not half an hour ago. She's off duty now until Boxing Day, I believe, an' I told her she could share my bed, not realising you meant to come home.' She peered anxiously at her daughter over the top of her spectacles. 'Did I gerrit wrong? I could have sworn you said you'd stay in Sydenham Avenue overnight, then come here tomorrer to give me a hand carryin' me cake an' so on back to your kitchen. Still an' all, when Fee sees you're here . . .'

There was a thundering on the stairs and Fiona, looking incredibly flushed and pretty, burst into the kitchen, stopped short, then flung herself at Marianne, waltzing her round, hand-fasted, as though they were still two little girls. 'Oh, Marianne, it's lovely to see you. We've not met for ages and ages,' she gabbled. 'But Mam said you were staying in Sydenham Avenue tonight! Oh, I feel right guilty, because I just put all me clothes into your half of the wardrobe and stuck me nightie under your pillow. But it don't matter – I can whip everything out again in two shakes and bring 'em down to the parlour. I suppose I could go back to me flat, but since we'll be movin' up to Sydenham Avenue tomorrow it don't really seem worthwhile.'

She turned as she spoke, but Marianne grabbed her arm. 'Don't be daft, Fee; I'll be just as happy sleeping on the sofa in the parlour as I would be in my own bed.' Now, you Wrens know more than most folk about ship movements. Any idea when the *Sea Spurge* will be docking? I had a letter a couple of weeks back and Neil said he hoped he'd get some shore leave over Christmas, but nothing's certain these days, is it?'

Fiona shuddered. 'No, nothing's certain, except that the wolf pack tend to hang around near the convoy routes,' she said. 'It's like some dreadful, dangerous board game, only it's real . . . but don't let's talk about it. He might already have docked, or it might be two or three days; there's just no way of telling. Does he know we're spending Christmas in Sydenham Avenue, though? Otherwise, he might waste time by coming here, and if he arrives on Christmas Day the trams will be running a Sunday service . . . but I'm sure you must have told him when you last wrote.'

'I did,' Marianne acknowledged. 'The trouble is, Fee, that he only gets letters when he docks so I can never tell for certain just what he does and doesn't know. But I'm pretty sure I mentioned something about spending Christmas at Sydenham Avenue when I told him Libby would be coming home, and I know he knows that because he wrote back absolutely thrilled at the thought of seeing her after so long.'

'Well, that's all right, then,' Fiona said. She crossed the kitchen and twitched her coat off its peg, sliding her arms into it and turning to speak to her sister as she did up the buttons. 'I'm just nipping round to Snowdrop Street to see me friend Madge. She's got three young brothers and they took a bus out into the country to cut holly. Mam said you'd got a little branch but I promised Madge I'd buy some of theirs, give the kids something to spend on Christmas presents.' She raised her fair brows enquiringly. 'How much shall I get? I should think a couple more branches would do us, wouldn't you?'

Marianne laughed. 'I certainly would – and you can jolly well get some drawing pins and put 'em along the picture rails yourself,' she said decidedly. 'I spent nearly the whole day baking, cleaning through and decorating, and I've had enough. In fact the only thing I didn't do was the Christmas tree.' She turned to her mother, still placidly darning socks. 'I'm going to beg your box of decorations off you, Mam, because Neil put ours up in the roof space last year and I don't fancy crawling around in the dark and getting filthy just for a few ornaments. Is that OK?'

'That's fine,' Gammy said comfortably. She addressed her younger daughter, who was just opening the back door. 'I know what you and Madge are like when you get together, so don't you go gassin' but come straight back, d'you hear me? I done a big stew, 'cos it's quick 'n' easy, but there's a mound of spuds to be peeled and a cabbage to be chopped and cleaned up.' She wagged a reproving finger. 'I ain't forgotten that enormous caterpillar what you managed to miss, an' nor has poor Limpy, I don't doubt.'

Fiona, halfway through the back door, let out a spurt of laughter. 'It were a bit of extra meat ration,' she said airily. 'I told him not to boast about it or all the others would want the same. Shan't be more'n a couple of hours!'

The slam of the door prevented any reply and Marianne, with a martyred sigh, went to the vegetable rack, filled the big colander with potatoes, perched the cabbage on top and returned to the sink. Gammy, darning away, shook her head reprovingly. 'You did oughta let that girl do her share, queen,' she said. 'Never were there two sisters more different, 'cos you're always willin' to give a hand whereas Fiona's main aim in life is to do as little as possible. I dunno where I went wrong bringin' her up, honest to God I don't.'

'She's spoilt, being so much younger than me,' Marianne said equably, running water into the sink. 'But it doesn't matter; she'll change when she's married, with a home of her own and a child tugging at her skirt. Let her have fun while she can, because it doesn't last.'

Gammy sighed. 'That sounds strange, coming from you, 'cos never was there a woman happier in her marriage than yourself,' she observed. 'Missin' Neil, are you?'

Marianne felt the hot colour flood her cheeks and was about to retract her last statement when the back door burst open and Neil catapulted into the room. Immediately, she dropped the knife she was holding and rushed towards him, then stopped short. His face was red and when she went to put her arms round him he warded her off. Marianne's hands dropped to her sides. 'N-Neil?' she faltered. 'What on earth . . . ?'

Neil glared at her. 'You changed the bloody door lock!' he shouted. 'What a fool you've made of me! I docked an hour ago and went straight to Sydenham Avenue because you said the whole family would be staying there for Christmas. Oh, I know today's only the twenty-third, so I couldn't be certain you'd be there, but I thought if you weren't I'd go in, light the fires and start airing the place through. So I march up to the front door, put my key in the lock – or try to – and struggle for five minutes before that interfering old bag from up the road comes waddling by our front gate and calls out that Mrs Sheridan had been in all day but had left a bare half-hour before. I told her my key didn't seem to work and she said you'd had intruders and had decided to change the lock.' He began to unbutton his coat. 'So that nosy old woman knows more than I do and I find myself locked out of my own home and made to look an almighty fool into the bargain. For God's sake, Marianne, why didn't you *tell* me? If you'd had a break-in, you can scarcely say it was so unimportant that you didn't think to mention it.'

'I did tell you about the break-in, when some of my ornaments were stolen, and I'm sure I told you I'd changed the locks,' Marianne said, uneasily aware that Neil's attitude had managed to put her on the defensive. 'But Neil, Mrs Shepherd saw someone entering the house with the front door key, a few weeks ago. That was why I decided to change the lock. I actually thought you might have left your key somewhere and an intruder had had a replica cut.' She took a deep breath. 'I even wondered if you might have let a fellow officer use our house when he was ashore for a few nights.

Only if that was the case, you didn't let me know and I found I didn't fancy walking in on a stranger and being frightened half to death.'

'I don't know what you're talking about,' Neil said sulkily. 'As if I'd lend the house to anyone and not tell you! It must have been Mrs Shepherd's imagination. And now let's forget it.' He took her in his arms and kissed her. 'Where's my little girl? I can't wait to see her face when I show her the presents I've brought.'

'Oh, dear! I cancelled her visit because of the bombing raids,' Marianne said, returning his kiss. 'The raids only happened two or three days ago, so there was no time to let you know. And look, I'm really sorry you didn't get my letter telling you I'd changed the locks, but you must admit you've had so little time ashore that it's not surprising it never occurred to me you'd go straight to the house and find you couldn't get in.'

Gammy had been sitting quietly in her chair whilst her daughter and son-in-law talked but now she got to her feet and came over to give Neil a kiss on the cheek. 'Wharra couple you are, gettin' all hot an' bothered over a perishin' door key,' she said. 'If you asks me it's all a misunderstandin', an' the less said the better. Why, Marianne never told *me* she'd had the lock changed!'

'No, because I didn't want to worry you,' Marianne said at once. 'I just felt I couldn't be comfortable, going in and out of the house whenever I got the chance, never knowing when I might find a stranger hiding away in there.'

Neil grinned suddenly, and took Marianne in his arms, giving her a hug and a very much warmer kiss. 'I don't blame you,' he said wryly. 'And now you'd better give me one of the new keys so this never happens again.'

Because Neil had come home, Marianne decided that the two of them would return to the house in Sydenham Avenue and spend the night there.

And when Fiona eventually returned, with her branches of holly, she said at once that she would go to Sydenham Avenue as well, and thought that Gammy should do so too. 'We'll eat our supper here and then get a taxi over to your place,' she said eagerly. 'The lodgers can come on tomorrow, as they'd planned, and this evening will just be for family. I bought a sack of chestnuts from Madge's brothers and we can roast them round the fire. Ooh, I do love roast chestnuts!' She turned to Neil. 'D'you remember that hot punch you made a few years back, when Libby was small? I know you needed lemons and oranges, and some sort of spirit, but could you make it again, d'you think? I managed to get hold of an orange, for Libby's stocking, but there's no point in hangin' on to it, so that can go in it, and Gammy's old pal, what owns Lily Logan's greengrocery on Stanley Road, sold her a couple of lemons under the counter like. She used one in the Christmas cake, but the other's in the fruit bowl.' She dimpled at her brother-in-law. 'And you, bein' in the Navy, can no doubt find some rum or whisky.'

Neil had to return to his ship on the 27th and the whole family went down to the dock to see him off. Walking back to the tram stop, Marianne reflected that it had been the worst Christmas of her life, though she assumed that everyone else had enjoyed it. They had all missed Libby dreadfully, of course, for as Gammy had remarked Christmas was really for children, and without the little girl's excited anticipation the day itself had fallen far short of its usual gaiety. They had tried to behave as they always had, but even the presents under the tree, the wonderful food, the scarlet and green crackers hoarded from the previous year, and the silver threepenny bits in the pudding had not compensated for the loss of Libby's company.

Neil, who had known nothing of the raids until the *Sea Spurge* docked, had missed Libby most of all, for he had not seen her once since her evacuation. He had assured Marianne that the very next time he got some shore leave he would go to Tregarth, but had asked her what he should do about Libby's presents. 'There's the prettiest baby doll I bought in New York, and a little wooden cot with woolly blankets and a proper pillow, which one of the crew sold me now his daughter is too old to play with such things,' he had said. 'And there's a skipping rope with musical handles and a white angora cardigan . . . should I parcel them

216

up and try to send them off, or hold on to them until I can deliver them in person?'

Marianne advised him not to trust such delightful items to the post. 'Give them to her yourself when you visit; she'll appreciate them all the more,' she had said.

Gammy and Fiona had decided there was no point in returning to Sydenham Avenue after seeing Neil back to his ship. Accordingly, they had let the fires out, packed away all perishable food in their marketing bags, and replaced the tree, looking a little jaded now, in its original position in the back garden, and the three women were now on their way back to Crocus Street. Marianne reflected that the house she had once loved had become more of a burden than a pleasure, not only because she had to check on it continually, but because she had been unable to rid her mind of the suspicion that someone had visited it in her absence. She had thought and thought, trying to find an innocent explanation for the oiled lock, and had finally decided to forget the whole incident. But in the back of her mind, unease remained.

She found she was looking forward to the return to Crocus Street, though of course going back to work would be a mixed blessing. As a supervisor she had to keep a certain distance between herself and her workmates whilst actually on the factory premises, but to her considerable relief once outside the other girls treated her very much as one of themselves. Marianne believed there were two reasons for this. One was her friendship with Betty Nolan. Betty was popular with everyone and made it plain that if they wanted her company when they went dancing, or to the cinema, then they must include Marianne.

The other reason, oddly enough, was another friendship, this time with Bill Brett. He frequently drove a number 19A tram, which many of the girls caught to the terminus on Stopgate Lane. Despite the leg injury which had kept him out of all three services when he had tried to join up at the beginning of the war, he kept busy. He had a large and thriving allotment and handed out vegetables to the factory girls whenever he had a surplus. When Heather Radcliffe, one of Marianne's workers, had her windows blown out during the Christmas raids, Bill had managed to acquire some glass and had put the damage right for her. He wielded a paintbrush pretty expertly and had shown Moira, another of Marianne's trainees, how to clean down and paint her kitchen after a large quantity of soot had descended into her fireplace, blackening everything in sight. He would always give a hand if a woman was struggling off his tram with a heavy basket, and though of course he never went dancing he had taken Marianne and Betty to the flicks on more than one occasion, saying that he felt a fool sitting in a cinema by himself. He was fond of what he described as 'a good comedy' and went to every one of the Marx Brothers' films, insisting on treating Marianne and Betty not only to the seats, but to pie and chips afterwards.

As a married woman, Marianne had been downright grateful that he always included Betty in any invitation to herself, though she knew she would have been perfectly safe going anywhere alone with Bill. She had complete trust in his reliability and good intentions. She thought he must have been very much in love with his Dora, for when he spoke of her it was with deep regret and affection, and so far as she knew he had never even contemplated remarriage. In fact, she told herself now, swinging along Stanley Road, Bill was that rare thing, a thoroughly decent man who would help anyone who needed a hand without so much as a thought for himself.

Ahead of her, Gammy and Fee sauntered along, Fee's hand tucked into her mother's elbow. As they passed the top of Pansy Street, however, Gammy stopped and turned back to address Marianne. 'I were just tellin' your sister that's where your pal Bill lodges. I forget the number but him an' me walked back from the shops together just afore Christmas. I told him there were no need for him to carry me messages all the way back to Crocus and he said since he lodged in Pansy it were nobbut a step and he'd see me right to me door and be home himself no more'n five minutes later.'

Marianne turned to Fiona. 'You've not met Bill, have you?' she said. 'He's ever so nice; well, everyone likes him. You do as well, don't you, Mam?'

'I do,' Gammy acknowledged readily. They were all well laden but Marianne seized her mother's bag so that the three of them might link arms. 'He's a real good sort, the kind what'll do anything for anyone. He and his wife didn't have no kids, so I reckon he's lonely. He keeps busy, though, what with his job and the allotment. Yes, Bill Brett's a real nice feller.'

Chapter Eight

1941

Bill was working on his allotment, barrowing manure from the pile he had built up to where he intended to plant his seed potatoes, runner beans and garden peas. He kept glancing at his watch because he was on shift at the tram depot later that day, and even though he caught a bus it was a half-hour's ride to the depot. However, it was a mild and sunny April day, and Bill spent every spare moment on his allotment. In fact, he virtually had two, since the old man who rented the plot adjoining Bill's could no longer manage the heavy work of digging and manuring the land. He was happy for Bill to do this for him and Bill, planting, weeding, digging and seeding, was glad to take payment in kind rather than money. Whenever he had the chance, he visited a nearby farm, buying sacks of manure and hiring the farmer's ancient cart, and even more ancient horse, to carry them back to the allotments. As a result of all this feeding, he knew that his fruit and vegetables would be considerably better than those grown by less ardent gardeners, and thought the result well worth the labour.

He still drove his tram, of course, and when-ever possible he would be at the terminus on

Stopgate Lane when Marianne's shift was finishing. He enjoyed her company and was proud to be seen with her, since he thought her truly beautiful. He liked simply looking at her, at the heavy silken fall of her burnished chestnut hair, the whiteness of her skin and her thickly lashed blue-grey eyes.

He was gratified that she clearly viewed him as a friend and did not hesitate to confide in him. She made him laugh with her stories of factory life, and talked lovingly and at length about the little daughter he had never met and about Tregarth, that strange, almost landless farm far away in its hidden valley. She told him of her childhood, when she and her sister Fiona had been close and loving companions, and though she did not say so, he gathered that this closeness had somehow dissipated as they grew older. Bill thought that Fiona's joining the WRNS had not helped their relationship, for although Fiona worked in an office and did an important job, Bill knew from what Marianne had told him that her sister's salary was scarcely half that earned by Marianne herself.

It had occurred to Bill, more than once, that there was something odd about this, for Marianne had told him that her sister's flat was very luxurious indeed. When she had first moved out of Crocus Street, Fiona had shared the flat with another Wren whose father had contributed to the rent, but ever since the previous Christmas, when the other girl had been seconded to work at a naval base in

Scotland, Fiona had been in the flat alone. Bill was at a loss to understand how she could afford it, and eventually decided that the other Wren must have continued to shell out in order to have somewhere to live if she ever returned to Liverpool. Otherwise, surely, Fiona would have needed to ease the situation by letting two or even three other Wrens share the flat.

Now, Bill tipped manure into the deep trench he had dug, then half filled it with earth. Did he have time to sow the peas, or should he leave them until another day? He had a little hut in which he kept a small piece of soap and an ancient towel, for there was a tap near the gate, enabling the owners both to water their produce when necessary and to clean up before making their way back to their own homes. Bill sighed, grabbed his barrow and returned to the hut. He would clean up, lock everything portable away and catch his bus. Later in the year, he would be able to take Marianne small gifts – a punnet of blackcurrants, or gooseberries; some delicious strawberries or broad beans – but right now all he could offer was his company. Though by no means a conceited man, he knew that this alone would please her, for her eyes always lit up when they met his and her pace quickened as she hurried towards him.

Thinking of the long summer evenings ahead, however, was not unalloyed pleasure, for as soon as the fruit and vegetables he was growing began to mature, the spivs and idlers, and even some little boys, would find the allotments as attractive as bees find honey. The previous year, whilst the Battle of Britain raged overhead, the allotment owners had realised that they would have to take action or see their plots stripped of everything edible. They had worked out a rota, armed themselves with a couple of airguns, and stood guard over their precious crops. At first they had thought the thieves would only come under cover of darkness, but this proved not to be the case, so they had extended their patrols to include any wife who would give up an hour or two in order to guard her husband's property.

The spivs and hangers-on had come, taken one look at the ancient airguns and the fierce expressions on the women's faces, and gone again. Of course they had come back later, but by that time a police constable or two had agreed to visit the allotments a couple of times a week, and the threat of being arrested was more than the thieves were prepared to risk.

As he cleaned himself up and began to walk towards the bus stop, Bill reflected that not only had the RAF won the battle for air supremacy, but Hitler had called off his threatened invasion of Great Britain, though that had not stopped the government from taking down or painting over road signs and generally making life rather more difficult than it need have been. Still, the thought of invasion was enough to chill Bill's blood and he found himself in full agreement with whoever had warned that an invasion called off one October might easily take place the next. Yes, it was better to be safe than sorry.

Bill began to hum a popular tune of the moment – *I found my thrill, on Blueberry Hill* – and smiled to himself.

Libby had been disappointed when the telegram had arrived putting off her Christmas visit to Liverpool, especially as it would have meant seeing her beloved father after so many months apart. She had quite understood that it was not sensible to return to the city when enemy bombers had attacked two or three nights running, but she had secretly hoped that her father might bring her mother to Tregarth to visit her over Christmas. It would have been marvellous to entertain them here, safe in the Welsh hills, but in a letter which had arrived in early January, Marianne had explained that such a visit would only be possible when Neil had a proper leave. *So don't be unhappy, my darling,* she had written. *Remember that we will come to you just as soon as we can. Daddy was terribly disappointed that you were not here to welcome him when he docked, but, like you, he knows that in wartime one must accept disappointment occasionally and hope for better luck next time. He says he will be due for leave – proper leave – when spring comes and will definitely visit you then.*

Libby, telling Matthew that she would not be going away for Christmas after all, had felt quite guilty over not being able to be truly sad. Oh, she would miss her parents, Gammy, and her aunt, but she knew that she would relish every minute of her first Christmas at Tregarth. So many things had been planned, including a visit to the nearest town to buy small presents on market day, carol singing round the houses, and a party which was apparently held yearly up at the castle, with a great tree, gifts for everyone, and a bran tub, something she had read about but which had never yet come her way.

And now it was the end of April; the weather was warm and sunny, and her father was coming to visit at last! She supposed that her mother would come as well, which would be lovely, but Marianne had spent three days with her no more than five or six weeks ago and she had not seen her daddy for over a year. He was coming, further-more, for a whole week, and in his last letter he had said he would be bringing the presents he had bought for her at Christmas, but had been unable to deliver. The presents were not impor-tant, she told herself strong-mindedly, though of course she could not help wondering what she would receive, but every night, as she lay in her small bed, she went over and over how she would take Daddy round the stables and cow byre, the meadows and lanes. He had been brought up in the country and would, she knew, appreciate everything in a way which Marianne could not, though she did her best.

'Libby, do stop dreaming and tell me if this looks right to you!'

Matthew's rather plaintive voice cut across Libby's thoughts, bringing her back to the reality of the Tregarth kitchen. She looked around guiltily; every inch of the table and sideboard were covered with ingredients, cake tins, jars of jam and other such things, for the children had despatched Auntie up to the castle, where Mr Ap Nefydd had sportingly agreed to detain her on the pretext of helping him with some government forms. Ever since the Christmas party at the castle, Matthew and Libby had been on good terms with Mr Ap Nefydd, frequently visiting him for a chat and a glass of his housekeeper's raspberry cordial, though they did not mention these visits to Auntie.

Mr Ap Nefydd had agreed to Matthew's suggestion when he had explained, bashfully, that he and Libby meant to bake a splendid sponge cake as a welcome for Lieutenant Commander and Mrs Sheridan's arrival at Tregarth next day. Mr Ap Nefydd's eyebrows had shot up almost to his hairline and he had asked why Miss Williams must be kept in ignorance of such a praiseworthy activity.

'Because she's bound to interfere, sir; Miss Williams doesn't know she can't cook and scorns recipe books as foolish and unnecessary,' Matthew had said, with a wry grin. 'She makes wonderful stews and roasts, but pastry, cakes and so on all come out the same: flat as pancakes and wet in the middle.'

'But you and Libby haven't done much baking, I'll be bound,' Mr Ap Nefydd had said, rubbing his nose, and giving Matthew a doubtful look. 'What makes you think you'll do any better than Ellie – Miss Williams, I mean?'

'We'll follow a recipe for a start and we'll make sure the oven is at the right heat,' Matthew had explained. 'Only we don't want to hurt Auntie's feelings, so it would be best if she wasn't around.'

Mr Ap Nefydd had grinned. 'I'll do it; and I'll get Mrs Bryant to make a plate of her famous sausage rolls. Miss Williams won't be able to resist a cup of tea and a sausage roll or two, especially if I'm not around, so that should keep her occupied until your baking is done. But I don't mean to oblige you without some sort of payment; I think I must have a large piece of your cake. You'll be far too busy entertaining the Sheridans, so I shall call for it myself soon after breakfast on Friday morning. Are you agreeable to my terms?'

They had been, of course, and they had made both children even more anxious to produce a perfect cake.

Now, Libby looked somewhat despairingly around the kitchen. They had adhered religiously to the recipe, though many of the terms used were strange to them. Creaming butter and sugar with a wooden spoon seemed a very odd thing to do and Matthew had had to forcibly prevent Libby from adding a measure of cream to the mix. They had whipped the eggs into a froth, though Matthew had complained bitterly that the book's idea of a large egg – six large eggs – might not coincide with those they had abstracted from the nests the previous evening, and the recipe's instruction to add the beaten egg to the creamed cake mixture a little at a time, with much vigorous beating in between to prevent curdling, seemed very strange indeed. So far as Matthew and Libby were concerned, only milk could curdle, and once again Matthew had to restrain Libby from adding milk to the mix. When it came to folding in the flour with a metal spoon, he had let Libby loose on the task whilst he greased two seven inch sponge tins, which they had borrowed from Mrs Bryant, since Auntie scorned such aids to culinary perfection and shovelled all her mixtures into any tin which would contain them.

'Well, that's finished and it looks all right,' Libby said, spooning the last smear of the mix into the tin. 'Want to lick the bowl, Matthew? The heat's just what the book said so I might as well put them in right away. The recipe says bake for thirty minutes but I think we ought to look after twenty, don't you?'

Matthew, smearing his finger round the large yellow bowl and licking enthusiastically, shook his head. 'No I do not,' he said decidedly. 'Don't you remember what Mrs Bryant said when we borrowed the tins? She said if we opened the door to have a peep and let cold air into the oven, the cakes might sink in the middle. You have to be strong and leave well alone.'

'Oh, but suppose it's a bit too hot and the cakes burn?' Libby wailed. 'My mother is a really good cook. It would be awful to give her burnt cake; don't you think perhaps . . . ?'

'Oh, Libby, use your loaf,' Matthews implored. 'You can cut burnt off, but there's nothing you can do if it goes all slimy in the middle and I must say,' he added, beginning to pile utensils into the yellow bowl, 'the mixture tastes absolutely delicious. I think raw cake is even nicer than the cooked sort.' He intercepted Libby's longing glance towards the oven and chuckled. 'You start the washing up and I'll dry, then we'll put all the things away, and by the time we've done that, the cake will very likely be cooked.'

The cake was a great success; Libby lovingly clapped the two halves together with raspberry jam in between, and wrote *Welcome, Mummy and Daddy* in her very best writing. Icing had not been available since the beginning of the war, but a piece of white card propped up on top of the cake was the next best thing.

However, it was only Neil who came striding across the yard halfway through Thursday afternoon. Libby and Matthew had been hanging about the lane all day but as luck would have it had gone back to the house to lay the table for high tea when their visitor arrived. Neil gave a shout, stood his suitcase and bag down and caught Libby as she flew into his arms, then shook hands with Matthew and came into the house to be introduced to his daughter's foster-parent.

Faced with anxious enquiries about Mrs Sheridan's absence, he assured them, with his pleasant smile, that Marianne was well but had been unable to get leave from her factory in order to accompany him.

'I did hope Mummy would be able to come with you, but I knew she might not,' Libby said loyally. 'We saw her in March and she did say that I might go home for a week or two in the summer holidays, so I really shouldn't grumble. I miss Gammy most awfully as well and wish she could come visiting, but she won't because of the lodgers. Mr Parsons says she's the best landlady in the whole of Liverpool and I'm sure he's right; she's certainly the nicest Gammy.'

'Yes, your Gammy loves looking after people,' Neil acknowledged. 'But what about your Auntie Fee? You must miss her. I know how fond you are of each other, and of course she's a good deal nearer your age than your mother or Gammy.'

'Who's Fee?' Matthew asked. 'I don't recall you mentioning a Fee, Libby.'

'Oh, she's my aunt, my mum's younger sister; she's a Wren,' Libby explained. 'But she almost never writes to me. She says she's too busy, so I don't write to her any more. Why should I? I'm busy too . . . well, we both are, aren't we, Matthew?'

Auntie, bustling about the kitchen with plates of sandwiches, some of Mrs Bryant's sausage rolls and a variety of the small cakes sold by the local baker, told everyone to sit down and start their tea. As the meal progressed, Libby bombarded her father with questions, largely concerned with his life aboard the *Sea Spurge* and friends and neighbours back home in Liverpool, though Neil admitted that he knew very little more about life in the city than she did herself. 'I'm ashore for such short spells that sometimes I'm only in Crocus Street for an hour or two,' he explained. 'Mummy and I try to visit Sydenham Avenue just to check that everything is all right there, but apart from that, the *Sea Spurge* takes up most of my time. But I'm rather surprised to hear that you and Fiona no longer correspond. I definitely got the impression that you exchanged letters quite frequently.'

'Well, we don't; in fact she's only ever written once and that was when I first came to Tregarth,' Libby said positively. 'But I don't mind at all, Daddy. She would only write about being a Wren and I think, myself, that it's more interesting making radios for the air force.'

Neil laughed but shook a chiding finger at her. 'Being a Wren is full of excitement; they do all sorts of interesting work so you may be sure I shall tell your aunt to pull her socks up and write often,' he said. He got up from the table and went across to his canvas holdall. Producing a parcel from its depths, he turned to Matthew and said: 'Now lad,

Libby tells me you've always got your nose in a book, so I bought you a copy of *The Last of the Mohicans*, which is an adventure story by Fennimore Cooper, and another one, *The Chums Annual*. I hope you've not read either.'

Matthew took the books and beamed. 'Thank you ever so much, Mr Sheridan,' he said a trifle breathlessly. 'And I haven't read either, though I've often wanted to. Thank you again.'

Neil continued to rummage in his bag, unearthing a golden-haired baby doll, a skipping rope and a white angora cardigan, with bunny buttons. Libby felt a great surge of disappointment, but threw her arms round her father's neck and gave him a hard hug, telling herself, as Gammy so often said, that it was the thought that counted. She had never been keen on dolls and one glance had told her that the cardigan was far too small, but she hugged it to her cheek, admiring its softness, then swung the skipping rope round. 'Oh, Daddy, what wonderful presents! Oh, I'm so lucky!'

She returned to her place at the table and caught a sympathetic glance from both Auntie and Matthew, both of whom realised that she had no time for dolls, the cardigan was babyish and too small, and skipping was an activity confined to the schoolyard. But before she could think of anything else to say, Auntie spoke. 'Sit yourself down, Mr Sheridan, for Libby has a surprise for you. Off you go, cariad.'

Libby shot into the pantry, returning seconds later

233

with the cake, squatting on Auntie's best cake stand. Raspberry jam oozed and a delicious fragrance hung about it. Whilst in the pantry she had looked, a little doubtfully, at the card with its welcoming message to Mummy and Daddy and had considered ripping it off, but had decided to leave it.

And now she stood the cake down in front of her father. 'Me and Matthew made it all ourselves,' she said proudly. 'We collected the eggs and stopped having sugar in our tea, or on our porridge, and we bought the flour from the baker in the village. Auntie gave us the cream and we made it into butter ourselves, in the churn, though you mustn't tell anyone, Daddy. And the raspberry jam came from Mrs Bryant, up at the castle; she's the housekeeper. She was going to give it to us for love, she said, only we explained that we wanted to get the ingredients ourselves, so she sold us half a jar. Wasn't that kind? And I wrote the card. I put Mummy and Daddy on it because I hoped you'd both come, but the day you leave I'll wrap a nice big slice in greaseproof paper and put it in a little tin and you can give it to Mummy when you get back to Liverpool.'

Her father stood up, walked round the table and gave her a loving kiss, then leaned across and shook Matthew heartily by the hand. 'You're a fantastic pair,' he said warmly. 'Why, that cake looks downright professional and I can't wait to taste it. As for taking a piece back to Mummy, I can't think of anything which would please her more, except being here herself of course. But who is having the honour of cutting the first slice? I'd love to do it, but men are no good at cake cutting. Shall we ask Miss Williams to do the honours?'

'It ought to be Libby or Matthew by rights, but perhaps I've a steadier hand,' Miss Williams acknowledged. 'Even if I can't pretend to bake a cake as good as this one.'

Neil, who knew nothing of Miss Williams's attempts in the baking line, laughed heartily. 'I dare say you could teach these youngsters a thing or two,' he said, and for a dismaying moment Libby wondered whether he bothered to read her letters, since she had told him, over and over, that dear Auntie could not bake to save her life. Then she realised that, being a grown-up, he was using what they called "tact"' and watched with bated breath as her father sank his teeth into the large and rather uneven wedge which Miss Williams had placed upon his plate.

And presently, when everyone was served, it was generally agreed that the cake was a masterpiece: light and fluffy, yet deliciously satisfying. As soon as tea was over, Miss Williams shooed their visitor and both children out into the yard, where they might explore whilst she cleared the table, washed up and began the preparations for supper.

Marianne had been bitterly disappointed when she had not been able to get time off to visit her daughter with Neil, but she told herself, severely, that fair was fair; she had seen Libby half a dozen times since she had been evacuated to Tregarth, and it would be nice, for both father and daughter, to have time together with no other distractions. Neil's ship had docked on the Wednesday and he had come round to Crocus Street to pick up the presents he had been unable to give Libby the previous Christmas. It was only then that Marianne had realised how their daughter had matured since Neil had last seen her. Libby never played with dolls now, only skipped with a rope in the schoolyard since there was nowhere suitable at Tregarth, and had long outgrown the angora cardigan. But she knew her daughter well enough to be sure that Libby would not dream of upsetting her father by letting him see her disappointment, and had looked forward to Neil's return, when he could tell her how Libby went on.

But within a very short space of time, Marianne was far too occupied to wonder what Libby and her father were doing, for on the night of 1 May, while Neil was safely ensconced at Tregarth, Liverpool suffered its worst raid of the war so far. The planes started coming over just before eleven o'clock, and bombs simply rained down on the city. Fires started almost immediately. The docks were hit and the constant whistle and crash as the heavy explosives descended meant that no one slept. Mr Parsons had been fire watching, though the other lodgers had been in bed when the raid started and had taken to the shelters along with Gammy and Marianne.

Mr Parsons told them, when he came wearily home at breakfast time next day, that he had never seen such destruction. By the end of the week, Marianne, making her way towards Pansy Street to make sure that Bill's lodgings were still standing and that Bill himself was all right, could scarcely recognise the streets along which she passed.

However, Pansy Street seemed relatively undamaged and when she knocked at Bill's lodgings his landlady, Mrs Cleverley, assured her visitor that Mr Brett, though extremely tired – and who was not? – was fine. 'He's just changed his job, though,' she told Marianne. 'He's drivin' buses now, instead of trams, because there's so many tramlines out of commission that he felt he'd be more use on the buses. And of course he's fire watchin' whenever he's norrat work. Want to come in for a drink o' tea, ducks? It's about all that's on offer, but I've just made a brew so you're welcome to a cup.'

Marianne declined, having a good deal to do herself before she could get a rest, but she felt much happier knowing that Bill was safe. Their friendship had matured into something precious to her, and she realised she could scarcely imagine life without him. She wondered whether Neil and he might actually meet at last, then dismissed the thought. Neil was in North Wales and Bill was clearly run off his feet; the meeting, like so many other things, would have to wait.

* * *

Bill returned home after a double shift on the buses, absolutely exhausted, and planning a couple of hours' rest before setting off for the warehouse from whose lofty roof he would be fire watching. He greeted Mrs Cleverley cheerfully, however, and asked if he could have a meal about half an hour before it began to grow dark, which was when he assumed the raiders would return. 'I want to get me head down for at least an hour, mebbe two, before I tackle your good grub,' he explained. 'But if you'd rather I had something cold right away, that would be fine.'

Mrs Cleverley, however, tutted and shook her head. 'Something cold indeed, for a feller what works every hour God sends,' she scolded. 'I'll do you a nice bit of bacon, a pan of chips and a pile of scrambled eggs for half past eight. Oh, and you had a visitor, a Mrs Sheridan. She were worried about you; I guessed she'd been looking for you on the trams – them that are still runnin', that is – so I told her you'd changed to buses. She's on nights tonight, but said you 'ud no doubt meet up when the raids are over.'

'Oh aye, I reckon you're right,' Bill said, heading for the stairs. He reached his room and took off his outer clothing, but did not bother with pyjamas, for it was a warm evening, and climbed into bed. Once there, he expected to sleep immediately, but instead his thoughts strayed to Marianne. From their very first meeting, he had been impressed by both her beauty and her courage. She had never grumbled or whined over her factory work, or the fact that as Gammy grew older Marianne was forced to take on many of her mother's tasks.

But Bill preferred to think of Marianne on the rare occasions when she had given way to his blandishments and allowed him to take her out for a day in the country, or down to the coast. The public were prohibited from visiting most beaches since they were sown with land mines, except for one or two places, and he remembered how, at the touch of sand on her bare toes, Marianne had seemed to become a child again, splashing joyfully into the little waves with her skirt bunched up in one hand, and shouting to him to join her. Together, they had collected shells and bits of seaweed, built a huge sandcastle and filled the moat with seawater, eaten their carry-out at the top of the beach and then trailed home, tired but happy.

'When Libby comes back from Wales, we must bring her here,' Marianne had said, and Bill had been thrilled at the use of the word we. He knew she trusted and liked him and wished, passionately, that she was not already spoken for, because for the first time since Dora's death he felt he had encountered a woman who he thought could take her place.

He had known Marianne for over a year now, but never allowed himself to reveal that liking was turning into something stronger. He must be content with her company, must never let her see that it was not mere liking which brought the smile to his face whenever his eyes fell on her. If he let his feelings

show, he was sure he would lose even her friendship, and that he could not bear.

Sighing, he told himself to think of the new
routes he had to learn in order to do his job as
efficiently as possible, and presently he slept.

Marianne knew that Neil must have heard on the
wireless that Liverpool was being bombed almost
out of existence and expected to receive a telegram
saying that he was coming home. Indeed, when
she had the leisure to think at all, she was sure
that he would come in person to give what help
he could to the stricken city, for normal life was
fast becoming impossible. Already, grim-faced
people, many with small children, were setting out
for the country, hopeful that there at least they
might get a night's sleep before beginning the next
day's toil. She had tentatively suggested to Gammy
that they might move out to Sydenham Avenue,
even if they went no further, but Gammy had jutted
her chin and refused to budge. 'I'll warrant you
aren't a-goin' to give up your factory work,' she
had stated. 'And my work's just as important in
its own way. Lookin' after me lodgers, doing me
ironing at the laundry, gettin' the messages for
them as ain't able to skirt round the bleedin' craters
left by that old bugger's bombs . . . oh aye, mebbe
I'm old, but I ain't useless. Why, as it is, there ain't
no trams or buses what can get through to your
factory, so you're having to walk. It's bad enough
walking from Crocus Street, but if you had to come

from the Avenue, you'd be no use to nobody by the time you arrived.'

Now, Marianne stood in the kitchen, stirring porridge in Gammy's largest pan. She was grey with exhaustion and longed for her bed, for she had had almost no sleep the night before, but she knew there would be little rest for anyone while the skies remained clear and the 'bombers' moon' bright. Last night, 3 May, had seen the worst raid so far, and she was actually contemplating sending Neil a telegram, begging him to return to the city. It had been one hell of a night, with a huge number of enemy aircraft bombarding the city with HE bombs, land mines and incendiaries. She knew that there must have been great loss of life and had been told by Mr Parsons, who was fire watching at his warehouse down at the docks, that an ammunition ship, the *Malakand*, had been hit not by enemy bombs but by one of our own barrage balloons, which had caught fire and broken loose from its moorings, falling across the ammunition ship as it lay in Huskisson dock. The resultant explosion had blown the dock to pieces and had sunk six other ships nearby.

Marianne feared that one of the ships could have been the *Sea Spurge*, but Mr Parsons was able to reassure her on that point; nevertheless, she agonised over what best to do. If she telegraphed and Neil came home and was killed, she would never forgive herself, but perhaps he would want to get his corvette out to sea before the next raid.

On the other hand, she had gained the impression that the *Sea Spurge* was in for repairs, in which case it might be impossible for Neil and his crew to take her to sea. She could not hope to ring the village, or the castle, nor would it be possible for either Libby or Neil to telephone her at present, since most of the lines in Liverpool were down and the system was in chaos. Marianne had heard that the telephone exchange had been hit, with many people killed, and though the authorities had promised to put things right as soon as they were able, she knew that this could take some time.

Upstairs, she could hear Gammy stirring, and she suddenly felt sure that Neil would come as soon as he heard of the devastation which had hit his home port.

The porridge was ready. Marianne pushed the pan to the back of the stove and began to lay the table.

On Sunday morning, Libby was awoken by someone shaking her shoulder. She opened her eyes and immediately realised that it was very early indeed, for dawn was only just streaking the sky. 'Whazzup?' she muttered. 'Whoozat? It can't be time to get up . . . anyway, it's Sunday. No school today.' There was a soft chuckle near her ear and even though it was too dark to see much she knew at once that it was her father and struggled upright. 'Daddy! What's happened? If you pull the blind down you can light my candle, then we can see

242

each other's faces. Is it – is it morning time? Only it looks pretty dark still.'

'No, sweetheart, it's not dawn yet,' Neil said, pulling the blind down and lighting her candle. 'But last night I heard on the wireless that Liverpool has been heavily raided. The Luftwaffe have bombed the city very badly. 'The dear old *Sea Spurge* is in dock for repairs but, darling, it's my duty to try to take her out to sea whilst the bombing raids last. Even if her engines are stripped down so we can't move her, there will be work for me there, simply lending a helping hand wherever it's needed. I've had a wonderful few days with you, pet, but I couldn't face myself if I didn't go back to help in any way I could. Can you possibly understand?'

Libby swung her feet out of bed and rubbed her eyes vigorously, hoping to hide the dismay in them. 'Yes, I do understand, but suppose you're killed, Daddy,' she quavered. 'And what's happened to Mummy? Is she all right? Was it just the docks that were hit?'

'I'm sure it was just the docks and Mummy will be fine; Gammy and Auntie Fee will be fine, too,' he said reassuringly. 'I gather that the telephone exchange is out of commission, which means I won't be able to phone you after I get home to let you know we're all right, but I'll get in touch somehow, so you don't worry. When Mr Ap Nefydd came for his cake the day before yesterday, he gave me his telephone number and said that either Mummy or myself could ring him at any time with a message for you, and he would see it got through. Obviously we won't be able to do that at present, but we'll contact him as soon as we can.'

As her father spoke, Libby was struggling into her clothes, and as she slid her feet into her slippers she seized his hand and tugged him towards the door. 'I'll make you some breakfast if you'll pour the hot water into the teapot,' she announced as they descended the stairs. 'Shall I wake Matthew? He could make you some butties while I do the toast; he's good at butties.' She glanced up at her father as they entered the kitchen and saw a hunted look cross his face, though she did not understand it. 'Daddy?'

'No, darling, don't disturb anyone; I've been wanting to have a word with you alone ever since I arrived,' Neil said quickly. He riddled the stove, added more fuel, and then pulled the kettle over the flame. 'I wanted to tell you how good I think you've been. It can't have been easy to accept such a total change in your circumstances. You've left your city home for a country one, and your own family for an elderly spinster and a boy in a wheelchair. You went to a rather smart school where you learned such things as French and geography and history, whereas now I gather it's pretty much the three Rs. You get taken out of school to help with farm work, and delightful though Tregarth is at this time of year, I know from your letters that you are often cut off in winter. And you must suffer from the cold, since Mummy told me fires are only lit in the best parlour over Christmas.'

There was a long pause while Libby assimilated her father's words before she answered. 'That's all true, Daddy, but I'm really happy here and having easy schoolwork is great. The teachers are awfully kind, and though Miss Williams may be a spinster – does that mean she isn't a married lady? – she couldn't be nicer. So you see, I haven't been particularly good, because I like everything here so very much.'

'Yes, I know. But what I'm trying to say, darling, is that change doesn't only take place when one is evacuated, it happens all the time, particularly when one's country is at war. There is going to be a big change in your life when the war is over and I want you to be prepared.'

Libby stared at her father, since the explanation – if it was one – seemed to have come to a shuddering halt. She waited and waited, and then realised that the piece of bread on her toasting fork had not only blackened and curled, but had burst into flames, and she hurried across the kitchen to throw it out through the back door. She impaled a fresh slice of bread on her fork and waited, this time, until it was a golden brown before laying it tenderly on her father's plate and addressing him once more. 'I don't understand quite what you mean, Daddy,' she said cautiously. 'Of course I know there will be changes when the war ends.

I'll have to leave Tregarth and go back to Sydenham Avenue, but you and Mummy will be there, and it'll be a change for you, too. I expect I'll have to go back to the convent as well, but I shan't be dreadfully behind with my work since Matthew does French and Latin and all sorts, and sets me exercises when I'm not in school.'

'Good,' Neil said, spreading butter on the toast. 'But that isn't exactly what I meant. Suppose, just suppose, that Mummy didn't want to give up her job at the factory and decided to stay with Gammy in Crocus Street. Suppose she and myself had changed so much that we didn't really want to go back to Sydenham Avenue.'

'Well then, we'd live somewhere else,' Libby said brightly. 'The lodgers are all getting on a bit; if they were to die, we could move into Crocus Street and share with Gammy. I'd really like that. The kids in Crocus Street are much friendlier than the ones in Sydenham Avenue. Well, there aren't many kids there, are there?'

'No, there aren't. But what about your Auntie Fee, Libby? She won't want to go on being a Wren when the war's over; how would you feel about sharing your life with her?'

Libby chuckled. 'It 'ud be an odd sort of life,' she observed. 'Auntie Fee can't cook, nor keep house, nor do marketing. I used to think she was really fun to be with, but I've heard Gammy say, over and over, that Auntie Fee doesn't pull her weight and it wouldn't be fair on Mummy, or

246

Gammy, to let them do all the work while Auntie Fee spent all her money on pretty clothes and wouldn't lift a finger. Here, Daddy, have another slice of toast. I've put the last of Mr Bryant's jam on it.'

Neil accepted the toast rather glumly, his daughter thought. 'Oh, well, I just thought I'd mention it,' he said. 'Don't say anything to Mummy when you next see her because I guess it wasn't such a good idea after all. Look, darling, I shall have to eat this toast on my way to the station or I'll miss my train and that would never do.'

Libby waved her father off rather forlornly, then returned to her own room. She did not expect to sleep again, having been so thoroughly roused, but lay down on the bed and had a little weep into her pillow, then settled herself to count her blessings for, after all, she had enjoyed every moment with Neil and told herself, stoutly, that there would be other visits, and perhaps next time Marianne could come as well.

In the middle of such cheery thoughts, she must have fallen asleep, only waking to the sound of Auntie's voice echoing hollowly up the stairs. 'Libby Sheridan, if we're going to church you'd best stir your stumps, young lady.'

Libby jumped off the bed and rushed to the washstand to slap her face with cold water and, hopefully, get rid of any sign of tears. She was still fully dressed since she had not bothered to take her clothes off when she had returned to her room after

Neil left. But she pushed her feet back into her slippers and hurried down to the kitchen, where she told Auntie, in a trembling voice, that Daddy had left to catch the early train at least two hours before.

If she expected Auntie to be shocked or even surprised, she was disappointed, for that sensible woman merely nodded grimly and began to pour the tea into two mugs. 'He said he must go after we heard the nine o'clock news last night,' she said. 'Well, you enjoyed his visit, and no doubt there will be another quite soon. Give Matthew a shout, dear. If we're going to church we need to stir ourselves because the horse won't attach himself to the cart without some effort on our part.'

Neil arrived in Lime Street, having had to get off the train at Edge Hill since the first night's raids had put the main line station out of action, and was shocked by the devastation all around him. He had known it would be bad, but had had no idea of the havoc which had been wreaked in his absence. There were huge craters in the road, severed tram lines reared up like angry snakes, and fires smouldered everywhere. Folk picked their way through the broken glass and rubble-strewn pavement, their expressions grim. Yet he was cheered by the fact that despite what they had obviously suffered, they made rude remarks about 'them bleedin' Nazis' as they met pals and neighbours. They shouted out to one another, giving information, cursing Hitler and the Luftwaffe and boasting that 'our boys in blue' would give the Nazis a bloody nose for what the bombs had done to their city.

Presently, Neil found himself faced with a huge bomb crater and asked a fat and cheerful woman in a stained floral overall how best to reach the flower streets. She pulled a face, advising him that he would have to walk, 'since the tram lines is buggered and buses rare as hens' teeth.'

Since she accompanied the words with a broad, gap-toothed grin, he answered her with equal cheerfulness, setting down his suitcase for a moment. 'I came into port last Wednesday and went straight out to North Wales,' he told her, 'so I had no idea of the extent of the damage. Shall I stick to the main road or would the side streets be a better bet?'

The woman considered. 'The trouble is, we've had three nights of this and with every raid the streets get worse,' she said. 'I know they say they're aimin' for the docks,' she chuckled richly, her fat cheeks pushing her dark eyes into merry slits, 'but if that's so, they're bloody bad aimers; wouldn't mind taking them on in a game o' darts. Why, they got the Mill Road infirmary last night. Must ha' killed dozens of poor buggers what were ill enough to start with, an' you can't say Mill Road is by the docks. Mind you, I've a cousin what fire watches there and she said the fire service an' the police an' that were wonderful. They got the mams and the babbies out of the maternity unit and into ambulances, and took 'em to other hospitals while the raid was still goin' on. One o' the fire fighters telled me appliances came all the way from Manchester to give a hand in puttin' out the flames. Aye, thinkin' on, you'd best stick to the main roads.'

Neil thanked her and took her advice, wondering where he should go in this neighbourhood to get information about his ship. He knew naval head-quarters, deeply buried underground, would be safe enough, but he did not mean to visit there until he had seen for himself how the *Sea Spurge* had fared, which he would do as soon as he had been to Crocus Street. He decided his best course would be to check Fiona's flat, because Gammy and Marianne would want to know how the younger girl had got on after last night's raid. Besides, he told himself, any man would look in on a sister-in-law when her home was surrounded by such destruction; people would think the worse of him if he simply bypassed the flat. At least the building appeared to be untouched, which was reassuring. Fiona lived on the first floor and he ran up the stairs and knocked on the door, suddenly aware that he was not in the least worried, but certain that Fiona was fine. She had probably spent the night in the bowels of the earth at naval HQ, but he waited anyway, and was not surprised when no one answered.

Feeling virtuous, Neil continued on his way, dodging bomb craters and tumbles of brick and cement, and presently arrived at Crocus Street. One glance was enough to tell him that despite its nearness to the docks, all was just as it should be.

However, as he walked along the pavement, he reminded himself that Marianne might have been at work, could easily have been caught up in a raid as she made her way to or from her factory on Long Lane. As it happened, he knew she had been working day shifts this week – earlies, too, so she should have been safe – yet nevertheless, he began to hurry. Because of her shifts, she played little part in local defence, particularly since the six-day week had come into force – and he knew sometimes the girls actually volunteered to work on their day off.

He glanced at the front door, then headed for the jigger. Reaching the yard, he ducked under the washing, banged on the back door and flung it open. As he had hoped they would be, both Marianne and Gammy were in the kitchen and clearly expecting him since Gammy, dispensing tea, simply smiled at him and reached for another mug, whilst Marianne ran straight into his arms. 'Oh, darling, darling Neil, I just knew you'd come,' she gabbled. 'There's such destruction, and the weather forecast is good, so the raiders are bound to come back, and I've been worried that they might sink your ship, but they haven't, it's OK.'

Neil returned her hug warmly, sliding a hand round the slender column of her neck and pushing his fingers up into her thick silky hair, telling himself that he was a lucky man to have such a beautiful, responsive wife. 'Thanks for the info, darling; that's a weight off my mind,' he said. 'I feel guilty that I didn't come home sooner, but the truth is I arrived at Tregarth, as you know, on Thursday afternoon and listened to the news that evening, and there was no mention of Liverpool. On Friday evening, when Miss Williams turned the set on, we found that the accumulator needed recharging, so we couldn't hear a thing. We took it down to the village yesterday, and when we heard the news last night we were horrified. I knew there was a train which left incredibly early, though it went to my heart to have to disappoint our darling Libby. She had made such plans . . . she and the crippled boy had baked a cake – there's a piece of it for you in my luggage – and introduced me to all their friends, and all the animals of course. But she was very good, very brave. I woke her in the early hours to explain that I must go and she hopped out of bed, dressed herself and came down to make me some breakfast.'

He grinned reminiscently. 'The first piece of toast burst into flames, but the second piece was delicious, and she insisted on spreading the third with some raspberry jam which she'd bought from a neighbour. I dare say some tears were shed when I wasn't around – she's only nine years old after all – but she showed me a cheerful face and waved me off just as bravely as I'd known she would. We're a lucky couple, darling Marianne, to have such a daughter.'

'I know we are,' Marianne said, leaning against his chest. 'But my love, you shouldn't refer to Matthew as "the crippled boy". He's got a name

– and you wouldn't like it if he were your child and folk called him a cripple, would you?'

Neil bit back the words 'but he is a cripple' and said: 'Sorry, didn't think. He's a nice lad; clever, too. Oh, by the way, I nipped up to Fiona's flat on my way here, just to check. She wasn't in, but the flat's undamaged so I guess she's all right.'

Marianne laughed. 'She heads for HQ like a rabbit bolting for its burrow the moment Moaning Minnie wails,' she said. 'Did you know she's got a new boyfriend? Someone quite high up in the service, apparently.'

Neil stared. 'Now how on earth would I know a thing like that?' he enquired. 'But I'm glad for her, of course. She's such a pretty girl, not the sort to be left on the shelf. What's his name?'

'I think it's Philip, but you know what with my working shifts and Fiona no longer living at home we hardly ever meet; two ships that pass in the night, you might say. And now, because of the raids, we see even less of each other.'

Gammy, sitting in her creaking old chair and sipping her tea, interrupted. 'I don't want to push you out, young Neil, but I think you ought to report to the nearest ARP post, 'cos that's what they're askin' servicemen to do. Believe me, the fellers want all the help they can get.'

'Right, I'll do that as soon as I've been to see the *Sea Spurge*,' Neil said immediately. 'I'll have to sleep aboard, of course . . .'

'Why don't you go home to Sydenham Avenue?'

Marianne asked rather plaintively. 'I could go with you, though it's an awfully long way to have to come to and from work. No, I suppose that was a stupid suggestion; I'm sorry I made it.'

Neil was beginning to reply, soothingly, when Gammy cut across him. 'No need for anyone to stay anywhere but here,' she said briskly. 'I'll sleep on the couch in the parlour and you two can have my double bed.'

Marianne beamed. 'It'll be grand to have you home for more than a few hours. As soon as you've drunk your tea and taken your case upstairs, you go off to the *Sea Spurge*. I'll come out with you – I'm helping the volunteers today. We're going to be roping off buildings which are in a dangerous condition, but it's difficult because a great many folk want to revisit their bombed homes and rescue anything not irretrievably damaged.'

Neil gazed at his wife with considerable respect. 'You're a great girl. I didn't know you had it in you,' he said admiringly. 'I shan't be two shakes of a lamb's tail; I'll just dump my suitcase and then we'll be off.' He turned to Gammy. 'And I won't refuse the offer of your bed; many thanks, Mother-in-law. You are good!'

By Sunday 11 May, the people of Liverpool were beginning to be cautiously optimistic that the Luftwaffe, having practically obliterated the city and the docks, had decided to move on to other targets. The weather remained fine, with a brilliant moon lighting up the city each night, yet the skies were silent. 'They're hitting London and moving further north,' Neil said authoritatively. 'They aren't going to waste their bombs when they think their job here is over. Now's the time to count the cost and start trying to put things right. What the Jerries don't realise is that despite the enormous number of deaths and the terrible destruction, they've not broken the spirit of Liverpudlians; quite the opposite in fact. Folk who grumbled and whined about rationing, shortages, long working hours and nothing to buy even if their pay was good are keener than ever to smash the enemy and prove that despite everything they're still in there fighting.'

He and Marianne were preparing for bed and Marianne, already clad in a thin lawn nightdress, turned to give him an impulsive hug. She thought he looked drawn and tired, yet there was a contentment in his face which had not been there for many months. She told herself that so many days of working side by side, whenever she was not on shift, had brought them closer than the eight years of happy marriage they had enjoyed before the war. Neil had told her he admired the way she coped, for though he had worked every bit as hard he did not have to do shifts at the factory as she did, which meant he usually got more sleep. However, the repair work on the *Sea Spurge* would be completed in a couple of days and she would sail for America, where she would pick up a convoy of merchantmen bringing desperately needed supplies to their beleaguered country.

'Darling, it's an awful thing to say, but I've enjoyed the last week more than I would have believed was possible,' Marianne said, her mouth close to his ear. 'Working together the way we have been has made all the tiredness and the stress worthwhile. I always miss you whenever you go away, but this time I don't know how I shall bear it. You're going into dreadful danger and I know there's nothing I can do to help you.'

Neil returned her hug warmly. 'You *do* help me,' he assured her. 'Just the knowledge that you care and are constantly thinking of me, and the fact that I'm making life easier for you when the convoys get through, is reward enough. And next time I'm home, please God, if there've been no more raids, Libby might be able to return to the city so that we can all spend time together.'

'I'm sure we'll manage something,' Marianne said, slipping into bed. 'Oh, Neil, we've only got two more days and then you'll be off, facing heaven above knows what dangers! If I think about it I'll drive myself mad, so I'll do my best to be sensible . . . but take care of yourself, my darling.'

Chapter Nine

October 1941

As Marianne emerged from the back door of the house in Crocus Street, the wind tore at the beret perched on her head and sent it skittering across the yard, so that wisps of her hair blew across her face, making her gasp with the strength of it. She ran in pursuit, snatched up her hat, then hesitated for a moment and decided to go back indoors to fetch a headscarf, for she and Fiona had arranged to meet outside St John's market and she knew that her sister, impeccably clad in her WRNS uniform, would expect Marianne to look as smart as she was herself.

As she re-entered the kitchen Gammy, who was sitting at the table, writing a letter, looked up in surprise. 'Well! You wasn't long, was you?' she enquired genially. 'Did you manage to get me some cookin' apples? And how about them chestnuts you was goin' to try to find? Me old teeth won't tackle 'em raw, nor roast, but I'll put aside a dozen or so and boil 'em in salt water; they're prime like that if your teeths is a bit wobbly like.'

Marianne laughed and pulled a face. 'Ha, ha, very funny,' she said. 'The wind's blowing a hooligan, as you used to say when we were kids, and my beret blew off, so I thought perhaps I'd do better with a headscarf; even the strongest gusts won't tear that off my head.' As she spoke, she picked up her headscarf and tied it firmly under her chin, then she opened the back door again and shot through it, shouting a farewell over her shoulder as she did so.

She hurried along to the tram stop and was almost there when she saw Bill Brett's sturdy figure ahead of her. She called to him but her voice was carried away by the wind, so she broke into a trot, grabbing his arm as she reached him. 'Bill!' she said breathlessly. 'Where are you off to? I'm going to meet my sister outside St John's market. We're having a girls' day out, doing a bit of shopping and having a bite of lunch.' She beamed up into his craggy, weather-beaten face. 'It's the last chance we'll get for a few days since Neil's ship should dock tomorrow, all being well. It's always a quick turn-round these days but he ought to manage at least one night ashore.'

'That's nice for you,' Bill said, grinning down at her. 'But how do you know when he'll dock? I thought that these things were state secrets, just about.'

Marianne returned his smile, her heart giving an anticipatory leap at the thought of seeing Neil so soon. They had had wonderfully loving times together ever since the May blitz, and she was hopeful that he might be able to get a few days off quite soon so that she could fetch Libby back to Crocus Street for a much longed for family reunion.

But Bill was still looking at her enquiringly and repeated his question. 'How d'you know when the *Sea Spurge* will dock? You sound pretty certain.'

'No one can be certain, but it's a great help having a sister who works at naval headquarters,' Marianne explained. 'The ships send signals, I suppose, so that the dockers can start unloading as soon the convoy steams into port.'

'Ah, I see. Well, as it's me day off I offered to do me landlady's messages, and while I'm out I'm goin' to see if I can find me some thick woollen socks ready for the winter,' Bill said as they climbed aboard the tram.

They found seats next to each other. 'Oh, Bill, there's no need for you to shop for socks,' Marianne said. 'If you buy some wool – make it thick, four-ply should do it – then Gammy and myself will knit them up for you with pleasure. In fact it would give us something to do in the evenings, when I'm not on shifts, and it's little enough in return for all you do for us.'

'That's awful good of you, but I don't like to impose,' Bill said gruffly. 'You've gorra husband to knit socks for, and it ain't as if I were in the services.'

'I'll knit your socks in a couple of evenings, if you just buy the wool,' Marianne said firmly. 'No argument. You'll need coupons, though.'

Bill thanked her and said he would get the wool

that very day, and the two conversed comfortably until they reached the city centre, when Marianne suggested he try a little shop she knew of on Bold Street, and they parted.

Fiona was already waiting when Marianne reached St John's market, looking truly glamorous in her uniform, apart from the hat. Marianne said as much. 'Someone told me they were going to change the pudding basins, but I see they haven't done so yet. I say, I wouldn't mind a couple of pairs of those black stockings. They're really nice, don't you think?'

'Oh, they're nice enough,' Fiona said. 'The trouble is they're part of our uniform, and if you've got slim legs like mine black stockin's make 'em look like liquorice sticks; at least that was what horrible Philip said the last time I met him off his ship.'

'He's a Jimmy the One on a destroyer, isn't he, like Neil was before he got his extra half,' Marianne said. 'I'd love to meet him, but what with my shifts and his sailings, I don't suppose I'll get the chance.'

'Oh, you'll meet him some time, I expect . . . if we go on seeing one another, of course,' Fiona said vaguely. 'If you've finished your messages, I'd like to take a look at some of the big shops; I could do with another lipstick and some face powder.'

The girls went from shop to shop, but no one had lipsticks or face powder in stock, so Fiona settled for a tiny jar of Pond's cold cream and a small pot of rouge, whose price tag made Marianne gasp, though Fiona paid the sum required without so much as lifting an eyebrow. Marianne, who had just bought a plain grey cardigan for her daughter with the last of her coupons and had spent rather more money than she had intended, envied her sister and hoped, ruefully, that Libby would appreciate the garment when winter set in.

After that, the two young women window-shopped in a desultory fashion before going along to Lyon's Corner House in Church Street and settling themselves in for a good gossip. Fiona said that she meant to pay for their meal, especially since she knew that the cardigan Marianne had bought for Libby had cost rather more than her sister had anticipated, so it was with a clear conscience that Marianne agreed to a proper hot dinner of steak and kidney pie, peas, carrots and mash, followed by apple tart and custard. Whilst they waited for their food to arrive, Marianne brought Fiona up to date with the happenings in Crocus Street and Long Lane.

'I've not yet told you, Fee, how grateful I am for the – the information regarding the *Sea Spurge*,' Marianne said, lowering her voice to a whisper. 'Ever since the May blitz, Neil and I seem to have fallen more deeply in love than ever. We went through a sticky patch when the war first started and we had to send Libby away. Neil really wanted me to stay in the country with her, or at least find war work somewhere less dangerous than Liverpool, and it was ages before I admitted that I'd moved in to Crocus Street with Gammy. Because he always seemed annoyed with me, I got terribly prickly and began to imagine things. Do you know, I'd almost convinced myself that he was taking a woman back to our house and sleeping with her in our bed!' She chuckled. 'Stupid, wasn't it? As though he'd do something so dreadful. But it was all in my mind, of course, because Neil is the most honourable man I know, and anyway, ever since the May blitz . . .'

At this point the nippy put two plates down in front of them, patted Fiona's shoulder in a familiar fashion, and asked if they wanted anything else. She waddled off when the sisters assured her that they needed nothing and Fiona, giggling, remarked that they would have to rename the nippies snailies, since young women had better things to do than to serve in restaurants and cafés.

'Oh, snailies is most unfair; I think they do pretty well,' Marianne objected. 'Now, Fee, tell me a bit about *your* life. Oh, I know your work is confidential, but you aren't in work twenty-four hours a day, seven days a week. You and I have one thing in common now which we didn't have before: we both spend a good deal of time waiting for our man's ship to dock. And when it does, of course, we can think of nothing else until his ship sails once more.'

Fiona stared at her. 'I don't know what you mean,' she said, rather huskily. 'Waiting for our man . . . oh, I *see*! But I'm not like you, tied to one feller. Of course I'm extremely fond of – of Philip, 'but I don't see any reason why I shouldn't accept other invitations when they're offered. He can't very well object – well, he doesn't know – and I'd go mad shut up in the flat when I'm not on duty.'

'Yes, and that flat,' Marianne said, reminded of a question she and Gammy had often discussed. 'How can you afford it, queen? I know you're pretty well paid now you're someone's secretary, but the girl you shared with left ages ago, and you've never replaced her, have you?'

'The girl I shared with – oh, you mean Mandy,' Fiona said. She pushed the pie round her plate, then cut off a tiny piece and ate it. 'Her father's a retired admiral, didn't I tell you? They've a big estate in Scotland, and loads of gelt. They've continued to pay the rent and I hand over what they call a small retainer. In a way, I'm a sort of caretaker. I keep the place clean, call in a plumber or an electrician if it's necessary, light fires in winter and open windows in summer . . . you know the sort of thing. I did suggest getting another Wren to share, but Mandy's parents said that they preferred to continue with the present arrangement. Any more questions, nosy?'

'Yes, lots,' Marianne said. 'Are you going to marry Philip? When the war's over I mean.'

To her astonishment, a bright flush burned up in her sister's face, and Fiona ducked her head and began scraping industriously at the remains of food on her plate. 'I dunno,' she muttered. 'Maybe . . .

maybe sooner than that. Anyway, it's my bleedin' business, not yours.'

Marianne stared, astonished by what seemed far too violent a reaction to a perfectly normal question. 'I'm sorry,' she said mildly. 'I didn't mean to intrude; it's the sort of question sisters ask each other, don't you think?'

'I don't know,' Fiona said, pushing her plate aside as the waitress returned with two rather small helpings of apple tart and custard. Marianne thanked the woman, feeling thoroughly uncomfortable and reflecting that she seemed to have a knack of rubbing Fiona up the wrong way. She looked down at the food before her. 'Goodness, there's scarcely enough on my plate to fill a hollow tooth! But it looks tasty.'

Fiona made no reply until the apple tart and custard had all gone, when she began to gather her gas mask case, hat and gloves in a rather final sort of way and Marianne thought, despairingly, that she would never understand the younger girl. Her sister had clearly taken offence over something Marianne had said and was about to storm off, so Marianne put out a detaining hand. 'Hang on, Fee. How about rounding off the meal with a nice cuppa? We don't meet often and if I've hurt your feelings by asking about your marriage plans, I'm sorry. Do sit down again, otherwise I'll have to leave as well, and this was supposed to be a girls' day out!'

Fiona, however, shook her head. 'No, I can't stop;

I've got to get back,' she said briefly. 'And you haven't offended me, I was being silly. If I decide to marry, I'll let you know.'

She turned away from the table as she spoke, but Marianne jumped to her feet and gave her sister an impulsive hug and a kiss on the cheek. 'Don't be cross, darling Fee,' she said coaxingly. 'Not when I'm so happy! Neil and I look like having two whole days together and we're planning to bring Libby home to Liverpool next time he gets leave, because the worst of the blitz seems to be over. Honest to God, Fee, all I want is for you to be as happy as us.'

Fiona jerked away, her cheeks flaming and her eyes suddenly hot and angry. 'For God's sake, Marianne, what a bloody stupid thing to do,' she hissed. 'What if someone was to see me being kissed in a public place, and me in uniform? I'd be in dead trouble, I'm tellin' you. As for leavin', there's no need for you to do so; you can stay here and sup your bloody tea till you're blue in the face, but I'm off, and don't you dare follow me.'

Marianne stared, suddenly feeling rage flower within her. She snatched up her marketing bag and gas mask case and shot to the cash desk, and, when Fiona would have stalked past, grabbed her arm. 'No you don't, my girl,' she said grimly. 'You can damned well pay your half of the bill even if you're no longer willing to pay mine – any more than I'd allow you to when you feel like this about me – and you can just apologise for the nasty, rude things you said, which I'm sure I'd done nothing to deserve.'

Fiona began to answer, choked, and leaned over in her turn to plant a kiss on Marianne's cheek. 'I'm – I'm real sorry,' she said humbly. 'I'm – I'm not very well, queen; haven't been meself for weeks. I worry something awful about – about my feller, and it breaks me up to think we might never have a chance of marrying. Will you forgive me?'

'Oh, darling Fee, of course I will,' Marianne said warmly, all her anger forgotten. 'You're my little sister, I'd forgive you anything.' She had thought that this would comfort Fiona, but instead her sister began to cry so hard that tears positively fountained from her eyes, and she gave Marianne a convulsive hug and shot out of the restaurant.

Leaving me to pay the entire bill, Marianne thought, with a mixture of amusement and annoyance. Oh, poor Fiona, will she never grow up? We all worry dreadfully over our menfolk, but we have to learn not to take it out on others.

She began to fish for her purse as the woman at the cash desk turned towards her. 'That'll be ten and fourpence, madam,' she said. Marianne paid and found her annoyance with Fiona had resurfaced. Now she would have to walk home, having spent even her tram fare on their two lunches. Returning to the table they had just vacated, she produced her last coin – a threepenny bit – and left it for the waitress, then went out on to Church Street sadly aware that her lovely day had been spoiled.

She turned towards Ranelagh Street, but had scarcely taken more than half a dozen steps when someone seized her arm and she looked round into Fiona's pink and tear-stained face. 'I'm sorry I lit out just now; I'm sorry for everything,' Fiona muttered. She thrust a rather tattered ten shilling note into her sister's hand. 'I can't think what come over me, leaving you to pay the bill, but that should pretty well cover it, I reckon. I'm a rotten sister to you, but I do love you, honest to God I do. It's – it's just the worry, you know, and – and – I forgot I had a message for you, from your Neil. If you're free tomorrow mornin' – and I know you are – he'll meet you under the clock just outside the dock gates at noon.' She gazed anxiously into Marianne's eyes. 'You'll be there, won't you? Promise me you'll be there.'

'Oh, Fee, of course I will,' Marianne cried, pleasure and excitement banishing every other feeling. 'Thank you, thank you! Outside the dock gates, under the clock. Oh, you are a darling! See you soon, I hope; come round to Crocus Street . . .'

But Fiona, with a brief wave, was heading towards Lime Street as fast as she could go and Marianne, burdened with her bulging marketing bag, did not even attempt to follow. Instead, she walked towards the nearest tram stop and was presently delighted to see Bill at the head of the queue. She would have joined him, but he spotted her and came to the back of the queue instead, triumphantly opening his canvas holdall to show her several skeins of thick and serviceable grey wool lying on top of the provisions he had bought for his landlady. 'As you can see, me shoppin' was successful,' he told her, glancing approvingly at her own large bag. 'Here, let me carry that for you; it looks perishin' heavy.'

'It is, but there's no need for either of us to carry it until the tram arrives,' Marianne said, standing it down upon the pavement. 'I bought Libby a nice grey cardigan for school and Fiona bought us a hot dinner in Lyon's, so I've done pretty well, all things considered.' She lowered her voice. 'Neil will be home tomorrow and I'm to meet him under the clock down by the docks at noon. I'm so excited! I shall pop into the butcher's as we pass and see if he's got any liver or kidneys, because offal's not on ration and Neil loves a fry-up. I've still got two of the onions left which you gave me a couple of weeks ago, too.'

Marianne was as good as her word and stopped off at the butcher's, though she had to get quite cross with Bill to prevent him from accompanying her, since he could not bear to think of her burdened by all her shopping. Marianne, however, laughed at him. 'Don't be so silly, Bill,' she said. 'How do you think I manage when you're not around? Are you on shift this evening? If so, I'll maybe see you later.'

Marianne considered it fortunate that the Wainwrights had always shopped at Mr Hartley's butcher's shop on Stanley Road, for she knew that if anything off ration was available it would be saved for his old customers. Sure enough, when she left his premises, it was with a small packet of liver and two sausages stowed away in her bag.

That evening, too excited at the thought of Neil's imminent return to settle to anything much, she began to knit Bill's socks and had actually turned the heel and was halfway up the leg before taking to her bed. Next day, full of delightful anticipation, she helped Gammy to make a liver casserole and got out a strawberry jelly and a tin of sliced peaches, which she had been saving for Libby's return. She made up the jelly, added the peaches, and stood the bowl on the slate slab in the pantry, whilst Gammy laughed at her indulgently and promised to have a meal ready on the table by one o'clock at the latest.

'Thank God it's not too windy today,' Marianne said, carefully combing her shining bob round her finger ends and slipping on her cream woollen jacket and a cheeky little scarlet beret.

'Come straight home, queen,' her mother called as she left the house. 'Good thing you're not on afternoon shift; I changed the bed this morning so that you've got nice clean sheets.'

'Thanks, Ma,' Marianne called, slamming the door.

She reached her rendezvous in good time. There were a great many people about but Neil was not one of them, though presently she saw him hurrying in her direction. He looked pale and worried, and when she ran towards him and tried to cast herself into his arms he held her back from him, staring seriously into her face.

'Oh, darling Neil, it's wonderful to see you! Fiona said she thought you'd be in port for a couple of days at least. Of course I hope and pray that you and the *Sea Spurge* got through without a scratch, but if your ship needs attention it would be grand if we could get to see Libby, if only for a few hours.'

Rather to her surprise, Neil stared at her as though he could not understand the words she had spoken. 'See Libby!' he said blankly. 'But – but surely you've seen Fiona? Surely she told you?'

'Oh yes, I saw her yesterday; she bought me a dinner at Lyon's and told me when and where to meet you,' Marianne said. 'But we didn't mention Libby . . . yes we did though, come to think! I had bought her a warm cardigan because it gets jolly cold in the Welsh hills in winter.'

Neil's blond eyebrows drew together. 'When and where to meet me?' he said, with what seemed like undue emphasis. 'I asked her to tell you – oh, dammit, are you sure she didn't say anything?'

Marianne frowned. 'She said all sorts of things,' she said slowly. 'She – she was in a funny sort of mood. She said she was so worried over her fellow – Philip, isn't it? – that she couldn't think straight.'

As they talked, they had been walking up towards the main road. People were pushing past them in both directions and Neil gave a snort of sheer annoyance. 'Your bloody sister!' he said furiously. 'This is just what I wanted to avoid; trying to have a serious conversation in a crowded place. Look, is there anywhere near here where we can sit down and have a cup of tea whilst I tell you . . . oh, hang it . . . whilst we talk?'

They were on the edge of the pavement and Marianne tried to tuck her hand into Neil's elbow and felt, for the first time for many weeks, his instinctive withdrawal. Her heart sank. Oh, not again, she prayed silently. Not more misunderstanding, ill feeling and consequent misery. 'What's wrong with Crocus Street?' she asked, after a moment's thought. 'We could go there . . .'

'Oh, sure. I can just see myself asking you for a divorce whilst your mother looks on,' Neil said savagely, then clapped a hand to his mouth before dropping it to his side once more. 'I told Fiona to warn you, begged her to do so, and now I end up having to tell you something I never dreamed I'd have to say.'

Marianne blinked. 'A – a divorce?' she quavered. 'Neil, you're joking, aren't you? You can't mean it! Why should I want to divorce you?'

Unconsciously, perhaps, Neil was gripping her wrists so hard that her hands ached. 'It is I who want a divorce, and I'm willing to give you grounds,' he said through clenched teeth. 'I've – I've met someone else, but I suppose you know that.'

Marianne jerked her wrists out of her husband's grip. 'But why now? I – I thought everything was right between us again, though before the May blitz you often got annoyed with me for no reason I could understand. What's happened to make you even consider breaking up our marriage?'

Neil sighed and looked round wildly, then pointed to the opposite pavement. 'There's a teashop over there,' he said, and caught Marianne's arm in a far from friendly grip. 'If you must have the truth, I fell in love with someone else within two years of Libby being born. It wasn't my fault. You weren't fun any more. All you thought about was the baby and the house, and I felt excluded. As far as you were concerned, you could take me or leave me. But my new friend was always a good laugh and I soon realised our whole marriage had been a horrible mistake.' He gave a short bark of bitter laughter. 'I'd married the wrong bloody woman! And then, last time I was home, she told me she was pregnant. She said either I married her, or got out of her life completely.'

'Then why don't you do that?' Marianne said, feeling the first stirring of hot anger break through the coldness of shock. 'Why don't you tell her to find some other sap?'

As soon as the words were out of her mouth she regretted them, but though Neil flushed, he answered her so quickly that she guessed the same thought must have occurred to him. 'Because you bore me,' he said, and there was a flick of contempt in his tone which stung like a whiplash. 'My friend is exciting, inventive, the perfect foil for a man who spends most of his life, at present, dodging danger. We married when you were just a kid and I wasn't a great deal older, and I thought a pretty, biddable girl would suit me down to the ground, but now I know I was wrong. I want my freedom and you've got to give it to me. The girl I mean to marry is due in March and I want everything shipshape and Bristol fashion by then. In fact sooner, if possible.'

'You claim to be in love with a lively young girl; why don't you say it's my sister?' Marianne said through trembling lips. 'I've suspected for a long time now . . . oh, my God, I can't bear it!'

For a second, he was so surprised that he let go of her arm and stepped into the road, seeing a gap in the traffic, but Marianne was before him. She darted away, almost blinded by the tears in her eyes, heard the squeal of brakes and the slither of tyres, the shouts of warning. She felt her feet slip on the road surface and heard a high, terrified shriek, though she did not know if it came from her mouth or another's. As she went down, a picture formed in her mind, a tombstone, vividly lit as if by a flash of lightning: *Marianne Sheridan, unbeloved wife of* . . . She stared at it, a moan of denial on her lips, but the tombstone was growing smaller and smaller and the darkness larger and larger, until at last the stone had completely disappeared and she was spinning down, down, down, into pain and unfathomable blackness.

*   *   *

For a moment shock froze Neil to the spot; then he ran forward and dropped to his knees beside his wife's inanimate form. There was blood everywhere; Marianne's hair was soaked in it, and a woman kneeling on her further side looked up, saw him, and told him crisply to get an ambulance. Above his head a man was telling anyone who would listen that the girl must have seen him, must have meant to do what she did. 'She turned her head and ran straight under me wheels,' he said, his voice hoarse with shock. 'And that there dray – well, the horse I mean – may have got her first; I aren't sure which of us . . .'

'It don't matter which of us gorr'er first 'cos the poor little bleeder's a goner,' the heavily built man at the horse's head said in a cockney accent. He stared belligerently at Neil. 'The lady told you to get an ambulance. You ain't doin' much good kneelin' there sayin' your perishin' prayers; it'll take more'n that to bring her rahnd.'

Neil stumbled to his feet. 'I – I'm her husband,' he said huskily. 'I've got to stay else they won't know who she is. Let someone else go.'

The woman who had commanded him to fetch help reached across and patted his hand. 'Sorry, chuck, I didn't realise,' she said. 'And don't you go despairin' 'cos it ain't as bad as it looks. The horse's hoof caught her across the skull and scalps bleed like crazy. I were a nurse years ago so I know better than to let anyone move her. We'll know more when the fellers . . . ah, thank God.' She got clumsily to her feet as a couple of uniformed men, carrying a stretcher, pushed through the crowd.

Neil stood up. 'She's my wife,' he said, 'though I think she's . . . she ran straight into the road and was hit by at least two vehicles. I don't want the drivers to bear the blame for her death.'

The elder man was already easing Marianne's body gently on to a brown blanket, and as the two men rolled her with the utmost gentleness on to the stretcher Neil saw her face for the first time and turned away, retching into the gutter. He would never have known her, for the face now turned towards him bore no resemblance to the woman who had run into the road no more than ten or fifteen minutes earlier. But the nurse who had first spoken to him grabbed his shoulders, shook him hard and propelled him towards where Marianne was being loaded into the ambulance. 'This is no time to give way,' she said briskly. 'Pull yourself together, man; I see you're an officer in the Navy, so you'll have seen worse. Gerrin that ambulance. I'll get names and addresses, 'cos even though it looked to me to be more your wife's fault than anyone else's – I see'd her bolt out into the road wi'out lookin' to right nor left – we'll still mebbe need statements from witnesses. The scuffers will come to the hospital and likely interview you, 'cos I can't see your wife bein' able tell anyone anythin' much.'

Neil thanked her and scrambled into the ambulance, keeping his gaze averted from Marianne's blood-boltered form. The vehicle jerked, then stopped, and there was a frantic banging on the back doors. The ambulance man opened them and peered out, and the woman who had spoken to Neil shouted: 'What's your wife's name, mister? The scuffers will want to know.'

'Marianne Sheridan,' Neil shouted, and the man closed the doors again. Neil looked across at him. 'She's gone, hasn't she?' he muttered. 'No one could live after that.'

'She's gorra pulse, mate,' the ambulance man said, rather austerely. 'I seen worse recover. Oh, I ain't sayin' she'll be cookin' your breakfast tomorrer morning, but she seems young and strong, so she'll mebbe come through all right.'

Neil tried to say she was not yet thirty, but the words would not come, and neither man spoke again until the ambulance had drawn to a halt. The driver ran round and opened the back doors, and the two men manhandled the stretcher into the building, whilst Neil followed. He told himself that if she was pronounced dead, he would go straight to Crocus Street, which was only a short walk from the Stanley, and break the news to Gammy before getting in touch with Fiona. He would have to find some good reason for the accident which did not include the truth, though he supposed that since he and Fiona would now be free to marry the truth would dawn on Gammy soon enough.

Then he remembered that he had been offered

the captaincy of a destroyer based at Southampton. He and Fiona would move south and take Libby with them. Fiona adored her niece and he knew the feeling was mutual, so he had no doubt that, once Libby had got over the trauma of her mother's death, what had happened might well be for the best. Of course, Libby must never know why the accident had happened, but as he followed the stretcher into the hospital Neil told himself that Marianne had run into the road deliberately. She had known her marriage was over, her husband in love with a sister she adored, and her future in ruins. She had been unable to face what lay ahead – the humiliation, and the knowledge that she had been unable to retain her husband's love – and had decided to end it all. It was not my fault, Neil told himself stubbornly. I have as much right to happiness as the next man. What was it the Duke of Windsor said when he gave up the throne of England? . . . *without the help and support of the woman I love* . . .

'Sorry, old man, but I can't let you go any further. I know she's your wife, but we need to see what's what and you'd only be in the way . . .'

Neil jumped as a man in a white coat, with a stethoscope round his neck, addressed him. For a moment, he just stared blindly at the tired face, then he felt relief wash over him. He had no desire whatsoever to follow the stretcher through the swing doors on his left, uncompromisingly labelled 'Theatre'. But what was he meant to do?

It would look extremely callous if he were to leave the hospital and go to Crocus Street; even more callous if she were still hanging on to a thread of life, though he could not imagine that that was possible. What he could do, however, was ring naval headquarters, for there was a public telephone in the foyer, and no doubt someone on the reception desk would give him change. Yes, he would ring through and ask to speak to Fiona, though perhaps he had better wait until the doctors had delivered their verdict. Once he knew Marianne was dead ... but he was suddenly shocked that he could even think such a thing. He had loved her once, God knew, and in an odd sort of way he loved her still. She was, after all, the mother of his beloved child, and he knew her to be both a good and loving daughter and a fond sister. He should be praying for her survival, but could she face life with both beauty and health gone? She might never be able to look after her own child again, might need help with the most basic tasks; might, in fact, be little better than a ... might never again recognise any of them as the family she once adored.

But the doctor was still speaking and Neil thought, savagely, that he must pull himself together. Whatever happened, he must never tell anyone, not even Fiona, that he had asked Marianne for a divorce seconds before the accident. From now on, he would be living a lie and must have his wits about him. He began to listen to the doctor's words.

'. . . next few hours are crucial,' the man was saying. 'You must have realised that your wife's accident was an extremely serious one. You've seen she's in a very bad way and I can tell you now that she has broken bones and probably internal injuries as well. In addition, the blow to the skull is almost certain to have caused a fracture, and such fractures are slow to heal. I can't give you a prognosis until we've taken a good look at her and this, I'm afraid, will take time. However, there is a comfortable waiting room three doors back along the corridor. I'll get a member of staff to bring you a cup of tea, and when we have news I'll either come to you myself or send a senior member of the nursing staff. If you leave the waiting room for any reason – you may want to telephone a relative to make arrange-ments – then tell them on reception that you are Mr Sheridan, husband of the road traffic accident in theatre three, and where you can be found.'

'Right. Thank you very much, doctor,' Neil said. 'I think I should get in touch with my mother-in-law, because she'll be expecting us for lunch and will worry when we don't turn up.'

The doctor, who had been turning away, paused. 'Do you have any idea of the time, Mr Sheridan?' he enquired gently. 'Unless your mother-in-law has her midday meal very late indeed, she will already be worrying. It's after two o'clock.'

By nine o'clock that night, Neil hated the waiting room more than he had ever hated anywhere before in the whole of his life. He hated the cracked brown linoleum on the floor, the peeling beige-coloured paint on the walls, the piles of tatty magazines and the unyielding and extremely uncomfortable Rexine-covered bench. When he had entered the waiting room, it had been packed. Weary men with anxious faces, women who cried into large handkerchiefs, a soldier who kept telling anyone who would listen that his wife had crushed her hand whilst trying to get a heavy sheet through the mangle, a couple of sailors who eyed Neil covertly and said they were there to see fellow seamen who had been badly burned when their ship had caught fire during a torpedo attack.

There had been coming and going, of course. Nurses in stiffly starched uniforms, doctors with bloodstains on their white coats, an occasional orderly, had bustled in and out, and every time the door opened Neil hoped that it would be news for him. Twice, indeed, he had been called into the corridor by Dr Redmond, the registrar who had admitted Marianne. On both occasions he had told Neil that his wife was still alive, though they now knew that she had indeed fractured her skull. 'When she goes up to the ward, you may see her for two minutes only,' he had said. 'You probably won't recognise her because we've had to shave her head, but that shouldn't worry you. The surgeon in charge thinks she'll be on the ward in an hour or so.'

Wearily Neil had returned to the waiting room.

He had managed to get hold of Fiona and thought he had explained the situation without giving anything away. He had told her that he and Marianne had met under the clock as arranged and had agreed to have a pot of tea and a plate of scones together at a little café on the other side of Stanley Road. He had told her he had had no chance to mention even the word divorce, had said that Marianne had been happy and full of pleasure at their reunion, so happy that she had dived into the road whilst chatting to him over her shoulder. The accident had been so quick, so totally unexpected, that he had had no chance to find out whether Fiona had mentioned the matter, but thought from Marianne's gaiety that she had not.

'Oh, thank God, thank God I said nothing,' Fiona had breathed into the telephone. 'At least I have nothing to reproach myself for, and nor have you, my darling. Will it be long before she's better, though?'

Neil had minimised the accident, and had asked Fiona to go round to Crocus Street and explain to Gammy what had happened, not forgetting to tell her that Marianne would not be allowed visitors until the next day.

'Mam'll want to come, but I'm too ashamed in case Marianne guesses about us,' Fiona had said. 'Of course I can't prevent me mam from joining you in the waiting room, but perhaps if I tell her she can't see Marianne till tomorrow she'll be sensible and stay away.'

Gammy had not been sensible, of course. She had come to the hospital, hoping to be allowed to see her daughter, had waited with her son-in-law for an hour, and by what for Neil had been a great piece of good fortune had been mistaken for somebody else. The fat little nurse who had come bustling into the waiting room had assured her that her daughter was doing well and would be pleased to see her for a short while after the doctors had done their rounds the following day. Gammy, much relieved, had hurried off home to get her lodgers their evening meal, and had actually suggested that Neil might leave his post for long enough to enjoy the liver and onion casserole which his wife had so lovingly prepared. Neil had laughed artificially and said she must save him a nice big portion, waved her off in the foyer and returned to his vigil.

Now, with the hateful clock on the hateful wall ticking its hateful way past nine o'clock, the waiting room was almost empty, save for Neil himself and a large, quiet man, who sat opposite, an elderly magazine spread out on his knees, though Neil noticed that he had not turned a page once in the last half-hour. The two men had sat in silence all that time, without once seeing a member of staff, when Neil decided he must speak or burst. He leaned forward. 'You've been here a while, mate. Is it your wife' – he jerked a thumb – 'on one of the wards?'

The man looked up and gave him a half-smile,

revealing crooked white teeth. 'No, it's an old pal,' he said. 'You?'

Neil had been eager that no one should know any more than was absolutely necessary, but all of a sudden he realised that to tell a total stranger the whole truth of how the accident had happened would be as big a relief as he could imagine. Ships that pass in the night, he thought confusedly. Two men thrown together by circumstance, who would almost certainly never meet again, for no matter what happened to Marianne he had accepted the command of HMS *Irascible* and his home port, in future, would be Southampton.

The man was looking at him enquiringly. 'Your wife, is it? I hope she's not hurt bad . . . or is she expectin', like?'

Neil leaned forward, elbows on knees, one hand cupping his chin. 'She ran into the road and was hit by a van and a brewer's dray,' he said heavily. 'I thought she'd been killed outright, but it seems not to be so. And . . . oh, God, it was all my fault! If I'd realised . . . if I'd thought . . . but she just turned away from me and ran into the road. If she doesn't recover I'll never know whether she was trying to kill herself or simply making for the café where we'd planned to have a cup of coffee and a chat.'

The man leaned forward and stared hard into Neil's face. 'Your fault? No, mate, you don't want to go blamin' yourself for what you couldn't possibly have prevented. Oh, I dare say it's natural that you should feel bad about it, but what could you have done?'

'It wasn't what I did but what I said,' Neil admitted heavily. 'I – I'd just asked her for a divorce.'

The man sitting opposite him looked appalled. 'A divorce? But she must have known things weren't right between you! And no woman would run into the road just because . . . though I've only ever known one woman real well, and that were me wife. But my feelin' is you're blamin' yourself for what ain't nothin' to do wi' you, not really.' Once more he leaned forward. 'I know wharrit says on the fillums an' that, but no sensible woman kills herself for – well, for love.'

'I hope to God you're right,' Neil muttered. 'But she's in an awful state . . . fractured skull, facial injuries . . . and she – she was the prettiest thing.'

'Then why did you ask her for a divorce?' the man said bluntly. 'It's clear as daylight you're still fond of her, or I dare say you wouldn't be waiting here now, lerralone admittin' to a total stranger that you're feelin' guilty over what happened.'

Neil frowned down at his shoes, trying to work it out for himself. Finally, he spoke. 'I guess it's because I'm in love with somebody else, someone younger and livelier. If I'm honest, I fell out of love with my wife after our kid was born, and into love with the other girl a couple of years later. I swear to you that I did my best to remain faithful, but it got more difficult as time went on. My wife

284

thought of nothing but the child, the house, nourishing meals and occasional trips to see my family in Devon. She never wanted to go dancing or to be alone with me. The truth is, we were just a couple of kids when we married, full of romantic ideas. It was all she wanted – her home, her child, her man – but it wasn't enough for me. I've been on Atlantic convoys since the beginning of the war and when I got into port . . . well, it was no excuse, I suppose, but things weren't good between us.'

There was a short silence, then the man scratched his head, looking doubtfully across at Neil. 'You've not said, but I guess you and this lively young gal had been carryin' on for some considerable time. So why had you not asked for a divorce before? Or can I guess?'

Neil nodded. 'She's expecting a child,' he said baldly. 'She told me I'd got to choose – my wife or herself. And dammit, there was no choice, not for me. So I asked my wife . . .'

The door opened. Dr Redmond stood there, looking tired to death, but he smiled as he gestured to Neil to follow him. 'We've done all we can for tonight, and we shan't be able to tell you anything much until she regains consciousness,' he said as they walked together down the corridor. 'I'll just let you have a peep at her, and then you really must go home. The operation has relieved the pressure on her brain, so she's out of the worst danger, for the moment at any rate.'

They reached the ward and Neil saw Marianne

lying flat on her back with tubes leading into her thin little wrists. She was covered in bandages, almost unrecognisable; he took only one quick, conscience-stricken glance before turning away, feeling his stomach heave.

'All right? Come back around eleven tomorrow,' the doctor said, steering him out of the ward once more. 'She's got more than a fifty-fifty chance, so don't despair.'

Neil muttered something appropriate and headed back towards the foyer. He popped into the waiting room as he passed, but it was empty, and he found he was relieved. He would go to Crocus Street and try to snatch some sleep before having to tell Gammy what had really happened and returning here tomorrow.

Outside, it was cold and clear, with a brisk wind blowing off the Mersey and a thin moon dodging the streaky clouds. She's alive, Neil told himself, and was surprised to find himself honestly grateful. No matter what happened now, if she lived he would have nothing to reproach himself for. Neil quickened his stride, optimism growing. It would be all right!

Chapter Ten

October came to the valley, as Auntie assured them it always did, with strong winds which tugged the coloured leaves off the trees and swirled them round at head height before dropping them in piles on the track. Libby was intrigued to learn both from Rhys and from other children at the village school that it was considered very lucky to catch a falling leaf before it could touch the ground. Consequently, she spent a good deal of time on the walks to and from the village leaping and bounding 'like a perishin' kangaroo', as Matthew put it. She managed to catch a number of leaves in this way – red, orange, yellow and crisp and crackly brown – and was proud of her good luck collection though Matthew, despite the disadvantage of his wheelchair, had managed to collect almost as many. Rhys, not the most agile of boys, barely got into double figures but said scornfully that catching leaves was for girls, though Libby was glad that he never so much as hinted at such a thing in Matthew's hearing.

Matthew was still Libby's best friend and the person she most enjoyed spending time with, but there was no doubt that he was no longer the cheerful, easy-going lad who had first introduced Libby to Tregarth. With his fourteenth birthday, it was as though he had decided that being stuck in a wheelchair, dependent upon others, was not for him. He got Rhys and Libby to help him out of his chair whenever Auntie was not around, and the three of them stomped around the kitchen, or rather two of them stomped whilst poor Matthew's white and skinny legs simply trailed uselessly behind him, twitching from time to time and causing Matthew to mutter beneath his breath words Libby had never heard uttered before. For the first time, he became impatient with himself and also with others. Reading had always been his greatest pleasure but sometimes he would shy a book across the room, saying that it was nonsense, that the author should be ashamed, that he had never read such twaddle in his life.

After some weeks of this, Libby buttonholed Auntie when she was milking in the cowshed, and asked her why Matthew had changed so much and was being so difficult. Auntie's head, in its old tweed cap, turned sideways so that she could look at Libby as she considered her question. 'Ever heard of puberty, my love?' she asked at length. 'That's what your poor old pal is suffering from.'

'Oh, poor Matthew!' Libby gasped, a hand flying to her mouth. 'Is it dangerous, Auntie? Can you catch it? Is it a boy thing or could a girl get it as well?'

Auntie snorted. 'It's not a disease, it's a way of saying that a boy or a girl is growing up,' she explained. 'Everyone has to go through it, usually when they're thirteen or fourteen. It's – it's difficult to describe and it's difficult to live through, because what it amounts to is . . . oh, dear, what is the best way to explain? Tadpoles turn into frogs . . . no, that won't do: you'll be expecting Matthew to go green and jump into the nearest pond. It's the time in a child's life when they are almost adults. They are leaving childish things behind but are not yet mature enough to be counted as grown-ups. They feel they are neither one thing nor the other; they aren't calves or lambs, but they aren't bulls or sheep, either. Does that make sense, Libby?'

'It makes a kind of sense,' Libby said rather doubtfully. 'Is it being a sort of half and half which makes Matthew so bad-tempered? But Rhys is a year older than Matthew, and I can't remember him being anywhere near as cross.'

'Rhys doesn't have Matthew's problems,' Auntie said. 'Besides, he knows what's happening to him and I don't suppose Matthew does. He just feels frustrated and misunderstood. Have you noticed his voice is changing? Well, that's another sign of puberty: when a boy talks like a boy one minute and like a man the next.'

Libby clapped a hand to her mouth, then spoke through her fingers. 'Oh, Auntie, and I told him to shut up when we were coming home two days ago, because we were singing "Blueberry Hill", with Rhys and Matthew doing the Fats Domino bits, and Matthew's voice kept going all squeaky and spoiling it. Goodness, will my voice go all deep? If it does, I'll have to resign from the choir.'

Auntie laughed, clearly hearing the note of hope in Libby's voice, but shook her head. 'And wouldn't it upset you not to have to attend church regularly! Not that you do; I've never met anyone more adept at thinking up excuses. But no, things happen to girls all right; you'll need a bust bodice – what they call a brassiere these days – as your figure changes, but your voice will stay the same. So do you think you can put up with Matthew being a bit scratchy for a year or so?'

'Gracious, will it take that long?' Libby asked, awed. 'But now that I know what's happening, it'll be much easier. It was not knowing why Matthew seemed so cross that was horrid.' She glanced quickly sideways at Auntie, then bent down and whispered in her ear. 'Matthew's never said not to tell you, so I'm not breaking a confiwhatsit, but he's trying to learn to walk. Is that part of puberty too?'

Auntie, who had continued to milk on and off throughout their conversation, stripped the teats, picked up her bucket, and got laboriously to her feet, her free hand in the small of her back. 'I'm getting old and rheumaticky,' she remarked, standing the bucket well out of harm's way, and returning her milking stool to its usual place. 'And yes, Matthew wanting to walk is all a part of growing up. Poor old Matthew, poor brave lad. But I'm sure that now you understand, you'll do everything in your power to help him to get through this difficult time, as I shall myself.'

Because children who lived at the head of the valley had so far to walk, they were sent home from school half an hour earlier than the rest. They had each been given a brand new exercise book and told that they were expected to use it as a diary which must be filled in every day. Matthew, Rhys and Libby felt cheated and were determined to make their diaries as boring as possible, which would serve Mr Tarporley, the headmaster, right, since he and other members of staff collected the diaries on Fridays and returned them to the children each Monday morning. However, despite these resolves, Libby and several of the other children found keeping the diaries engrossing, the evacuees finding the marshalling of facts a great help when they were writing their weekly letters home.

On this particular day they were in luck, for as they emerged from the schoolyard Rhys's father, who had been picking up sacks of animal feed in the old farm cart, stopped beside them and bade them jump in. 'You'll want to get on with them diaries,' he remarked with a slow grin, helping his son to hump the wheelchair and its occupant aboard. 'I know our Rhys can't wait to get on paper that Millie give birth to five dog pups and two bitches last night.'

Libby giggled. She knew Rhys hated writing and usually produced no more than half a page a day, whereas she covered sheet after sheet and was already on her second exercise book, but she also knew that their pal could wax eloquent over farming matters. Since Millie's progeny, all excellent, intelligent border collies, who seemed to know by instinct how to control a flock of sheep, would be much in demand, Rhys would enjoy describing each one in his diary. The fact that he was to be allowed the pick of the litter would also be mentioned and the pup of his choice described in much detail.

'Thank you ever so much for waiting, sir,' Matthew said as he settled himself and saw his wheelchair propped up amongst the feed sacks. 'We'll write up our diaries and then have a bit of time to ourselves outside before it's too dark.'

Mr Evans dropped them off actually in the Tregarth yard, Rhys having first extracted a promise from them both that they would come up to the Evanses' farm as soon as they had done their chores so that he could show them Millie's pups. Libby and Rhys jumped down, hauled the wheelchair off the cart, and helped Matthew into it. Then Rhys got back into the cart and Libby ran ahead to open the back door so that Matthew could wheel straight in. There was a slight step from the yard to the kitchen but Matthew knew exactly how best to enter, lifting his front wheels up and crashing them on to the kitchen floor, and then hefting the back wheels bodily and pretending not to notice Libby's tactful shove from behind. Indeed, Libby reflected as they entered the warm kitchen, his arms were so strong that he scarcely needed any help with the wheelchair now.

Auntie was washing eggs at the sink but turned a surprised gaze on them as Libby shut the door. 'You're early,' she remarked. 'Guess what's for supper?'

Both children grinned and answered in chorus, 'Casseroled rabbit and onions!', Matthew adding: 'I'd know that smell anywhere. I guess Dewi got lucky with his traps in the long coppice.'

'That's it,' Auntie said. 'What'll you do? It's too early to collect today's laying, and no point bringing the cows in. Better write your diaries, get it over with.'

Matthew gave a martyred sigh and fished his diary out of his satchel, but Libby produced her own with some satisfaction. There were more red marks in hers than in Matthew's – spelling was not her strong point – but then there were more stars, too, and some very nice comments. Today, she reflected, she would only do a page now, and then she could add to it after she had seen the newborn puppies.

For half an hour the kitchen was silent. Matthew wrote a line, chewed the end of his pencil, gazed out of the window, wrote another line. Libby scribbled away, though she also chewed the end of her pencil from time to time as a word or a phrase escaped her. Auntie turned to stare, curiously, at the two exercise books.

'You didn't write much, Matthew,' she commented. 'Goodness, boy, you've only managed three lines and young Libby here has done a whole page. Still, perhaps by this evening . . .'

'Oh, her!' Matthew said dismissively. 'She's got a whole life to write about; I've only got half.'

The remark was so bitterly said and so unlike Matthew that Libby gasped; how could he say such a thing? His life was as full as hers even though there were things she could do which he could not. She glanced quickly across at him and saw that his face was red, and guessed that he had embarrassed himself probably even more than he had embarrassed her. But Auntie took the remark at its face value. 'Life is what you make it,' she said quietly. 'There are folk round here who would tell you I only had half a life because I'm a spinster and have no man or child of my own. But I'm telling you, Matthew, that it's not so. My life is different from that of a married woman because I only have myself to rely on, only myself to please and to blame, but it's the life I've chosen and I wouldn't change it or give any man the power to say do or don't.'

'But it's not the same for me,' Matthew mumbled. 'You say you chose not to marry. I had no choice, Auntie. I got infantile paralysis and it took away my legs. I don't s'pose I'll ever want to marry – yuck, I don't fancy it at all – but who's to say I could, even if I would? *That's* what's beginning to get me, that I'm going to be different all my life. D'you know, when I lived in the city and someone wheeled me along a busy street, folks spoke to the person pushing the chair, smiled at him or her, cracked a joke, but hardly ever looked at me. You don't count as a person, you see.'

'But no one treats you like that here,' Libby pointed out. 'Anyway, just you remember how strong your arms have grown, because you're using them all the time. Your muscles are bigger than Rhys's – arm muscles, I mean – and one day you'll walk again. I'm sure you will, because you're so determined.'

Auntie sat down at the table and beamed at Libby and Matthew. 'You're a sensible girl, Libby Sheridan,' she said. 'Never give up and never say I can't, and now let's all go over to the Evanses' and see Millie's pups.'

Two days later, Matthew and Libby were piling leaves into a great heap for Dewi to barrow away. A good deal of mirth was occasioned by the wind which kept swirling their efforts back into the corners of the yard, but they were beginning to think they were winning when someone came round the corner of the house, pushing a bicycle. Libby recognised him at once, dropped the hay rake she had been wielding, and shot across to the cowshed, where Auntie was treating a wound on Bluebell's flank. The cow had just dropped a heifer calf and turned to gaze dreamily over her offspring's head as Libby arrived in her stall.

'Auntie, Auntie, it's Jimmy from the village, with a telegram,' Libby gabbled. 'Oh, it'll be from my daddy, saying he's coming to see us and bringing Mummy. He said he'd try to get some leave before Christmas . . . oh, do come out so you can read it and reply.'

Auntie finished spreading ointment, covered the wound and headed for the yard. Libby noticed that the older woman looked a little anxious, and for the first time it struck her that the telegram might be for Auntie herself, or even for Matthew, and might not contain good news. She watched anxiously as Auntie perused the message, which seemed to be quite a long one, and looked up at Jimmy. 'Come into the kitchen while I write a reply,' Auntie said. 'You'd better come too, Libby. I'm afraid it's not good news.'

'Well, here we are, my love! Gracious, it's years since I last visited Liverpool. I hadn't realised anywhere could be so crowded. Just you hang on to my hand, dear, and look round for your father, though I dare say he's gone back to sea. If so, I think we'd best catch a taxi cab and go straight to your grandmother's house. No point in going to the hospital until we know a bit more.'

Libby, clutching Auntie's hand, gazed helplessly about her. She, too, was astonished at the crowds on the platform, most of whom seemed to know exactly where they were going. Although the telegram had come from her father, she did not truly expect to see him waiting, since she knew he was seldom ashore for long. Besides, she thought that, had he been able, he would have come to Tregarth to fetch her himself.

'Well? Any sign?'

'No, and I can't see Gammy either, nor Auntie Fiona,' Libby said. 'Remember, Auntie, when you replied to the telegram, you had no idea which train we'd be catching. I think you're right and we should take a taxi to Crocus Street. Come along, it's this way.'

Auntie followed Libby's small, determined figure, trying to fight off a feeling of dread, for the telegram had merely said that Mrs Sheridan had been seriously injured in a road traffic accident and that Mr Sheridan thought that his daughter should return to the city, for a short while at least. Auntie had immediately replied that she would personally bring the child to Liverpool as soon as it could be arranged. Then she had sunk her pride, gone up to the castle and begged Mr Ap Nefydd to take over at Tregarth just for a few days, until she could leave Libby in safe hands. 'And I can't leave Matthew alone at Tregarth, either,' she had said. 'Can he come to you, Frank? He'll be no trouble, I promise you, and Dewi will see to the beasts.'

Mr Ap Nefydd had agreed to everything she had suggested, as she had known he would, which meant that she had left Tregarth with a quiet mind. Now that she was in Liverpool, however, black bat wings of worry seemed to be closing about her head. She had told Libby that her mother had been badly injured, but doubted her own ability to explain and comfort if the worst should happen and Mrs Sheridan die before they reached her bed. This had been her main reason for deciding to go to Crocus Street before visiting the Stanley hospital. She would find out from Mrs Wainwright how things stood and guessed that the older woman would visit the hospital with them. As a mother herself, she would be in a better position to deal with Libby's reaction should the worst occur.

'Join the taxi queue,' Libby whispered as they emerged from the station. 'And when we get near the front, say you want to go to the flower streets. Then we might share if anyone else is going that way – and they nearly always are.'

Feeling that she was the child in this city and Libby the adult, Auntie agreed meekly with her suggestion and presently found herself deposited on the pavement beside a number of terraced houses, with a salt wind blowing in her face and Libby tugging impatiently at her hand.

'We'll go round the back, because Gammy hardly ever opens the front door and the bolts are awful stiff,' the child said, leading the way. 'I just hope she isn't hospital visiting . . . but that's evenings, I think.' She pushed open a small wicket gate and crossed a tiny cobbled yard, ducking under a line of washing. 'Here we are.'

*   *   *

The moment the back door opened, Libby flung herself at Gammy. 'We're here, we came as soon as we possibly could,' she said. 'How's Mummy? Does she know I'm coming to visit her? Oh, Gammy, I'm so sorry, I forgot you'd not met Auntie . . . I mean Miss Williams.' She turned to her companion. 'Auntie, this is Gammy; you know all about each other but you've not met before.'

'How do you do, Mrs Wainwright?' Auntie said, holding out her hand. 'I wish we could have met in happier circumstances. How is your daughter? I realise it's early days, but . . .'

'I'm afraid she's very poorly still, and hasn't yet come to herself,' Gammy said formally. 'Because she has been so ill she's in a private room, so we can visit her any time. I expect you know that I make my living by taking in lodgers, so as soon as I'd finished clearing away the breakfast this morning I went across to the Stanley. It's been six days now since the accident, and the staff say that in such cases the patient benefits from hearing familiar voices, which is why me son-in-law wanted us to get Libby home.'

Auntie nodded. 'I've heard that hearing is the last of the senses to go and the first to return,' she agreed. 'I suppose Mr Sheridan is at the hospital now?'

Gammy shook her head, and to Libby's horror she saw tears form in the old woman's eyes. 'No, he's had to return to his ship,' she said. 'He's in command of a destroyer, the *Irascible*. Her home port is Southampton, but he's hoping that the Navy will allow him to return to the corvette he commanded before, since that would mean he'd be coming into Liverpool once more. But it all depends on them admirals and that; it ain't a decision he can make himself.'

'Oh, Gammy, but surely the Navy will understand that Daddy should be able to visit Mummy whilst she's in hospital?' Libby said, her voice trembling. 'It's Daddy's voice she'll want to hear more than anyone else's; even more than mine or yours.' She looked round the kitchen, but there was no sign of a meal in preparation. 'Can we go now? Before you start making the lodgers' supper?'

Gammy nodded, but looked anxiously at Auntie, then sent Libby up to the bedroom, telling her that she should stow the smallish suitcase, which was all the luggage the pair of them had brought, out of the way before they left.

Alone in the kitchen, the two women exchanged speaking glances before Gammy leaned forward and spoke with some urgency. 'I dunno what young Neil told you in the telegram,' she said in a low voice, 'but me daughter's gorra fractured skull, a broken tibia – wharrever that may be – a broken collar bone . . . oh, no end of damage. Her poor face looks like a railway line with stitches, and her head is a great big white puffball of bandage. When Neil said he'd sent for Libby, I were that cross I could have hit him, but I dare say he's in the right of it and the kid's gorra know how poorly her mam is. Only she's goin' to get the devil of a shock when she sees her for the first time. Me daughter's pal Betty, what works with her, walked straight past her bed and then the silly young cow went and fainted, which weren't no help to nobody. And her a grown woman wi' an important job assemblin' wireless parts! Still, there you are, it teks all of us in different ways, but I don't mind tellin' you I'm scared stiff of what Libby will do when she sees her mam.'

'I think maybe you underestimate her,' Auntie said. 'If you tell her that Mrs Sheridan looks very different because of stitches, bandages and the like, but that she will be her old self when her wounds heal, then I think you'll find she will accept it without too much fuss. Children are resilient . . .'

She stopped speaking as Libby came running noisily down the stairs and back into the kitchen. 'Ready, pet?' she asked. 'Would you rather I stayed here or shall I accompany you?'

Marianne floated in darkness. Even the tiniest movement was so painful that her mind screamed, though her lips could not utter a sound. Sometimes voices, faint and strange, came to her out of the darkness, but they were hollow and echoing, speaking no language she could understand. Sometimes she thought she might feel cold, sometimes hot, yet neither feeling remained with her for long, or seemed real. Once she thought she was in a place in between, waiting to be told what

301

was to become of her; mostly she simply floated, longed for light, knew only dark.

The lady on reception looked doubtfully at Libby until Gammy had leaned over the counter and told her that they had Dr Redmond's permission to bring the child to see her mother. 'She's Mrs Sheridan, in room eight.'

'Ah, I see. Very well, I'll just ring through and make sure the doctor isn't in room eight,' the receptionist said. 'If you'll wait a moment . . .'

They waited. Libby clutched a corner of Auntie's coat with one hand, and Gammy's plump little paw with the other. A nurse bustled up and gave them all a bright, meaningless smile. 'Visitors for Mrs Sheridan?' she said. 'Follow me.'

They obeyed and were presently ushered into a small white room. Libby stole to the side of the bed and stared and stared into her mother's deathly pale face with its tracery of stitches running across it like the railway lines under Bankhall Bridge, and the great white mound of bandage which was her head. 'Mummy?' she said gently. 'Mummy, it's Libby. Auntie brought me up from the country to come and see you because Daddy's had to go back to sea. You do look poorly, Mummy, but the doctors say you'll be better soon.'

Gammy sighed. 'No matter what the doctor says I doubt she can hear you, queen,' she said lugubriously. 'I come in here t'other day and the nurse said that some feller, likely a hospital visitor, had been chatterin' away to her and there were no sign she so much as knew he were there, lerralone heard a word he said.'

'Well, I think she can hear if the doctor says so,' Libby said obstinately. 'Auntie thinks so too, don't you, Auntie? The last of the senses to go and the first to return, you said.' She leaned over and spoke to her mother once more. 'Next time I come, would you like me to read to you? We're keeping a diary at school and I get top marks for mine; I put it into our suitcase so I shan't fall behind. Then, when you begin to get better, you'll know what I've been doing.'

Libby lay in Gammy's large bed and let tears slip silently down her cheeks and soak into her pillow. Auntie had stayed for three whole days, but then she had had to return to Tregarth, explaining to Libby that it would not have been fair to remain away for longer.

'It's not as though Mr Ap Nefydd and I have been on good terms these past years,' she had said gruffly. 'The truth is, I took advantage of our old friendship because I needed someone to look after Tregarth whilst I brought you back to Liverpool and learned how things stood. I had hoped that Mrs Sheridan would come to herself and agree to my taking you back to the valley with me, but that hasn't happened. I asked your grandmother whether it might not be best to take you with me until your mother comes round, but she was adamant that you should stay in Crocus Street and I dare say she's right. I'm afraid I was being selfish when I suggested you should return with me, because your Gran is getting on in years. What's more, apart from yourself, she has no family here at present able to help and support her spirits. Your father is at sea, and your aunt is with the Wrens somewhere in the south of England. And of course, if anyone's voice will bring your mother back to consciousness, it'll be yours. So you see, my dear, I shall have to go back to Tregarth without you.'

Libby had said she understood, adding that as soon as her mother was her old self, she would bring her to Tregarth. 'Because I'm certain that quiet and country life will be what she most needs,' she had said earnestly. 'I know her war work is important but I don't believe she'll be well enough to go back to the factory for a long time and you did say she would be welcome at Tregarth, didn't you, Auntie?'

Auntie had agreed that this was so and Libby had waved her off at the station, calling out messages for Matthew and Rhys as Auntie had leaned out of the train window and waved.

She had acknowledged that both the older women were right when they said that her place was here, but nothing could reconcile her to the sudden change in her life. Not only did she miss Tregarth – the animals, the people, and in fact the valley itself – but even in the three days which had passed since their arrival she had realised that Gammy was not her old self. Several times she had addressed Libby as Marianne and had harked back to incidents in her mother's childhood, clearly expecting Libby to remember them as Gammy did herself. Auntie had not noticed but Mr Parsons, who had lodged with Gammy for over ten years, did. 'I'm glad you're back, queen, because this has hit your grandmother harder than most folk realise,' he had told Libby, whilst he had been chopping kindling in the woodshed and Libby had been taking the washing off the line. 'Mrs Wainwright's that forgetful now that she has to take a list of her messages, and even then she comes home without the half of 'em. Why, the other day, when we come down for our breakfast, she picked the porridge pan off the stove, made as if to ladle the stuff into our dishes, and realised the pot were empty. She were that astonished . . . well, we all had a good laugh but I knew in me heart it weren't that funny.'

'She seems all right since I've been back, apart from muddling me up with my mother and telling me Auntie Fiona would be fetching her some apples when she got home,' Libby had said rather doubtfully. 'She'd forgotten Auntie Fee had been posted down south.'

'Oh aye, she's been almost her old self since you come home,' Mr Parsons had agreed. 'That's why I think you'd best stay at least until your mam gets out of hospital. I know you're only a kid, but you've a good head on your shoulders and Mrs Wainwright relies on you.'

So now here she was, visiting the hospital two or three times a day, showing everyone a cheerful face and helping Gammy in every way she could. Only at night, when Gammy was asleep, could she allow herself the luxury of tears. Gammy had suggested, half-heartedly, that she might return to school, but Libby had pointed out that this would severely limit both her hospital visiting and her helpfulness in Crocus Street, and since the authorities had no idea that she was back in the city, no more was said of a return to school. Libby, however, spent every evening writing her diary and composing long letters to Auntie and Matthew, in which she talked, wistfully, of her return to Tregarth.

She had written to her father too, explaining that she was now living back in Crocus Street, and hoping that he would come back to Liverpool before she returned to Tregarth, but so far she had received no reply, and guessed that his ship was still at sea.

Beside her, Gammy gave a little snorting gurgle and turned over. She muttered something about pigs' trotters, then about the apples which someone had promised her. Libby lay still and rigid, frightened that Gammy might wake properly and realise that she had been crying, but after a few moments tiny, regular snores began to issue from the old woman's open mouth, and presently both occupants of the big bed slept.

'Everything's spoiled! Oh, I know it wasn't Marianne's fault – if anything it was yours – but even so, she's ruined everything. You say you can't get a divorce but I don't see why it's so impossible. She isn't being a wife to you, after all. Oh, if only she would come round, I'm sure she'd divorce you. Marianne's always been very generous; she wouldn't want to make me unhappy.'

Fiona and Neil were sitting on a stile in a country lane which led up to the Downs, and Neil turned to gaze incredulously at his companion. 'Fiona Wainwright, I've heard folks say some wicked things in my time, but that beats the band,' he said. 'Your only sister has been lying at death's door and all you can do is think about getting her to give me a divorce. It's the most heartless thing I've ever heard and you should be ashamed of yourself.'

Fiona sniffed, then began to cry. Tears poured out of her eyes and a vivid blush rushed up her neck and invaded her face. She turned and flung her arms round Neil's neck. 'Oh, darling Neil, I didn't mean a word of it. It's my condition and the fact that I can't do anything to help myself, lerralone poor Marianne,' she muttered. 'I'd love to go home and see me mam and give Marianne any help I could, but one look at me and the whole story would come out.' She patted her extended stomach.

Neil gave her a hug, kissed the side of her cheek and shook his head chidingly. 'It wouldn't come out because your mother has never had the faintest suspicion that there was anything between you

307

and me but normal friendship. Everyone thinks you had a boyfriend called Philip something or other, and when they see you're pregnant they'll naturally assume it was him.'

'Marianne won't,' Fiona said. 'As soon as she regains consciousness, she'll remember you asked her for a divorce.'

'She might, though the doctors don't think she'll remember anything which happened directly before the accident. Besides, I never said it was you . . . I never used your name. If you wanted to go back to Liverpool, you could do so safely. Once the baby's born and you've had it adopted, you could even re-join the Wrens, I believe, if you wanted to do so.'

'I don't know what I want,' Fiona wailed. 'If only you weren't in the Navy and there wasn't a war on, we could run away to France, or Greece or somewhere, change our names and live happily ever after. Marianne's ever so pretty and ever so sweet, and I love her lots, so I'm sure if she thought you were dead she'd remarry quickly enough. But the way things are, everything's spoiled.' She fished a tiny hanky out of her gas mask case and mopped, fruitlessly, at her tear-swollen eyes.

Neil sighed and produced a large white linen square, which he thrust into Fiona's hands. 'Look, everyone in the village thinks we're a respectable married couple. Since you left the Wrens, you've had a nice little job in the local bakery, and when I'm home folk are friendly and eager to get to know us. As for Marianne being pretty, I don't deny that she was and I'm sure she will be again, but right now she doesn't really enter into it. If you remember, this conversation started because I'm worried about Libby. At the moment, Gammy is looking after her and she seems content enough, but I can't help worrying over what will happen when Marianne's better. In normal circumstances – if we were divorced, I mean – I should expect to have Libby to stay with me for a couple of weeks during each school holiday, but if I do that she'll find out about you, and that is a can of worms I dare not even contemplate.'

'But if you and Marianne divorce . . .' Fiona began, only to be hushed by a finger placed across her lips.

'If, if, if,' Neil said impatiently. 'I happen to love my daughter and I've not seen her for months. Next time I get a few days' leave, I'm going back to Liverpool. I shall spend time in Crocus Street with Libby and go to the hospital to see Marianne. I know last time I suggested it you threatened to kill yourself, or do something drastic to get rid of the baby, but I've thought it over and I'm afraid for once in your life your threats just won't work.'

Fiona tightened her lips and glared at him, all traces of tears gone. Then she slid off the stile and set off down the lane in the direction from which they had come. 'If your daughter means more to you than I do, and if you can forget my delicate condition, then Marianne won't be the only person looking for a new feller,' she shouted furiously over her shoulder. 'There are times when I hate you, Neil Sheridan.'

Marianne had been hearing the voices now for hours or days, she had no idea which. One was a child's voice, sweetly familiar, though she could not put a name to it. The other was a man's voice, deep, rumbling and, she felt, reliable. The sharp and terrible pains in her head, which had made concentration impossible, had eased, sometimes almost left her. She was aware, too, that she no longer floated in limbo. Hands touched her, and she felt their touch. Some hands were rough, quick and uncaring, others gentle and soothing, handling her poor body with compassion. Somewhere, deep in her mind, a word floated and was presently joined by others. Nurse. Hospital. Doctor. She could not, as yet, make any sense of the words, draw any conclusions, but she knew that one day she would be able to do so. Oddly, she shrank from the knowledge, even shrank from the fact that the darkness was no longer black but pale grey, and that sometimes, just for a moment, she could see brilliant white, a blob of blue, a streak of pinky-gold. Such moments of revelation did not last but again, deep in her mind, she knew that one day they would, and though this frightened her she realised that it was yet another sign; she would get better, even if she did so despite herself.

*　　*　　*

Christmas came and went and in mid-January Neil got leave and came back to Crocus Street. He did so in the teeth of fierce opposition from Fiona, for she was suffering all the miseries connected with the seventh month of pregnancy. She had terrible heartburn and varicose veins, complained that she was the size of an elephant, and, though Neil had assured her she was still beautiful, thought herself the ugliest of ugly sisters. Her hair, which had always been a bush of bright curls, became greasy and limp, and for the first time in her life her milky complexion was covered in spots. She ate ravenously, then discovered a boil in her armpit and stopped eating at all. She was given to fits of weeping, alternating with a sort of wild gaiety, and had left her job at the bakery because she said the trays of loaves were too heavy and customers stared at her as though she were the fat lady in a freak show.

For the first time since they had moved into their cottage in the village, and had been accepted there as man and wife, Neil realised that to get away from her, even for a week, would be a real relief. Feeling guilty, he was honest enough to admit – if only to himself – that had Fiona not been pregnant, had the lies not mounted and mounted, he would not dream for one moment of divorcing Marianne. She had been a good wife to him, a good mother to Libby, and when compared with the whining, savagely complaining Fiona, she was a far more appealing life partner.

Of course, he was not always with Fiona, since a great deal of his time was spent at sea, but then he was too busy and preoccupied to appreciate and enjoy Fiona's absence. Now, stepping off the train at Lime Street Station, he was suddenly conscious of feeling ten years younger. He knew that Fiona's constant nagging, complaining and bad temper were all the result of her condition, and that, naturally enough, she blamed him for her pregnancy. But once again he could not help remembering wistfully how very different things had been when Libby was on the way; delighted anticipation had been his young wife's first emotion, though she had suffered very much as Fiona was doing. But without complaint, Neil thought grimly. But once the baby was born, surely Fiona would revert to her old sweet self ? He certainly hoped so, and on the spur of the moment told himself that if she did not, he would return to his wife and hope that, between them, they could once more build a good marriage.

Emerging from the station, Neil joined the queue for taxis. He looked around vaguely, and realised that a good deal of clearing up had taken place since his last visit. The road was clear of rubble, as the cold fresh air was clear of dust. The queue shuffled forward and Neil glanced at his wrist-watch. It was late afternoon, and though he had meant to give Gammy warning of his imminent arrival, somehow he had not managed to do so. The village in which he and Fiona lived was small and remote, and because she had refused to believe that he would really leave her with a baby due in the near future Fiona had prevented him from travelling into Southampton until he had gone to catch the train, and then it had been too late to send a telegram. Besides, one never knew in wartime; he had hoped to reach the city before dusk fell, but missed connections and enemy action might have prolonged the journey into a second day.

The queue moved forward again and Neil, who had stood his case down, picked it up and followed suit. He wished he and Fiona had parted on good terms, but unfortunately this had not been the case. When she had actually threatened to accompany him and let everyone believe 'what they bloody well pleased', he had lost his temper. 'You're nothing but a nasty, spoilt kid,' he had shouted furiously. 'You don't give a damn about your mother, or Libby, let alone poor Marianne. And what about the baby? I know you said you'd have it adopted and tell everyone that it had died, but what normal, decent woman could even consider giving her baby away if she could keep it?'

'I hate kids,' Fiona had shrieked. 'Look what happened to Marianne the moment Libby was born; you bleedin' well lost interest in her and don't attempt to deny it, 'cos I should know! Oh, go back to Liverpool and bleedin' well stay there.'

Now, Neil reached the head of the queue, gave his destination as Crocus Street and hopped on to the cracked leather seat, setting his suitcase down at his feet. The taxi started off and Neil tried to dismiss that last angry disagreement with Fiona from his mind. He knew she hadn't really meant it, but it still rankled that she could say such things.

However, it did not do to dwell on thoughts of Fiona, since he had decided to say, if he was asked, that he had not even been aware that she had moved down from Liverpool to the south of England, and had certainly seen nothing of her. He had never given his mother-in-law, or his daughter, his village address, so they had continued to send their letters to the *Irascible*, knowing he would be given all his correspondence soon after he docked. Some of the men lived aboard while their ship was in port, whilst others went to the nearest Sailors' Home. Local men, of course, went home, glad of the comforts this afforded, even if it was only for a few days.

If I'd not been posted to the command of the *Irascible* I'd still be berthing at Liverpool every five or six weeks, he reminded himself almost wistfully as the taxi carried him along Byrom Street. He knew that the worst of the bombing had happened months before, but of course rebuilding was not only impossible for lack of materials, but would have been foolish; no one could guarantee that the Luftwaffe would not return and attack the city once more. Neil knew that some of the docks were still unusable due to sunken shipping, and that approaches to Liverpool were treacherous for the same reason; knew, too, that the wolf pack

314

lurked in the Irish sea, near the mouth of the Mersey, making the job of the convoys more difficult than that of shipping which sailed from the southern ports.

But today the evening air was cold and crisp and he suddenly realised that he would see Libby in no more than ten or fifteen minutes, and felt excitement rise within him. She was his beloved daughter and he had not seen her for months and months. He knew from her letters that the move back into Liverpool had not been a welcome one, save for the fact that it enabled her to see her mother. She had made no secret of the fact that Tregarth was where she would much prefer to be, and had confided in him that Gammy had days when she seemed extremely muddled, forgetting there was a war on, leaving pans to burn dry on the stove and hanging on the line linen which she had not yet washed. Neil had dismissed all this as absent-mindedness brought on by old age and, he supposed, her daughter's accident. Mrs Wainwright had always been brisk and capable, needing help from no one, running her home and seeing to her lodgers without any apparent effort. He hoped that Libby was not having to do too much but knew there was little he could do about it, even if it were so. Surely Marianne must be getting better? It was three months since the accident.

At this point, the taxi drew up in Crocus Street. Neil grabbed his case, paid the driver and set off down the jigger. He crossed the back yard in half a dozen long strides, beat a tattoo on the door and flung it open. Libby, peeling potatoes at the sink, dropped her knife and flew across the room, leaping into his arms and squeaking: 'Daddy, Daddy, oh, Daddy!' whilst his mother-in-law, sitting by the fire, knitting what looked like a long, mud-coloured scarf, beamed at him and pushed her spectacles down her nose in order to survey him over the top of them.

'Neil. You never said . . . did you? . . . but I dare say it were a sudden decision to let you have leave, so you couldn't warn us,' she said. 'Well, I don't reckon you said anything in your last letter, anyroad. Eh, lad, it's grand to see you, an' lookin' so well, too. Marianne will be over the moon when you visit the hospital.'

Libby was still in her father's arms, but he stood her down gently and raised his eyebrows. Regretfully, his daughter shook her head. 'I think it's what they call a manner of speaking,' she said. 'Mummy hasn't come round yet – well, she doesn't open her eyes, so far as I know – but something really exciting happened this morning, Daddy. I went in early and I took my diary so I could read her yesterday's entry. I took a letter from Matthew as well because honestly, Daddy, although she can't talk or do anything, I'm beginning to know how she feels about things.' She smiled affectionately across to her grandmother, who had returned to her knitting. 'Gammy thinks it's my imagination, but I'm sure I'm right. I think her mind must be like a deep pool, with different levels, so that the very bottom-most one is black and as she gets better and begins to come up to shallower water the colour goes from charcoal to a pearly grey. That's what she's in now and I do think we understand one another.'

Gammy laid her knitting down and came over to give Neil a peck on the cheek and a squeeze of the hand. 'It's grand to see you, lad, bleedin' wonderful in fact,' she said huskily, and Neil saw that her eyes were full of tears. 'We knew you'd come when you could and our Libby is convinced that it only needs your voice to bring her mam back to her senses, so let's hope she's right. I hate to see her lyin' there, white as a corpse, with all her lovely hair cut off and tubes everywhere.'

'Yes, but because she can't eat she needs the tubes and things; they're helping to make her better,' Libby explained and it occurred to Neil that his daughter spoke as an adult speaks to a child, rather than vice versa. 'But let me tell Daddy my good news, Gammy; then he can put his suitcase in the parlour and go up to our room to have a good wash, because Mummy always used to say that railway journeys were mucky things. After that, I think we ought to go to the hospital so Daddy can see Mummy for half an hour or so, and then come back here in time for supper with the lodgers.' She turned back to her father. 'It's a wonderful vegetable pie; Gammy heard the recipe on *The Kitchen Front*, so you won't want to miss that.'

'And your good news?' Neil asked, seeing the teasing sparkle in his daughter's eyes and realising that he was expected to be afire with curiosity. 'Don't tease your old daddy; God knows there's been enough bad news lately, so don't withhold the good!'

'Well, I pull up a chair by Mummy's bed each morning, take her hand and ask her how she's feeling, what sort of night she's had and whether the doctor has done his rounds. She doesn't answer, of course, but once or twice I've thought her eyelids have sort of flickered. Then I always ask if I should read yesterday's entry in my diary and I take her hand whilst I read. And this morning, when I went to take her hand, it moved! It came towards me instead of just lying limply on the top sheet, and when I caught hold of it, she squeezed my fingers, honest to God she did. I rang the bell for a nurse, but the one who came was Hodges. She's bad-tempered and rough; I don't like her. Still, she is a nurse so I told her what had happened and she gave a rude sort of sniff and said I was probably imagining it. Daddy, I didn't imagine it, I promise you. So anyway, I waited until she'd gone out of the room again and then I bent over and whispered in Mummy's ear that I would read the diary and then fetch Sister Andrews, because she's wonderful and was thrilled to bits when I told her.' Libby stopped speaking and beamed up at Neil, her eyes bright with the anticipation of his pleasure.

Hastily, Neil fixed a smile to his own face, though he thought it quite likely that the child had been mistaken. And even if she had been right, it was difficult to be thrilled because his wife had squeezed his daughter's hand. Then he remembered the crushed and broken figure he had last seen three months earlier, and was able to put more enthusiasm into his voice as he replied. 'That's wonderful, darling, the best news in the world! It shows she's beginning to respond, beginning to get better. Thank God you were there and not miles away at Tregarth. And now let's get over to that hospital so I can see Marianne for myself.'

Marianne heard the child's voice, felt the touch of the child's hand, and was comforted. The child was saying something which she could not understand, but presently there came to her ears another voice, a man's voice this time. She was beginning to realise that she was in hospital and assumed the voice must belong to a doctor, then decided this was unlikely since doctors were not in the habit of indulging in conversation with their patients and this voice went on and on.

Usually, she made no attempt to understand what was being said, but today, something in her mind decided that what the man was saying might be important, so with a tremendous effort she began to try to make sense of his words. After a few moments, however, she gave up and concentrated, instead, on the voice itself. She decided that it was familiar, and that she did not much like its owner, which was strange, because whenever the

319

other voices – including the child's – came to her ears, there was a sort of warmth . . .

This had not happened at first, she realised, but it had come upon her gradually so that now she looked forward to hearing certain voices . . . the child's was delightful, the other man's deep, rather shy tones welcome, and the old woman's, though sometimes it worried her by quavering away into sniffs and sobs, was still the voice of someone she loved. This man's voice was lighter, pitched a little higher than the voice of the man who spoke to her most often.

Someone touched her hand, though only for a moment. Then the voices faded and she was alone once more. As a general rule, when visitors left, she simply sank back into sleep, or at least indifference, but now she began to think; she *was* getting better. She was suddenly aware that her lids, though heavy, could probably lift if she tried hard and concentrated. She decided that the next time the child or the deep-voiced man came visiting, she would make the huge effort it required and open her eyes, see where she was, who sat by the bed. It frightened her even to think of it, but she told herself, resolutely, that she had never been a coward and must not let fear cramp her recovery. When she saw the child and the deep-voiced man, surely recognition would blossom and she would begin to drag herself back to the real world.

*   *   *

By the time Neil was ready to return to Southampton, the staff at the hospital assured him that Marianne had regained consciousness and, though weak, would soon be able to remember who she was and what had happened to her. Neil pretended to be delighted, but really he felt both annoyed and puzzled by his wife's behaviour. Libby always visited her mother first thing in the morning and the two had exchanged conversation, though of a very basic sort. Marianne had asked the child: 'Who am I? And who are you?' And Libby, tremendously elated, had answered her on both scores.

His wife had spoken to the nurses once or twice and was beginning to eat thin gruel when someone held the feeder to her lips, yet Neil himself had only to enter the small private ward for Marianne either to be overtaken by sleep or to become unconscious once more. Neil could not understand it. Everyone assured him that Marianne could remember nothing of her life directly before the accident, so why did she not respond to the sound of his voice? But he felt he could scarcely complain, should in fact be grateful, that her patchy and still distorted memory had not thrown up the recollection of the half-hour or so before the accident. Because the doctor advised it, he sat by the bed and talked to her about the happy early days of their marriage, but he could not tell whether she understood him, though occasionally a gentle smile flitted across her face and gave him hope. Libby, however, assured him that when she read to her mother from her diary Marianne responded, sometimes even giving a little laugh when something amused her. The staff did not encourage more than one visitor at a time since they said that several voices – and several personalities – might confuse the patient, so Neil had to be content with what his daughter and mother-in-law told him.

Now, after a week of daily visits, he told Gammy and Libby that he thought Marianne was beginning to respond to him. Oh, he didn't invent lively conversations, since he did not wish to be revealed as a liar; he simply said that when he told her some story of their past she nodded, smiled and squeezed his hand as though she remembered. She had not, so far, squeezed his hand, but she had nodded and smiled, which he felt was a good sign. He was happy for her to remember everything, save for the fatal ten minutes or so before the accident. Surely God would not be so cruel as to let her recall the one incident he most wished to remain for ever forgotten.

He had expected to be questioned about Fiona since they were both in the south of England, but it did not occur to anyone that he might have seen his sister-in-law. Highly daring, he asked Libby whether her aunt wrote often. They were walking hand in hand home from the hospital to Crocus Street and Libby gave him such an angry glance that he released her fingers for a second and stopped walking to stare down into his daughter's small, pointed face. 'Auntie Fee only writes to Gammy, not to me,

322

because I wrote to her and told her she should come and visit my mum,' Libby said furiously. 'She writes to Mum, of course, sometimes quite long letters and sometimes little short ones, but she's never been to the hospital, not once. Daddy, she's supposed to love Mum like you and I do. If you love someone, you make a big effort to help them get better, don't you? But Auntie Fee says she's too busy and can't get leave, so I told her if she was too busy to visit my mum, I was too busy to write to her. And anyway, I asked someone from naval headquarters about leave to visit a sick sister, and the officer I asked said Auntie Fee could get compassionate leave if she wanted.' She snorted, tucking her hand into her father's once more and beginning to pull him along the pavement. 'Even Gammy was a bit disgusted and she thinks the sun shines out of Fiona.'

Neil looked covertly at his daughter. Was this the moment to try to pour oil on troubled waters, and to explain to Libby that there are sometimes reasons why a person suddenly behaves in a way that seems to go against their nature? He began to say that he had always thought Marianne and Fiona to be the most loving of sisters, that there must be some reason for Fiona's extraordinary behaviour, that it was possible she could not visit because she had been posted abroad and was thus unable to come back to Liverpool, no matter how she might long to see her sister.

Libby gave another contemptuous snort. 'If that's true, why hasn't she told Gammy so?' she demanded indignantly. 'I think Auntie Fee can't be bothered to come all the way back even though she knows her sister has been unconscious for such ages. I expect all she thinks about are parties and dances and lots of young men. But we'll get Mummy better without her, see if we don't!'

'The job she's working on may be frightfully hush-hush,' Neil said feebly. 'Don't condemn her too soon, my pet. War changes everything.'

He saw his daughter compress her lips, but she said nothing and presently they reached the house in Crocus Street and the subject was dropped.

Neil visited the hospital for the last time the following day, and on this occasion Libby was allowed to accompany him since she meant to come to the station to see him off. They arrived very early, and for the first time Neil saw his wife with her eyes open, sitting propped up by pillows as a nurse held the spout of the feeding cup to her lips, chatting to her in a quiet voice of hospital matters. Neil went over to the bed, suddenly aware that he was feeling every kind of fool. What if Marianne said something he would prefer Libby not to hear? But she was smiling at her daughter and did not seem to have noticed him.

Libby darted to the side of the bed and gave her mother's cheek a kiss. 'Hello, Mummy; it's me, Libby.' She turned to her father. 'Sometimes she can't remember my name, but she knows I'm her little girl,' she turned back to the figure in the bed, 'don't you, Mummy?'

A frail white hand came up and gently removed the spout of the feeding cup from between her lips. 'I 'member Libby,' her mother said, her voice so low that Neil had to lean forward to catch the words. Marianne's eyes flickered over Neil, then returned to focus on her daughter's small face. 'You . . . school . . . now?'

'Not today, Mummy. Today Daddy's going back to his ship. I'm going to see him off at the station, but I knew you'd want to say goodbye as well, because now his home port is Southampton he can't get to see you as often as he would like.'

Marianne looked at Neil curiously for a moment, then a smile touched her lips. 'Neil?' she said. 'It *is* you!'

Libby beamed. 'Yes, it's Daddy, but he's going back to his ship today, so you must say goodbye for a bit,' she said. 'Do you remember me telling you that his home port is Southampton now? So you must say goodbye until his next leave.'

'Goodbye, Neil,' Marianne said, and just for a moment Neil thought he saw a puzzled, almost antagonistic, gleam in his wife's eyes. Fortunately, Libby seemed to have noticed nothing but bade him briskly to give her mother a kiss, since they must be on their way or he might miss his train.

Feeling uncomfortable, for he was sure he had not misinterpreted the look he had been given, Neil leaned over the bed. He felt her withdrawal and kissed air an inch from her cheek, then straightened up and told the nurse, breezily, that she might get to work again with the feeding cup since he and his daughter must leave at once.

The two of them hurried out of the hospital. Libby was chattering gaily about the enormous improvement which had come about since his arrival but Neil, as he hailed a taxi cab, admitted that he did not think it was his presence which had brought Marianne back to full consciousness. He decided to be frank, since he suspected that the medical staff were well aware that Marianne had not appeared to know him at first, and this fact might easily get passed on to his daughter. Indeed, Marianne herself would probably give the game away by asking who the devil he was.

'Oh!' Libby said. 'But of course she's been seeing me two or three times a day for weeks, so I suppose you're almost a stranger . . . no, I don't mean that, but I could see that she wasn't really taking it in, that you were going back to Southampton, I mean.'

They left it at that, and presently Neil caught his train and was waved off, whilst Libby returned to Crocus Street and her grandmother.

Chapter Eleven

June 1942

'Any post for me, Auntie?' Matthew, eating his breakfast at the kitchen table, looked up hopefully as Miss Williams entered the kitchen, holding several envelopes. 'You've no idea how I miss that Libby kid. She writes a damned good letter but it's not the same as having her chattering away on the opposite side of the table.'

'There's one for each of us from Libby; all the rest are seed catalogues or bills, or other such boring epistles,' Auntie said, flicking a bulging white envelope across the table and sitting down heavily, pulling her porridge bowl towards her. 'You read your letter to me and I'll read mine to you, only I mean to get outside this porridge first. Milking the cows gives one an appetite, I find.'

'Righty-ho,' Matthew said breezily, ripping open the envelope. 'Hey, it's not just a letter, it's a perishin' book. Oh, I see, she's enclosed her diary.' He squinted at the first page. 'She says to get Mr Tarporley to read it and send it straight back so she can get on with her Monday entry as soon as possible.' He grinned across at Auntie, shovelling porridge. 'How much will you bet me that her mother's out of hospital? I can't think of any other

327

reason for her writing such pages and pages, and for sending her diary back when there are still a few blank sheets at the end. Oh, Auntie, if I'm right, we could see her here in a couple of weeks, maybe less, because she said ages ago that the doctors think a spell in the country would get her mother back on her feet again. And I dare say Mrs Sheridan might be quite useful if we gave her quiet things to do.'

'Read me the letter and stop conjecturing,' Auntie said impatiently. 'If there was ever a more aggravating boy than you, I've yet to meet him. Guessing butters no parsnips, or whatever the saying is. Go on, read it or I shan't let you see mine.'

Matthew laughed. 'You're like a kid, wanting things now and not tomorrow,' he said, and then, as Auntie half rose from her chair: 'All right, all right, I'm going to read it. Just let me sort out the pages, and then we'll start.

'Dear Matthew,
    'My mummy will be allowed to leave the hospital at the end of next week if she continues to get better, and I'm sure she will. She knows us all, the people who are able to visit her I mean, though when we mention Fiona – Gammy does, I won't – she looks so bewildered that the doctors have said we mustn't confuse her by mentioning names until she can put a face to them. Gammy showed her a wedding photograph with Mummy

328

in her long white dress and Daddy in his uniform, but it made her cry. She said it was because once she had been pretty and now she was not, but that's rubbish. She's still pretty, truly she is, though the stitches have left lines on her face and her hair hasn't grown back everywhere yet. But it doesn't matter, truly it doesn't, because Nurse Russell was a hairdresser before the war, and she's teaching Mummy to comb her hair in a certain way. It looks as good as ever and I'm sure once she's out of the hospital Mummy will know nothing has really changed.

'As you may have guessed, Gammy isn't at all keen that Mummy and myself should come back to Tregarth. She says she can't manage the lodgers by herself any more, and keeps complaining that the laundry work her too hard, though as you know, she stopped working for them before Mummy's accident. I hope this is just an excuse and that now Mummy is out of danger Gammy will be able to cope as before, but Mr Parsons thinks not. He knows her best of everyone and says if we mean to go ahead and leave Crocus Street for a while, then Gammy will have to employ a helper to do the things I do at present. It isn't that I work terribly hard, I just keep an eye on things. I get pans off the stove before they boil dry, remind her of the correct time when she gets out of bed at two in the morning and trundles down to make breakfast, and see she puts her coat and hat on before leaving the house. It's nothing very difficult but it does mean Gammy needs someone actually on the spot.

'Because of the bomb damage, there are lots of people in Liverpool without homes of their own who would be glad to move in for a few weeks just to give an eye to Gammy until Mummy is well enough to take over once again. The house in Sydenham Avenue was let to somebody else ages ago. Our furniture went into storage but the warehouse was bombed and everything was destroyed.

'When I mentioned it to Gammy – having help whilst we're away I mean – she thought about it for a bit and then said: "How about cousin Edith?" I didn't know she had a cousin Edith, but apparently she does. She's not a lot younger than Gammy, but the two were quite friendly once. Edith has been living in Bootle with her daughter, but they were bombed out in the May blitz. They've moved in with other relatives but are miserably cramped, so Gammy thinks her cousin would be delighted to move to Crocus Street. When I told Mummy she laughed and said that when they were younger the two cousins had fallen out over a young man but that must have been ages and ages ago, so I suppose it will be all right now.

'Oh, Matthew, you don't know how much I miss Tregarth and everyone. I can't wait to see you all again, even though Mummy may only be able to stay a short time before she has to come back to Gammy.

'Say hello to Auntie for me and say, "See you soon."

'Your old friend,
'Libby Sheridan.'

Matthew laid the rustling pages down and beamed across at Auntie. 'Isn't that good news?' he said exultantly. 'And if Libby really brings her mother here, it would be nice for you to have another grown-up about the place instead of just us kids. Oh, I know there's Dewi, but he doesn't think of much besides farming matters, and of course he's part time so sometimes you don't see him for a whole week. I say, you know Mr Ap Nefydd's huge carthorses? Dewi told me yesterday that Duchess is in foal and Duke is the father. It'll be their first foal for five years and Mr Ap Nefydd is delighted because the last foal, Prince, is one of the best workers he's ever had.'

'Yes, yes, very interesting,' Auntie said testily, scraping the last of her porridge from her bowl and picking up her own letter. 'Do you want me to read to you, or not? Though it beats me how the child can find so much to say.'

'Oh, that's easy,' Matthew said at once. 'Libby knows we're interested in different things. Most people write letters without giving a lot of thought to the receiver, if you get me, but Libby isn't like that. Go on then, Auntie, read away!'

'Dear Auntie,

'As I told you in my last letter, Mummy is doing very well indeed and would like to accept your kind invitation to visit Tregarth after she leaves the hospital. She really is a great deal better and talks of returning to her factory job, though I think she would find shifts and being on her feet so much very exhausting. I would rather she stayed with Gammy, though helping in the house, cooking, cleaning and getting the messages may seem like quite hard work after lying in bed for so long.'

Auntie looked up from her letter. 'Sensible child,' she said approvingly. 'If you ask me, that cousin coming to Crocus Street would be the best thing that could happen. If her grandmother got someone young and energetic in, then Mrs Wainwright would simply let her take over. But someone of her own age will make her want to compete. She'll pull herself together and probably be able to manage without her cousin after a few weeks.'

Matthew grinned wickedly. 'You should know,' he said demurely. 'Being so old and wise yourself.'

Auntie aimed a playful swipe at him across the table. 'Do you want to hear the rest of my letter, or do you not?' she demanded, and upon Matthew's nod, began to read once more.

'I've told you before about Mummy's friend, Mr Brett, who is a bus driver. He says he will miss

her but agrees she should come to Tregarth. He used to be on the route which took the workers to the factories on Long Lane, but because so many tram lines were blown up he now drives a double-decker bus. He's old and a bit ugly, but very, very nice. Mummy's face lights up when he comes on to the ward; she says he's her friend, no matter what she looks like.

'Give my love to all the animals, especially to Buttercup, my favourite cow, and dear old Dapple. Oh, and Matthew and Dewi of course.

'The hospital won't say when Mummy can be released – it's something to do with tests – but as soon as they tell us for certain, you may be sure I'll write.

'Your young friend,

'Libby Sheridan.

'That's good news, isn't it?' Auntie said, getting rather stiffly to her feet and beginning to clear the table. 'I don't think it will be long, Matthew my boy, before there will be two extra people in this kitchen!'

'If only it wasn't for clothes rationing, I'd rush out and buy Mummy something pretty to wear for her homecoming,' Libby said longingly as she, her grandmother and Mrs Edith Robinson carefully removed Marianne's clothing from the chest of drawers and spread everything out on the bed. 'I won't take a great many clothes because there's no point. I've noticed that Mummy hates making decisions, or having to choose anything. I'll have to do her packing for her when we go to Tregarth.'

'True,' Gammy said. 'And you won't want to take too much to Tregarth, either, or Miss Williams will think you're planning a long stay.'

'I am,' Libby said rather defiantly. 'I know the bombing isn't anywhere near as bad as it was last year, but the docks do get attacked from time to time and bombs get dropped on the city as well. I'm sure Mummy will want me out of it.'

Mrs Robinson – only she had told Libby to call her Aunt Edith – turned and grinned. She was a tall, thin woman, with hair dyed an unconvincing ginger, very white skin and a habit of singing to herself, out of tune, but with great enthusiasm, as she worked around the house. Libby had liked her on sight and within a few hours of the stranger's arrival had realised that Mr Parsons knew just what he was talking about when he had said, unconsciously echoing Auntie, that the introduction of a woman her own age would put Gammy on her mettle. As a result of the competition between the two old women, cooking grew more inventive, and shopkeepers were bullied into parting with such sought-after items as lemons, pigs' kidneys and sugar-coated biscuits. Mr Parsons, giving Libby a wink, had remarked quietly that they would eat like kings whilst she was away, and he did not grudge having to give up his favourite armchair, to which Mrs Robinson had laid claim on her very first day in Crocus Street.

The final selection made – a blue cotton dress, suitable underwear, a pair of ancient sandals and a worn, navy cardigan – the women trooped downstairs and Libby took her mother's coat and hat from the hook on the door, then turned to beam at her companions. 'I'll be back in about an hour. You'd best lay an extra place for supper because Mr Brett has hired a taxi and it would be only polite to ask him to share our meal,' she said happily. 'He's been so good, visiting Mummy at every possible opportunity, taking her little presents and reading to her, as well as fetching any messages she wanted. It isn't as though he were a relative or a real friend – he's just the fellow who rescued her when she was attacked. Ever since then, he's kept an eye on her, that's all. I just wish Daddy could be here today – well, I'm sure he would if he could – but maybe he'll come up to Tregarth if he can get a few days off.' She flung open the back door. 'Aren't we lucky that it's warm and sunny? It's nice to think that Mummy's first venture out will be into sunshine. See you later!'

Marianne had taken the clothing which her daughter had brought, pulled the curtains round her bed, and slowly, but without any help from anyone, put on the underwear, the blue cotton frock, the cardigan and the ancient sandals. Then she had added the dark grey coat and the small

335

grey hat trimmed with artificial violets and looked, shrinkingly, in the mirror she had found in the black leather handbag her daughter had provided.

She could not see her whole figure, of course, but only her face. Still criss-crossed with scars, still pale as milk because she had not put a foot out of doors for months and months, the eyes still frightened, the mouth trembling. She wanted to leave the ward, of course she did, yet the thought scared her half to death. But she tightened her lips at herself in the mirror and slitted her eyes, determined that no one should guess how the thought of normality terrified her.

With a confidence she was far from feeling, she swished back the curtains and smiled at Libby, who was sitting on an empty bed further down the ward, a fact which would have horrified Sister had she known. 'I'm ready, darling,' she said, trying to sound gay but knowing it was a poor effort. 'I'd love to be able to walk to Crocus Street, which isn't really very far, but I'm afraid I couldn't possibly make it. Oh, it's awful to feel so weak, but I dare say there will be a taxi on the rank.'

Libby tucked her arm into her mother's, smiling brightly. 'Oh, Mummy, this is a great day, so your carriage already awaits,' she said. 'Wait till you see!'

Marianne had already said her goodbyes to the staff and handed over the small presents which were all they could manage because of restrictions and rationing. They would have liked to buy rare and precious gifts for all the nurses, with the possible exception, Libby said, of Nurse Hodges, but Auntie had saved their bacon by sending them a quantity of shell eggs, as they were now being called, to differentiate them from the dried sort. She had also sent several large slabs of home-made toffee, which Mr Brett had hammered into bite-size pieces and Libby herself had weighed into quarter-pounds before slipping them into brown paper bags, and they had managed to buy a couple of pairs of silk stockings for the sisters.

Now, Marianne clutched her daughter's fingers nervously as they traversed the corridor, crossed the foyer and emerged into the summer sunshine. Directly opposite them, there was a taxi, its rear door already opening, and for a moment of blind panic Marianne thought that the figure beginning to emerge was that of Neil, the man she knew to be her husband. Yet she had seen him so rarely since her accident that he was almost a stranger – and strangers still frightened her. She stepped back, heart hammering, perspiration prickling along her scalp. Having been shown her wedding photograph, she was forced to believe that it was true: she and Neil had once been in love, but she doubted that this was still the case. Perhaps he had loved her for her beauty, for she could tell from the photograph that she had been a very pretty girl indeed, and now that her looks had gone his love had cooled.

She knew, of course, that she was still not herself,

was deeply confused. She could see no sign of love in the brilliant blue gaze he turned on her, yet thought that perhaps the accident had made her over-sensitive. She had hinted as much to the nurse with whom she was friendliest, Sister Paula Jones, and Sister had told her that men frequently found the hospital atmosphere inhibiting to the natural emotions they knew they should be feeling and that this would pass when the two of them were in familiar surroundings once more.

Marianne could only hope that the sister was right, but secretly she did not believe a word of it. Her looks were not going to improve simply because she had left the ward, and if Neil had truly loved only her beauty, and was indifferent to her character, then leaving hospital would not change a thing.

'In you get, Mummy,' Libby said cheerfully now, as Bill Brett, grinning and red-faced, scrambled out of the taxi, pushed her small case into the front, took his place facing them and slammed the door shut.

The taxi started off at once, clearly having been told in advance to head for Crocus Street, and Bill grinned reassuringly at her. 'Feel kind o' funny?' he asked in his deep, rumbling voice. 'It must seem mortal strange to be in the open air again, lerralone seeing all the folk and traffic. I had a word wi' Teddy Brassnose, him what were in hospital for the best part of a year while they got him fitted up wi' artificial legs, and he said he were fair terrified every time he poked his nose outside his front door. His advice to you, Mrs Sheridan, was to make haste slowly. Get used to being inside your own house, then nip into the yard now and again to fetch in kindling, or get the washing off the line. After that, a little walk along Stanley Road . . . but I reckon you know what I mean.'

'Yes, I understand, and it's good advice,' Marianne assured him. 'As you know, Libby and I are going in the country for a few weeks. I thought I'd be all right to leave the city after a couple of days, but I was mistaken, I know that now. I could no more get aboard a train than fly to the moon. So I'll do as your pal says and make haste slowly.'

They knew they were in for trouble when the enemy aircraft swooped low over the convoy. Black against the rising sun, it circled them twice, then raced off, to be followed, half an hour later, by two others. Messages whirled around the convoy, because everyone knew where the planes had gone and what the result would be. Because of their very nature, fully laden convoys moved slowly, so all the enemy aircraft had to do was pinpoint their position and direct any ships in the vicinity, particularly U-boats, to the sitting duck.

The escort had done their best to bring the aircraft down but had had no luck, and though they changed course immediately the planes were out of sight they knew that, unless there was a miracle, they could not possibly escape the attack that was to come. Neil did everything that he should do, including sending up a prayer for bad weather – heavy rain, a fierce tropical thunderstorm, a thick rolling white fog, even a high wind to cause heavy seas – but it remained calm, the sea like a millpond, the sky above innocent even of a wisp of cloud.

The escort knew it was useless to try to hurry the convoy, yet they circled the merchantmen impatiently, like snapping dogs round a flock of sheep, and they must have made some impression, for the first enemy shipping was not spotted until mid-afternoon. Desperately, hastily, the convoy began to weave as full steam ahead was ordered, but within a couple of hours the battle had begun. Sea battles are terrible things, reminding Neil of a fight between dinosaurs, for both attacker and attacked can only move ponderously and end up simply slogging away at each other like a couple of old, worn out pugilists, scarcely aware of what is happening through the smoke.

Neil gave his orders to the gunnery officer and saw them carried out. The crew fired their torpedoes and watched them sizzling through the water, giant silver fish of destruction. The *Irascible* was fast compared to her charges, but the Jerries had a cruiser which would outstrip them all; it was possible they were doomed, but in the confusion it was hard enough to tell friend from foe, let alone calculate the enemy's superior firepower.

Night came. Neil thought, though he could not

be sure, that three of the convoy which he was protecting had been sunk. Despite the darkness, he had seen the death throes of the SS *Santa Katrina* and had noted, with pain, how men had tried to scramble aboard the lifeboats only to be dragged down as the mother ship plunged to the ocean bed.

The night wore on. Other ships suffered similar fates to that of the *Katrina*. There were screams amidst the thunder of the guns and the crash of wounded shipping, and Neil gritted his teeth until his gunnery officer said, flat-voiced, that they had run out of shells, which was the signal to get as far away from the battle as was humanly possible. Without firepower, they were useless to the escorts and to the merchantmen; all they could do was skedaddle, and that quickly.

They were leaving the convoy when they were hit. Neil imagined that one of the U-boats had noticed their change of course and followed, eager for the chance of another kill. Her torpedoes, two of them, slammed into the *Irascible* below the water-line. They had no defence, not so much as one depth charge remaining, and very soon, Neil realised, there would be no *Irascible* either, for she was already low in the water and sinking rapidly.

The bo'sun approached him, his sandy eyebrows lifting an enquiry which he did not need to put into words. 'Pipe abandon ship,' Neil said quietly, though already he could see the queues of men forming up to get aboard their lifeboats. He watched, fighting a sort of sick despair, as the boats were lowered. The first one was fully laden as it went over the side; the second was so near the water because of the list of the ship that the men mainly chose to jump down into it as it settled on the calm sea. He would be last off, naturally, but the bo'sun shouted to him to hurry and he realised that the *Irascible* was going down fast; realised, too, that unless the boats managed to get well clear they could easily be dragged down in the ship's wake. He was in the cockleshell craft when the U-boat fired another torpedo. It struck the first lifeboat, cutting it neatly in half, and staining the sea with debris and blood, but some of the men managed to struggle to other craft and climb aboard. There was a good deal of cursing, since there had been no need for the U-boat to fire that last torpedo. The *Irascible* had gone; all that remained a circle of oil and a great deal of debris, and Neil told himself that no British submarine would have fired on defenceless men in lifeboats, though he had to acknowledge that in the confusion of a sea battle mistakes could occur.

But the bo'sun and the other men were looking towards him, waiting for him to tell them what to do. He looked around the boat. There were oars, life jackets under the seats, and of course iron rations, so they might yet come out of it with whole skins. He pointed to two of the sturdiest seamen. 'We'll take turns in rowing whilst it's still night,' he said. 'In the dark it's too easy to make a mistake and approach enemy shipping. I've no idea what's happened to the others, but when daylight comes we'll know a bit more.'

There were murmurs of agreement from the men around him and presently Neil sank into a state which was neither proper sleep nor wakefulness, and began to relive again what had occurred over the past few months.

It had started with his visit to Libby and Marianne, of course. Fiona had not wanted him to go at all, had actually admitted to being jealous of Libby – jealous of a nine-year-old child! He had not understood it but had told himself that it was simply the result of her pregnancy. He remembered, or thought he did, how fond of Libby Fiona had been before the war. She had adored her little niece, always buying her presents and planning treats such as trips to the theatre or a shopping spree.

So he had travelled back to Southampton, secure in the knowledge – or so he thought – that his darling Fiona would welcome him with open arms and would be eager for news both of Libby and of Marianne herself. He had planned to tell her immediately that Marianne would be scarred for life, might never become her old self once more, because he thought that this would dissipate any jealousy she might feel towards her older sister. He had sat in the train, putting Marianne completely out of his mind, not even remembering how sweet Libby had been, nor how kindly old

Gammy had welcomed him to her home. If she had known . . . but fortunately she had not.

He had left the train at Southampton, filling his mind with thoughts of Fiona, her beauty and liveliness, and longing to get a bus or a taxi to the village, but knowing he could not do so immediately. First he had to visit the *Irascible*, make sure that all was well there, and confirm his orders.

He had arrived on board to be met by his second in command with what had once been sealed orders in his hand. At the sight of his skipper, a relieved smile had broken out over Simpson's face. 'It's great to see you, sir; I opened the orders just in case you'd missed your connection and wouldn't be back in time,' he had said breathlessly. 'We're to sail immediately.'

'Immediately?' Neil had said, feeling his heart sink. 'But my wife doesn't know I'm back in Southampton, let alone going straight to sea. Is there time for me to get into a taxi and rush home?'

Simpson had pushed the papers into his hand, shaking his head. 'Not a hope, sir,' he had said. 'Send a telegram.'

Neil had done just that, knowing how upset and disappointed his young love would be, and doing his best to explain his helplessness in the face of orders. He had been horribly aware that Fiona's baby – their baby – might easily arrive in his absence and had hoped Fiona would understand that he had no choice. The telegram had cost him a small fortune, but if it cooled Fiona's wrath it

344

would have been worth every penny, he had told himself as he left the telegraph office and hurried back to the *Irascible*.

That voyage had been relatively uneventful and they had found themselves back in Southampton by mid-April. Now Neil remembered how, the moment they had docked, eager with anticipation, he had run to the nearest taxi and ordered the driver to take him to the cottage. Wondering what his reception would be, he had paid off the taxi and rushed up the path to the cottage door. It had been mid-afternoon, so he had not been unduly surprised to find the door locked, and had bent over to fish out the loose brick behind which Fiona always hid the key. He had unlocked the door and gone inside, and known immediately that the place was empty; had been empty for a while. It smelled damp, and despite the fact that it was a chilly spring day the ash of the kitchen fire was damp too.

He had dumped the small bag he carried on the kitchen table and had then seen the envelope. It was addressed to *Neil Sheridan* in Fiona's large, unformed handwriting and Neil had subsided on to the nearest chair, slit open the envelope and begun to read.

Dear Neil,
    Your telegram was the bloody end, so I'm off. Shan't tell you where I'm going because I don't want you following me. If you are around when

345

the baby comes, I know you'll nag me to keep it,
which I won't do. Once it's born and off my hands,
I might come back to you or might not, depending
how I feel. At the moment, I'm so angry with you
I can't think straight. You say you have to obey
orders, but I'm sure that's not true. Other women
have babies; don't tell me their fellows go to sea
and leave them to cope alone.
   Fiona.

He had been staggered and horrified by the
letter, of course he had, yet he had known, sham-
ingly, that there had been an undercurrent of relief.
He would go straight to the nursing home and
find out where she had gone after the baby's birth;
they would doubtless know. He had cursed himself
for letting the taxi go, but just as he had been
locking the cottage door behind him he had heard
a bus draw up at the nearest stop and had managed
to get aboard.

Fiona had not been at the nursing home, had never
been there. Matron had been quite annoyed but had
told him that his wife – and here she had given him
a shrewd and unfriendly glance – had said she was
returning to Liverpool where her parents would
support her whilst her husband was at sea.

He remembered his indecision and how he had
not known what to do for the best. The *Irascible*
would not be in port for long enough to allow him
to return to Liverpool, and anyway, he had not
believed for one moment that Fiona had returned

to Crocus Street. He had known she might do so after the baby's birth – she had said as much – but now he realised that this was probably an empty threat. Fiona loved to be popular, hated disapproval, and if she had simply turned up in Crocus Street too many questions would have been asked. No, wherever Fiona had fled to, it would not have been back to Liverpool. When he had returned to the *Irascible* it was to find that she was once again to sail on the evening tide.

It had been April when he had discovered that Fiona had left him and now it was June. Grimly, he had continued to escort the convoys across the ocean, trying not to worry about his lost love. Fiona, he told himself, would always land on her feet and the *Irascible* would somehow manage to avoid trouble.

The weeks had passed without incident and the convoy had been proceeding calmly on its way when their luck had run out, which was why he was sitting in the lifeboat right now, telling himself that things could have been a good deal worse. He was alive, uninjured, and when day dawned someone would pick them up and this time, when he returned to port, he really would find Fiona.

Looking up at the stars twinkling above him, he wondered what Fiona would say if she could see him now. He could not believe she would wish him harm, wanted to believe that she missed him, as God knew he missed her. He found he was forgetting the irritable, edgy Fiona and her ridiculous demands, remembering instead the girl he had fallen in love with, not only for her beauty and liveliness, but for her sweet disposition and loving ways.

Next to him, on the hard wooden seat, the bo'sun pointed to the horizon. 'It's getting light; dawn will be breaking in an hour or so,' he said in a low voice. 'I think the fellows ought to stop rowing now, then we'll have a better chance of being picked up by one of our own craft.'

'Right,' Neil said, and gave the order. The bo'sun was right, the light was definitely strengthening in the east.

Three hours later, they were picked up by a somewhat battered corvette. She was not one of the original escort but had simply seen one of the crippled merchantmen and headed for it, passing so close to the *Irascible*'s lifeboat that their hail had been heard and the corvette had dropped a rope ladder and got the crew aboard. When one of the seamen told Neil that they were heading for Liverpool, he felt that fate had taken a hand. He and the other survivors had really suffered remarkably little, for the June night had been warm and the sea calm. Neil was aware that they had been extremely lucky, particularly when he considered the fate of the rest of the convoy. He guessed that the shipping would have scattered and would now be doing their best both to regroup and to get into safer waters as soon as possible, and here he was, going back to Liverpool, where he would certainly discover his darling Fiona's whereabouts.

Oh, he did not think for one moment that she would have returned to the city, but he was pretty sure that she would have given Gammy, and probably Marianne, her new address. Once he had that, he could make up his mind what would be best to do, for he had realised that the next move really should be Fiona's. He could write to her, suggest a meeting, explain that the *Irascible* was no more, that he would certainly get some leave before being given another command. She might reply or she might ignore his letter, but one thing he was determined she must do. She must tell him if she had borne a healthy child, and whether she had kept it or given it up for adoption. He knew he had no rights, would not have dreamed of making any claim; it was simply the knowing that was important, and surely Fiona would not deny him that.

Thinking of Liverpool made him think of Marianne. He had received a bundle of mail the last time the *Irascible* had docked; three of the letters had been from Libby, a couple from Gammy and a couple from his own parents. Libby had been delighted that her mother had improved so much, had said that by the time Daddy received this letter she and Mummy would probably be back at Tregarth, but if not they would certainly be in Crocus Street. She had given him a delightful account of the woman she had been told to call Aunt Edith and thought that Gammy was very much better now that she had another grown-up to give her a bit of a hand.

They aren't like any other grown-ups I've ever come across, she had written. *They argue over everything, but Mr Parsons says women are like that and it doesn't mean they don't love one another. He said to watch carefully, so I did, and I think he's absolutely right. Daddy, they enjoy arguing! I hope it doesn't upset Mummy when she comes out of hospital, but Mr Parsons doesn't think it will; he thinks it will make her laugh. She laughs often now, which the nurses say is a good sign.*

Neil decided that if Marianne was in Crocus Street, he would take a room at the Sailors' Home whilst he was in the city. The little house would be dreadfully crowded and he did not mean to make things worse. If she was at Tregarth, of course, he would visit her there, but only for a day at the most. He longed to see Libby, but that longing was offset by a deep desire not to see his wife. Since his January visit, he had begun to be convinced that she remembered more than was good for him. He knew of course that he had behaved badly, that it was at least partly his fault that she had been knocked down, but he wished, fervently, that his behaviour should not become known to anybody but Marianne.

Perhaps the worst part was not being absolutely certain just what she did know. He had been careful not to use Fiona's name but he remembered what Marianne had said just before she ran into the road:

*You claim to be in love with a lively young girl; why
don't you say it's my sister?* she had asked. *I've
suspected for a long time now . . . oh, my God, I can't
bear it!*

She had turned blindly away from him and run
into the road, and when she came round Neil had
waited helplessly for the accusation which he
acknowledged he deserved. Yet he knew from
Libby's and Gammy's letters that she had said
nothing. At first this had been comforting, for he
had assumed she had forgotten what had sent her
flying into the road, but now he felt sure she
remembered at least part of what had happened.
So, really, it was a bit of luck that he was on his
way back to the city. He made up his mind that
he would ask Marianne straight out. Oh, he would
not quote his very words, but he would ask her if
she remembered their quarrel; they could go on
from there. Feeling better for having made a decision, he settled down to compose a short speech,
even deciding upon the moment when he would
kiss his wife and congratulate her upon her
recovery. He told himself severely that of course
he was glad she was better, even though he knew
that the love he had felt for her once had died. But
there was no reason why friendship should not
take its place, he decided.

Of course if Fiona did decide to return to him,
he would have to come out with the whole story,
or at least a good part of it, but that was not an
insuperable obstacle to good relations. War, with

its long absences, would be responsible for a good
few marriage break-ups, he was sure, so there was
no reason why folk should not accept that his
marriage was simply a casualty of the conflict. The
fact that he had been unfaithful with his wife's
sister need never come out, for when the war was
over he intended to return to Plymouth, where he
had been born and bred. If Fiona returned with
him, it would be as Mrs Sheridan, and since his
parents had never met his sister-in-law, it might
be possible to keep her identity a secret. It was
irritating that Libby, who was very fond of her
grandparents, might spill the beans, for he knew
she would want to visit him once he was settled.
But none of this could happen until the war ended
and he told himself, optimistically, that by then
Libby would be older and wiser. He would talk to
her, explain the situation, and she would surely
understand.

Satisfied, he walked across the deck of the
corvette to stand in the bows, gazing ahead. Not
long now, he thought. It'll be grand to see the Liver
Birds looming up as we turn into the Mersey
estuary; grand to see Liverpool again.

Marianne had been home a week and was settling
in nicely. She was however puzzled by the fact that
Bill took up far more of her thoughts than Neil,
despite the fact that the latter was her husband.
Somewhere, in her subconscious perhaps, she
realised that she trusted Bill completely and did

not trust Neil at all. She searched her mind for some reason for what seemed an illogical distrust, but could only come up with a vague memory of finding a pillow on her bed at the house in Sydenham Avenue which smelt of a perfume not her own.

But this was plain ridiculous, the result of too much thinking, too much imagining. Bill was her good friend but Neil was her beloved husband . . . yet she realised that even the thought of Neil's hand on hers was no longer comforting; instead it made her feel apprehensive, as though some part of her knew all was not well.

After a couple of weeks in Crocus Street, Libby thought her mother was quite strong enough to make the journey to Tregarth, though Marianne had warned her that she did not mean to stay there for longer than a few days at the most. So the two set off, continuing their conversation as the train chugged towards the village. 'I'm so much better that I want to try to return to work at the factory,' Marianne said. 'Bill thinks it's a good idea and you know I have a great respect for his opinion. He thinks that spending time doing nothing in particular, pottering round the house, getting the messages and so on, gives me too much time to feel sorry for myself, and I believe he's right. At any rate, when I'm busy I seldom feel anxious and I'm sure – well, I know – that Mr Reynolds would be glad to have me back.'

'But when I'm at Tregarth, you'll have lots to do because you'll have all my work as well as your own,' Libby pointed out. 'I know you love the factory, Mummy, but I don't want you to overdo it and get ill again. The doctors did say to take things gently.'

Marianne nodded, smiling. 'Make haste slowly was the way Bill put it,' she observed. 'Well, we'll talk about it when we return from Tregarth.'

Libby opened her eyes very wide at this. 'We?' she squeaked. 'But won't I be staying, Mummy? I thought you wanted me to be away from the city until the war was over.'

'Well, I do want you to be safe, of course,' Marianne said. 'But you know Aunt Edith only agreed to come to Crocus Street for a few weeks, and now she's getting quite eager to move on.'

'But Gammy told me that Aunt Edith's cousin's house was simply crammed with relatives, which was why Aunt Edith agreed to come to us,' Libby said. 'What has changed? Have some of them moved out?'

'No, no. Aunt Edith has a sister who lives in Southport. Her husband – Aunt Edith's brother-in-law, I mean – was a good deal older than his wife and died a couple of weeks ago. Don't you remember Aunt Edith and Gammy going off to a funeral? Well, that was him, and whilst they were there, Beryl, that's Aunt Edith's sister, asked Edith to move in with her and she agreed to do so as soon as we get back from Tregarth. So you see, darling, I think we shall need you in Crocus Street, though of course if the raids start again you'll have to go back to Tregarth.'

The train pulled into the station and they were met by Dewi with the horse and cart, and went straight up to the castle, since there had been great changes in Libby's absence. Matthew now seemed to be living there five days a week, and when Libby questioned this and said that Auntie must miss him horribly, he had laughed and given her a poke in the ribs. 'Auntie's up here almost every day for one reason or another,' he told her. 'You see, Uncle Frank – he's told me to call him that, so don't look so surprised – has agreed to help me with my work so that I can go to university, perhaps as much as a year early. And when I do go into the village to school one of the men harnesses up the pony and trap so I can ride in it. It's the life of Riley, I'm telling you.'

'Old Mother Riley?' Libby questioned, genuinely puzzled. 'I shouldn't have thought . . .'

'Twerp! It's an expression. I don't know where it comes from but it means . . . oh, well, it means things are going your way,' Matthew said, somewhat confusedly. 'Now you're back I reckon you'll get a lift down to school whenever I'm going into the village. Uncle Frank's ever so nice, honestly he is. Even Auntie agrees, and you know how she used to feel about him.'

'I don't think I shall be staying,' Libby said sadly. 'My grandmother is finding things difficult and

Mummy means to go back to work just as soon as she can. So they'll need me, you see.'

Matthew pulled a face. 'So do we need you,' he said. 'But I can't believe your mother will let you live in that horrible great city when you could be safe here, at Tregarth, with Auntie and me.'

'Except that you're hardly ever at Tregarth,' Libby reminded him. 'Still, I expect you'll come back in the school holidays, won't you? Oh, Matthew, I do hate change and war seems to change everything. But perhaps you're right, perhaps Mummy will let me stay. She'll see what a help I am when Mr Ap – I mean Uncle Frank – starts cutting the hay.'

'I hope so,' Matthew said rather doubtfully. 'I've missed you ever so much and so has Auntie. But if you don't – stay, I mean – then letters are the next best thing, and you're an awfully good letter writer.'

The two young people were sitting in the breakfast parlour of the castle whilst Marianne, Auntie and Mr Ap Nefydd talked in the drawing room. Libby wondered if they were asking about her father but hoped that Auntie was trying to persuade Marianne to let her remain at Tregarth. After all, she was only ten years old and surely could not be expected to take responsibility for Gammy and the lodgers once Aunt Edith had left. She determined to buttonhole Auntie when her mother was not around and try to persuade the older woman to suggest that Gammy employed someone to help her after Aunt Edith left.

But when she did so it was in the hayfield, and Auntie's mind was clearly on the harvest tea she was spreading out beneath the trees for the workers. She did listen, but professed herself unable to interfere. 'If your mother and grandmother truly need you, and I'm sure they do, my dear, because you are sensible beyond your years, then I can scarcely claim that I need you more,' she said. 'From what your mother has been telling me, a paid helper would not be the answer since your grandmother needs someone to give an eye to her twenty-four hours a day. Your mother said that on one occasion Mrs Wainwright cut the coupons out of her ration book and threw them on the fire, saying they were out of date.' She had been cutting a fruit loaf into rather uneven slices, but now she turned and gave Libby a hug. Libby stared, round-eyed, since Auntie was not a demonstrative person, but she recognised that the hug was to offset a disappointment in store. 'My dear child, I'm truly sorry to say this and I'm sure you realise that both Matthew and I will miss you sorely, but we cannot steal you away from your family when they need you. Besides, there may well be changes to come at Tregarth.'

Libby must have looked as puzzled as she felt for Auntie, her cheeks reddening, said: 'I can't tell you more just yet but I promise you, my dear, that as soon as I'm able to do so, I will write you a nice long letter, explaining how things are. And in the meantime, I know you will do everything you can

to make your mother's life – and your grandmother's – as easy and pleasant as possible.'

To Libby's dismay, Marianne, though fascinated
by every activity the farm offered, did not change
her mind about leaving her daughter at Tregarth.
They stayed for only a week, and when it came to
bidding Auntie and Matthew goodbye, Libby's
tears flowed freely and she saw that Auntie, too,
had the over-bright eyes of one who considered
herself too old to burst into tears, but could not
entirely refrain from weeping.

Chapter Twelve

Back in Crocus Street, as they were all sitting round the kitchen table drinking tea, Aunt Edith announced chirpily that she was packed and ready to leave and intended to go that very evening. It meant that Marianne could sleep with her mother whilst Libby used the small truckle bed, though Marianne sighed at the thought of the three of them in the small room. She had had a room to herself at Tregarth and did not relish sharing with two other people, particularly as Gammy thought night air injurious to health and would never open the window, though the summer nights were warm and the room grew steadily stuffier as the hours progressed.

Aunt Edith left, as she had intended, immediately after tea, and Bill came round early the following morning, shaking hands with Marianne and then with Libby, his face wreathed in smiles. 'Glad to have you back,' he said heartily. 'I reckon you'd be feeling pretty flat now your little holiday is over, so I thought I'd treat you to a trip to Prince's Park and a high tea. Unless you've other plans, that is, o' course?'

'Oh, Bill, you are kind,' Marianne said gratefully, beaming at him. She reflected that he had proved himself the best of friends, visiting her regularly in hospital and never allowing her to dwell on her scarred face or to worry over the clumsiness she had shown when first attempting to do the small simple tasks which had, to begin with, taxed her mending bones and muscles. 'But I don't think we ought to leave Gammy . . .'

'Of course I meant Mrs Wainwright to come as well,' Bill said quickly. 'Sorry, I should have said. I know she gives her lodgers a Spam salad and a big plate of bread and butter on a Saturday, and that don't take much preparation, so she'll be able to come, won't she? What time shall I call for you? My taxi driver pal has offered to take us to the park, though he can't guarantee to be around when we want to come home. Where's Mrs Wainwright now?' he asked curiously. 'I don't think I've ever entered your kitchen before without her being here.'

Marianne laughed. 'Aunt Edith ruled my mother with a rod of iron and got her up early seven days a week. Now she's gone, Gammy decided to have a really good lie-in and, so far as I know, hasn't yet put a foot out of bed. But I'll ask her as soon as she's up and I imagine she'll jump at the chance of an outing. Oh, Bill, you do spoil us,' she said gratefully. 'We'll be ready and waiting from half past two onwards, if that's all right.'

Bill said that was fine and left and Marianne, glancing at the clock, sent Libby upstairs to wake her grandmother, and pass on the invitation.

But an hour after Bill had left, when Gammy had come downstairs and was sitting at the kitchen table dipping fingers of toast into her tea and telling Marianne and Libby how much she would enjoy the trip to the park, someone banged on the back door and it shot open to reveal a man's tall figure, grinning at them.

'Daddy!' Libby squeaked. 'Oh, Daddy, we didn't even know you had leave. Oh, why didn't you send us a telegram? You're most awfully lucky. We only got back from Tregarth yesterday.'

She hurled herself across the kitchen and into his arms, kissing any bit of face she could reach, and he responded heartily, then stood her down and turned to his wife. 'What a welcome! Marianne, you look so *well*! Do you realise this is the first time I've actually seen you on your feet since before your accident?'

He crossed the kitchen in a couple of strides. Marianne remained rooted to the spot, so shocked and astonished that she simply could not move, but when he took her in his arms and kissed her, she shrank back a little, holding her hands defensively before her. 'Be careful, Neil; I'm very much better but I'm somewhat frail,' she said, her voice shaking a little. 'Oh, how lovely it is to see you – and what a surprise! We had no idea you had come ashore.'

Neil stepped back. 'Sorry, old girl, I was forgetting,' he said gruffly. 'I expect I scared you, bursting in when you thought I was still at sea. The poor old *Irascible* went down in mid-Atlantic a couple of weeks ago. I was one of the lucky ones and got picked up by a corvette whose home port was Liverpool. She was quite badly damaged herself, but limped back into port and I came straight here after I'd reported to naval HQ. I knew you meant to go to Tregarth so I was hoping against hope that I'd be in luck and catch you either before you left or soon after you returned. It may be a week or two, or even more, before I get another command, so we'll be able to spend some time together as a family.'

He gave her a coaxing smile and took both her hands, drawing her gently towards him. 'Am I allowed a proper kiss?'

Marianne gave a tiny nod. He kissed her cheek, then stepped back and she thought she saw relief in his bright blue eyes. Quickly, she turned away from him and addressed her mother. 'Put the kettle on, would you, Gammy? I expect Neil is longing for a cup of tea.'

'That's true; I could do with a cuppa,' Neil said heartily. He turned to his daughter. 'Any chance of a biscuit, or a bit of cake, sweetheart? Then I'll tell you what's been happening to me since we last met, and you can tell me your stories.' He laughed. 'Doing that will probably last us until bedtime.'

Gammy had bustled over to the stove and lit the flame under the kettle, whilst Marianne got mugs and the jug of milk and stood them on the table and Libby ran to the pantry for the remains of Gammy's apple cake. Gammy turned to Neil, reaching up to kiss his cheek. 'Grand to have you home and safe, lad,' she said. 'Only we's off to Prince's Park when we've had us dinners. A pal's picking us up in a taxi; how about that, eh?' She laughed comfortably. 'Your wife's gorra feller what spoils her rotten, 'cos you ain't here to do it.'

Marianne was amused to see Neil looking put out, but said soothingly: 'It's the fellow I told you about, Neil, the one who saved my bacon when I was attacked outside the factory. He's been a good friend to us all and because he knew we'd be missing Tregarth, he suggested a bit of an outing to cheer us up.'

'You could come too, Daddy,' Libby said, hanging on to her father's arm. 'Mr Brett wouldn't mind. He's ever so nice.'

Marianne suddenly realised that the last thing she wanted was for Neil to share their outing. Bill's friendship was disinterested, completely unthreatening. He thought she was happily married, longing for her husband's return from sea. If he spent time in their company, he would soon realise that this was not the case, for though Neil had kissed her, though he had tried to give her a hug, she had looked into his eyes and had seen the wariness there. Furthermore, Bill would realise that her own reaction to Neil was hardly that of a loving wife. If only I could remember clearly what had happened just before my accident, she thought.

363

I know there was something, some sort of quarrel, but it's as though it happened in another life, to another person. I just know that the love we felt for one another seems to have died. I don't know whose fault it was or if there really was another woman – I never managed to prove, even to myself, that he had taken a woman to our house in Sydenham Avenue – but even in hospital I could feel his remoteness. I'm sure he came, not because he wanted to, but because it would have looked bad to stay away.

'Daddy? Do come with us!' Libby pleaded, tugging at her father's arm and doing a little dance of excitement.

But to Marianne's relief, Neil was shaking his head. 'No, darling, I couldn't possibly do that, not today at any rate. I've got to book myself into the Sailors' Home or find some other lodgings, for the time being at least. You are quite crowded enough in this little house; I wouldn't dream of making it worse.' He looked ruefully at his wife. 'It's a pity we gave up the house in Sydenham Avenue . . .'

'Yes; I believe you had a use for it which had nothing to do with me.'

Marianne heard her own voice saying the words and could scarcely believe she had spoken, but having done so she did not mean to retract. She stared at Neil challengingly and saw the colour creep up his neck and invade his face.

For a moment, you could have heard a pin drop, then Neil said awkwardly: 'I – I don't know what you mean. If we had continued to pay the rent in Sydenham Avenue, then I would have had somewhere to lay my head.'

'Well, I suppose you could rent another property out in the suburbs,' Marianne said politely, 'but I wouldn't be living in it. I'm going back to work next week and Crocus Street is on a direct bus route to my factory.'

The blush was fading from her husband's face and she saw his glance dart uneasily around the room, though when he spoke it was placatingly. 'My dear Marianne, we agreed long ago that you should live in Crocus Street whilst you continued to work at the factory, and clearly I should not have mentioned Sydenham Avenue, since it was a bone of contention between us. But I gave way because I could see you were right; living in Crocus Street was best for everyone. As for renting somewhere else, we'll leave that until after the war, shall we?'

'I suppose so,' Marianne said dully. 'But you and I must have a talk, Neil, a long talk and in private. I'm – I'm not myself yet, you know.'

'I agree that we must talk,' Neil said quickly. 'But not right here and now.' He smiled at his daughter and rumpled her hair affectionately. 'You have to understand, darling Libby, that when two people have lived through great danger and unhappiness, even if they have emerged unscathed, they need time to sort themselves out. That's what Mummy means when she says we need to talk. Can you see?'

Libby nodded, though Marianne saw the look of doubt on her daughter's small face. 'Yes, I think so, Daddy,' she said. 'Your ship was sunk, which must have been truly frightening, and Mummy's been in hospital for more than six months, which is as bad, if not worse. So now you want to tell Mummy about your time at sea and she wants to tell you about being dreadfully ill for so long. Have I got it right?'

'More or less,' Neil said. 'What time is this jaunt to Prince's Park going to take place?' When Marianne said that they were to leave at half past two, he glanced at the kitchen clock. 'It's not yet twelve, so if you'll slip your coat and hat on, we'll go for a bit of a walk and talk things over.'

Marianne agreed, but their talk solved nothing. Neil continued to insist that their marriage was not, as she claimed, on the rocks. 'We've been parted for so long that we are almost strangers,' he said. 'I still love you, Marianne, and want to make a go of things, but you have erected a wall around you, so I can no longer get near. We need time together, to relearn each other – can't you see that?'

'Perhaps you're right,' Marianne said wearily. She realised that she was not emotionally strong enough yet to face a head-on collision with her husband. She feared that he would lie without compunction, if it suited him to do so. Feared, too, that she would probably have to pretend to accept such lies. When she was truly strong again it would

366

be a different matter, but for now she would have to prevaricate a little.

As they returned to the house in Crocus Street, she said falteringly that she was not yet ready for a 'real' marriage and was relieved, but not particularly surprised, when he agreed at once. It was the first positive sign he had given that he thought their marriage was rocky, for Neil had been an ardent and persistent lover, at least for the first half-dozen years of their life together.

Upon one more thing they agreed: that for the time being at least, Libby should be kept in ignorance of their difficulties, so they entered the kitchen with linked arms and smiles on their faces. 'All sorted,' Neil said brightly as he closed the door behind them. 'I'm going off now to find myself some lodgings, and when I've done so I'll buy fish and chips and be back here around six, if that's all right. And although I shan't be sleeping here, I'll be back each morning so that we can be together as much as possible.' He turned to Libby. 'Mummy's starting work again next week, but you and I, Libs my love, will find a thousand ways of amusing ourselves whilst she's saving the country.'

Gammy looked up sharply and Marianne guessed that her mother had recognised the sarcastic note in Neil's voice, even if Libby had not. 'Less o' that, young man,' she said. 'And as for draggin' me granddaughter off on h'expeditions of pleasure, you can forget that. She's come back from that there Tregarth to give me a hand, ain't that so, Marianne?'

Marianne laughed; it was the first time she had felt like laughing since Neil had come home. 'You're right, of course, Gammy, but I'm sure Neil will be happy to take you along to whatever form of entertainment he suggests,' she said. 'And don't worry about fish and chips for us, Neil, because Mr Brett is going to give us all high tea when we've been to Prince's Park. We'll see you tomorrow.'

It was dismissal, which would normally have annoyed Neil very much indeed, wives being, in his opinion, the ones who obeyed orders but did not issue them. However, he had been considerably shaken by Marianne's attitude, and did not mean to argue with her until he had thought over the situation. He had not dared to so much as mention Fiona, but intended to do so as soon as Marianne was back at her beloved factory.

So now he slung his borrowed ditty bag over his shoulder and set off to find himself lodgings. He would choose somewhere decent, within walking distance of Crocus Street, but not too close. Buoyantly, totally unaware of the accommodation crisis caused by the May blitz, Neil whistled as he set off along the Stanley Road.

'Morning, Gammy! I take it Marianne's gone off to her beloved factory?' Neil came into the kitchen and began the ritual of taking off his coat and cap, hanging them on the door, and crossing the room to give his mother-in-law a big kiss and to bend over Libby to ruffle her hair. She was squatting on a low stool, holding out a toasting fork upon which was impaled a thick slice of home-made bread.

Libby jumped to her feet and pressed her hot face against his, then examined the slice of bread, slid it off the fork, handed it to her father, and speared the next piece. 'I got up early to see Mummy off, so I've had porridge as well as toast, but by the time Gammy was washed and dressed the porridge had gone so thick and sticky that she wouldn't eat it,' she said. 'What'll we do today, Daddy? First, though, if you'll stay here with Gammy, I'm going round to Mr Brett's lodgings. Did I tell you he'd got an allotment? He's ever so generous and has saved us some onions and a nice bunch of young carrots. There was some cold mutton left over from Sunday and of course with potatoes at only a penny a pound we've got lots, so Gammy's going to make shepherd's pie' – she looked up at him and gave him what she fondly imagined to be a wink – 'and then old Mrs Nebb is coming round to keep her company while you and I go off on our own.'

'How nice to have my life mapped out for me,' Neil said. He had been beginning to think that Libby and her mother were determined that he should have no chance to question the old woman regarding Fiona's whereabouts, but now the opportunity was being handed to him on a plate.

Libby finished the last slice of toast, jumped to her feet and ran over to the back door. 'I promised I'd fetch Mrs Nebb because she's a bit shaky on her pins, after I go to Mr Brett's,' she said. 'You stay here with Gammy; I shan't be gone long.' And without waiting for a reply, she grabbed her coat off the peg, struggled into it and shot out of the back door, slamming it behind her.

Gammy, sitting at the table eating toast, reached for her teacup and shook her head disapprovingly. 'That child! She never walks if she can run and she behaves as though I were in me dotage, which I ain't. I told me daughter the kid had gorra go back to school 'cos she's bright, is Libby, and I won't have her missin' out on my account. After all, school only lasts till four in the afternoon and I reckon if I get one o' me neighbours to pop in during school hours, I'll be able to manage.' She sighed and shot Neil a rather sly look. 'Don't think I don't know what they're sayin' about me, but it ain't true. Oh, I get confused sometimes – who doesn't? – but I know what o'clock it is, as we used to say.'

'I'm sure you do,' Neil said soothingly. 'And I agree with you that Libby ought to be in school. Marianne thinks so too. She told me the other day that she meant Libby to go back to the convent when the September term starts. But I suppose everything depends on whether Marianne can continue her factory work without making herself ill.'

Gammy drained her tea, licked her finger and absently picked up the crumbs of toast on her plate, then collected the used crockery and carried it over to the sink, speaking as she did so. 'Marianne was always a strong young woman; she'll tackle anything she wants to do, and do it well. My other daughter – well, you know Fiona as well as I do – is a different kettle of fish altogether. I dare say you've noticed that her name's never mentioned. Well, it's partly because of Libby, who's taken a real dislike to her auntie. You see, Fiona never was much of a letter writer so didn't bother to answer Libby's screeds when she were at that there Tregarth. Marianne never said a lot, but when she first began to know who she was and where, she asked why Fiona never popped in to visit her in hospital. I told her and told her that the Wrens had sent her sister down south somewhere, but when Marianne were a bit better she said Fiona could have got a few days' compassionate, which she never done.'

'I see,' Neil said thoughtfully. 'And she's not been back since Marianne has been up and about?'

Gammy shook her head sadly. 'No, never a once, though she do write to me reg'lar,' she said. 'Not that you can blame her, 'cos you know what the services are. They've been an' gone an' sent her to the north of perishin' Scotland, so she's got as much chance of comin' home on leave as I have of flyin' to the moon.'

Neil hid the stab of dismay which arrowed through him and spoke lightly. 'Poor old Fiona; as I recall, she always hated the cold and Scotland is renowned for its low temperatures. But you said she writes regularly, which must be some comfort. Just where is she living, by the way? You never know with the Navy: when I'm posted it might be to Scotland too.'

'I think it's somewhere north of Inverness,' Gammy said. She got to her feet and crossed to the dresser, pulling the middle drawer right out and ferreting around behind it. She produced several envelopes, then fished in the pocket of her overall, produced the tiny steel-rimmed spectacles she wore for reading, and turned the top envelope over, slowly reading out what was written on the back flap: *'Leading Wren Fiona Wainwright, Mountfort House, Invergordon, Scotland.'* She turned to grin at her son-in-law as she replaced the envelopes and slid the drawer back into position. 'She likes it up there, even though you're right and it gets awful cold. But I reckon it don't freeze up 'cos it borders on something called the Cromarty Firth, which is like the sea, only from what she says sort o' calmer. She tried to describe it in one of her letters, sayin' it's what the Scots would have called the Mersey estuary, only there ain't a river as far as I know. I keep me letters hid 'cos if young Libby knew where they was, she'd probably burn them, she's that set against her auntie.' The old woman sighed deeply, toddling back towards the sink, into which she proceeded to pour hot water from the kettle. 'And they used to be that fond of one another,' she mourned. 'But I don't deny Fee's not behaved well.' She began to wash the breakfast dishes, clattering them noisily on to the wooden draining board. Still with her back to Neil, she added: 'I used to think you had a soft spot for me youngest . . . mebbe more than a soft spot. I used to think if you'd met her first . . . but mebbe I'm wrong.'

Neil laughed; even to his own ears it sounded false. 'When I first met Fiona she was a kid of eleven or twelve,' he pointed out. 'And right now I'm as annoyed with her as Libby is. She might at least have written to her sister, seeing how ill Marianne was.'

'She did write – still does – but she don't visit,' Gammy said briefly, continuing to clatter the dishes, and presently, having got what he wanted, which was Fiona's address, Neil adroitly changed the subject so that by the time Libby and old Mrs Nebb entered the house, Gammy and her son-in-law were deep in a discussion of where he and Libby should go that day.

That night, in bed in his lodgings on Fountains Road, Neil tried to decide what was best to do. Naturally he longed to catch the first available train up to Scotland, for it was pretty clear from what Gammy had told him that his little love had rejoined the WRNS. This meant of course that she must have had the baby adopted, and with an inward chuckle he wondered what farrago of lies she had produced in order to disguise the real reason for her absence from the service. Or of course she might have admitted the truth, for one could never tell with his Fiona. He caught himself up on the thought. His Fiona? She had behaved disgracefully towards him, never even relenting to the extent of sending him her new address. But then he remembered that they had parted on bad terms, with him wanting to keep the baby, though he knew perfectly well that it was the last thing Fiona desired. He had done his best to see, whilst they lived in the cottage, that Fiona wanted for nothing, but even that had not been enough.

So what was his best course? He knew he no longer loved Marianne as he once had; knew, too, that it was nothing to do with her scarred face, or the way she dragged her leg. He thought, trying to be fair, that no one else would have noticed her limp, but he had done so because he had had to slow his pace to fit in with hers. He had met her out of the factory a couple of times, whilst Libby had remained at home with Gammy, and had been aware that despite the scars she would still be considered a very pretty girl by most men. Neil, however, told himself that he was a perfectionist; once Marianne had been perfect; now she was flawed. Yet he knew that her looks alone would never have made him feel so uneasy, for his discomfort was caused as much by guilt as by her scars.

Yet he could not help admiring her. She was brave, never complained and went out of her way to help Gammy without appearing to do so. She was an excellent mother, teaching Libby from books she had got out of the library, for the factory had agreed that for at least two or three months she might work part time. Nevertheless, much though he admired her, he and Marianne could never live as husband and wife again. When love dies, he told himself, it cannot be resurrected for the asking. Therefore, the very next day he would set out for Scotland, saying that he had been called before a tribunal to explain exactly what had happened to the *Irascible*. In his mind's eye, he saw Fiona, neat in her Wren's uniform, her bush of glowing red gold curls spread out upon her shoulders, her green eyes wide with delight and her mouth curving into the welcoming smile which showed the tip of her tongue, and her small white teeth. Yes, by going to Scotland, he was sure he would be doing the right thing.

Presently, he slept.

However, the next day a shock awaited him. His first task each morning had been to report to naval HQ in case his new posting had arrived, and today they greeted him with the news that he was to command HMS *Sorrel*, one of the flower class corvettes, gave him a travel warrant, and told him to report to Southampton immediately.

Sick at heart, he went to Crocus Street to explain the situation. He did not have to pretend dismay and disappointment, for his heart had sunk into his boots at the realisation that the signal meant he could not possibly get up to Scotland, on this occasion at least. He looked round the room. 'Where's Gammy?' he asked.

'She's gone round to the Hudsons'. I thought you and I were having a trip out today, Daddy – well, you said we were – so Gammy's taken her knitting and a packet of butties, and gone round to spend the day with her old pal. So if you want me to come with you, to wave you off, I can.'

'That would be lovely, darling,' Neil said. 'But we'd best go round to Mrs Hudson's and explain about the signal. Fetch your coat and we'll be off.'

As they made their way to the Hudsons' house on Snowdrop Street, Neil explained that the Navy called any sort of correspondence between ships or men 'signals' since in the old days the only means of communication between shipping was by running up signals to the masthead, 'the signals being flags, of course,' he ended.

Libby nodded thoughtfully. 'I like that, it's really romantic,' she said. 'Daddy, can I ask you a question?'

'Of course, darling,' Neil said, though he felt a prickle of apprehension. 'Though I don't know if I shall be able to answer. Fire away.'

Libby hesitated for a moment, then spoke bluntly, her eyes fixed on her father's face. 'Why aren't you and Mummy true friends any more? When she's in the kitchen and you come in, there's a – a sort of stillness for a moment before either of you speaks, and when you do speak your voices don't sound the way they do when you're talking to me or Gammy. Is it – is it because Mummy looks different now? I think she's as pretty as ever, I scarcely notice the red lines any more, but Mummy thinks she's really ugly. Perhaps if you came into the kitchen and told her she was beautiful and gave her a big kiss, she'd begin to believe what I keep telling her, that she's very pretty indeed.'

'Oh, darling, I'd do it willingly, except that I shan't be here when Mummy comes home tonight,' he said. He hesitated, then plunged into speech once more. 'And, you know, Mummy doesn't like being kissed or hugged . . . not since the accident.'

Libby nodded slowly. 'Some of her bones still hurt,' she admitted. 'Sometimes, if I put my arms round her neck and pull her head down to give her a kiss, she says: "Careful darling, that's a bit painful." But she doesn't say that to you because you don't try to hug her, do you?'

Neil bit his lip. This was getting more and more difficult. As they turned into the Hudsons' yard, he decided he'd better pull rank before Libby's questions got too searching. 'No, I don't try to hug Mummy because I know hugging hurts her. And now, young lady, Mummy tells me that you'll be returning to school in September. Are you practising arithmetic and English language from the books she fetched out of the library? I'm sure, if you go up to the school and explain, they'll give you work to do during the summer holidays, so you won't have fallen too far behind other girls of your age.'

The gambit worked. Libby began to argue that she had no need of extra lessons, that if the convent knew she was back in the city they would want her to start school at once, even though it was only July. They knocked at the Hudsons' back door and Gammy herself answered it, raising her brows enquiringly when she saw who waited on the step. Behind her, Mrs Hudson called a greeting, inviting them into the kitchen and saying that since they were here, she would just nip up and make the beds.

Libby and Neil came into the room and Neil opened his mouth to explain, but Libby was before him. 'Daddy's had a signal from naval headquarters; he has to return to Southampton to take up command of HMS *Sorrel*,' she said importantly. 'Mummy doesn't know yet. Now you stay just where you are, Gammy, because I mean to go with Daddy to his lodgings to help him pack, and then we'll catch a tram to Lime Street so I can wave him off. And after that, I'll get a bus out to Long Lane. I'll tell Mummy that Daddy's had to leave, and then I'll go home and start making the supper. What do you say?'

Gammy laughed. 'You're as bossy as I were when I were your age,' she commented. 'And what makes you think they'll let you go waltzing into your mam's factory? I can't see it happenin' meself.'

Libby laughed too. 'Course they won't. They'll make me send in a message,' she explained. 'Otherwise, if it's something important, they sit you down in the foyer and fetch your mother out to you. Only I shouldn't think this is particularly important.'

'Thank you very much,' Neil murmured. He was beginning to think Libby needed taking down a peg or two. She had simply taken over, ignoring his superior right to say what should happen. He realised that there was no sense in voicing his thoughts, however, since he would have told Libby to do exactly as she had done. So he assured Gammy that he was sorry to be leaving without any prior warning, gave her a kiss, promised to write, and took his daughter's small hand. 'Off we go,' he said cheerfully. 'I hope it won't be too long before I'm back in Liverpool, so I won't say goodbye, but au revoir.'

He and Libby were letting themselves out when the kitchen door opened and Mrs Hudson reappeared. 'You ain't stayed long,' she said in a somewhat aggrieved tone. 'Me son Ben's in the Navy; I were going to ask you . . .'

'Daddy's been recalled,' Libby said quickly. 'Gammy will tell you all about it,' and with that she closed the back door firmly behind them, and she and her father set off across the courtyard, along the jigger and back to Fountains Road.

As it happened, Neil was in luck, for he and Libby no sooner arrived at Lime Street station than they realised his train was waiting alongside the platform. 'Get aboard, get aboard,' Libby shrieked. She knew how easy it was to miss a train. 'I'll run

379

along to the buffet and get you some sandwiches, Daddy, because you might not get a chance to buy anything to eat on the journey.'

'Most stations have someone selling paper cups of tea . . .' Neil was beginning, as he climbed aboard the train and let down the window to lean out, but he was speaking to empty air. His bossy little daughter had already gone, though she turned back suddenly. 'Money, Daddy, quick! I've only got my tram fare, and another shilling in case I see something off ration. Is that the guard about to blow his whistle? No, it's all right, he's having a word with the engine driver. Thanks, Daddy,' she added, as money changed hands.

Neil had put his ditty bag on a corner seat, and now he heard a voice behind him saying admiringly: 'She's a bright 'un – knows what's what and don't waste time wonderin'. Your daughter? She don't favour you much in colourin', yet there's somethin' . . .'

'Yes, she's my daughter; she gets her bossiness from me and her colouring from her mother,' Neil said, grinning at the young sub-lieutenant squeezed in beside him. 'Apparently, she's afraid I'll starve if I have to travel all the way to Southampton without a packet of sandwiches and a cake or two.'

The younger man laughed. 'She's probably right,' he observed. 'I'm going to Southampton meself, and it's a pretty tedious journey. My wife's working in munitions, but my signal arrived yesterday, so she had time to make me a pile of sarnies before I set out. Ah, here comes your young lady; looks like she's bought the shop.'

Libby, panting up beside the window, beamed at her father. 'Two fish paste, two cheese and two blackberry jam,' she said triumphantly. 'I didn't buy tea because I knew I'd only spill it. Oh, heavens; quick, take them!'

The carriage had jerked, and even as Neil seized the packets of food the train began to move and Libby stepped hastily back. Neil, who had still been feeling a little resentful over the way his daughter had masterminded his departure, felt all his resentment disappear in a flood of love. He leaned further out, as his fellow officer withdrew back into the carriage. 'Thank you, darling. Give Mummy my love and say goodbye to her from me,' he shouted. 'See you soon, I hope . . . take good care of yourself!'

Neil wrote to Fiona as soon as he got to his new command, and posted the letter before he set sail. He did not receive a reply for several weeks, and though he supposed, doubtfully, that Fiona's eventual response was perfectly friendly, it could certainly not have been described as a love letter. She had taken exception to his saying that she had deserted him, and also to the questions he had asked about the baby.

Since I had it adopted, it was taken away from me immediately, so I never actually saw it, she wrote.

They said it was a boy, so I suppose it must have been. I saw no reason to get in touch with you since I felt, once I was free, that I wanted to move on. So I rejoined the WRNS, saying I wanted an immediate posting. After all, you still have a wife and daughter in Liverpool, and perhaps it would be best if you and I forgot we had ever been more than friends.

Neil had not known what to think but had written again and again, each letter more loving than the last. He had suggested that Fiona might have some leave and use it to come back to Southampton when he was ashore. Once again, he had had to wait a long time for a reply, and when it came it was unsatisfactory. She pointed out that the journey from Invergordon to Southampton would take days and added, waspishly, that she had better things to do with her free time, rare as it was, than to spend it aboard trains or buses.

Next time he wrote, winter had come, and Neil knew that Scotland was deep in snow, but he suggested that since he had a week's leave he might spend it travelling to Invergordon, even if he only had a few hours in her company. This time Fiona must have written almost by return of post, but once again, her reply to his suggestion was, to say the least, unsatisfactory.

If you come here, I'll make myself scarce and certainly shan't welcome you, her letter said bluntly. *When the war is over, I may want to meet you again, to see how we feel about one another then, but whilst the war continues the WRNS comes first, so far as I'm concerned. I have a good many girls who rely upon me as I rely upon them. Please try to understand, Neil, that I have a life of my own which has nothing to do with the life we once shared. I enjoy getting your letters and hearing your news, but I can never quite forget that, had it not been for you, I would be able to return to my family and receive a warm and loving welcome. You've been back to see Marianne and Libby, but I'm just terrified that if I turn up on the doorstep it will trigger something in Marianne's mind, and she'll know about you and me. When the war is over, everything will be different, so please don't even consider meeting up with me again until then.*

Neil had no choice but to go along with Fiona's wishes, and as the weeks turned into months he grew reconciled to not seeing her until peace broke out.

At Christmas, he managed to snatch a few days' leave when the *Sorrel* needed repairs to her engine room, and hurried up to Liverpool. Libby welcomed him but with less than her usual ebullience. She was back in school and spent a good deal of time with her pals, or with Gammy. She helped with the cooking and cleaning and was, Gammy assured him, as capable of making a meal, or baking a loaf, as Gammy herself had once been.

Marianne was working shifts once more and, though she was always polite, he could not kid himself that she considered him as anything but an acquaintance. Or perhaps that was a little too cold. He hoped she thought of him as a friend, but there were moments when he doubted even that. She seemed to be on very good terms with a fellow called Bill Brett, a bus driver. Neil had seen them once, from the top of a tram, when they had gone shopping in the city centre. Marianne's hand had been tucked into the chap's elbow, and they had been gazing at something in a shop window, and even as he watched, Marianne had turned to her companion, laughing over something he had said, and had squeezed his arm.

Neil had been angry, telling himself that Marianne was his wife and had no right to so much as smile at another man. Oh, this Bill Brett was no Adonis, from what he had been able to see, which wasn't much, but that did not matter. Jealousy reared its ugly head at the mere thought of Marianne's being fond of another, even though Neil knew he was being ridiculous. His mother would have scolded him for being a dog in the manger, not wanting the young woman himself, but not wanting anyone else to have her either.

That evening, when he got back to Crocus Street, he mentioned, he hoped casually, that he had seen Marianne with an elderly chap, looking into a shop window. Marianne looked at him, her expression infuriatingly amused. 'Did you? Then you've seen Mr Brett,' she said, with unimpaired calm. 'I've told you before, Neil, that he's been a good friend to Libby, Gammy and me.' She chuckled. 'He does all sorts of things which Gammy and I can't manage; replaces washers in the taps, unblocks the sink, nails down loose boards – and he's a dab hand at chopping kindling. In fact, I don't know what we'd do without him.'

Neil thought it would have been nice to be able to say she should save such jobs for him, but of course such a reply was out of the question. Instead, he said stiffly that she must convey his thanks to the fellow, since he did not intend to waste a moment of his leave calling on strangers. Then he stalked out of the kitchen, pretending not to notice the hurt look on Libby's face, or the puzzlement on Gammy's.

Chapter Thirteen

March 1943

'Did you have a good day, darling? Gammy's feeling a little better, so I think she'll probably come downstairs tomorrow, but for now Nurse Thompson has told her she'd best stay in bed,' Marianne said. She always worried when her mother was ill, knowing how the older woman fretted, feeling sure she was needed downstairs, and trying to insist that she would be just as comfortable lying on the sofa in the kitchen. On this occasion, however, because she both liked and trusted Nurse Thompson – and, Marianne suspected, because she had felt so ill – Gammy had agreed to stay quietly in bed until she was given permission to come downstairs for an hour or so.

Libby smiled across at her mother as she entered the room, then closed the back door softly behind her. 'I'm so glad Gammy's beginning to pull round,' she said. 'As for me, I had a wizard day, thank you, Mummy. We're doing this "Wings for Victory" thing, so the school sent us out in little groups to visit houses in the neighbourhood. We're asking everyone to give up some of their savings stamps to buy bombers and, in a way, it's to help

Daddy, because the bombers will be attacking those horrible U-boats and the ports in France where they live when they're not at sea. So Gilly, Fanny and I from our class, and Annette and Ruby from the fifth, went all the way out to Prince's Park, where the rich people live. We got ever so many savings stamps and tomorrow, in assembly, they'll be added up and we'll be told which group got the most. The groups were named after zoo animals – we were the zebras – and I wouldn't be at all surprised if we turn out to be the winners. I'm glad Gammy's better, though; I think Nurse Thompson was worried yesterday because Gammy was talking wildly and her face was as red as a beetroot.'

'Yes, she was very poorly,' Marianne acknowledged, turning to smile at her daughter. 'I never realise how much we rely on her until she's ill. Oh, I know we have Mrs Addison in to keep her company when you're in school and I'm on shift, and she's a great help, of course, but it's Gammy who keeps the place running smoothly, you know.'

'Yes I do know, and I know who's been working like a slave today, when she should be in bed,' Libby said. Marianne was peeling potatoes at the sink and now Libby dropped her satchel on to the kitchen table, walked across the room, and took knife and potato firmly from Marianne's hands. 'You go up to bed, because when you're on nights you truly need at least four or five hours' sleep, otherwise you'll make mistakes. Go on, Mummy,

387

up the wooden hill to Bedfordshire. I can finish these and put them on to cook, only you'll have to tell me what else needs doing.'

Marianne sighed and rubbed her hand across her forehead, which was beginning to ache. 'You are a good girl, the best daughter a woman could have,' she said gratefully, drying her hands on the roller towel which hung from the back door. 'I'm afraid I couldn't buy anything off ration from the butcher, but I thought I'd make up some dried egg, mash the potatoes with a bit of margarine, and then fry up a rasher of bacon each. I've made an apple pie for a pudding, and there's dried milk and custard powder in the pantry, but you'll have to sweeten it with saccharin. Oh, how I bless kind Bill Brett! Every time he goes over to see his pal he brings back a few Bramley apples.'

'Oh, Mum, why not go to bed at once? I'll finish peeling the spuds. Shall I bring your supper up to your room or shall I leave you to cook something for yourself before you go off to the factory?'

Marianne smiled at her small daughter, thinking how strange it was to be called Mum instead of Mummy, but remembering that she, too, had shortened Mammy to Mam, perhaps even before going from the juniors to the seniors. 'I shan't be going upstairs, sweetheart. Don't you remember? I've been sleeping in the parlour ever since Gammy was taken ill. And don't bring me any food through because I'll make myself a sandwich and have some apple pie before I leave for work.'

Libby giggled. 'I did forget you were sleeping in the parlour,' she admitted. 'I won't make you a sandwich before I go to bed myself because it will only curl up and dry out. Besides, if you've got time you might want to make yourself scrambled egg on toast. Now you go off, Mum. I'll do my homework first – I haven't got much – and then get on with the supper.'

Marianne blew Libby a kiss and left the room. She reflected that she slept far better on the sofa in the parlour than she did when she shared her mother's bed, for Gammy snored when she was well and kicked and wriggled when she was ill. However, because of Marianne's shifts, they only had to share the bed one week in three. Gammy always stoutly denied that she snored, said it must be Marianne herself, or even Libby, and in fact got so defensive when the subject was mentioned that Marianne and Libby had told each other that they would simply have to grow accustomed and had stuffed their ears with balls of cotton wool when Gammy really got into her stride.

So it was with the anticipation of getting four or five hours' really good sleep that Marianne took off her outer clothing, rolled herself in her blankets and cuddled down on the couch. There was no fire in the parlour, of course – fuel was rationed like everything else – but despite the chill Marianne soon warmed up and presently fell asleep. Almost immediately, she began to dream, strange muddled dreams, though not unpleasant, in which Libby was the headmistress of a convent school and she herself a very young and nervous pupil. Waking, she chuckled to herself; Libby's tendency to bossiness was even entering her dreams now.

She had set the alarm, though she woke twenty minutes or so before it went off, and when it sounded she got automatically off the sofa and began to dress, for she could scarcely go through to the kitchen in her underwear, knowing that the lodgers might still be sitting around the table, drinking cocoa and discussing their day. When she did go through, it was to find only Mr Parsons still there. Despite the fact that there had been no air raids on Liverpool since January of the previous year, the civil defence still continued their patrols.

Mr Parsons looked up from his perusal of the *News Chronicle* crossword and got stiffly to his feet. 'I heard your alarm go off so I knew it were time for me to get to the warden post,' he said. 'Oh, and there's a message for you. It's from your father-in-law.'

Marianne, who had picked up the kettle and was filling it at the sink, turned round so sharply that she splashed water on the floor. 'My father-in-law?' she repeated incredulously. 'But he lives in Devonshire, miles and miles away. Oh, do you mean a letter or a telegram?' She laughed. 'I thought you meant Mr Sheridan himself had called, but of course that's impossible.' She turned off the tap, tipped a good deal of water out of the kettle, and carried it to the stove, explaining as she did so that she fancied a cup of tea before setting off for Long Lane.

She put the kettle over the flame just as Mr Parsons spoke once more. 'It were Mr Sheridan, large as life. He's just like his son – I recognised him at once,' he said positively. 'And don't imagine it's bad news, 'cos it ain't. He's up here on some business connected with his war work; I remember your husband telling us that his dad was doing something connected with the war office. So anyway, I told him I'd wake you but he said not to do so since you were on nights, which meant of course that you'd not be working tomorrow morning. He said to ask you to meet him down at the docks at noon tomorrow, under that there old clock, and he'll take you out for your dinner – only he called it lunch, come to think – and tell you how the family is keepin'.'

'I say!' Marianne said, very impressed. 'Fancy him coming all the way up to Liverpool: I suppose it's some sort of conference or other, about the war. Probably all sorts of people will be converging on the city.' She sat down on the nearest chair. 'Oh, I do like Mr Sheridan; it will be lovely to see him again. We used to go and stay with them, you know, before the war, but though we've exchanged regular letters Libby and I haven't seen them since – Neil's mother is nice as well, but she's something very important in the civil defence world, and what with that, and the long journey down to Devon, visiting them has been out of the question. Now, if I tell

Libby her grandpa is in Liverpool, she'll want to miss school and come with me to the docks, which is just what I don't want, so don't say a word, will you, Mr Parsons? I'm sure Mr Sheridan will make time to see his beloved granddaughter before he goes back to Devon, but I'd rather see him alone first.'

'Understandable . . .' Mr Parsons was beginning when Marianne suddenly gasped, her hands flying to her hot cheeks.

'Oh, my God, I'd completely forgotten. He hasn't seen my face, doesn't know about – about the scars and the limp. It'll be the most awful shock. Do you think I ought to get in touch with him, tell him he may not recognise me? But I don't suppose he told you where he was staying, did he?'

Mr Parsons tutted disapprovingly and wagged a finger. 'You're a foolish young woman, that's what you are,' he said roundly. 'Apart from a couple of pink lines, your face is just exactly the same as it was before the accident. As for that limp, what rubbish you do talk, queen! Considering how bad you were hurt, a little bit of a limp ain't even noticeable, provided you don't try to walk too fast. Honest to God, young Marianne, it's time you took a long hard look at yourself. You're . . . well, if I'm honest, you're downright gorgeous and that there Mr Sheridan will think he's the luckiest feller in Liverpool to be takin' such a looker to some posh hotel for dinner.'

Marianne laughed, but leaned across the table

and squeezed Mr Parsons's hand. 'You're a dear, Mr Parsons,' she said gratefully. 'Libby said the other day that I should stop behaving as though I were as ugly as a witch, and Mr Brett has said over and over that I haven't changed, so even if Mr Sheridan doesn't know me at first, I shall tell myself it's because he's not seen me for almost four years.'

At that moment the kettle boiled, and in making the tea and cutting a thick slice of bread and margarine the subject was dropped, though Mr Parsons's parting shot was that he would eat his hat – and hers as well – if her father-in-law failed to recognise her the next day.

Marianne had hoped to catch Bill's bus up to Long Lane, but on this occasion was out of luck. Through Bill, she now knew most of the drivers and conductors who worked on this particular route, so was able to ascertain that Bill was on early shift that week. 'You'll mebbe see him when you catch the bus back in the morning,' the conductor told her. 'How's Mrs Wainwright? Bill told us she were down wi' that flu which is goin' the rounds. She's a game old gal; I hope as she's feelin' better.'

'She's a good deal better, thank you, only I think she had bronchitis,' Marianne said, smiling at the small cheerful man. 'Thanks for the information, Mr Andrews. My father-in-law is visiting Liverpool and I'd like him to meet Mr Brett, who's been a good friend to us. Neil doesn't get back here much now his home port is Southampton, so he's never had time to visit Mr Brett, but I do feel someone, other than myself of course, ought to express our thanks for all his help.'

The conductor agreed, though he said that Bill enjoyed helping others and probably expected no thanks. The bus drew to a rumbling halt and the girls climbed down and began to jogtrot towards the factory, all of them eager to clock in as quickly as possible. Marianne hurried with the rest, anxious to get out of the cold March wind and into the warmth of her assembly room.

The talk amongst the workers was all of a recent speech by Mr Churchill, and Marianne joined in, though her mind was actually seething with speculation. Mr Sheridan had undoubtedly come to Liverpool on important business connected with the war, and Mr Parsons had made it quite clear that her father-in-law was not the bearer of any sort of ill tidings. She knew that Neil visited his parents if he had sufficient time when he was in port and she wondered, rather apprehensively, if she was to be questioned about her marriage. If so, she decided, she would tell the truth, or as much of it as she was able to remember. The Sheridans were a delightful couple and Mrs Sheridan wrote regularly each week, keeping Marianne up to date with the family's doings. Marianne and Libby wrote whenever they could and, thinking back, Marianne was sure, or almost sure, that the picture she painted of their lives in

Crocus Street was a cheerful and pleasant one. She began to wonder, though, whether her descriptions of Neil's rare visits might have been a little too clinical, for most wives she knew greeted their husbands' return with ecstasy.

I do try though, she told herself now, walking slowly along behind the girls at the long benches, and peering over their shoulders to make sure that the work was being done correctly. I tell Neil's parents about our outings, and when Libby was at Tregarth I told them all about Miss Williams, Matthew and the place itself. However, time will tell why Father-in-law has decided to pay me a visit. I shall soon know what he has to say.

Next day, dressing for her meeting with Neil's father, Marianne put on her best frock and cardigan, and the court shoes which she hardly ever wore because she thought they made her limp more obvious. Gammy had gone downstairs and was sitting in the kitchen, talking to Mrs Addison, so Marianne was able to get ready in solitary splendour. Having brushed her hair into its pageboy and decided that she looked as respectable as one could in wartime, she got out her tiny supply of make-up, dabbed powder on her cheeks and examined herself anxiously in the dressing table mirror. Then, with a sigh, she rubbed the powder off again. Stupid to try to disguise the scars, though she did apply a tiny bit of lipstick.

Presently, she made her way into the kitchen,

where Gammy smiled approvingly and said she looked "a fair treat", and Mrs Addison remarked: 'Pretty as a picture,' before bustling over to pour Marianne a cup of tea.

'I won't have one, thanks,' Marianne said quickly. 'I'm meeting Mr Sheridan under the clock and it will take me ages to hobble there in these bloody ridiculous shoes.'

'Then change 'em,' Gammy said briskly. 'Don't be a fool, girl. A fat lot of good it'll do any of us if you trip over an uneven paving stone and break your bleedin' leg.'

Marianne agreed, rather reluctantly, to change into the worn but comfortable brogues she wore for work. Then she set off for the clock tower. It was strange to be standing there waiting for Mr Sheridan on the very spot where she had so often waited for Neil, and when someone touched her shoulder she actually gave a squeak before turning to face her father-in-law. For some reason she had expected him to approach from the roadway, but in actual fact he had come, as Neil had so often come, from the vicinity of the docks.

He beamed at her, shook her hand, then leaned forward and kissed her cheek. 'My dear, how grand it is to see you again, and looking so well, too, after your dreadful ordeal. Mollie sends her love and wishes she could have accompanied me, but of course this is really a business trip to see their lordships and Mollie is tremendously busy with her civil defence work. I know your own raids, back in '41, were horrendous, but we in the west are very vulnerable from both the sea and the air, being so much nearer to the Channel ports.'

'I do understand, Father Sheridan,' Marianne said warmly. Her father-in-law was superficially very like his son, for both were blond-haired and blue-eyed, but now Marianne saw that the elder Sheridan had a firmer mouth, a more determined chin and a gentler look in his blue eyes. 'I wish Mother Sheridan could have come up with you, of course, but I knew it wasn't possible. Now that Libby is no longer in the wilds of Wales, though, we might manage a quick visit to Devon when I next get time off from my factory. Libby would love it and so would I.'

'That would be marvellous,' Mr Sheridan said, tucking her hand into the crook of his arm as he spoke. 'Now, my dear, your knowledge of the city must be a great deal better than mine so you must tell me where you would like to lunch and then lead me in the right direction. I know you and Mollie exchange letters regularly but not everything that happens can be passed on by post, so I'll fill you in as best I may.'

The two of them set off, and presently arrived at Stanley Road, pausing on the pavement's edge, for the traffic at this hour was heavy. As they stood there, Mr Sheridan asked Marianne if she remembered Neil's cousin Eva and her husband, Danny. Marianne remembered them both, blonde, bubbly Eva and her rather more serious husband, and said

397

politely that though she had never known either well, she remembered them both with affection.

'Well, Danny says he's met someone else and has asked Eva to divorce him,' Mr Sheridan said gloomily, as they stood on the kerb. 'I suppose their marriage is going to be another war casualty, though nothing is . . .'

Marianne pulled herself free of his arm and put both hands up to her face. 'I can't bear it,' she heard her own voice say in a strangled gasp. 'Oh, I can't bear it!' And then, when her father-in-law began to say she must not upset herself, she shook her head violently and turned to face him. 'He . . . Neil . . . asked me for a divorce because he said he'd fallen in love with someone else,' she said in a small voice. '*That* was why I ran into the road and got knocked down! And I'd forgotten all about it until you told me about Danny and Eva.'

Mr Sheridan stared at her. 'Neil asked you for a divorce? Oh, my dear, are you absolutely certain? Mollie and I have always considered you the perfect couple and Neil has never given the slightest indication that there was anything wrong with your marriage.'

'I'm afraid I am certain,' Marianne said positively. 'I don't know whether you realise, but everything that happened, including the accident itself, was simply wiped from my memory. I could remember my sister Fiona telling me that Neil's ship would be in the following day and saying that Neil would meet me under the clock, where we had often met before, but I couldn't remember anything about the meeting itself. And now it's all come back to me. When we met, I remember that he made no attempt to take me in his arms, but I suppose I thought it was because he was in uniform, though it had never stopped him hugging me before. Then – then he broke the news and said some pretty unforgivable things. He said he'd fallen in love with a girl quite soon after Libby was born; she was lively, great fun to be with, and I was boring. He said I was so wrapped up in the baby that I never gave him a thought.'

Her voice broke and she would, once again, have tried to cross the road, except that her father-in-law prevented her. 'You've had a very nasty shock,' he said firmly. 'When there's a gap in the traffic, we'll cross over and go into that little café – see it? – and talk quietly over a cup of coffee.'

Marianne actually moaned. 'That was where Neil and I were going when I was run down,' she said. 'Oh, Father, I'm so sorry! I suppose it was the coincidence of meeting you under the clock – you are very like Neil at first glance – and then you talking about divorce. If I'd realised my memory would come flooding back, I'd never have upset you by telling you what Neil said; it was the shock which made me come out with the truth.'

By this time they had crossed the busy road in complete safety and were taking their places in the small café, not at a window table but at one well to the back. Once they were settled, with cups of coffee before them, Mr Sheridan spoke. 'I believe every word you've uttered, dear Marianne,' he said gently. 'But has Neil said nothing of this since your accident? If he wanted a divorce before, then I suppose he must want one still. Why has he not continued to press for it now that you are back on your feet and in command once more?'

'I'm not absolutely certain, but now, thinking it over, I imagine there may be two reasons. He told me his – his young lady was expecting a baby. Whilst I was in hospital, of course, and in a coma, divorce was impossible, and by the time I regained consciousness the baby had probably been born, so the urgency was over.' She looked undecidedly at her father-in-law, then pressed her hands to her hot cheeks. 'Oh, dear, I shouldn't be telling you all this. After all, Neil is your son, and I know how much you and Mother love him. But I suppose I'd better make a clean breast of it. I – I know the girl he loves, and thinking back I realise that she left the city whilst I was still in a coma and has not come back once, either to visit me or to see her old mother.'

On the opposite side of the table, Mr Sheridan nodded gravely. 'Are you talking about your sister Fiona?' he asked quietly. 'As you know, Libby has been writing to us ever since war broke out, and my wife remarked that the child had written scathingly of her Aunt Fiona's failure to visit you while you were in hospital. We knew, of course, that she was a Wren, but we also knew that she could have put in for compassionate leave and would almost certainly have been granted it.'

Marianne nodded dumbly. Denial was useless since she imagined that Neil would ask for a divorce as soon as the war ended and then the Sheridans would have to know that Neil intended to marry his sister-in-law. 'Yes, it's Fiona that Neil means to marry,' she said. 'To tell you the truth, Father, I've been unhappy in Neil's company ever since the accident, though I could not have said exactly why. His attitude towards me has been so different! Colder somehow, and of course my attitude to him must have been coloured by what I knew subconsciously.' She smiled tentatively at the man sitting opposite her. 'Honestly, though, I'm downright glad that everything's come back; it explains so much. Indeed, when Neil next comes into port, we'll be able to talk openly, because now that I've remembered I'll be only too willing to give him a divorce.'

'But suppose he doesn't want one now?' Mr Sheridan said hopefully. 'I wouldn't be at all surprised to learn that he's changed his mind, recognised your worth. My dear, most marriages need a deal of understanding and hard work from both parties. Won't you give my boy a chance? If he's changed his mind and still loves you, of course?'

Marianne sighed deeply but shook her head. 'Life isn't that simple, Father,' she said quietly. 'Even if Neil still loved me – which I'm certain he does not – I don't love him. Indeed, there are times when he frightens me, when I catch him giving me a glance of such dislike that I can scarcely bear to remain in the same room . . . And now perhaps we had better go along to the Adelphi, or we'll be too late for that lunch you promised me. And if you don't mind, we won't mention Neil, marriage, divorce or my sister Fiona again.'

Mr Sheridan agreed and they enjoyed an excellent meal, though conversation was understandably a little stilted. When it was over, however, and he was accompanying her back to the tram stop, he raised the subject again. 'My dear, I understand that you would never have mentioned Neil's behaviour to me under normal circumstances,' he said. 'But I think I must beg you to let me share the knowledge with my wife. I won't tell her the whole story because I couldn't bear to see her faith in her son so totally destroyed. I'll just say that you have grown apart and that at some point there may be a second divorce in our family. I shall make certain Mollie knows that it's not your fault and we shall welcome your visits, with little Libby, at any time. But my dear, you are a very pretty girl, with a great deal of charm. Is it possible that you, too, have met someone? Oh, I don't mean to reproach you, but if you were both to remarry . . .'

Marianne shook her head. 'You're thinking of Neil's career, and your family's reputation,' she said frankly. 'But I'm afraid I can't help you there; after what I've been through, the thought of marrying anyone makes my stomach churn. Don't get me wrong, Father, but right now I simply don't like men. No, I'll stick to the single state after the divorce comes through.'

For a couple of days after her memory had returned, Marianne could think of nothing else. Her mind worried at the problem and what she should best do. She slept badly, constantly waking from nightmares in which she fought imaginary beasts and fell prey to irrational terrors. But on the fourth day she woke calmly and found that her mind had made itself up during the first stretch of uninterrupted sleep she had enjoyed since her father-in-law's visit.

She realised that since she and Neil no longer loved one another – and of this she was quite certain – a divorce was the only sensible solution. The question which now reared its ugly head was so obvious that she was astonished she had not thought of it before. She had been well now and back in work for a long time and had received both letters and visits from her husband. And never once in all that time had he given her the slightest hint that he was thinking of divorce. Why not? Could it be that her sister had fallen out of love with him, as she herself had done? It seemed possible that if this was so Neil had looked, with his usual calculation, at his options. She did not think that he would jettison his comfortable married life for bachelorhood, though if Fiona could be persuaded to marry him, she had no doubt that his urge for a divorce would come to the fore once more.

Having thought things through so far, Marianne realised that she could not possibly contemplate living with Neil as man and wife. The thought that he might – almost certainly would – fail to concur with her wishes horrified her. What on earth should she do?

But another night in which she slept the sleep of exhaustion found her waking calm but resolute. She would write to Fiona and persuade her to come home. It would mean admitting to her sister that she knew about her affair, but she would promise there would be no reprisals, explain that they must sort the problem out and trust to Fiona's affection for her family to bring her home.

She wrote that evening and waited hopefully for Fiona's reply, which came almost at once, agreeing to return as soon as she could get leave. Once more, Marianne slept without nightmares.

Matthew was sitting in the small parlour at the desk which Mr Ap Nefydd had found for him. His books were spread out before him, and he was frowning over a difficult problem when the door opened. Auntie's head appeared round it. 'Hello, Matthew,' she said gruffly. 'I want a word . . . or has Frank already spoken to you?'

Matthew grinned at her as she sidled into the room, thinking how different this approach was from her usual one. Normally, she would have flung the door open and come crashing into the room, apologising for interrupting his studying, but not meaning a word of it. She always had news of some sort to impart, for ever since Libby's departure and his own removal to the castle she had agreed with Mr Ap Nefydd that she should house the land girls he was now employing, though they came up to the castle kitchen for their main meal. Since Auntie came up as well, this meant that a day seldom passed when she did not pop in to see Matthew, so that they could exchange news. 'I haven't seen Uncle Frank since breakfast,' he said now. 'Why, Auntie? What's up?'

Auntie drew up a chair and sat down, but instead of answering his question pointed to the familiar beige-coloured envelope lying on the desk. 'You had a letter from Libby, didn't you?' she said, almost accusingly. 'So did I. She's obviously excited and pleased that her mother has got her memory back – I never even knew she'd lost it – and says how happy they all are that she can remember everything, because of course it means she has completely recovered. I'm delighted that all is now well.'

'Mine's the same,' Matthew confirmed. 'That's pretty well word for word what she said in her letter to me. Oh well, so long as she's happy . . .'

Auntie leaned forward inquisitively to look at the pages of Libby's letter spread out upon Matthew's exercise book but he covered them firmly with his hands. 'It's not Libby's letter which has got you all of a tizzy,' he said accusingly. 'What's up?'

Auntie sighed and sat back in her chair. Matthew noticed that her cheeks were very pink and her eyes very bright and wondered just what she had been up to, for he knew her well enough to recognise both excitement and just a trace of guilt. Was it some minor household disaster? Had one of the land girls decided to leave, or to lodge elsewhere? But Auntie was beginning to smile. 'I'm getting married,' she said, all of a rush. 'Frank needs another land girl, or so he says, someone to supervise the others, I believe. Even one more soul would make Tregarth somewhat crowded, so I suggested I might come up to the castle; God knows there are enough bedrooms here. Frank said that would be fine, but only if we got wed.' She shot him a shy, almost pleading glance. 'And you know, I really do miss you, Matthew, especially now you don't always come to Tregarth at weekends. Frank said if we were married, we could adopt you, only I said maybe you'd not want that. If you hate the idea, maybe I'll not marry Frank at all,' she ended defiantly.

Matthew was both touched and delighted, but he was also amused, for it had been pretty clear to everyone that the relationship between Frank and Auntie was getting closer with every day that passed. They rarely squabbled now and were usually on the best of terms. He was fairly sure that the thought of adoption was to give the couple a good reason for marrying, but nevertheless, he felt tears come to his eyes. 'I think I'm a bit old to be adopted,' he said gruffly. 'But if I'm not – I mean if it's all right – there's nothing I'd like more than to be a proper part of your family.'

'Too old to be adopted? What nonsense!' Auntie said at once. 'Come to that, I'm too old to be married, though I shall take umbrage if you agree with me, young man.'

Matthew laughed, breaking the slight tension. 'I wouldn't agree at all,' he said stoutly. 'You can get married at any age, particularly if you' – he saw Auntie stiffen, saw a martial look appear in her eyes, and hastily changed what he was about to say – 'if you get on well,' he finished lamely.

Auntie relaxed. 'Good. I was sure you'd see it our way,' she said expansively. 'And now I'll come to the point. Naturally, it's going to be a quiet, private wedding, just yourself, Frank and me, but I'm told we need a couple of witnesses; something to do with signing the register I believe. We shan't get married in the village because you know what folk are, they'll come in droves and maybe snigger behind their hands. After all, Frank and I have known one another for years and years.'

Matthew grinned across at her. 'Can I give you away? Or am I too young?'

Auntie chuckled. 'I'd love you to give me away, but I don't know if that will be necessary as we're getting married in a register office. But what

I wanted to ask you was whether you thought I might invite Libby and her mother. I'm really fond of Libby, you know; I still miss her and enjoy her letters immensely, and her mother is a delightful woman. What do you think?'

'I think it's a very good idea, only will it be possible for Mrs Sheridan to get time off?' Matthew asked rather doubtfully. 'It's a heck of a journey, Auntie . . . well it is to reach Tregarth, at any rate.'

Auntie waved a dismissive hand. 'We aren't getting married in the village; it'll be in Wrexham, which is much nearer to Liverpool than the valley. Frank plans that we'll get married at half past eleven, then we'll all go along to the Wynnstay Hotel on Yorke Street for a nice luncheon.'

'That sounds wonderful,' Matthew said appreciatively. 'When do you mean to tie the knot? Because the Sheridans will need time to make arrangements, I'm sure.'

Auntie looked doubtful. 'We've not discussed dates, but I think Frank would like us to be married as soon as possible. And please don't say "tie the knot", Matthew, because it makes me think of captives and prisoners and things. What a good job the castle is on the telephone! I shall send an open invitation to Mrs Sheridan by the very next post, and ask her to telephone me as soon as she possibly can, giving the dates when she and Libby would be able to join us.'

Matthew smiled. 'How very unusual, to let the wedding guests choose the date of the wedding,' he observed. 'Novel, but nice, because you, myself and Uncle Frank could manage any date, just about. Were you thinking of including Libby's dad in this invitation, though? Because if so, that really will complicate matters.'

Auntie, however, shook her head. 'No indeed. For one thing, we scarcely know the man, and for another he spends most of his time at sea. No, it is just Mrs Sheridan and Libby herself whose names will be on the invitation.'

Matthew agreed that the invitation could scarcely include a man who was nearly always at sea, and then he returned to his work whilst Auntie, whistling, set off in search of Frank to tell him that all was now arranged.

As she left the room, Matthew called after her, 'Hey, Auntie, remember what you tell the land girls? *A whistling woman, a crowing hen, is neither good for God nor men.* You mustn't flout your own rules.'

'It's not a rule, it's a silly old saying,' Auntie said. 'See you at suppertime.'

It was a fine day in early May and Libby was wandering around Paddy's market. She was wildly excited because, on the following day, she and her mother were to catch the train to Wrexham, where they would attend Auntie's wedding. In itself, that would have been excitement enough to drive most things out of Libby's head, but now she had the additional pleasure of being sent out alone, with money in her pocket, to see if she could find a suitable dress for the occasion. Fiona, who was home on leave for the first time since Marianne's accident, had offered to go with her, but Libby had said politely that she would prefer to go by herself. She had never been much interested in clothes and had thought that her best frock, blue cotton with a white Peter Pan collar, would do very well, but Marianne had insisted that she should try it on and with the best will in the world Libby had not been able to do the buttons up, or convince herself that the skirt was anything but far too short. Naturally, she did not mean to disgrace the wedding party by turning up in her grey school skirt and blouse, so she had set off alone that morning on her shopping expedition, determined to prove to everyone that she was quite grown up enough to choose the right garment.

As soon as she had got off the tram she had headed for Paddy's market, for no one bought new, using valuable clothing coupons, if they could buy second-hand, and very soon she had cast her problem upon the motherly bosom of Mrs Arthur, who had had a stall in Paddy's market for as long as anyone could remember and was one of Gammy's oldest friends.

'A wedding, eh?' Mrs Arthur said when Libby explained the situation. She looked critically at her customer. 'White's nice, but not much use after the event, so to speak. Gets grubby too fast, and likely you'd spill something on it which

410

would stain. Pink's nice and so's blue, so long as it ain't too dark, but I reckon I've got the very thing.' She rummaged amongst a pile of clothing and produced a full-skirted cotton frock in sunshine yellow. 'Gorrany white sandals?' she demanded. 'Them brown 'uns lowers the tone, if you get my meaning.' She held the dress up and shook it. 'It needs a good iron, I won't deny it, and the hem's comin' down at the back, but your mam can cobble that up in ten minutes, an' I reckon it's about your size. Come over to the back of the stall and try it on.'

Libby was happy to oblige and presently left the stall clutching a brown paper parcel. Mrs Arthur, bless her, had charged a modest sum for the dress, so there was still money enough for white sandals, if she could find a pair.

As she left the market and headed for the tram stop she was feeling very proud of herself and looking forward to the praise she expected to receive in Crocus Street, but when she entered the kitchen she found Gammy and her mother both looking solemn. Her first thought, not unnaturally, was that something had occurred to prevent their journey to Wrexham the next day, but that proved not to be the case. Marianne smiled when her daughter produced her new possessions, then put an arm round Libby's shoulders and gave her a squeeze. 'Darling, Auntie Fee's had a signal from her officer, saying she must return to Invergordon at once. She was awfully sorry to leave without

411

even saying goodbye, but I promised I'd pass on her love to you and explain.'

'Oh, Mum, what a shame,' Libby said, though she felt a lightening of the heart because the wedding had not been called off. Besides, though she had promised to forgive Fiona, she still felt upset when she remembered how her aunt had behaved. 'Can I nip into the parlour and try my new things on?' she said. 'The frock needs ironing and the hem's coming down at the back, but otherwise it's really rather nice.'

'Of course, pet,' Marianne said, and presently, having approved both frock and sandals, she got out the ironing board, whereupon Gammy said bossily that she was the professional so far as garment pressing went, and took over.

Libby would have tried the dress on again when Gammy and her mother had finished with it, but this she was forbidden to do. 'It'll likely get crushed in the perishin' train,' Gammy said gloomily, 'but we must look on the bright side. Mebbe if you sit real still, and don't eat nothin' till after the ceremony, you won't disgrace us entirely.'

Libby giggled. 'I'll sit still, I promise, and keep my coat buttoned up even if I nearly die of the heat,' she said. 'Then, when we arrive at the register office and I take my coat off, everyone will think I'm Auntie's bridesmaid!'

Marianne laughed too. 'If I know Auntie – Miss Williams, I mean – she'll probably turn up in her old brown coat and wellington boots,' she said.

'And no one in the Wynnstay will even guess we've been to a wedding, let alone that she's the bride.'

'They'll think you're the bride, Mum, because you're younger then Auntie and you haven't changed since you and Daddy married . . .' Libby was beginning, when her grandmother interrupted her, holding out the purse in which she kept her housekeeping money.

'Don't you go sayin' ridiculous things what might upset Miss Williams, or Mr Ap Nefydd,' she said crossly. 'Just you nip down to the corner shop and buy me half a stone o' spuds. I mean to make a Woolton pie for us suppers tonight.'

Libby took the purse and her grandmother's marketing bag and set off, wondering why Gammy had interrupted, and what was wrong with mentioning Marianne's wedding to Neil. Now she came to think of it, though, Libby realised that she herself had been feeling a bit uncomfortable about the whole business of marriage ever since she had overheard the quarrel between her mother and her aunt on the day of her friend Adelaide's party. Frowning, she wondered why Gammy, too, thought the subject should be avoided.

Dawdling along Stanley Road now, heading for the greengrocer's, she let her mind stray back to the day of the party and the argument she had overheard. Auntie Fee had returned a couple of days before – Libby thought that her mother must have written to her, explaining that Gammy had been poorly and was pining for her youngest child, but whatever the reason, her aunt had returned to Liverpool and the house in Crocus Street.

Libby sighed, and peered hopefully into the greengrocer's window. She had not been meant to hear a word of the quarrel, of course; Marianne and Fiona had believed her to be at Adelaide's house but, unfortunately, she had forgotten to take with her the quarter-pound of aniseed balls which were to have been her birthday gift and had returned to the house in Crocus Street. Gammy had been visiting her friend Mrs Nebb so the kitchen was deserted, and Libby had been about to grab the little parcel when the sound of raised voices had come to her ears.

'But I don't *want* him. I don't want to get married to anyone,' Fiona had wailed. 'Remember how young I was before the war. People change, honest to God they do.'

'Well I don't want him either,' Marianne had said crisply. 'Do I take it then that you've reeled in someone else?'

'Don't be so unkind,' Fiona had said tearfully. She had sniffed. 'I don't suppose I've been the only one playing the field. Oh, I shouldn't have said that, because I know it isn't true. Marianne, I'm as sorry as I can be. I'd do anything to turn back the clock.'

'So would I,' Marianne had interrupted. Suddenly the heat had gone out of her voice, leaving it wistful. 'We were such good friends, you and me. But the way you behaved put a stop to all that.'

'Oh, Marianne, I've done my very best to explain and I've said how dreadfully sorry I am for what I did. I've even told you the biggest secret of all, which was the reason why I dared not come back to Liverpool . . .'

'I didn't know at the time, though I found out when my memory returned, and I'm doing my very best to forgive and forget, but it's really hard,' Marianne had interrupted, her voice still calm. 'I know some women in that condition go a little mad and I think you must have been one of them. But Fee, your affair started years ago. I've honestly done my best to forgive, but forgetting is a whole lot more difficult.'

'I know I behaved really badly,' Fiona had said, her voice thick with tears, 'but you know, Marianne, when we were kids I always looked up to you and envied you. I wanted to be just like you, to have what you had, a nice house, a handsome husband, a dear little girl . . .'

'Well, you're welcome to everything but Libby,' Marianne had said. 'I don't want anything but her.'

'Nor do I,' Fiona had said quickly. 'Ever since leaving Southampton I've known I made a terrible mistake. I've met someone who really matters to me – one day I hope you'll meet him – so all I want now, dearest and best of sisters, is for you to forgive the past and for us to resume our old friendship. We were very loving sisters, weren't we? Oh, Marianne, please, please forgive me. Surely, now that I've told you everything, you can understand?

Isn't there anything I can do, or say, to put things right?'

There had been a longish pause which Libby, shifting uneasily from foot to foot, had thought would never be broken. Then Marianne spoke. 'Yes, there is something you could do for me. I realise it's a lot to ask, but . . .' Here her voice had dropped to a whisper and Libby, suddenly realising that she was eavesdropping, or rather had been, moved towards the back door just as she heard her aunt and her mother begin to giggle; heard, also, their footsteps approaching the kitchen door.

Libby fled precipitately into the yard. Then, with studied casualness, she had pushed open the back door and re-entered the room, calling out as she did so. 'Mum, I've been and gone and left my present for Addie behind . . . do you know . . . ? Ah, here it is.' She grabbed the little bag of sweets off the kitchen table just as her mother and aunt, both very red in the face, had come into the room. Hastily, Libby had blown them a kiss and made off as fast as she could, praying that neither woman would realise she had heard their raised voices and known they were quarrelling.

That had been two days ago. Thinking it over as she walked back to Crocus Street with the potatoes, she admitted to herself that she had no idea what the quarrel had been about, nor why they had been giggling like a pair of schoolgirls as they entered the kitchen.

When Auntie Fee had first returned, Marianne had treated her coolly and even Libby had positively cold-shouldered her, but after the row the sisters seemed to have resolved their differences and Libby had accepted Fiona's explanation of her failure to visit Marianne when she had been so very ill. 'I'm terrified of hospitals, and though I kept meaning to come I couldn't quite bring myself up to scratch,' Fiona had said, hanging her beautiful red-gold head. 'And then my job is truly important and very hush-hush. I dared not leave it in other hands and maybe see ships sunk as a result. Darling, try to understand and don't hold it against me! Your mammy has said she's forgiven me.'

So naturally Libby did likewise, glad that the tension between her mother and her aunt had disappeared. Indeed, their relationship seemed to have regained its old friendly footing, for Libby frequently saw them exchanging quick, amused glances, saw them both stifling giggles. If her mother could forgive Fiona, then so could she. It was useless to dwell on something in the past which she would probably never understand, and it was lovely that everyone was friends once more.

Right now, Libby had more important things on her mind. Auntie's wedding, for instance, and of course seeing Matthew again. They had corresponded, even spoken a couple of times on the telephone, but they had been best friends ever since her arrival at Tregarth and she knew that when she saw him face to face she would be able to talk freely, to discuss problems which she would not dream of mentioning to anyone else.

She was still worried that her parents seemed ill at ease with one another, and had tried to confide in Adelaide. But her pretty, plump little friend had not understood. 'Mums and dads always quarrel,' she had said, opening her round brown eyes in astonishment. 'My mum and dad used to remind me of Punch and Judy, because they were always yelling at one another over the tiniest things and sometimes they'd have a real fight and I'd go up to my room and hide under the bed until it was over. That was before the war, of course, which is why I don't hate the war as much as most kids do. My dad's in the Navy, like yours – well, you know that – and when he comes home he's so pleased not to be bucketin' round in his old destroyer that he's really nice to Mam and me. The only time he gets cross is when he's havin' a lie-in and someone starts makin' a row under his winder. And even then he don't blame our mam, but just yells through the glass at whoever's makin' the row. Ain't your dad like that?'

'No,' Libby had assured her friend. 'It's just . . . oh, I don't know, it's too difficult to explain. It's just that they aren't . . . well, loving any more.'

'It's the perishin' war,' Adelaide had said wisely. 'Besides, you're not with 'em all the time, are you? I expect they do the lovin' bit when you're at school, or in bed.'

Libby had decided not to tell her that her dad stayed in lodgings when he was in port, even though Gammy had offered, over and over, to move herself and Libby down to the parlour, just for a couple of nights. But Neil had muttered that he would not dream of disturbing her and had suggested that Marianne might like to join him in his lodgings. On the first occasion, Marianne had been darning a pair of her husband's socks and had stared across at him with an expression so hostile that even Libby had recognised that her mother resented the remark. But all she had said was: 'No thank you, that would not do at all,' and Neil, his face blotching with red patches, had muttered some excuse, got to his feet and left the room.

Now, Libby turned into the jigger, reflecting that with Auntie Fee gone life could return to normal once more, and though she felt vaguely ashamed that the thought pleased her, she knew that it was true. Fiona had been sweet and loving to everyone, had bought little presents and taken Gammy and Libby herself on a variety of outings. Because Marianne was working, she had not been included in such trips, but Libby thought her mother would not have wanted to go in any case. Marianne enjoyed the quieter outings that Mr Brett arranged, though they never went far or spent much money. When Auntie Fiona had suggested taking the whole family out for Sunday dinner, Marianne had said firmly that she was on days the following week so would lie in late on Sunday and probably spend the afternoon getting ready for the week ahead. Libby had opened her mouth to say that her mother could easily spare the time to accompany them, but had closed it after a quick glance at Marianne's set face. Grown-ups, she had concluded, were a weird lot, who made decisions for no reason that a practically minded child could fathom.

Crossing the yard, she pushed open the back door and thumped the potatoes down on the kitchen table. 'I'll peel them later,' she said to the room in general. She turned to her mother. 'I think I'll wash my hair because I can see we shall be pretty busy tomorrow, with the wedding an' all.'

Marianne smiled. 'You're right; we'll be leaving the house very early so there won't be much spare time,' she said. 'I'm going to wash mine immediately after we've had our supper.'

Libby smiled. 'Friday night is Amami night,' she said, quoting the advertisement. 'Oh, I can't wait for tomorrow; it'll be wonderful to see Auntie and Matthew again.'

All the way to Wrexham in the train, Libby was so excited that only her promise to Gammy kept her quietly in her seat. Marianne bought two sticky buns and produced them when they changed trains at Bidston. Libby ate hers with great care, anxious not to mark her clothing.

On reaching their destination, she helped her

mother down on to the platform, 'as though I were a very old lady,' Marianne said, and the two of them set off, Libby at least afire with excitement, though her mother seemed calm enough. They were a little early, but as soon as they reached the register office they saw that Auntie, Mr Ap Nefydd and Matthew had already arrived, and to Libby's astonishment and pleasure a familiar figure stood beside the wheelchair, chatting to Matthew. It was Rhys Evans. He had been tall, broad and fair-haired when she had seen him last and she was sure he had not changed at all.

Libby broke away from her mother to hurl herself at Auntie, then turned to Matthew – and stopped short. He had changed! Instead of the boy she had expected, a young man sat in the wheelchair, smiling at her. His dark hair, which used to flop over his forehead, had been cut very short, and – gracious! – his upper lip was covered in dark down so that it looked as though he was trying to grow a moustache. Libby went towards him and was relieved when he stuck out a hand, took hers, and shook it firmly, showing that he had no intention of kissing or being kissed. 'Hello, Libby, you've grown,' he said. 'I expect I have too, but it's hard to tell when a fellow is sitting down. Ah, they're opening the doors. Rhys will give me a hand up the steps if I need one.' He tutted impatiently. 'You'd think people in wheelchairs never attended weddings, but I dare say I'll manage.'

In fact he did not need to do so. The man who

had thrown open the doors must have noticed the wheelchair, for he disappeared for a moment and then came back with a stout wooden ramp which he positioned on the steps. From force of habit, Libby went to take hold of the handles, but Matthew waved her away. 'It's all right; if I take a run at it I can do it without anyone pushing,' he said.

And Libby, flushing, remembered that Matthew had been growing more independent even before she had left Tregarth. Meekly, she followed him into the building, turned into the room indicated by a tall gentleman in a dark suit and dazzling white shirt, and presently watched as Uncle Frank and Auntie became man and wife.

Libby felt a bit cheated; this was the first wedding she had attended, and despite knowing that it was to be what they called a civil ceremony she had expected the sonorous, well-known words to ring out: *Dearly beloved, we are gathered together here in the sight of God . . . wilt thou have this woman to thy wedded wife . . . with this ring I thee wed, with my body I thee worship . . .* presumably followed by a suitable hymn which, in its turn, would blend into the Wedding March. However, the ceremony was short and to the point, one thing in its favour, and when they left the building Mr Ap Nefydd had actually arranged a wedding car for himself and his bride, explaining that they were supposed to arrive at the reception ahead of their guests, in order to greet them as they entered the building.

'Of course, if we sprinted we could easily beat you all,' he said, grinning at them. 'But I felt a wedding car would be more dignified.'

Auntie, getting into the back of the elderly limousine, snorted. Libby heard her mutter: 'Lot of fuss about nothing, and why do they call it a wedding breakfast, pray, when it's eaten at lunchtime?' However, once ensconced, she waved to left and right in a very regal manner before she was whisked off.

Libby had time to assimilate that Auntie really had made an effort and was wearing a blue silk suit and matching hat, the latter decorated with a bunch of pale blue feathers which drooped coquettishly over one ear. She had not noticed her footwear but poked her mother in the ribs. 'What price her old brown mac and wellies now?' she hissed. 'I think she looks lovely. Even her hair is done differently, not screwed into that horrible bun.'

Before Marianne could reply, Matthew twisted round to grin up at her and for the first time Libby saw a glimpse of her old friend in this strangely mature Matthew. 'Rosalie, one of the land girls, told me Auntie's been putting it in pipe cleaners for the last three nights,' he said. 'Rosalie showed her how. Of course, Auntie pretended it was just a bit of fun, but really it was in preparation for today.'

'Gosh,' Libby said inadequately. 'I never would have thought it, though I didn't really believe she'd turn up in her wellies. I mean, she doesn't wear them for church, does she?'

'True,' Matthew said and began to wheel himself across the road and on to the opposite pavement. 'Uncle Frank has booked a private room at the Wynnstay Hotel and ordered a splendid meal; I can't wait, because we left home this morning without any breakfast. Mrs Bryant offered to get up early and make porridge and toast and that, but Auntie insisted that she would set her alarm and be up at the castle in time to see that we were all fed. Only, of course, once she was in that blue silk suit – it's the one she wore at a cousin's wedding thirty years ago – there was no chance of her risking messing it up by splashing porridge down the front. Then she burnt two lots of toast and announced that since she wasn't hungry nobody else could be, not at that hour of the morning at any rate. I thought Uncle Frank would have blown his top because he enjoys a good breakfast, but he just laughed and hurried us all out to where one of the farmhands was waiting with the pony and trap.'

They were almost at the Wynnstay by now and see could Mr Ap Nefydd and Miss Williams – no, Mrs Ap Nefydd – standing beneath the arched entrance. Marianne, who had been walking on one side of Matthew's wheelchair, tapped him on the shoulder. 'Are they having a honeymoon?' she asked. 'Surely they'll have a few days together before returning to the valley?'

Matthew shook his head. 'Uncle Frank wanted to go to the seaside for a couple of days but Auntie said it would be a waste of money and she'd prefer to go straight home to the castle.' He pulled back on his wheels for a moment, slowing the chair, and looked up into Marianne's face with a twinkle in his dark eyes. 'Only I happen to know Uncle Frank has booked them in at the Royal Hotel in Llangollen. He's hired a taxi to take them there.'

'Are Mr and Mrs Evans coming to the wedding breakfast as well?' Libby asked eagerly. 'It will be like old times for me if they are.'

Matthew, however, shook his head. 'Afraid not. Too much to do on the farm, Mrs Evans said, but she was glad that Rhys could come and represent the whole family.'

At this point they reached the Wynnstay and were warmly greeted before being ushered into a private dining room, where the table was laid with a crisp white cloth and napkins and cutlery for six persons. Everyone sat down and to Libby's joy wine was poured into every glass, including her own, by an attentive waiter. However, her mother beckoned the waiter back and said that her daughter would prefer lemonade, though she did allow Libby a sip of the dark red wine before pushing the glass towards Mr Ap Nefydd. Libby pretended to be disappointed but was really quite glad, and presently the whole party was served with plates of delicious tomato soup, followed by roast turkey and all the trimmings. The meal concluded with treacle pudding and custard, because Auntie said it was Uncle Frank's favourite. Then there were tiny cups of coffee and after that a big bowl of nuts and raisins, and everyone abandoned the table and went into a pleasant sitting room, where they caught up on each other's news until one of the staff entered to announce that the taxi had arrived.

Auntie kissed Marianne and Libby, and extended an invitation to them both to come to the castle for a visit. Libby thought this a wonderful idea, for it made it easier to say goodbye to everyone, believing that she would be seeing them again quite soon. She shook hands with Matthew and Rhys, though the boys assured her that they meant to accompany the Sheridans to the station. 'Then we'll come back and tour the town, and see a flick,' Matthew said. 'But we won't abandon you until your train leaves. Ah, Auntie's getting into the taxi; I wouldn't like to be in Uncle Frank's shoes when she finds out she's having a honeymoon after all.'

Marianne laughed. 'I think she's so mellowed by that excellent meal and all the wine she drank that she'll probably think she's at home,' she said. 'When I saw that turkey, I thought that no one would ever realise there's a war on.'

Matthew grinned up at her as they began to make their way towards the station. 'If I had said the words "black market" before the meal, it might have turned to ashes in your mouth,' he said. 'But actually, it was probably all quite legitimate. Hotels are allowed a good deal more leeway than private folk like us. And I believe Uncle Frank provided the turkey and probably quite a few of the vegetables.' He turned to Libby. 'Did you enjoy your lunch, my child?'

Libby felt her cheeks grow hot. So he considered her a child, did he? Once, they had been equals, or so she had thought, but Matthew seemed to have sprinted into adulthood, whilst she had remained behind. 'It was very nice,' she said stiffly. 'I don't think you should bother to come to the station though, Matthew, because Mum and I remember the way and you did say you wanted to look at the shops.'

Marianne and Rhys had drawn slightly ahead, giving Libby the opportunity to have a few private words with Matthew, and now she said what had been on her mind all day. 'You're different,' she said plaintively. 'You're ever so much older than me . . . no, I don't mean that, but I don't suppose you ever play games and muck about the way we once did.'

'I'm still only five years older than you,' Matthew pointed out, grinning. 'But I know what you mean, and it's true, of course. If I tell you you'll catch up in four or five years you probably won't believe me, but it's true. Tell you what, we'll have a pact. We'll meet again when you're say, oh, nineteen and I'm twenty-four, because by then you'll have taken the big leap into being a grown-up and with a bit

of luck – and a lot of hard work – I'll have qualified as a doctor. How does that appeal to you?'

'It sounds all right,' Libby said doubtfully. 'But
we'll meet before then, surely? At Tregarth, I mean.'

'Well, I don't know,' Matthew said. 'There's talk
of me going to a boarding school, so that I can take
exams more easily, but there're the holidays, I
suppose. And we'll write – don't forget to write,
young lady!'

'I will, but you must write as well,' Libby said.
She felt suddenly lighter, as though a weight had
been lifted from her shoulders. Matthew understood, that was the important thing.

'I'll write,' Matthew promised. 'And now let's
catch up with the other two. It's nice to have had
a chance to talk . . . but of course we haven't
covered everything by a long chalk. Why don't
you catch that later train? Your mother might like
a look at the shops.'

But Marianne explained that she wanted to catch
a particular train since they would be met at the
other end by a friend who owned a taxi and Libby,
agreeing quickly, as they arrived at the station,
found that she was quite glad to say goodbye to
the new, grown-up Matthew, and to wave through
the window as the platform began to recede. It
had been a great disappointment to realise that
never again would they be able to pick up the
casual, easy-going friendship they had shared, but
she supposed it was all part of growing up.
Perhaps, Matthew was right, and by the time she

was sixteen or seventeen, and he twenty-one, they would be on the same wavelength once more.

She told her mother what Matthew had said and Marianne gave her hand a discreet squeeze. 'I'm sure he's right, darling; it's always painful when friends begin to grow apart. Usually girls mature more quickly than boys, but of course with you and Matthew there's the age difference to take into account. But as he says, when you are both young adults your friendship will return to its old footing.'

Libby was relieved to think that all would be well one of these days, and turned to more practical matters. 'Who's meeting us though, Mum?' she asked as the train began to pick up speed. 'I don't know anyone with a taxi, do I?'

'Well, no; but Mr Brett said he'd meet us, and he has a pal who drives a taxi if you remember,' Marianne said. 'Besides, those lads probably had all sorts of things planned which didn't include a couple of females, and I certainly didn't want to go to the cinema! I wonder how Gammy's got along without us?'

Chapter Fourteen
Victory, 8 May 1945

With the war in Europe officially over and the
Tuesday and Wednesday both declared public holidays, Libby and her pals begged, borrowed or stole
anything flammable they could lay their hands on
to add to the bonfires which would blaze up as
soon as darkness fell. On that first night, every
ship in the docks blasted away on its sirens, church
bells pealed continuously and cars, buses and other
vehicles sounded their horns. Bonfires were built
wherever it was safe to do so and effigies of Adolf
Hitler were joyously burnt to a cinder. It was almost
midnight before Libby returned to Crocus Street,
to find herself in disgrace. Marianne and Gammy
had guessed she would be late but, as her mother
put it, midnight was too late for a girl only just in
her teens. 'But I was with my pals, so there was
no danger, and they must have got home even
later than me since they saw me to my very door,'
Libby said. She flung her arms round Marianne's
waist. 'Oh, don't be cross, darling Mum, because
if you are it'll spoil all my pleasure in the party
tomorrow. Say you forgive me!'

Marianne laughed and rumpled her daughter's
smooth chestnut bob. 'I'm not cross, queen, but

you know Gammy's been very poorly and anxiety makes her wheeze. And now off to bed with you because we've a load of cooking and preparation still to do for the street party tomorrow. And don't think that you'll be let off helping because it's a public holiday. You've had your fun today, but I mean to enjoy tomorrow; after all, even the factory will be shut.'

'I thought Mr Brett would come round and keep you company,' Libby observed, helping herself to one of the buns her mother had made earlier. 'Wasn't he on holiday too?'

Marianne shook her head. 'No. The bus company asked for volunteers because, as they said, folk from out of the city would want to come in to join in the celebrations and those in the city might want to visit friends and relations in the country. So Bill volunteered to work all day today and a half-day tomorrow. As he said, it's not as though he's got family to think of, but only himself.'

Libby stared at her mother. 'Oh, but Bill never thinks of himself. He's the most unselfish man I know,' she said. 'I say, Mum, that bun was delicious. Can I have another?'

'No you can't,' Marianne said. She began to pile the buns into an old toffee tin. 'Now stop making excuses and get to bed, otherwise you'll be no use to me in the morning.'

The Crocus Street party to celebrate the end of the war in Europe had been planned for weeks.

Everyone who had a secret store of food willingly produced it and the women of the street got together to cook, to supply chairs and tables, and to pray that it would not rain on their festivities.

Gammy's bronchitis had kept her in bed for a week, but she announced that she felt well enough to get up and totter downstairs. Bill Brett had supplied them with logs and chopped-up branches for their kitchen stove, since fuel was extremely hard to come by and Gammy needed both warmth and hot food. 'You aren't to venture out when the street party starts, though,' Marianne had warned her mother. 'Too much excitement isn't good for wheezy chests.'

Now, Libby was cutting a loaf for sandwiches at one end of the table whilst Marianne was making jam tarts at the other. She looked up and smiled at her daughter. 'We'll take it in turns to sit with Gammy, shall we, darling? Only I really don't want her to come out of doors. It wouldn't do if she were to catch another chill, especially now she's getting better.'

'True, but if we wrap her up really warmly I don't see why she shouldn't join in the fun,' Libby said. 'It's a once in a lifetime experience, Mum, you said so yourself.' She turned to her grandmother, who was sitting beside the fire, glancing from one face to the other as each spoke. 'You'd like to come out just for a little, wouldn't you, Gammy? You can wear your big old winter coat, and the woolly hat Mrs Nebb knitted for you, and if you're cold you can have a blanket for your shoulders, only I don't think you'll need it because it's a warm day with almost no wind, for a miracle.'

Libby put corned beef on a round of bread as her grandmother replied that nothing, norreven handcuffs, would keep her from the street party. 'There ain't a wheeze left in me chest,' she assured them. 'An' I've got me appetite back; hungry as a hunter I am, so don't you try to bar me from the fun, me girl, even if you do think it's for me own good.'

'Oh, Gammy, we'd bring grub in to you even if you couldn't face the street party,' Libby protested, noticing for the first time how old and shrunken her grandmother looked. 'But I know you, you'd stagger out there if you were half dead, and you'd enjoy everything, especially the singing and dancing which will start when the food's finished.'

'Aye, you're right there,' Gammy said. 'I wonder if our Fiona will get back in time for the celebrations? Eh, and there's your dad, queen. Not that he'll be back yet awhile, 'cos it teks a good deal longer to get from Germany to Liverpool than from Scotland.' She chuckled wheezily. 'But they're sendin' the prisoners o' war back as quick as they can, so I guess it won't be that long before your da is home.'

Neil's ship had been torpedoed back in the autumn of '44 and again he had been one of the lucky ones picked out of the water, this time by a German vessel. Libby had written regularly to her father, usually enclosing her letter with those penned by Gammy and her mother, but they had received very few replies. They also sent Red Cross parcels and knew that most of those had reached their destination, but there had been no news, as yet, of Neil's return. Only the previous day, Libby had remarked to her mother that Daddy would be astonished at how she had grown and had added, tentatively, that she supposed that now the war was over they would go back to Sydenham Avenue.

Marianne had smiled but shaken her head. 'We stopped paying the rent on Sydenham Avenue ages ago,' she said. 'Darling, when Daddy comes back we shall have a great deal of talking to do. Things have changed, you know. I dare say my factory job will finish but I've been independent for so long that I can't imagine myself not working. War changes people and I think that Daddy and I are so different now that we may not want to live together any more.' She had given her daughter a quick, almost shy glance. 'I've always thought you knew that all wasn't right between Daddy and me.'

When this conversation had taken place, Gammy had been ill in bed, so mother and daughter had been able to talk freely. Libby had nodded. 'I did know you weren't really friendly any more. Well, even that time when Daddy came home for a whole week's leave, he stayed in lodgings and you stayed here. And when I mentioned it to one of the big girls at school, she sort of

434

grinned and then gave me a hug and said that things would take their course, whatever that might mean.'

'Yes; well, she was right, and I'm sure when Daddy gets home we'll sort something out,' Marianne had said vaguely, but then her tone had strengthened. 'But whatever we do, I should like you to realise that we shall do it apart, which means of course that you will have to choose whether to live with me or with Daddy.'

'I'd rather live with both of you,' Libby had said dolefully but then, remembering the atmosphere which had prevailed whenever her parents were together, thought better of it. 'No, I don't mean that, I mean I'd rather live with each of you in turn,' she had amended firmly. 'That way, I'd still have a mum and a dad, but you'd both be happy and – and relaxed, not all tense and wary, the way you are when you're together.'

Marianne had stared at Libby with what looked like respect. 'You wise child,' she had said wonderingly. 'Still, no point in meeting trouble halfway. What would you like for dinner? It'll have to be something cold, since the power's off and I don't mean to light the fire until Gammy comes downstairs again.' She had sighed, poking her head round the door of the pantry and seeing its empty shelves. 'Although the war in Europe is won we'll still have to manage on our rations. But things can only get better, I tell myself.'

Right now, however, the room was warm and

inviting, thanks to Mr Brett, with the smell of cooking making the kitchen seem almost as delightful as it had done before the war, and Libby finished making the last sandwich and went to the oven to examine the jam tarts baking within. They were done to a turn and she was taking them out and standing them on a wire tray to cool when the back door banged open and a cheerful voice said: 'Hello-ello-ello, I smell me mam's bakin'! I don't suppose you expected to see me today, did you? No warnin', I'm afraid, but I raided the Naafi before I left Invergordon and I bet no one else has got chocolate bars and biscuits to add to the feast!'

'Fiona!' shrieked three voices, and Gammy actually struggled up out of her chair to throw her arms round her youngest child. Libby put down the tray of jam tarts she was holding and charged across the room to clutch her aunt round the waist and Marianne quickly followed suit.

'Oh, Fee, me darlin',' Gammy said breathlessly, sinking back into her chair as Fiona reached across and picked up a sandwich, starting to eat it as though she were starving. 'It's that grand to see you! But how did you manage to get away?' She looked at her daughter's neat uniform and at the new sailor hat perched at a jaunty angle on the braided red-gold hair. 'You've not left the service, I see; not that we expected you would, of course.'

'Well, you're out there, Mam,' Fiona said cheerfully. 'I shall be demobbed some time in the next month, but I've been given a week's leave, so you're landed wi' me for a bit. I dunno what I'll do now that peace has come, but I doubt I'll come back to Liverpool on a permanent basis like. There's a feller I'm really keen on . . . but I'll tell you about him some other time.' She turned to Libby. 'Gracious, queen, how you've grown!'

'Everyone says that; I expect it's the first thing Daddy will say when he walks in,' Libby said resignedly. She glanced at the clock above the mantelpiece, then turned back to her aunt. 'You'd better borrow one of Mum's overalls, Auntie Fee, and give a hand, because the street party starts in an hour and we're nowhere near finished yet.'

Fiona chuckled. 'Are you testing my abilities as a cook?' she asked teasingly. 'Because making sandwiches was something I could do even before I joined the Wrens.' However, she got down one of Marianne's overalls and put it on, then began to spread margarine as Libby started to slice another loaf. 'Heard anything from Neil?' she asked Marianne. 'I believe they're sending the POWs home just as fast as they can, so it won't be long now before he's back.'

Neil lay on his bunk, gazing at the rough concrete ceiling above his head. Everyone knew that the war would soon be over; the attitude of the guards at the POW camp could have told them that. Ingratiating was the word, Neil thought with an inward grin. He guessed that as soon as peace was declared, the guards would simply melt away, try to dissociate themselves from anything to do with the war. It was common knowledge that the Allies were advancing, would probably arrive within a few days, maybe hours, and that would mean, praise God, a speedy return to England and to the arms of his beloved Fiona. He thought of his last leave before his ship had been sunk and he had been taken prisoner; indeed, the memories of that leave were what had made his time in the POW camp bearable.

Now, he let his mind wander where it would, which was chiefly to Fiona and that memorable last leave. It had been absolutely wonderful, a magical time which he thought he would never forget. Before it, he had honestly believed that everything was over between Fiona and himself and he had been in a state of miserable anxiety. It had looked as though she was no longer even slightly interested in him, had put the whole affair behind her. She had answered his letters, to be sure, but usually long after she had received them, and had signed off not *your loving Fiona*, as in the early days of their relationship, but simply *Fiona Wainwright*.

Considerably the worse for wear after taking part in the Normandy landings, his ship had limped into Southampton and he had gone to naval HQ to discover how long he should expect to be ashore, only to be told that it might take anything from three days to a week before he could sail once more. It was not long enough to go up to Invergordon to talk things over with Fiona, but possibly too long to hang about in Southampton. On the spur of the moment, he had decided to visit his parents, and he had actually been at the ticket office, enquiring about train times and meaning to send a telegram to the older Sheridans warning of his impending arrival, when someone had taken his hand and a voice murmured into his ear: 'Darling Neil! Don't say you were thinking of buying a ticket to Scotland!'

He had turned, his heart thumping madly, and even as he had done so, soft arms had encircled his neck and a red-gold head had nestled beneath his chin. It was Fiona.

After that first quick, passionate embrace, they had broken guiltily apart, Neil taking off his cap to push his hands through his thick blond hair. He had glanced around quickly, though he knew very well that fellow naval personnel would pretend they had seen nothing, for was not everyone in the same boat? Others would assume that the slender, delicate creature in his arms was either his wife or his girlfriend, and though one was not supposed to behave as they had just behaved, most superior officers would turn a blind eye.

However, no one seemed to have noticed anything untoward, so Neil took Fiona's small hand in his and led her out of the station. 'I can't believe it, I can't bloody believe it!' he kept repeating. 'Oh, my dearest, darling girl, whatever are you doing in Southampton? In your last letter

439

– the only one I've received for months – you said not to come up to Scotland because you had leave due to you and were going to spend it in Liverpool.'

By now, they had left the station behind and were on the broad main road, and Neil noticed for the first time that his little love had a duffel bag slung over one shoulder which must mean, surely, that this was not a flying visit. Perhaps she intended to stay for a day or two, which meant – his stomach curdled with delighted anticipation – a night or two as well. But Fiona was speaking, dragging him along towards the queue for taxis.

'I went to Liverpool and saw Gammy,' she said rapidly. 'And then I thought, why not visit my old pal Neil? They don't know I've got nearly a week, so why not give meself a treat? And I jumped on a train and here I am.'

'I can't believe it,' Neil breathed again, gripping her hand and then making little circles with his forefinger on the inside of her wrist. She squeaked and giggled, then returned the caress. 'But how did you know I was in port?'

'Oh, I keep an eye on your comings and goings, you gorgeous brute,' Fiona said airily, as they reached the head of the queue. She sank her voice to a whisper. 'A pal told me about a delightful country hotel – expensive, I fear, but really good. We could stay there if you'd like. Oh, Neil, darling, we'll have a fabulous time, I promise you. The weather's wonderful, and the countryside round there is truly beautiful. We can go for long walks, fish in the river, enjoy the sort of food that you can still sometimes find in the country . . .'

'. . . and love one another,' Neil breathed and thought to himself that perhaps all his dreams were about to come true. He wanted Fiona desperately, but still needed to remain on good terms with Marianne. He enjoyed being a father, but guessed that should he and Marianne divorce he would see far less of Libby. I'm not being selfish, but kind and practical, he told himself, with his arms full of yielding, supple Fiona. Yes, if she would consent to become his lover once more, they could begin to plan for the future.

But she was looking at him enquiringly. What had she just said? Ah, he'd got it. She'd been talking about a country hotel . . . 'Oh, Fiona, that sounds wonderful. I can't tell you what this means to me. I've missed you so dreadfully; you're all I can think of! And to have you to myself is my idea of heaven.'

A taxi drew up alongside and Neil helped her into it, then paused. 'You'd best direct the driver.' Then, dropping his voice: 'I take it you've got civvies in your duffel bag?'

Fiona nodded. 'And the sexiest black nightie you've ever imagined,' she breathed.

Neil was about to ask her how she happened to find him on the station when it occurred to him that the hotel to which they were heading would certainly be expensive and he had very little cash on him. He put it to Fiona that he had no idea what the cost of this clandestine treat would be, and she gave him a laughing, wicked glance. 'Had we better stop off at the nearest branch of your bank so you can get some money?' she asked, telling him what she anticipated they would be charged.

Neil realised a visit to his bank would be essential. He cashed a cheque, happy to be doing so, thinking that it was worth ten times as much just to know that Fiona loved him, longed to be with him, missed him as much as he missed her.

They reached the hotel and booked a double room. Neil admired the view of the rolling countryside, but his mind was chiefly taken up with the large bed, the soft pink blankets and the crisp white sheets. A porter had brought up their bags, but as soon as he left Neil sat down on the bed and reached hungrily for Fiona. She laughed and wriggled, but escaped from his grasp, telling him firmly that dinner would be served in ten minutes and surely he could save 'that sort of thing' until they had the time to enjoy it.

Neil agreed that perhaps this would be sensible, so they cleaned up and went down to the dining room. There were a good few other guests, mostly couples, many in uniform, and Neil saw with pride how enviously the men stared at him and how the women's eyes took in every detail of his companion's appearance.

The dinner they enjoyed was probably excellent

but Neil was almost indifferent to the food. Soon, very soon now, he and Fiona would climb into that big bed and then . . . and then . . .

They had wine with their meal and, at Fiona's insistence, a brandy to follow. Perhaps that was why Neil felt so extremely tired that he undressed and tumbled into bed as soon as they reached their room. He remembered catching a glimpse of Fiona in something transparent and black, remembered her sitting on the edge of the bed and brushing out her long red-gold curls. He remembered trying to tell her to take that wisp of black off and then there was something warm and soft in his arms. He was still trying to work out why Fiona had suddenly become plump and cushiony when he fell into a deep and dreamless sleep.

Next morning, he awoke because something was tickling his face. For a moment he could not think what it was, for the room was bright with sunshine and not at all like his cabin on HMS *Sorrel*, but then he remembered. He turned his head and there was Fiona, sitting up in the bed they had shared and eyeing him impatiently. 'Do wake up, darling Neil, and try not to look as though you've spent the whole night making love to me, which you have,' she hissed. 'They serve breakfast between eight and nine o'clock, and you slept so soundly after our frolics that I couldn't wake you in time, so I ordered breakfast in bed, on a tray, and it will be along at any moment.'

Even as she spoke, there was a knock on the

door and upon Fiona's calling: 'Come in!' the door opened to reveal a pretty young woman in a black dress and frilly white apron, carrying a heavily laden tray. Behind her came a man in dark trousers and waistcoat, also carrying a tray, which he set down on Neil's bedside table. Neil turned his head sideways to look at Fiona's tray just as she turned towards him. The man, backing away from the bed, held the door courteously for his colleague to pass through, and they left the room, closing the door softly behind them.

'Shall I be mother?' Neil asked playfully, since the coffee pot, milk and cups were on his bedside table, whereas toast, scrambled egg and marmalade graced Fiona's tray.

She looked across at him, smiling apologetically. 'Oh, Neil, I am so sorry. I did order bacon and eggs, but I suppose it's a set breakfast in bed, so we'll have to make do with what they provide. Goodness, that coffee smells good.' There was a bathroom adjoining their bedroom, and whilst Neil was still eating toast and marmalade Fiona had a bath and dressed, returning to say she would meet him downstairs in half an hour. He protested, naturally, but though Fiona was very sweet and loving, she was also extremely firm. 'I don't mean to give anyone cause to say I behaved like a trollop and not a wife,' she said. 'Did you know this hotel has boats for hire? The weather's just perfect for a day on the river.'

Accordingly, they ordered a packed lunch and

hired a rowboat, while Fiona talked merrily of the fun they were having, and had had the previous night, until Neil began to remember it, though not with much clarity. He decided to refuse wine with his meal when they returned to the hotel, then capitulated when Fiona pouted and said that they could share a half-bottle if he felt a full one was too much. Neil agreed – he would have agreed to almost anything to please his love – yet despite the best of intentions he finished his meal with coffee and brandy. Because of the physical exertion of rowing the boat he was already tired when they reached their room, but he undressed and got into bed, sure that tonight he would prove to Fiona that even a day on the river could not diminish his ability to make love to her.

Presently, Fiona joined him between the sheets, putting warm arms round him, talking soothingly . . . and the next thing he knew, it was broad daylight and Fiona was standing by the bed, dressed in her uniform, her duffel bag on her shoulder. 'What's going on?' Neil mumbled. 'Why are you wearing your uniform? What day is it?'

Fiona laughed. 'Darling, I've never known anyone sleep so soundly! It's ten o'clock and I told you yesterday I'd have to leave for Invergordon today. Oh, my sweet, I'm awfully sorry, but if I get back late they'll put me on a charge, and so far my record's been pretty good. I've ordered a taxi – it's waiting – so you'll have to make your own way back to Southampton when you're ready to leave.' She swooped down on him, all warmth and affection. 'I'm so sorry we can't leave together as we'd planned, but you know how it is. We don't have to vacate the room till noon, so there's no hurry; not for you, you lucky thing. But I must be off.'

Neil tried to grab her, but she laughed, pinched his cheek and headed for the door. He began to say he could be ready to leave himself if she'd just wait five minutes, but reaching the door she turned to shake her head at him. 'It's no use, darling; by the time they've made out our bill, and you've settled it, I shall be in Southampton, maybe even on the train.' She gave him a bright smile and a tiny wave. 'Goodbye for now, Neil; don't forget to write!'

Neil stared at the closing door, then jumped out of bed. He would wave her off, give her one last kiss, then return to the room to pack, for the last thing he felt he needed was a couple of hours kicking his heels in the hotel.

But even this last moment was denied him. He dressed rapidly and clattered downstairs, just in time to see the rear of the taxi disappearing down the drive. Disconsolate, he retraced his steps, then changed his mind and approached the receptionist sitting behind a small desk, apparently totting up figures in a large ledger. 'Excuse me. My – my wife had to return to her base this morning and didn't want to wake me, so I missed breakfast. Is there any chance of some porridge, or toast and coffee?'

446

But that wonderful episode had been months ago, something to remember and linger over during his long grey periods of imprisonment and, he told himself now, a magic time which would doubtless recur when he was home again. He glanced at the tiny window, greying with dawn. Soon he would hold her once more, feel her soft body yield to his. Neil drifted into dreamland.

The street party had been a great success, and when Fiona had produced her chocolate bars and given one to each child it had set the seal on a perfect day. Gammy had spent a couple of hours during the afternoon at the long table, though at Marianne's insistence she had gone indoors at four o'clock. Her daughters had tucked her up on the sofa in the parlour and she had slept until eight, then she had insisted upon returning to the street to join in the communal singing, though to her regret she could not participate in the dancing. Marianne had been worried that the unaccustomed exertion would bring on a recurrence of the bronchitis which had laid her mother low, and insisted upon taking the old lady up to bed at ten o'clock.

Libby protested volubly when she, too, was packed off to bed, but Marianne pointed out that she would be in school next day and that ten o'clock was late enough for anyone. Then the two sisters settled down in front of the fire for a good gossip.

This was interrupted, before it had really begun,

by a knock on the back door. Marianne hurried to answer it, guessing who stood without, and ushered Bill Brett into the kitchen. Fiona stood up and came towards them, looking uncertainly from her sister to the newcomer, and Marianne realised that the two had never met. 'Fiona, this is the friend I've told you about, Bill Brett. Bill, my sister Fiona.'

The two shook hands, murmuring conventional greetings, then Marianne told Bill to sit down and Fiona pulled the kettle over the dying fire. 'I gather we've got you to thank for the wood, but I'm afraid you'll have to wait a while before the kettle boils,' she said. 'Well, Mr Brett, you're quite a surprise! My sister's talked about you a lot, but somehow my mental picture of you was quite different.'

Bill laughed and pulled a wry face. 'I can imagine. I expect you thought I was tall, dark and handsome – and young, of course – but your sister seems to have grown accustomed to me lack of looks.'

Marianne watched with some amusement as her sister's face turned slowly scarlet and she began to stammer out a denial of Bill's words. 'It's all right, Fee, he's teasing you,' she assured the younger girl. 'Remember what Gammy used to say when we were kids? *Handsome is as handsome does*, and believe me, it's very true. Besides, though Bill keeps saying he's plain as a boot, I think he's got a very nice sort of face.'

'So do I,' Fiona said hurriedly. She turned to Bill as the colour began to fade from her cheeks.

'I am sorry; one should never make personal remarks.' She crossed to the pantry and returned with the old toffee tin, taking the lid off and offering one of the remaining buns to their visitor. 'Have one of these; Marianne made them yesterday, and they're very good.'

Bill helped himself to a bun, then turned to Marianne. 'I'm awful sorry I didn't come round earlier, like I promised, but the chap who was doing the afternoon and evenin' shift went down with flu, so bein' as how I knew you'd be pretty busy with the street party, I offered to stay on.' He grinned at both girls. 'But I guess Gammy and Libby are in bed and the lodgers are still out enjoyin' themselves, so if you'd like to go out and join in the dancin' and that, I'd be proud to take you both, one on each arm.'

At this moment the kettle boiled and Fiona jumped up and made the tea, pushing a large mug towards Bill, who received it gratefully. 'Thanks for the offer,' she said, 'but I don't think I could cope with any more jollity. In fact, if you'll forgive me, I'll go to bed. Marianne and I agreed earlier that I should share with Gammy tonight, so if the two of you go off you won't disturb anyone when you bring Marianne home.'

Bill drained his mug, then let out his breath in a long sigh of satisfaction. 'That were grand. I didn't know I'd be workin' a double shift, so I didn't take a flask wi' me when I set out this morning, and I've been dying for a cup of tea for the past three hours,' he explained. 'I don't suppose we'll be long, because I reckon we've both had a pretty full day.'

Once out in Crocus Street and heading for the Stanley Road, Marianne tucked her arm into the crook of Bill's elbow and smiled up at him. 'Well, now you've met my sister. Isn't she the prettiest thing?' She snuggled her face against his shoulder.

'She certainly is, but for meself I prefer dark-haired girls,' Bill said. 'Now where would you like to go first? They were lettin' off fireworks up by St George's Hall, though God knows where they got them from.'

Fiona stole quietly up to Gammy's bedroom, determined not to disturb the old woman, but Gammy was still awake. Libby had taken her truckle bed down to the parlour when Gammy was first taken ill, and slept there still, so Fiona undressed whilst chatting quietly to her mother. 'You've been wonderful today, Mam; no one would ever think you'd been so ill,' she said, as she slipped between the sheets. 'I bet it's a day you'll remember all your life, won't you?'

Gammy chuckled quietly. 'It ain't the first victory celebration what I've lived through,' she reminded her daughter. 'You won't remember the ending of the Great War – you were barely a year old, though Marianne was around seven, I suppose – but of course there were dancing in the streets and parties for the kiddies,'

'I bet there was a lot more food then than there is now,' Fiona exclaimed, but Gammy shook her head.

'You're wrong there, queen. We had rationin' in that war too and there were a lot less money about. As I remember it, the party for the kiddies were mostly potted meat sandwiches, bread and jam and slices of the plainest cake you ever did see. Your poor father was still in France; it were weeks an' weeks before he came home and of course when he did come, he'd been quite badly wounded and was still walkin' on two sticks. But we knew on Armistice night that he was alive and that was all that mattered. In our street, all us women had agreed to wear bright colours. Most of us had something red on, an' we were havin' a grand time doin' the Lambeth Walk, when all of a sudden some young feller in hospital blue started to scream and point. It seems he thought the red were blood, thought he were back in France. They took him back to the hospital, but I reckon it brought home to us that though the war might be officially over, the effects of it still went on.'

'Oh, Mam, you never mentioned that before,' Fiona breathed. 'So perhaps you'd do better to forget the Great War and to remember the victory celebrations which are going on now.'

'Aye; what happened after the eleventh of November certainly weren't no picnic,' Gammy said. 'The flu epidemic, which them poor buggers brought back from France, killed more folk than the war itself. It weren't only the Allies, either; it hit everyone, includin' the Huns of course. There were one bishop – I can't remember his name – who claimed the flu were God's punishment for countries goin' to war, but I don't believe it myself. Kiddies died like flies, and they didn't have no part in the conflict.'

'I don't believe God would punish the whole world in such a way,' Fiona agreed. 'Don't you think about it, Mam, because everything's different now. Doctors know more and they've got medicines to cure almost anything. And the Great War ended in November, when folk spent more time indoors, I imagine, so a whole family would infect each other. Oh, I know you've had bronchitis, but you're getting better, and you'll get better even faster if you think nice, cheery thoughts.'

Gammy sighed. 'Aye, it were November, and it were pretty cold in the streets,' she said dreamily. 'Dark came early, of course, but the bonfires kept us warm and the excitement too. I had you on me hip and your Aunt Ruby give our Marianne a piggyback, and we danced until the flames began to die down. We'd all brought a few spuds to push into the embers, and as the fire cooled we fished 'em out with bits of plank and carried them back indoors. They was charred on the outside, but cooked nicely within, so we sat down at the kitchen table, stuck a scattering of salt and a knob of margarine into each spud, and gobbled them up.' She sighed reminiscently. 'I can taste 'em still. I dunno whether anyone put spuds in the fire out there last night, but I doubt it; it's too early in the year and new spuds don't bake, they just shrivel up.' She began to hum the Lambeth Walk, kicking out feebly at the appropriate time, causing Fiona to give a squeak of protest as a hard heel landed on her toes. 'Oh aye, that were a night to remember, and memories are about all you've got when you reach my age.'

Fiona yawned and heaved the blankets up over her shoulder. 'I've got some good memories meself,' she said drowsily. 'Mam, I've never said anything before because of the war, but now it's over I'd like you to know that I've – I've met a feller who really matters to me. He's asked me to marry him and I mean to do so. Some time in the next few weeks, I'll bring him to visit and introduce you . . .'

Beside her, Gammy sat up on one elbow. 'I thought I already knew him,' she said drily.

Fiona twisted round. Her eyes had grown accustomed to the darkness and she stared, incredulously, into her mother's pale face. 'You thought you already knew him?' she squeaked. 'Why, I've only known him myself for a year and I'm jolly sure I've never even mentioned his name.' For a moment, she honestly thought that her mother must be losing her mind, but somehow the dryness in the older woman's voice did not sound like insanity.

'Good God, girl, d'you think I'm blind?' Gammy said. She sounded amused as well as slightly offended. 'You began casting out lures to your brother-in-law when you were no more'n sixteen or seventeen. I were right flummoxed, not knowing whether I should interfere, because letting you know I knew might have made things even worse. I were afraid the pair of you would run off together, leaving poor Marianne to cope with Libby alone. Besides, I weren't sure that Neil were the right feller for you either, and it were plain as the nose on your face that Marianne were still crazy about him. Then, when she had that turble accident, I thought mebbe everything would come right. You kept away but Neil visited the hospital every time he were in port, and I was sure all would be well. So it ain't Neil, then?'

'Mam, you're a perishin' wonder, knowing so much and never letting on,' Fiona said, scarcely able to believe her ears. She smiled to herself, thinking how horrified both Marianne and Neil would have been had they realised the extent of the old woman's knowledge. 'No, it certainly is not Neil. Oh, I don't deny that we did go through a stage of – of believing we were in love, but that ended a long time ago.' She hesitated, then plunged into speech once more. 'Would you be pleased if Marianne and Neil made up their – their differences, and settled down to married life again?'

Gammy considered. 'It 'ud be better for Libby in a way, you might think, but I don't believe you can mend a broken pot so the cracks don't show,' she said at length. 'I'll tell you one thing, my girl:

454

right from the time you could toddle you wanted anything your sister had got and mostly Marianne just handed over 'cos you were her baby sister and she loved you. Then she began to realise that it wasn't just dolls and clothes you were after but her man, and that was a different kettle of fish altogether. She had closed her eyes to what was going on, but after her accident all that changed, though I'm not sure exactly why. She began to look at Neil real cold and keep him at arm's length. She was never rude, that's not my girl's way, but it was plain as a pikestaff that trust had died, and when trust dies, love goes too. Even liking can't live without trust, and poor Marianne would have felt very alone had it not been for meself and Libby.'

'And of course I made things worse by never visiting her in hospital,' Fiona said. 'But I was so ashamed, Mam. I knew what Neil and I had been doing was wrong, but I was sure if I came back to Liverpool you would all guess and hate me for ever, and though I knew I deserved it, I couldn't bear to lose my whole family at one stroke. If I'd known you already knew . . .'

'But you didn't know, and mebbe it were kinder in the end to stay away,' Gammy said comfortingly. 'At least you wrote reg'lar, though the letters were pretty short. I know Marianne were very cool with you when you first come home back in forty-three, so I reckon she'd guessed, but now you're friendly as anything, always laughing over nothing and going off arm in arm to look at the shops, like you used to do before the war. That has me puzzled, I must confess. Are you going to tell me what's been going on?'

Fiona considered, then giggled. 'I don't mean to tell you the whole story now because you're tired and so am I, and it's rather a long one,' she said. 'But you'll know everything quite soon. Now, as I told you earlier, I've met this feller who means a lot to me, and I think I mean a lot to him. His name's Hamish McDonald and we're going to get married as soon as we're demobbed and can find ourselves somewhere to live. So will it be all right if I bring him to visit you? You'll like him, I'm sure of it. He's the best thing that has ever happened to me.'

'Course you can bring him,' Gammy mumbled, her voice thick with sleep, but then it sharpened. 'And it would serve you bloody well right if he fell for Marianne and whisked her back to Scotland with him.'

'I know it would, because Marianne's a much nicer person than me,' Fiona admitted. 'But now we really must go to sleep, Mam, or we'll be like a couple of chewed rags by morning.'

Fiona came downstairs when she heard someone stirring in the kitchen below. She felt guilty for having slept late, guessing that Marianne would have had to cope with the lodgers' breakfasts before going off to her factory, but instead she found her niece at the kitchen table, making carry-outs for the three men, who were gathered around her. 'I'm afraid it's mainly what was left over from the street party: Spam and pickle sandwiches, a couple of buns each, and of course a flask of tea,' Libby was saying apologetically. 'I'd have done you some bread and jam but we ran out of bread yesterday and I've not had time to get to the shops.' She swung round as her aunt entered the room. 'Good morning, Auntie Fee. Gammy awake yet?'

'Not yet; she's snoring like a pig in muck,' Fiona said cheerfully. 'Morning, gentlemen. Sorry I wasn't down in time to make the porridge. Mam and I talked half the night away, but I'm sure Marianne fed you before she left.'

'Now you're wrong there, missy,' Mr McNally said gruffly. 'Mrs Sheridan were on the early shift, but Libby managed all right, didn't you, queen? And Mr Parsons here found a stale loaf at the bottom of the bread bin, so we had toast 'n' all.'

'Of course, I forget how useful Libby has become now that's she's older,' Fiona said. 'Me mam often remarks on it in her letters.' She peered hopefully at the stove as the three men took the packets of food and the flasks which her niece had prepared and disappeared into the yard, shouting their goodbyes as the door shut behind them. 'Any porridge left for me? And I'd be glad of a cuppa. I dare say Gammy would too.'

'I'm afraid the porridge is all gone but I'll make some more before I leave for school,' Libby said. 'I'm awful sorry about the toast, Auntie Fee, but

I could nip next door and see if I can borrow three or four rounds of bread; what d'you think?'

Fiona shook her head. 'No, no, toast isn't necessary, and I'll make the porridge if you'll take a cup of tea up to Gammy. She always used to say her day couldn't start without a brew.' Fiona crossed the kitchen, poured a mug of tea and handed it to her niece. 'By the time your grandmother has drunk this, I shall have made the porridge. Shall I take it up to her room or do you reckon she'd rather get up?'

'Dunno,' Libby said briefly, taking the cup. 'I'll ask her. Shan't be a mo.'

Fiona was mixing porridge oats, water and a judicious amount of dried milk in a pan when she heard a crash and a muffled shout. She crossed the kitchen and went to the foot of the stairs just as her niece began to hurtle down the flight. She was white-faced and breathing hard, and she tumbled straight into Fiona's arms. 'Oh, Auntie Fee, Auntie Fee, it's awful,' she gabbled. 'She was half sitting up and as I got near the bed she sort of slumped over . . . I said, "Are you all right, Gammy?" but she didn't answer or move . . . oh, Auntie Fee, I think she's dead!'

'I knew our mam was popular, but I never realised that half Liverpool loved her,' Marianne said, as they left the cemetery. She produced her handkerchief and dabbed at her damp eyes. 'I wish we could have asked everyone back for tea and a bun,

458

but it just isn't possible. As it is, every woman in Crocus Street has brought biscuits or cakes or buns, loaves of bread, or butty fillings, so at least we shan't be shamed by putting on a poor show.'

She was speaking to Bill, who had tucked her right hand into his elbow, but Libby, clinging to her other hand, spoke before he could answer, eager to reassure her mother. 'Oh, Mum, as if anyone would think badly of us! After all, it isn't just the flower streets that have their power cut off today, and we aren't the only ones having a hard time of it, with the men coming back, rationing no better, and almost nothing in the shops.'

'Oh well, we're doing our best,' Marianne said. 'I've got to see the landlord and explain that I want to take on the house, because of course it's always been in Gammy's name. Mr Parsons has already said that all three men want to stay on, so there'll be no problem with the rent. But if my factory stop making radios I could be out of a job.'

Fiona arrived beside the little group just in time to hear Marianne's last remark. 'With the rents coming in from the fellers and the allotment which the Navy sends you out of Neil's pay, you shouldn't need to work,' she observed. 'I dare say Lewis's would take you back in their gowns department, but would you like that? You've got used to telling other people what to do; how would you feel if the boot were on the other foot?'

'I suppose I'd have to get used to it,' Marianne

said rather doubtfully. 'But you're right, of course; while the lodgers are happy to remain in Crocus Street, I should be able to manage financially. However, I don't intend to shut myself away like a – a housekeeper. I actually like being with other people of my own age and I like feeling I'm doing important work. In fact, Fee, I like earning my own money and having some independence, and I don't mean to give it up.'

'I do know what you mean,' Fiona said. 'I feel the same myself, more or less, and anyway when Hamish and I are married I shall have to work for a bit. He's very keen to start up a business of his own, but he'll need capital so we've agreed that we'll both work for a couple of years, and not start a family until his business is up and running.'

Bill turned to stare at her. 'Wish I could start me own business,' he said wistfully. 'Small chance o' that, though. It ain't easy to pay your way on a bus driver's salary, lerralone to save.'

Libby, who knew all about Hamish, for Fiona liked nothing better than to talk about her beloved, smiled up at Bill. 'Auntie Fee's feller comes from one of the islands off the Scottish coast. He wants to buy a boat and take holidaymakers on trips around the islands, to show them how beautiful they are,' she explained. 'If you had your own bus, Mr Brett, you could drive the trippers up to Scotland. Then they could get aboard Hamish's boat and you could wait around for a couple of days, and then drive them back to Liverpool. I bet

Gammy would say, "Let's keep it in the family," wouldn't she, Mum? Or is it disrespectful to talk about her when – when we've just been to her funeral?'

They had been making their way out of the cemetery to where a large black funeral car was parked. The driver opened the door for them and they piled in. 'You're quite right, that's exactly what Gammy would have said,' Marianne replied as the car began to move forward. 'And, darling, don't ever stop talking about Gammy, because it's talking about her which will keep memories of her alive. Never forget that.'

As the car traversed the familiar streets and the adults chatted, Libby's thoughts reverted to the totally awful thing she had said to her mother after she had accepted that Gammy was dead and would never again share a joke with her granddaughter, or need Libby to accompany her to the house of an old friend. She had said: 'I'm really sad about Gammy, Mum, but surely I can go back to Tregarth now? I mean, you only kept me at home so I could keep an eye on her, didn't you?'

As soon as the words were out of her mouth she had regretted them, especially when she had seen a tear trickle down her mother's scarred cheek. 'Oh, Mum, I'm so sorry!' she had said remorsefully. 'But it *is* true that I couldn't go back to Tregarth whilst I was needed here, isn't it? Of course I wouldn't desert you, but if you're working all day, and I'm in school . . . I thought – I thought . . .'

Her voice had petered out as she realised what her words implied, which was that she would rather be at Tregarth than in her own home. She had begun to stammer out an apology, but her mother had cut her short. 'You were evacuated to Tregarth because Liverpool was a dangerous place to be in wartime,' her mother had said quietly. 'Darling Libby, the war is over, the danger is past and I doubt very much whether a thirteen-year-old girl would find much employment on a Welsh hill farm. Of course at the time we took you away you were unhappy because you loved the country and the farm and that. But surely by now you've grown accustomed to city life again? You said yourself that the teachers at the village school were mainly intent upon getting everyone to read, write and do simple arithmetic, whereas at the convent lessons are far more interesting. Indeed, if you had still been at Tregarth, you would have had to leave on your fourteenth birthday, whereas the convent expect you to take your School Certificate, and possibly go on to further education after that. But if you'd like to visit the castle, I'm sure that could be arranged.'

Poor Libby had been abject in her apologies and promises that the remark had been made thoughtlessly, had not been meant as it had sounded, and now she reflected that it was a good job her mother appeared to have forgotten about her suggestion of spending time with Auntie and Uncle Frank, for Libby had realised that a good deal of her urge to return had been because she wanted to see Matthew again. He had been her good friend and ally, and without him the castle, even Tregarth, would hold little allure.

And Matthew was at boarding school, somewhere in the south of England. He had matriculated with ease the previous summer and was taking Higher School Certificate in a year, and if his results were good enough he would take up a place at a Cambridge college where he wanted to read medicine, thus following in the footsteps of both his parents. Libby had gathered from Auntie's letters that Matthew usually brought friends with him when he came home during vacations, or went to their homes, sometimes for several weeks. Though at first Libby had written often, and Matthew had replied, the letters had gradually dwindled.

The car drew up outside the house in Crocus Street, bringing Libby abruptly back to the present. Her grandmother's death had been in the obituary column not only in the *Liverpool Post*, but also in a national newspaper, and Auntie had sent a letter to say how sorry she was to learn of Marianne's loss. She had also said, with typical generosity, that Marianne and Libby really must come and stay some time. Now that the war was over it would doubtless be easier to arrange. Libby supposed, however, that the invitation was merely politeness, and that her mother would not dream of taking Auntie up on it. She must accept that things had changed, and she would probably never see Auntie, Uncle Frank or indeed Matthew again.

But they were all getting out of the car now and hurrying down the jigger and into the kitchen. A couple of neighbours, who had volunteered to remain behind, were boiling kettles on borrowed primus stoves, to fill the tea urn lent by the church hall. Mrs Nebb, Gammy's oldest friend, was red-eyed but greeted Libby with a rather watery smile. 'Did it go off awright, chuck?' she asked wistfully. 'I reckon they gave her a grand send-off; and now, queen, you'd best start getting the food out of the pantry, 'cos I reckon the place'll be full to burstin' in twenty minutes.'

Chapter Fifteen

Autumn 1945

Within three days of coming home, Neil had sorted himself out and was on a train bound for Scotland. He had been kitted out with civvies by the Navy, had signed papers and been interviewed, and at last was told that he might go home. Fortunately for him, things were still somewhat disorganised, and his request for a travel warrant to Invergordon, in Scotland, had been granted with no awkward questions asked.

So now Neil sat in a corner of the crowded carriage, and tried to tell himself that he was doing the right thing. The fact was that he had written several times to Fiona since his release from the POW camp, whilst he waited to be repatriated, each time begging her to reply. She had not done so, however, and he was beginning to think that she must have been posted elsewhere. Of course, if she had gone in the last weeks of the war, she would never have received any of his letters, and it was this which had finally decided him. He must go to Invergordon himself. He remembered the address of her Wrennery and knew that only a personal visit would get her new address out of the girls who had been her friends. They would understand that he and Fiona were in love and think that they hoped to wed – for Fiona would certainly not have told anyone that her lover was already a married man – and this, he was sure, would soften the hardest heart.

But as he travelled the long miles, as the autumn countryside grew wilder and less inhabited, doubts – and even fears – began to trouble Neil's mind. What if he was wrong? Suppose the reason that Fiona had not replied to his letters was because, in the year which had elapsed since their last meeting, she had met someone else, changed her mind about him? Remembering those wonderful days in the hotel outside Southampton this seemed extremely unlikely, but Neil could not help recalling how she had fled from him whilst he was away at sea, how she had put their child up for adoption. Suppose, just suppose that she, so much more fickle than himself, had forgotten his deep and abiding love for her? If she had . . . but that was something he preferred not to think about. Instead, he must convince himself that once he reached Invergordon all would be well. He had intended to go to whatever address he was given by her friends just as soon as he could – if she was not still in the area, of course – and persuade her to come south with him. Now, with doubts niggling at his mind, he decided that he would cross-question her friends, hopefully without appearing to do so, as to the welcome he was likely to receive from his young love, and if she was carrying on with someone else . . . Well, no point in meeting trouble halfway; he would simply have to wait and see.

On this thought, surprisingly, he fell asleep and had a peculiar dream in which it was not Fiona he found when he reached Invergordon, but Marianne. Not, however, the Marianne of his most recent visits to Crocus Street, but the one he had met, fallen for and married thirteen – no, fourteen – long years ago. And she was so sweet that not even his recollection of her sister's supple and willing young body took away his pleasure in her. She smiled at him, cuddled up to him, was sweetly compliant with all his demands . . .

He woke, groggily, to find that his head had fallen sideways, on to the shoulder of an extremely embarrassed young sailor who was trying – vainly, it seemed – to free himself. Neil apologised, red-faced. 'I've only just come ashore from spending a year in a POW camp in Germany,' he mumbled. 'I'm on my way to see my wife . . . I reckon I was more tired than I knew.'

The grins did not disappear from the faces of the other passengers, but the sailor said: 'It's OK, mate; I reckon we're all pretty weary,' and stood up to get a newspaper down from the rack, which he spread out and began to read. Neil was able to scan the headlines surreptitiously when he was not staring out at the passing scene.

After another hour or so the train drew into a small station, and looking through the smeared and dirty window Neil saw a man with a handcart, upon which were displayed a number of what looked like rock cakes, a large tea urn and some weary-looking sandwiches as well as a supply of paper cups and plates. Neil's mouth watered and he unwedged himself from his companions and hopped down on to the platform. He had just managed to purchase a bun, a sandwich and a mug of tea when the train jerked and he had to hurl himself back aboard, spilling a good half of his drink. He waved reassuringly to the guard, pulled the leather strap up to close the window and returned, breathless, to his seat, where he devoured his cheese sandwich and the bun before drinking what remained of the tea. The sailor looked enviously at his supplies. 'You're a jammy bugger, you are,' he said grudgingly. 'If I'd got down on to the platform I'd ha' been left behind for sure. Oh aye, you're dead lucky.'

Neil agreed rather loftily that he was indeed fortunate, but the small incident had given him food for thought, as well as a sandwich and a bun. For the first time it occurred to him that he truly was lucky; two women, both of them beautiful in their own way, were waiting for him to return. To be sure, Marianne had been rather cool with him on recent leaves, but her letters to the POW camp had been very much more friendly. She had written delightfully of Libby's various ploys as well as her own, had passed on titbits of gossip, amusing comments, all sorts. She had been, in fact, like the Marianne of his recent dream, the girl he had married.

So if the worst came to the worst and Fiona had found other fish to fry, then he saw no reason why he should not mend his marriage with Marianne.

Oh, he acknowledged that it might not be easy; he would have to agree with all her suggestions, tread carefully, use diplomacy where once he would have commanded. But it would be a good deal better than living alone, and with Gammy gone and her sister out of the way, Marianne would be easily persuaded to give up her job and return, if not to Plymouth, at least to somewhere a good deal more salubrious, he thought, than the flower streets. But if he and Fiona married, then it would be a matter of indifference to him where Marianne and Libby lived, though it would have to be within reach of wherever he was himself, since he hoped to have his daughter with him for at least part of the school holidays. Surely Marianne would agree to this; she might even marry again and be glad for him to have the child with him for even longer. He admitted to himself now, as the train chugged onwards, that his love for Libby had never faltered. Yes, it was as well that he had decided to sort this tangle out, for Libby's future was of paramount importance to him. He adored his daughter and was just thankful that Fiona loved her as well.

Sighing to himself, he closed his eyes; how wonderful it would be if Libby decided that she would rather live with her aunt and her father than with her mother! He began to imagine a pleasant cottage, close to the sea but also in the country, and Fiona wrapped in a large white apron, cooking a delicious meal, whilst Libby came happily back from school, chattering about her day.

Presently, despite the cramped conditions and the stuffiness of the compartment, he slept once more.

Twenty-four hours later Neil was again on a train, but this one was going south, and he was in a far from pleasant mood. In fact he was so furious that he could scarcely think straight but sat in his corner seat and glowered at the world, now and then grinding his teeth, an occupation which he had thought belonged only to villains in novels.

He had found Fiona, after getting directions from one of the girls in the Wrennery. She was living in a village, in the middle of a row of terraced cottages whose front doors opened straight on to the muddy street. He had caught a taxi from Invergordon and almost stopped the driver from leaving him, believing himself to be in the wrong area altogether. Yet this was No. 6, and the girl had seemed in no doubt that Fiona was indeed living in this small, poor-looking place.

Because of its appearance he had approached the door somewhat cautiously and tapped lightly, preparing an apology if a stranger answered his knock. But the woman who had appeared, clad in a grey skirt and blue jumper, was undoubtedly Fiona. She had frowned at him for a moment, then smiled.

'Neil! I hoped you'd take the hint and keep away when I didn't answer your letters, but I guess I was being unduly optimistic. Well, we can't talk on the doorstep; I suppose you'd best come in, but whatever you've got to say, make it short. I'm cooking a meal and I'm not yet used to doing so over an open fire.'

Neil had had to duck his head to enter the low doorway, and had stared round him, relieved to find that the cottage was reasonably decent, though the floor was of earth and the furniture consisted of a large wooden table, two kitchen chairs and a dresser, upon which stood a variety of plates, dishes and cutlery. There was an open fire, with a large black pot suspended over it from which emanated a delicious aroma. Fiona had obviously been peeling potatoes at a low stone sink and now she returned to her task, jerking her head at one of the chairs. 'Sit down,' she said brusquely. 'I must get on; Hamish will be home in an hour.'

'Who the hell is Hamish?' Neil growled. 'What the devil's going on?'

He had seated himself as directed and now Fiona turned from the sink, giving an impatient sigh and casting her eyes towards the ceiling. 'Oh, Neil, don't be such a complete idiot! As soon as I was demobbed, Hamish and I got married. I take it you've not been back to Crocus Street? They would have told you, because we went down south so that I could get married with my friends and family around me. That was back in August and now it's October!'

Neil stared at her. 'Married? But . . . but . . .'

'Well, you didn't expect me to hang around so

that you could be one of my wedding guests, did you?' Fiona asked sarcastically. 'Why didn't you go back to Crocus Street as soon as you reached England? I'm sure I thought you would, if only to see Libby. Marianne has always said that your love for your daughter is the best thing about you, but it seems she was wrong.'

'Married?' Neil said, his voice rising. 'You're *married*? I can't believe it! My last leave ... that wonderful hotel ... remembering our lovemaking was the only thing which kept me going in the camp. But of course, I suppose you couldn't wait for a fellow who wasn't around to gratify ...'

Fiona turned so quickly that Neil had no time to dodge the flying potato which she hurled at his head with extraordinary force. It hit him right between the eyes, and whilst he was still gasping Fiona followed it up by slapping his face so hard that he fell off the chair, clouting his head on the table leg and giving an outraged shout. 'Why, you vicious little bitch! All I said was ...'

'Don't you dare repeat what you were about to say,' Fiona said threateningly. She looked magnificent, all sparkling eyes and pink cheeks, whilst her bush of hair stood out round her head as though it, too, had a life of its own. It made him think of Medusa and certainly, had her hair been able, he was sure it would have bitten him. But he was lying on the floor, nursing what would undoubtedly become a bump the size of an egg on his forehead, whilst Fiona bent over him, looking quite capable of murder; he could not help noticing that though she had flung the potato, she still held an extremely sharp-looking knife in one hand.

Feeling at a distinct disadvantage, Neil began to scramble to his feet, saying sulkily as he did so: 'All right, all right, I'm sorry. But what was I to think? You were all over me . . .'

He righted the chair and sat down on it, cringing back as Fiona made a movement towards him. But it appeared that she did not mean to wreak more havoc upon his person, but merely to remove a tea towel from a pile on the dresser. She went over to the sink and dipped the cloth into the pail of water which stood beneath it and offered it to him, though with a lurking grin which, in other circumstances, he would have found offensive. As it was, he accepted the cloth and wiped his face before returning to his point, though he now realised that Marianne was not the only woman with whom diplomacy would have to be employed.

Accordingly, he thought hard before beginning to speak once more. 'Look, Fiona, I don't want to offend you, but you must admit that the last time we met we were – we were more than friends. I came up here meaning to beg you to return down south with me so that I could get divorce proceedings under way. Yet I find you married to another man. It's enough to make any fellow begin to doubt the evidence of his own eyes.'

'Doubt away,' Fiona said, her voice muffled by the fact that she was crouching on the floor and fishing a potato out from under the dresser. 'Ah, here it is!' She stood up, tossed the potato back into the bowl and sat down opposite Neil. 'You conceited fool!' she said scornfully. 'I didn't give tuppence for you then and I don't give tuppence for you now. How I laughed when you believed what I told you about how we'd made love, when I knew we had done nothing of the sort. Didn't you wonder why you fell asleep so quickly? It's a miracle you woke at all; I put a sleeping tablet into your brandy and you never noticed a thing. Then I gave you a pillow to cuddle and went and slept on the couch. The second night was the same, even though you drank very little wine – I put another tablet into your brandy and you were off to the land of Nod the moment your head touched the pillow.'

'But . . . but . . .' Neil stuttered, 'but *why*, for God's sake? I don't see the point – if you're speaking the truth, that is.'

Fiona laughed. 'I was doing a favour for a friend, someone who wanted you out of the way for a few days,' she said. 'We laughed for hours, me and my pal, when I described what had happened and how easily you were fooled.' She glanced at the little clock which stood to one side of the dresser. 'You'd best get off,' she said abruptly. 'There's a bus back into Invergordon which passes here in about ten minutes. You can wave him down and be aboard before Hamish gets back for his dinner.' She leaned forward and examined him curiously, then began to splutter with laughter. 'Wharra sight you look,

474

Lothario! If Hamish were to walk in now, he'd jump to the wrong conclusion and black your other eye for you. Do you know, you're going to have a black eye – you've got a bruise already. And a bump on your forehead as big as a hen's egg.' She began to giggle helplessly. Then, seeing him open his mouth, she walked over to the door and held it open. 'Skedaddle,' she said briskly, 'and don't you ever show your face here again, or I'll make you sorry. Ah, I can hear the bus. Gerra move on, 'cos there ain't another till tomorrow and I dare say you don't fancy sleepin' under a hedge.'

Neil had left the cottage, wishing that he had had the courage to shout some rude but truthful remark about the sort of girl who would behave as Fiona had done, but if he had screamed an insult then she would probably have battered him, and if he had waited until he was safely aboard the bus he would have been insulting empty air. He had longed to ask her the name of her pal and the reason the man – it must be a man – wanted him out of the way, but he had realised that there was nothing he could do or say to force the information from Fiona. He had heard the cottage door slam behind him as the bus crawled round the corner and had flagged it down, then climbed aboard, glancing back at the cottage as he did so. He could see no sign of movement from within, though he had been certain that Fiona was watching his departure.

The bus had not been crowded, but the passengers had stared curiously at him as he had taken his seat. It had not been until he descended from the vehicle in Invergordon that he realised he had left his cap on Fiona's floor.

The train, jerking to a halt at a small station, brought Neil's thoughts abruptly back to the present. The recollection of Fiona's mocking laughter had soured even the memory of the happy times they had shared in the past, and it astonished him how totally love had turned not just to dislike, but to hatred. The only pleasurable moments of his journey south came when he was imagining Fiona being whipped at the cart's tail around the streets of Liverpool, or hearing her branded as a common whore for her behaviour towards himself.

He also wondered whether Fiona had told Marianne about their time together, then was sure that she had not. Such knowledge would not only have upset Marianne, it would have amounted to telling tales. He might be furiously angry still with Fiona, but he did not think that even she would sink so low. However, he should have explained to Fiona that since she was no longer interested in him, he intended to try to mend his own marriage. After all, it had been a good marriage once and could be so again. He had never told Marianne about Fiona and he was sure that she had completely forgotten the acrimonious remarks he had made when asking her for a divorce – at least she had never spoken of it. He breathed a sigh of relief – there was still hope – and reminded himself that Marianne had always been generous. If he told

476

her, humbly, that he had once been unfaithful but would never fall from grace again, he was sure she would forgive him, particularly since he believed she had made no effort to meet other men during his long absences at sea and in the POW camp, so he feared no rival.

Then there was Libby, his beloved daughter. A child should be brought up by both its parents, surely Marianne would agree with that? Libby was as much his child as hers; he should choose her school, her friends, her pets, her pastimes. Yes, Libby would be on his side, would want a return to her pre-war life now that the conflict was over. They might not be able to rent the house in Sydenham Avenue again, but there were other pleasant streets, other delightful houses. He did not mean his family to remain in Crocus Street with the lodgers taking up more than their fair share of the house. He meant eventually to persuade Marianne to move to Plymouth, where they would be within easy reach of his parents. Marianne loved both his mother and his father, as did Libby, and it would be easy to get a job in Plymouth, where he was known.

Soothed and comforted by such thoughts, he decided to take the bull by the horns and go straight to Liverpool, where he would doubtless learn his fate. He told himself that Marianne would never reject him totally, particularly since she knew nothing of his affair with Fiona, or his request for a divorce.

* * *

The train steamed into Lime Street station. Neil stood up to get his case down from the rack and saw his reflection in the small mirror. Horrified, he stared. The lump on his forehead looked the size of an ostrich egg and the black eye was purpling up horribly. Quickly, he revised his plans. He would give it a couple of days before visiting Crocus Street. He was actually emerging from the station and about to head for Nelson Street, where he knew he could get cheap lodgings, when another thought occurred to him: the sympathy vote! He would tell Marianne, and his daughter, that he had jumped down from the train to help an old lady with a heavy case and had tripped over it, landing face first on the platform. Yes, it would be a hard-hearted woman indeed who did not rush for the arnica to spread on his hurts. It would also explain the absence of his cap, which he would say had rolled away down on to the track. Smiling at his own ingenuity, Neil hailed a taxi. 'Crocus Street!' he said briskly.

It was Marianne's day off and she had gone out early to get her rations from the grocer on Stanley Road who held her books; then she meant to get as many vegetables and as much fruit as she could carry and have a baking day, making sufficient pies and puddings to last the week. As it was October, the greengrocer would be well supplied with apples, pears and a wide variety of vegetables, and Marianne planned to bottle any extra fruit she might obtain and pickle onions, cucumbers and red cabbage.

Her factory was gradually turning productivity to wireless sets for the home market, but the girls had all been told that when the men came home, their jobs would finish. Marianne had made enquiries and, though they could not commit themselves, the management at Lewis's thought there was a good chance of employing her in one capacity or another. She had dreaded the thought of leaving the factory, but to her own surprise she was becoming reconciled to the change.

There was still very little in the shops. Public services, such as electricity, were cut off at certain times, and rumour had it that things would get worse before they got better. The fact that the dockers were on strike did not help matters, and Marianne had seen with her own eyes the queues of ships waiting to come into port to be unloaded. She felt a certain sympathy for the strikers, but she feared that much of the food the waiting ships carried might go bad before the dispute was resolved. Still, no point in worrying about what she couldn't change, and today she would be able to do her baking, since the power was on.

By the time Libby came in from school, Marianne's lust for cooking was beginning to wear a little thin. When her daughter bounced into the room and eyed the laden table longingly, however, Marianne told her that she might have a scone, a plain bun and a slice of the new loaf. 'I used our margarine ration on the pastry and the cakes,' she explained, 'but there's a jar of raspberry jam in the pantry and some blackberry jelly as well. As soon as you've eaten, you can get on with your homework.'

'Thanks, Ma,' Libby said, helping herself to the bun and the scone, and speaking rather thickly through a mouthful of the latter. 'But have you forgotten? It's Elsie Smith's birthday and she's invited me to her party. Good thing I didn't go there straight after school or you would have wondered where on earth I was. Mrs Smith's giving us tea in her house and then taking six of us to the flicks. Well, it will be ten because there's Mrs Smith, Elsie, her brother Tom, and her sister Ethel. And don't worry about the film – Tom is only six so it will have to have a U certificate to be all right for him!' She had hung her school coat and hat on the peg by the door whilst she was talking and now she headed for the hall. 'I'll have a wash and brush my hair,' she called over her shoulder. 'Mrs Smith is a real sport; she says Trevor Howard and Celia Johnson are appearing in a film called *Brief Encounter* sometime before Christmas and she'll take us older ones then.'

'I wouldn't mind seeing that myself; I adore Trevor Howard,' Marianne called. 'You're quite right, though, I'd forgotten you were off partying. But what time does the film end? I don't like the thought of you walking home alone after dark.'

She went to the foot of the stairs and Libby, now

at the top of the flight, turned to beam at her. 'It's all right, Adelaide has been asked as well. We'll catch a tram, of course – the stop is right outside Adelaide's house – and Adelaide says her big brother Jack, or her father, will walk me home from there.'

'That's good,' Marianne said, relieved. 'I would have come to the cinema and collected you, but I must say I'm glad you've made other arrangements. I always look forward to my baking day but end up worn out.' She chuckled to herself as she returned to the kitchen, remembering that Bill had offered to take her out tonight since he knew it was her day off. She had refused the treat, but guessed he would come calling when his own shift finished. They would sit in the kitchen and talk and plan, just like an old married couple, though of course they were no such thing.

Libby clattered down the stairs and burst into the kitchen. 'You are quick!' Marianne said wonderingly, seeing her daughter's hair loose, with a couple of kirby grips holding it back from her face. 'Is it cold outside? If so, you'd best wear your old Burberry.'

'My mac will do,' Libby said. She crossed the kitchen, kissed her mother on the cheek, and headed for the back door. 'I'm going to call for Adelaide, so I'd best get a move on. See you later, Ma.'

'See you later,' Marianne echoed, beginning to put her baking into a variety of tins. She wondered how long Libby had been calling her Ma instead

481

of Mum; yet another sign of her daughter's maturity, she supposed. Glancing at the clock, she saw that it would be at least an hour before the lodgers came in, and even then they would go to their rooms to have a wash before coming down again for their evening meal. She had made an apple tart for pudding and meant to give them corned beef hash as a main course, because the butcher had shaken his head sadly when she had asked for stewing steak.

Deciding that she might as well make herself a cup of tea and rest for an hour, she put the kettle on the stove and was about to sink into the most comfortable of the creaking old basket chairs when someone knocked on the back door. Wondering if Bill had got away early, Marianne crossed the kitchen and pulled open the door, reflecting that it was just like her old friend to knock rather than come straight in. The man who stood on the doorstep, however, was not Bill, but Neil Sheridan.

Marianne was so surprised that she stepped back and Neil obviously took this as an invitation, since he smiled at her, entered the room, and took her in his arms before she had a chance to repulse him. 'I'm back, darling,' he said. 'I'm sorry I couldn't let you know, but with the release of so many POWs, things are in a bit of a mess. I had to draw civvies because the things they give you to wear in the camps . . . well, they're more like rags than clothing, and far too thin for winter wear. I suppose I could have sent a telegram, but all I wanted was to get home as soon as possible.' As she pulled away from him, he cocked his head on one side and gave her what he no doubt considered to be a charming and rueful grin. 'Oh, darling, we've got so much talking to do, so much explaining, but you've not said you're pleased to see me!'

Marianne was beginning to get over the first shock of surprise, but she had still not quite made up her mind what she should say when the kettle began to hop. Hastily, she crossed the room, picked up the teapot, added another small spoonful of tea leaves to those already within, and poured on the boiling water. Then she went and got another mug from its hook on the dresser, reached for the tin of dried milk, and spoke with a calmness she was far from feeling. 'I'm glad you're back, of course, Neil, because I wouldn't want anyone to be held prisoner now that the war is over. But I'm sure you realise that our marriage ended the day you asked me to divorce you. You told me you had a young lady, who was in the family way . . .'

'But you'd forgotten – you'd forgotten everything!' Neil said. He sounded astonished and rather peeved, Marianne thought. 'And anyway, I only said what I did in a moment of madness. Why, you and Libby mean more to me than anyone else on earth and our marriage, my memories of our love, were all that kept me going in the camp. Honest to God, Marianne, if you throw me over I might as well chuck myself in the Mersey, because I'll have nothing left to live for.'

'Yes you will, Neil,' Marianne said, pushing a mug of tea towards him and indicating that he should sit down in one of the basket chairs. 'You've your career for a start . . .'

'I've chucked the Navy and mean to get a job ashore, so don't think you'd be having a part-time husband. Oh, Marianne, you were always the soul of generosity; give me a chance!'

'I'm sorry, Neil, but I'm afraid it's too late,' Marianne said gently. She knew, in her heart, that his distress was just an act, but she still felt sorry for him. She wondered if he knew Fiona was married, then guessed that he must do so. He would scarcely have visited a wife he no longer loved before the young woman who had been his mistress. So she hardened her heart. 'Don't think this is a quick decision. I really couldn't live with you again, knowing what I know.'

'But I'm telling you, I'm a different man from the one who was fool enough to fall for a pretty young face,' Neil said wildly. He glanced at her and she could read the calculation in his narrow, handsome face. 'Just what *do* you know? I had every intention of telling you I'd had an affair and that it was over, dead and buried. What else can I do to convince you that my marriage means more to me than anything else in my life?'

'Look, Neil, I don't have to answer any of your questions because I'm not at all sure that I believe a word you say,' Marianne said. 'I thought we had a good marriage, then I found it was just a hollow sham. And the truth is, I'm going to marry someone else.'

Neil gave a sneering laugh. 'Oh yes? But since you're still married to me, that's one plan, my dear, which would need my wholehearted co-operation. You can beg me to divorce you, but I shall do no such thing, so you'd best grow accustomed to following my lead in trying to mend our marriage.'

'You're quite wrong, Neil. I applied for a divorce some while ago, and you will be served with the papers as soon as you return to your parents' home, since that was the only permanent address I had for you,' Marianne said, keeping her voice level with an effort. She saw the colour rise in Neil's face and noticed, for the first time, that he was sporting an incipient black eye and had a huge lump on his forehead. 'Let's change the subject,' she said brightly. 'I see you're wounded. What happened?'

She saw Neil's hand stray to his face and guessed he had forgotten all about whatever accident he had suffered. But the reminder had made him look at her with more attention, and when he spoke a good deal of the anger had left his voice. 'Oh, I fell, helping someone with a heavy suitcase off the train,' he said vaguely. 'But that reminds me: last time I saw you, your face was scarred, but now it's as smooth and beautiful as ever. I'm glad. But now kindly tell me, dear Marianne, how you expect to get grounds for a divorce from a man who has been incarcerated in a POW camp for nearly a year?'

Marianne smiled; she couldn't help it. 'Remember

the Riverside Hotel, just outside Southampton?' she said softly. 'The waiter and waitress who brought you breakfast in bed? You might have forgotten them, Neil, but they remembered you – and your lady friend. Fiona agreed to do it when I asked her, because she wanted nothing more to do with you and I suspect she wanted revenge for the way you had treated both of us. So I'll get my divorce all right, and we'll be free of each other.'

Neil jumped to his feet. His face was red, except for his nostrils and a thin line about his mouth, which was white and bloodless. His eyes blazed, and when he came towards her Marianne looked round wildly for a weapon, because his whole demeanour was that of a man driven to extremes. She grabbed the poker and stood up, trembling in every limb, but determined not to show that she was afraid. 'Don't you come one step nearer, or it won't only be a black eye and a lump on your head,' she said. 'If I scream . . .'

Even as she spoke, someone knocked on the back door and she felt the breath whoosh out of her in a long sigh of relief. It was Bill, she was sure of it, suddenly feeling his nearness as a sort of glowing warmth. She shouted: 'Come in!' and saw the door swing open and Bill's large, reliable figure enter.

He glanced round quickly, clearly taking in her visitor's furious face and her own grip on the poker. He grinned at her, his slow, steady grin, then turned courteously to Neil. 'Hope I'm not interruptin' anythin',' he said cheerfully. He crossed the room and held out a large hand. 'I'm Bill Brett, a friend of Marianne's, and you be . . . ?'

'I'm her husband, Neil Sheridan, and I'll thank you . . .' Neil stopped short and stared at the other man. He had extended his hand as though to shake Bill's, but now dropped it to his side, clenching his fingers into a fist. 'I'm sure I've met you before, though we didn't exchange names,' he said. 'I can't quite call it to mind . . . give me a moment . . .'

'It were in the hospital waiting room at the Stanley,' Bill said helpfully. 'It were the night your wife were injured . . . we got to talkin', if you remember.'

Marianne, watching on the sideline, so to speak, saw Neil's expression change from puzzlement to icy fury. His head shot forward, reminding her sharply of a snake about to strike, and his words emerged in a hiss. 'You bastard. You told her, didn't you? Oh yes, kind old Bill Brett, who'd never stand a chance with a woman like Marianne unless he held some secret that she wanted! You spilled the bloody beans, told her every word I'd told you in confidence, turned her against me . . . why, I could . . .'

Bill's deep voice cut in. 'I told her nothing, norra word of what you said to me that evening,' he said quietly. 'Why should I tell her something which would only distress her? So you can forget that, me laddo. I don't go tellin' tales out of school; ask anyone.'

'I don't believe a word of it,' Neil said viciously.

487

'She forgot everything after the accident, every bloody thing; so if you didn't tell her, who did?'

'I remembered,' Marianne said. Her voice trembled a little and she paused to steady it. 'Your father came to Liverpool for a conference and suggested that we meet so that he could give me lunch. We met under the clock, where you and I, Neil, had met so often in the past. He's awfully like you, superficially at least, and when we reached Stanley Road, he told me your cousin Eva was getting a divorce. Suddenly it all came flooding back; how you had explained about your lady friend and her – her situation, how you wanted a divorce . . . oh, everything you said.' She lowered her voice. 'Even that you thought I was boring and no longer any fun.'

For a long moment Neil simply stared straight at her; then she could almost see the calculation begin. 'But that was years ago,' he mumbled. He had dropped his eyes and was staring down at his clenched fists. 'I was a fool, I admit it. Can't you bring yourself to forgive and forget?'

Marianne laughed. 'Of course I can't,' she said, her voice light and amused. 'Neil, you really had better go. I've told you I'm divorcing you, and as soon as the decree absolute comes through I'm going to marry Bill.'

Neil stared wildly from one to the other. 'You're throwing yourself away on a fellow old enough to be your father, who'll probably never earn more than a bloody dustman,' he gasped. 'Right, if you're prepared to sink that low, I want nothing more to do with you.'

He was halfway to the back door when something seemed to strike him, and he turned back. 'Where's my daughter? What will she have to say when she knows you've turned me away? I'll fight you for custody, you may be sure of that.'

Marianne laughed again and saw Neil's expression become positively murderous. She might have shrunk back but Bill put his arm round her, so that they faced Neil together. It gave Marianne the courage to speak. 'If you fight for her, then I shall be forced to tell her the truth,' she said quietly. 'Incidentally, your father knows everything. Oh, I didn't mean to tell him, but I was so dreadfully upset when I remembered the things you'd said to me that it all came out.'

Neil turned a face, suddenly haggard, towards her. 'You . . . you . . .'

Bill suddenly moved ponderously forward and it occurred to Marianne that though he might be older than her husband, he was also considerably larger and probably a good deal stronger. She put a detaining hand on his arm, then realised that it was not necessary. 'I think you'd best leave,' Bill said, and there was a note of authority in his voice that Marianne had never heard before. 'Libby's a nice kid; I've no doubt she'll keep in touch with you, though of course she'll live with me and her mother. If I were you, I wouldn't hang about Liverpool; there's too many folk here know too much for your comfort. Best get back to Plymouth and your parents.'

'I'll do as I bloody well please,' Neil growled, but this was so plainly a meaningless flourish that Bill and Marianne ignored it, and after a second's hesitation Neil slammed out of the kitchen.

Marianne heaved a sigh of relief and smiled up at Bill. 'Thank God that's over,' she breathed. 'At least I hope it is! You don't think he'll come back, do you?'

Bill chuckled, but shook his head. 'You'll never see hide nor hair of that fellow again,' he prophesied. He glanced at the clock above the mantel. 'Best get the table laid,' he said. 'The lodgers will be back in ten minutes and meeting your husband has made me devilish hungry!'

Marianne and Bill got married on a beautiful May day, with Libby and her friend Adelaide acting as bridesmaids. Bill had bought Marianne a tiny diamond solitaire engagement ring and Marianne had joyfully parcelled up the much larger ring Neil had given her so long ago, and sent it back to Plymouth. Neil had never acknowledged receipt of it, but she knew he had got it because Libby had gone down to Plymouth during the Easter holidays and had asked Grandma Sheridan.

'Yes indeed; he received it weeks ago,' her grandmother had said wonderingly. 'Dear me, how extremely forgetful your father can be! He promised faithfully that he would write and thank your mother for returning it, but I dare say it slipped his mind. Indeed, his first reaction was to send it back to Marianne, telling her to wear it on her right hand, but I dare say he forgot. As you know, my love, his new job is very demanding, but I do believe he enjoys it. At first, Father and I thought him foolish to leave the Navy, but I'm sure now that he did the right thing.'

Libby had agreed with her grandmother, but when she returned home she had been able to give Marianne a somewhat fuller account of what had happened to the sapphire cluster which Marianne had posted off so blithely. 'He's been and gone and got himself a lady-friend,' she had told her mother with a wicked grin. 'I suppose some people might think her pretty – she's got shoulder-length blonde hair, big blue eyes and a little tiny rosebud mouth – but I think there's something hard about her face. At any rate, she rules poor Dad with a rod of iron and I'm telling you, Ma, she doesn't like me one bit. And of course, when I noticed the ring on her engagement finger and said it was yours once, she was absolutely furious. She tried to snatch it off, only she's got big knuckles and it wouldn't come. She had to grease her finger with soap, and when she flung it at Dad and said she didn't want a second-hand ring Dad told her he'd bought it from a Plymouth jeweller only days before and that, though it might be similar, it had never belonged to his ex-wife. I don't think she believed him and I was really tempted to say again that it was your ring, but Dad gave me such a pathetic look that I changed my mind and pretended I'd made a mistake.' Libby had glanced shyly at her mother. 'I loved visiting Grandpa and Grandma Sheridan, but if Dad marries that woman and moves out I don't mean to visit *them*. She'd probably poison my coffee, or spit in my porridge when I wasn't looking.'

Marianne and Bill had both laughed, and Marianne had promised that she would not insist upon her daughter's visiting her father and his new friend, though she hoped very much that Libby would continue to spend time with her Sheridan grandparents. 'They were very good to me when I was married to their son, and in fact Mother Sheridan still writes regularly.'

Libby loved the freedom of the big house in Plymouth, with the beach and the sea close at hand, and the countryside a short walk away, but she was serious when she said she had no intention of staying with her father and his new wife once they were in their own home. At present, Neil was living with his parents, but Mrs Sheridan had said in her latest letter that he had put in an offer for a small house in the nearby village of Meavy, and meant to remarry at once.

Libby was very fond of her father, but seeing him with his new lady-love had opened her eyes to faults in his character that she had not previously known existed. He told fibs – no, large lies – if it suited him to do so, and he was quite prepared to disappoint his daughter if his lady-friend, whose name was Mirabelle, demanded that he should. Besides, there were other people Libby wanted to see even more, like Fiona and Hamish. They had moved from the village near Invergordon to a cottage perched on the very edge of the firth, and when the summer holidays arrived Libby meant to visit them, for she had never been to Scotland and longed to see the places which Fiona, in her letters, had described so graphically.

Then there was Auntie, and Tregarth. At first Libby had planned to go to the castle when Matthew was certain to be there, but she had revised this scheme. It would be best if she went when Matthew was off somewhere with his friends, because she had sense enough to realise that though she might catch up with him one day, a fourteen-year-old who had not yet taken her School Certificate and a nineteen-year-old studying medicine at a Cambridge college were still poles apart. It would be wonderful, however, to see Auntie, Tregarth and the castle once more. Yes, she would definitely take up Auntie's invitation just as soon as her mother could spare her.

Chapter Sixteen

February 1951

Libby woke to hear the rain pouring down and bouncing off the cobbles, as it had done for pretty well the whole of the month. Groggily, she sat up in bed and peered at the small face of her alarm clock. She had gone to the Grafton Ballroom the night before and had come home later than she had intended because Cyril, who had taken her to the dance, had insisted upon staying to the bitter end. This was annoying because she had to be up early to catch a train to go to Tregarth, where she was to spend a few days.

She got out of bed, being careful to lower her head as she neared the washstand, for her room was an attic, with a sharply sloping ceiling, and a long window at knee level. Bill and Marianne had bought the house when they left Crocus Street. Marianne was now working in Lewis's and enjoying the challenge, for she was a buyer in Gowns and spent a good deal of her time travelling to London to the big fashion houses, where she selected garments which she thought her customers would like.

'Libby? I know you aren't going to work today, but don't forget you're going off to Auntie's to

494

spend a long weekend at the castle. Do you want some porridge, or are you going to have a lie-in and catch a later train?' As Marianne said the last few words, she must have been climbing the stairs, for Libby's bedroom door shot open and her mother's face appeared. She smiled at her daughter. 'Oh, you *are* up! Thank goodness; I should have felt really mean if you'd changed your mind about catching the early train and were trying to have a lie-in. I heard you come in last night, awfully late, so I did wonder if you'd changed your plans, especially as it's still pouring with rain.' She bent to look out of the window. 'My goodness. If this goes on, Bill says he plans to build an ark.'

Libby, pouring water from the jug into the basin, turned to smile at her mother. 'You're right about coming in late, but I still mean to catch the earlier train,' she said cheerfully. 'It's an awful time of year to go visiting but at least it means that Uncle Frank and Auntie will have more time to spend with me than they did last year, when I went in June. And of course the boss was quite happy for me to take the time off when no one else wanted to be away.' She was working in the Accounts Department of a big insurance company and in a few weeks would be taking examinations which could lead to her becoming, one day, a qualified accountant, and her boss had no time for what he termed 'slackers' or 'bad time-keepers'.

She began to wash, stripping off her nightgown and throwing it on to the bed. 'I packed everything

495

last night so all I've got to do is gobble some breakfast before I go. In fact, I'll probably catch the same tram as you.'

'That'll be nice. And now, madam, you'd best answer my question or you won't be gobbling anything, save bread and water. Do you want some porridge? I could do you some toast as well, if you feel you've got time to eat it before we leave. I wish I could offer you an egg but we've only got the dried sort.'

Libby laughed. 'I'm going to the land of plenty, where I can collect my own egg fresh from the hen before breakfast, and eat it with a slice of Auntie's home-cured bacon,' she said gaily. 'Porridge will be fine, Ma.'

Presently, neatly arrayed in a bright yellow jumper, a charcoal-grey skirt and high-heeled black court shoes, Libby ran down the stairs, dumped her suitcase by the back door, and sat down to eat the porridge her mother had made. 'Where's Uncle Bill?' she demanded, as she finished the bowl and began to sip her tea. 'I bet he was on earlies, wasn't he?'

'That's right,' Marianne said. 'I meant to ask you before: will you be seeing Matthew this time, or is he still in the States?'

'He only goes to the States to visit some distant relatives of his father's,' Libby pointed out. 'He was there last summer and the summer before, but now, as far as I know, he's a junior houseman at some hospital in London, working all the hours God sends and getting almost no time off, so it's not likely he'll be at the castle.' She drained her cup and stood it down on the table. 'We'd better get a move on, Ma, or you'll be in trouble with your boss and I'll miss my perishing train.'

'I used to wonder about you and Matthew,' Marianne said, as mother and daughter walked towards the tram stop. 'You were fond of one another as children and I thought you'd remain close. But it doesn't seem to have happened.'

'Well it wouldn't, would it?' Libby said rather crossly. 'He's five years older than me, Ma, and five years is a lot when one of you is fourteen and the other nineteen. Think of me and Lucy next door. We might like each other – well, we do – but we're poles apart, wouldn't you agree?'

'Yes, of course. I was being silly,' Marianne said as they reached the tram stop. 'Though Lucy isn't even thirteen yet. But I do see what you mean. I remember you saying that Matthew had suddenly become a young man whilst you were still only a kid. That must have been the last time you saw him . . . at Auntie's wedding, wasn't it?'

Just then the tram drew up, and the usual scrum to get aboard started. The vehicle was crowded, so mother and daughter had no further chance to talk, and a quick glance at the clock by the station caused Libby to grab her suitcase, give the briefest of waves and run into the concourse. She must have been just about the last person to board the train and was amazed to get a corner seat, though the pane was so steamed up and dirty on the inside,

497

and coated with raindrops on the outside, that she reflected she would be lucky to catch more than a glimpse of the passing scene. She rubbed herself a peephole but could still make out almost nothing, so she gave it up as a bad job and leaned back, thinking with delightful anticipation of her little holiday. Auntie had made great improvements at the castle, for many of the women who had joined the forces or worked in factories during the war had returned to the village and were happy to earn money working for the Ap Nefydd estate. Neither Auntie nor Uncle Frank wanted their home to be a showplace, but they decided that fresh curtains, clean carpets and a roof which was proof against the wildest of weathers would suit them.

'We're not spring chickens any longer,' Frank had told his wife. 'As we get older, we'll need the place to be warm and comfortable and easy to run; looks really don't matter. If we aim to deal with say half a dozen rooms, then the rest of the place can go hang. What both of us really care about is the land and the stock, and thank God both are in good heart and, with the men coming home, should stay so.'

As a result, when Libby stayed at the castle she had a large and comfortable bedroom, draught free and embellished with an enormous radiator which was turned on when the weather was cold. The central heating system was run by the Aga in the kitchen and that room also had been 'dealt with' so that it was warm, cheerful and stocked with a number of labour-saving modern appliances, such as the very first washing machine Libby had ever encountered, a Calor gas cooker, which they used in summer when the Aga was allowed to go out, and a refrigerator, which stood in one corner, clicking and spluttering away to itself, but keeping food fresh in the hottest weather, and supplying Uncle Frank with ice cubes to float in his nightly glass of whisky.

All this was very pleasant to contemplate, but Libby could not help being sad for Tregarth. The castle was very grand, of course, and very comfortable, but she had been so happy at Tregarth! When she had first visited the castle, after the war, the land girls had still been in residence at the old house. Then a farm manager and his wife and four children had moved in. Mr Malone's wife had been a cheerful, slapdash Irish woman, who let her children run wild and had not, she had told Auntie sunnily, believed in housework. After four years of Malone occupation, Tregarth had been in a poor state and the next farm manager had elected to live in the village, leaving the house to moulder sadly away, its roof no longer proof against the dripping trees and the wild winds and snow of the valley in winter.

Libby knew that Auntie wanted the house made habitable once more, but at present the money to do such extensive work was just not available. Uncle Frank had promised that he would start work on Tregarth as soon as a would-be tenant came forward but as yet, so far as Libby knew, this had not happened.

The train drew in at the small station and Libby

got down. She went out to the taxi rank and waved to the elderly man in the driver's seat of the waiting cab. He was the same one who had ferried Libby and her mother to and from the village during the war and he got slowly out of the car, a welcoming grin spreading across his grizzled face. 'Nice to see you it is, missie,' he said. 'You'll be wantin' Tregarth, of course. Hop in. I'll stow your case and that there bag in the back, if you'd like to take the passenger seat.'

It was on the tip of Libby's tongue to say that she was going to the castle when she paused, irresolute. She had been shut up in that stuffy train for ages and was longing to stretch her legs. From the station, one reached the castle by way of the main road, a far longer journey than if one simply went to Tregarth, and then climbed up and over from one valley to the next. If she did this, she would arrive at the castle more or less when she was expected, and could have a look at the old house where she had once been so happy at the same time.

Abruptly, she made up her mind. 'If you can take me as far as the village, Mr Morrow, I'll walk the rest of the way,' she said. And then, when he protested that she would get soaked to the skin, she laughed at him and shook her head. 'It will be like old times to walk, Mr Morrow, and I don't mind a bit of wet. Remember, Matthew and I used to go to and from the school in the village every day, come rain or shine, and so far as I can recall, we never caught so much as a cold.'

'Ye-es, but in them days you often got a lift,' Mr Morrow pointed out, helping her into the passenger seat and stowing her case away. 'It's a fair old walk from the village; it must be all of three or four miles.'

'That's true, but I mean to call on my old friend Rhiannon. I'm told she's working in Mr Jones's shop in the village, and it would be good to catch up with her news,' Libby said.

'Ah well, in that case I'll drop you off at the shop,' Mr Morrow said, chuckling comfortably. 'I know you girls, chatter chatter you do, so I dare say the rain will have stopped by the time you and young Rhiannon have talked yourselves dry.'

Accordingly, when they reached the village, Mr Morrow stopped the taxi right outside the shop, then hurried round to help Libby out with her suitcase. Since it contained winter clothing and wellington boots, it was quite heavy, and Mr Morrow suggested that he might drive her case to Tregarth and dump it in the front porch. It was clear he had no idea that the house was deserted and Libby certainly did not intend to tell him. Instead she said, untruthfully, that the horse and cart could be sent to the village to pick it up, and Mr Morrow, nodding wisely, drove off satisfied.

As soon as he was out of sight, Libby hefted her suitcase and glanced around. The rain was still falling steadily and the wind was rising, and for a moment she hovered, thinking that perhaps she would indeed have a chat with Rhiannon before setting out on her long walk. But if she did, she guessed that it would be growing dusk by the time she reached the castle, and she had no intention of facing the long climb and the steep descent in the fading light. She did glance quickly into the shop's dark interior, but could see no one behind the counter and guessed that Mr Jones and Rhiannon were in the back room, eating their dinner.

She set out, glad she had not brought an umbrella, for the wind which met her as soon as she was clear of the houses would have turned it inside out before she had gone more than a couple of yards.

In a way, it was a nuisance that the weather was so wild, because she had looked forward to seeing the valley which she had once known so well. She knew, of course, that it had not changed; trees pressed close to the narrowing roadway, and now and again a stream actually ran clear across the path, and there were huge puddles everywhere. Even above the wind and the rain, she could hear the tinkling of water as it ran down from the banks which reared up on her left. Libby reflected that in another month or so, if something was not done, the trees and bushes would begin to invade the lane, and make the passage of any vehicle larger than a bicycle difficult, if not impossible. As it was, she had to keep a weather eye open for branches which overhung the path and would have impeded her progress had she not spotted them in time.

She had gone about a mile when she realised that the rain now contained flakes of snow. She wondered whether she should turn back, swallow her pride and ring the castle from the telephone in Mr Jones's shop. Then she scolded herself. Ridiculous to be put off because of a bit of sleet. She, who had traversed this road when the snow had drifted across it, when she and Rhys had had to dig a way through so that the cart might take them to and from school. And anyway, it was far too wet for snow. She would certainly not let this sort of weather put her off.

She was, however, getting soaked. Fortunately, her mackintosh had a hood, though the wind kept trying to blow it off her head, so that she was forced to clutch it beneath her chin which meant a good deal of manoeuvring when she wanted to change her suitcase from her left hand to her right.

Libby plodded on and she began to see, when she turned her head sideways, that despite the month and the weather there was still beauty here. Fat cushions of moss, their tiny cups quivering in the wind, starred the big boulders fringing a nearby pool that she could see through the trees; she remembered that pool well. It was fed by a tiny stream which dried up in summer, and was far too small even in spring to hold any but the tiniest inhabitants. But she and Matthew had perched on the boulders – Rhys had lifted Matthew to his lofty seat – and hung lengths of fishing line baited with bits of bread, expecting, with the innocence of youth, that one day a fine trout might be hooked out and proudly presented to Auntie.

Further along were the great beech trees, amongst whose gnarled roots the three children had indulged in wildly imaginary games. Rhys was clever with his hands and had made tiny boats, and manned them with matchstick men. There was one particular root pool which actually disappeared inside the tree itself and Matthew, who had a gift for story-telling, had woven many adventures which he said had overtaken the boats and their matchstick occupants when they disappeared into the dark bowels of the earth.

Libby emerged from beneath the beech trees and glanced to her right. In spring, the thinner woodland here would be alive with wild garlic and Solomon's Seal and she remembered, with a little snort of amusement, a remark she had made when she had first come to the valley. 'I smell a lovely dinner,' she had told Matthew, as the garlic gave off its strong and pungent odour. 'Someone is going to have a delicious stew presently.' How Matthew and Rhys had laughed and teased her, and how foolish she had felt herself to be, a real townmouse, as Matthew had called her, and how desperately she had wanted to be a country person, like them!

But now she was approaching the turn-off which led to Tregarth, so she kept her attention on her surroundings and was glad to have done so, for she very nearly passed the gap in the trees through which one had to go to reach her destination. It was sadly overgrown and the track, for it had become little more, had narrowed so that at first she thought she had paused too soon, and almost went on. Then she remembered the state of the rest of the lane and stopped for a closer look. Yes, this was it; there could be no doubt.

Libby set off under the dripping trees, with the wind apparently resenting her intrusion and seeming set to blow her off her feet. She continued despite it, however, and presently the house was before her.

Poor Tregarth! She saw peeling paintwork, the porch roof hanging at an odd angle, a litter of smashed slates where a previous storm must have weakened the roof and sent them hurtling to earth. The window to the right of the front door was glassless, but someone had nailed plywood over it so that the rain might not penetrate.

Slowly, almost hesitantly, Libby approached the porch and stood under its frail shelter. Would the door be locked? If it was, she could go round the back. She knew where the back door key was always kept . . . yet she decided she would feel like an intruder if she did so. Of course she knew the house had been empty for many months, yet who could say that this was still the case? A tramp might have made his home in the kitchen or the scullery, or the latter been invaded by black beetles and worse. No, she would not go round the back . . .

The porch roof creaked, the rain fell, the wind howled . . . and suddenly Libby turned and hammered on the oak of the old front door. Illogically, she felt certain that someone was within and would answer her knock and sure enough, just audible above the noise of the storm, she could hear what sounded like dragging footsteps, accompanied by tapping. Libby remembered blind Pugh in *Treasure Island* and felt the hairs on the back of her neck prickle erect. She took a couple of steps away from the dubious shelter of the porch; the rain hammered down and the wind snatched spitefully at her hood. Hesitantly, she stood still, waiting. A poem, learned at school but she had thought long forgotten, ran through her head.

'Is there anybody there?' said the traveller, knocking on the moonlit door, and his horse in the silence champed the grasses of the forest's ferny floor.

But there was no horse and the floor of this particular forest was thick with fallen leaves and mud, so Libby gathered her courage round her like a cloak and stole back into the porch, staring at the front door.

It creaked open and Matthew stood before her, as she felt she should have known he would. All fear and uncertainty fled and warmth invaded her. Matthew was smiling at her, balancing on two crutches, and so tall that she had to tilt her head to look into his face. She began to return his smile, to open her mouth to speak, but he shook his head.

'Not now,' he said gently. 'Don't rush anything. We've got a lot of catching up to do, and all the time in the world to do it.'

And then he took her hand and drew her into the house, closing the front door behind them.